SWEET SEDUCTION SURRENDER

SWEET SEDUCTION BOOK FOUR

NICOLA CLAIRE

ISBN-13: 978-1493683451

ISBN-10: 1493683454

❀ Created with Vellum

ABOUT THE AUTHOR

Nicola Claire lives in beautiful Taupo, New Zealand with her husband and two young boys.

A bit of a romance junkie, she can be known to devour as many as half a dozen books a week if she drinks too much coffee. But her real passion is writing sexy, romantic suspense stories with strong female leads and alpha male protagonists who know how to love them.

So far, she's written well over 50 books. She might have caught the writing bug; here's hoping there's no cure!

For more information:
www.nicolaclairebooks.com
nicola@nicolaclairebooks.com

ALSO BY NICOLA CLAIRE

Kindred Series

Kindred

Blood Life Seeker

Forbidden Drink

Giver of Light

Dancing Dragon

Shadow's Light

Entwined With The Dark

Kiss Of The Dragon

Dreaming Of A Blood Red Christmas (Novella)

Mixed Blessing Mystery Series

Mixed Blessing

Dark Shadow

Rogue Vampire (Coming Soon)

Sweet Seduction Series

Sweet Seduction Sacrifice

Sweet Seduction Serenade

Sweet Seduction Shadow

Sweet Seduction Surrender

Sweet Seduction Shield

Sweet Seduction Sabotage

Sweet Seduction Stripped

Sweet Seduction Secrets

Sweet Seduction Sayonara

Elemental Awakening Series

The Tempting Touch Of Fire

The Soothing Scent Of Earth

The Chilling Change Of Air

The Tantalising Taste Of Water

The Eternal Edge Of Aether (Novella)

H.E.A.T. Series

A Flare Of Heat

A Touch Of Heat

A Twist Of Heat (Novella)

A Lick Of Heat

Citizen Saga

Elite

Cardinal

Citizen

Masked (Novella)

Wiped

Scarlet Suffragette Series

Fearless

Breathless

Heartless

Blood Enchanted Series

Blood Enchanted

Blood Entwined

Blood Enthralled

---

44 South Series

Southern Sunset

Southern Storm

Southern Strike (Coming Soon)

DESCRIPTION

"Don't for a minute believe I want you any other way, Jason Cain. The second you stop being you is the moment you should fear most."

For several months now Katie Anscombe has tried to hide her attraction to Jason Cain. That's what everyone expects of Katie. And of course, it helps that he basically ignores her too. But something about the ex-special forces soldier has caught her attention. And dreams are free, aren't they?

Forced into a lock-down for forty-eight hours, with no one to come between them and stop the tension from exploding inside her small house, things become volatile. And a volatile Jason Cain is really something to witness. But the closer she gets to Jason, the more it becomes apparent that he's unlike any other man she has ever met.

A sexy, dominant, but slightly broken soldier. A Pandora's Box of desire and fervent need opened. Katie and Jason must face up to their fears, in order to embrace what feels right. But with overprotective brothers and an eccentric millionaire art dealer throwing spanners in the works, surrendering to each other isn't as easy as it sounds. Fighting their attraction has been second nature for too long, so when they finally give in to their base desires, will it be everything Katie dreamed about? And will it last?

Love at first sight has never been so dangerous and so very delicious at the same time.

*For: Those readers who wanted desperately to hear
Katie & Jason's story and hounded me through Facebook.
This one's for you and keep those requests coming!*

CHAPTER 1

AND I SWEAR MY HEART LEAPT FOR JOY

THE INSISTENT BUZZ OF MY CELLPHONE INTERRUPTED MY concentration. It rattled its way across my desk, making an amusing combination of whirs and chirps, interspersed with one long beep. A text message. I ignored it. If I didn't get this particular proposal finished, my client was likely to throw a hissy-fit.

The one downside to being the interior designer *du jour*, was only those customers with deep pockets could afford me. And as we all know, deep pockets often led to demanding people. It didn't make any sense to me. Manners were not something that should fall by the wayside in the presence of a large bank account. Papa would never behave like that and he's one of the wealthiest men in Auckland.

But the newly titled Mrs Montgomery-Smith was not cut from the same cloth as Jacob Anscombe. New money. Ugh! Not that I let Mrs, or Mr for that fact, Montgomery-Smith know that I was on to them. They strove to meet all the requirements of today's über rich, including the attitude. But, Anscombe Interiors did not concern itself with how people obtained their money, we - or at least me, I'm a one-woman show - aimed to please.

Which meant here I was slaving away on the final presentation of

Mrs Montgomery-Smith's sitting room, in order to email the details to her by five. She'd only given me the outline for this particular room five days ago. That didn't stop her from insisting I have the design completed by end of business today though, did it?

It wasn't an unusual request, most people expected miracles to occur in minutes and wanted to pay peanuts for the final product in the end. Not that my final drawings today would be that - *final*. No, I expected, at a minimum, half a dozen revisions before Mrs Montgomery-Smith was appeased. Still, I'm a professional, I take pride in my work. So, I'd been up since four working on this diligently. Even if my first design was shot down by the woman, it would be a design I was proud of all the same. I never gave less than one hundred percent. Papa taught me that.

My cellphone chirped and whirred and buzzed a few more inches across the polished surface of my desk, this time accompanied by ASI's ringtone; Avril Lavigne's *"Here's To Never Growing Up."*

I sighed, hit 'save' on my laptop and picked the phone up, swiping the screen with my thumb to activate the call.

"Darlings," I answered when the line connected, putting as much Katie Anscombe cheer into my voice as I could muster. Considering the early wake-up call and the pressure to get this particular design completed, it was a wonder I could do chirpy at all. "To what do I owe this delightful pleasure?"

"Katie, sweetheart. You didn't answer my text." A genuine smile graced my lips. Somehow Eric's continued flirtations and ridiculous term of endearment for me always made me smile.

"Eric, you know if I had been aware the text was from you I would have replied instantly."

"Then you *were* aware a text had been sent to your phone?" he asked, tapping away on a keyboard in the background. Eric, the IT control-room guy at my brother's security and investigations firm, could carry out a conversation, trace a GPS signal and hack into government computers all at the same time.

"I was busy," I admitted. "If someone really wanted me, they'd phone. Evidence of this is in the conversation we're currently having."

"Oh, Katie. If only you knew how much I want you."

I stifled a chuckle. It would only encourage the man.

"What's up, darling?" I asked, getting us back on more stable ground.

Eric sighed. It sounded weighty. "We're on lock-down, sweetheart."

A chill raced down my spine. I could count on one hand how many times my brother Nick has placed ASI and those who fall under its indefinite protection under a lock-down. He'd told me that to do so cost his firm in the region of tens of thousands of dollars each day. Not something he contemplated unless absolutely necessary. And the type of work my brother does, means that to be absolutely necessary, is to be life threatening.

"That's not good news, Eric," I said softly.

"Don't worry about a thing, Katie," he replied instantly. With false bravado I might add. "We're all good here, Adam's at Sweet Seduction with Dom, your parents are out of the country sunning it up as you know in Fiji, so that just leaves you."

"Me," I said uneasily. Just who would they send to protect me?

Eric sighed again. This one wasn't so much weighty as downright ponderous.

"Katie, the closest operative I have to your address is Jason Cain."

I didn't say anything for a moment. I couldn't. My mind had blanked and my heart had faltered. I cursed my ridiculously romantic and utterly misguided heart, but still couldn't find the wherewithal to make a sound in reply to Eric's statement.

"Katie?" Eric asked, his voice breaking through the mild panic attack I was having. "Listen, I know he can be a pain in the butt, but he's very good at what he does," he added.

"I know," I replied. My voice didn't sound like mine.

"Sweetheart," Eric cajoled. "Nick wouldn't think to send someone he didn't absolutely trust."

"It doesn't sound like he had much of a choice, now does it?" I managed to say, in a somewhat recognisable voice. "Being as Jason was the closest operative and all."

"Katie," Eric chastised gently. "I wouldn't send Jason if I didn't believe he could protect you. You've got to know that."

It's not that I didn't think Jason Cain, former Captain in the New Zealand Army's SAS, was capable of protecting me. That wasn't the problem at all. No, Jason was more than capable of taking on a plethora of terrorists with stealth, zeal and a dedication to the task only the elite soldiers of the country's premier military special forces unit could have.

No, my sudden desire to run and hide had nothing to do with Jason Cain's professional abilities, but everything instead to do with the man himself. Not that I would admit that aloud to anyone.

"Of course, darling. Where is he now?"

"Um," Eric stalled. "He's actually on your porch waiting for you to open the front door."

My head swivelled to look out into the hallway off my office, as though I could see the front door from my seat at my desk - which I couldn't. Then to my mortification, my hand went to my hair, to ensure it was suitably presentable and my eyes quickly scanned down the front of my top, seeing if everything was still in place. I closed my lids slowly and shook my head from side to side.

Well fudge. This was not how I had expected today to go at all.

"OK, darling," I said with false cheer. "I had best let him in then."

"Katie," Eric said softly. "As soon as the lock-down's lifted I'll let you know." It was the only solace he could offer and we both knew it.

"You just take care of business there, Eric. I'll entertain the Captain for as long as it takes."

Eric chuckled. "God, now you've got me considering becoming an operative again. If only my heightened level of intelligence wasn't needed in the brains of the organisation, I could have been the one being entertained by you today."

I laughed, my smile returning to my face at last.

"We go where we are needed, Mr Shaw."

"Would you hold it against me if I said I need you, Ms Anscombe?"

"You are incorrigible, darling." A banging started up at the front of the house, my heart skipped several beats and I completely missed Eric's next comeback line.

"Ah, Eric, I better get that."

"OK, sweetheart. I guess there's only so long we can leave him out in the cold." Had Eric been purposely distracting me at Jason's expense? My lips tipped up further.

We both rang off and I carefully put my cellphone back down on the desk. I stared blankly at my laptop screen, which had switched to the screen saver at some time during my conversation with Eric. I watched the cosmic pattern of brightly lit stars for several seconds, then jumped at the sound of further banging on my front door.

Taking a deep breath, I stood up whilst opening my desk drawer and pulling out the sheathed knife I kept hidden there. Nick had taught me to fire a gun, as he had my older brother Dominic. But whereas he allowed Dominic to carry a pistol when needed, he resolutely refused to let me obtain a firearms licence. I understood his reticence, but I also understood the world he now traversed in. I loved my brothers, I knew the reason for their over protectiveness was because they loved me. But I am not one to leave my protection up to others. I like my independence too much. So for the past three years I've been studying Eskrima, or more particularly Arnis and the modern version of knife wielding, Kombatan. A mixture of Filipino and Japanese martial arts.

I could handle a knife as well as Nick could handle a gun. So far I hadn't had cause to use my chosen form of weaponry outside of training. But with ASI on lock-down, and Jason Cain at my front door, there was no time like the present to be prepared.

I walked out of my office and strode with purpose towards the front door and the now insistent banging coming from outside. The glass rattled in the frame with the effort Jason was putting into pounding on it. I rolled my eyes, flicked the blade of my knife up along the sleeve of my shirt to conceal it, and checked the peep hole to make sure the baboon on the other side was who I suspected it was.

"Open up the god-dammed door, Kate."

Yes, Jason Cain, the only person to call me Kate. Not Katie. Not sweetheart. Not even Catherine. But Kate. Short, abrasive and abrupt. That was Jason.

"Don't get your fatigues in a knot, Captain," I muttered under my breath, flicking the lock on the door and taking a hurried step back as Jason barrelled through the opening.

He stood over me with fury in his eyes. I half expected to see steam coming out in puffs from each ear. My lips edged up at the vision.

"You think a lock-down is humorous?" he growled.

I tried not show my amusement. It didn't work.

He took a menacing step towards me, while kicking the door closed with his booted foot. Big thick soled booted foot. The type of boot only military personnel wear. Jason hadn't quite let go of the Army, even though the Army had definitely let go of him.

All levity left me. I flicked a steady gaze up to his face, allowing myself to see what I'm sure he thinks he hides from everyone else. Sadness hid in the corner of his rich chestnut coloured eyes. Sometimes you'd see a deeper chocolate colour, but most of the time the hardness he wears across his façade hides the melted tone and you're stuck with unforgiving chestnut instead.

His lips were pressed in a thin frowning line, creases marred his forehead. Jason wasn't always angry, I'd seen him laughing once or twice with his sister Gen, but around me he can't seem to control his temper, as though I'm the catalyst to his rage, the spark that ignites the fire. Something arced between Jason and me, something electric and dangerous and exciting. It fascinated me and, I think, it scared him. Neither of us willing to test that connection further.

His hair had grown out slightly, I noticed, not quite the buzz cut blond of before. He may still dress like a soldier, but at least he'd embraced a more relaxed look with his hairstyle. Small curls had started to grow at his neck, brushing curved tendrils across unblemished tanned skin. I felt my fingers twitch with a desire to do the same.

I sucked in a shaky breath, tried to ignore my overpowering hormonal response to this man and crossed my arms over my chest in an effort to give as much attitude as I could manage. I'm not known for my attitude, so I was sure the move was lost on him.

Until he spotted the knife.

"What the fuck?" Jason exclaimed suddenly, reaching out in lightning quick moves to capture my hand, thereby immobilising my arm, so he could turn my wrist up and display the long six inch blade clearly.

His fierce eyes came up to mine and stared at me intently. I swallowed thickly under a magnetic trance.

"Planning on gutting me with that, Kate? Careful," he taunted. "You might break a nail."

I don't know why I retaliated. Jason had been pushing my buttons for months now, this current barb was nothing new. Maybe it was the fact that I held my knife, my weapon of choice, while he mocked me that did it. When my fingers wrap around the hilt of a blade I become someone else.

I ran my free hand up his arm, the arm attached to the hand immobilising me. Watched as his nostrils flared at the intimate action, then he released his grasp preparing to pull back. I'd counted on that. You think Kombatan is all about wielding a knife? It's not. The knife is only part of the equation. My instructor took great means to ensure we used *all* of our skills to overcome an enemy. I wasn't above using my feminine wiles to achieve that goal.

I took advantage of the gap and freedom Jason had created, and flicked the knife out and up under his chin. The tip of the shiny blade dug in infinitesimally. I hadn't drawn blood, but you wouldn't know that by the colourless look to his cheeks.

We both stilled. Neither of us breathing. Then he smirked. A condescending smile meant to unnerve me. I gave as good a glare as I could muster, but the smirk just spread further.

"Well now," Jason drawled. "This is an interesting development indeed. Does Nick know you play with sharp implements, like a wannabe ninja warrior princess?"

I took a step closer, not shifting the knife tip at all, but using my increased heart rate to fuel my anger. This may not have been part of my Kombatan training, but I didn't care. Jason made a part of me, long thought buried, rise up like a snake from a charmer's basket.

I smiled, it was probably calculating and snarled, "Back off, Cain!"

I don't really know what happened next. It was quick, so sudden, and my body was spun around several times that the dizziness created added to the confusion of seeing my knife on the floor discarded and feeling my back pressed up firmly against the wall several feet down the hallway. Without a pause for my mind to catch up to the change in dynamics and the new position I now found myself in, Jason's body slammed flush against mine.

"Kate, Kate, Kate," he purred above me, one hand still holding my knife arm at the wrist down by our sides, the other wrapped around the front of my throat: palm hot and heavy, yet gentle against such a vulnerable part of the body. "That was uncalled for," he added with a soft shake of his head.

I blinked, tried to still my thunderous heartbeat and sucked in a short, sharp stab of air. None of it settled my nerves or gave me any clarity. How the hell did he disarm me so easily?

"We've got at least twenty-four hours in each other's company," Jason murmured, shifting his face closer, relaxing his body against the length of mine. I was sure it was all an act, purely designed to throw me off balance. *I think.* Whatever it was, it was working. Damn it. "If you want to fight me the entire time I'm here, then let's get a couple of things straight."

He leaned in further, his hot breath washing over my cheek. At every point on my body where his touched I felt hot streaks of lightning shoot past. I could feel the measured rise and fall of his chest, the slow, steady beat of his heart through his shirt. The firm and powerful strength of his thighs against mine. I wanted to close my eyelids and savour the sensations he created. But I would not give him the satisfaction.

"Anything you can do, I can do better," he whispered.

And maybe it was his cheesy choice of words, or maybe it was just time for me to grow a pair, as my brothers would say, but I woke up from the fantasy his proximity had created and let my body relax, giving the impression of capitulation. Playing possum, something Nick would approve of, I was sure.

I felt Jason's body mould further into mine, I kept my eyes averted from his face, which was now mere centimetres from my own. His hand at my throat began a slow caress; it was so unexpected, I almost tensed. Then he shifted, slightly, moving his large frame to the side as his hand holding my wrist released its grip and moved. I have no idea where he intended it to go, but I took the opportunity of distraction to twist beneath his grasp, raise my free non-dominant hand up and punch him hard under the chin with the palm of my extended arm.

I'm not particularly good at close hand-to-hand combat. I have practised with my trainer, but always with a knife in my grasp. The principle, even unarmed, is the same though. His head shot back with a grunt pressed through his lips, his chest shifted with the momentum, and I gave a swift jab with my dominant right hand into the side of his torso, near the vicinity of his kidney.

He doubled over and I used the increased space between us to escape, coming to rest a meter down the hall to watch him recover. When his furious eyes rose up to meet mine I finally spoke.

"You are welcome in my house, Jason. But if you ever touch me again, I *will* gut you."

He slowly stood upright, his gaze running over my body in a way I had never seen him do before. It was blatantly sexual. Hungry, full of desire and longing, carnal in nature. He hid nothing. And it was everything I thought Jason would be, but had never shown me. He tried his utmost to offer me only indifference mixed with a smattering of disdain normally. Sure, occasionally I'd think I see a hint of something else, but Jason worked damn hard to maintain that icy façade between us. This, right here though, was entirely new. Something I'd dreamed about, but never thought I'd witness. And now that I did, it left me feeling decidedly anxious. Fearful of the craving he chose to let me see.

"Is that a challenge, Kate?" he asked, taking a seductive step closer.

I knew how to handle a disgruntled Jason. I even had experience in how to handle an irate Jason. But the Jason who prowled towards me did not come with an instruction manual. I had no idea how to combat *this* Jason. I swallowed thickly, he watched the move with a predatory gleam in his eyes. Which, incidentally, were now full on deep chocolate brown. And I swear my heart leapt for joy.

Traitorous organ.

"What are you going to do now, Kate?" Jason murmured, his voice several octaves lower than before.

My eyes darted around the small space we were in, spotted my knife on the floor, closer to Jason than me. Then finally, after admitting I was stymied, I lifted a defiant gaze to his face.

He chuckled, relaxed back on his heels and let the smirk have free rein.

"Kate," he chastised in a rough, but clearly amused voice. "If you can't handle the fire, then don't pick up a fucking knife."

And OK, that was absolutely the most god-awful bastardisation of a saying I had ever heard, but he was right. Jason Cain was fire, and I was truly well out of my league.

CHAPTER 2

YOU DON'T KNOW THE REAL ME

JASON LEFT ME IN THE HALLWAY WITH NOT SO MUCH AS A backwards glance. He strode off into the lounge to no doubt investigate security there. Which was confirmed as I heard him rattle several locks on the windows and test the handle on the rear kitchen door. I let a slow breath out and attempted to still my rapidly beating heart.

This day just kept getting worse. And I still had a design to finish for Mrs Montgomery-Smith. I shook my head in bewilderment and stepped forward to pick up my now pathetic looking knife off the floor.

"Careful with that, Kate," Jason called from the next room. "Can't take you to an A&E if you slice yourself. Lock-down means you get me stitching up any injuries and I don't much care for anaesthetic. Waste of time."

I glared at the doorway to the lounge. I couldn't see him, so how he knew I'd picked up my knife, I don't know. But the glare helped me contain my anger and stopped me from biting back... exactly what he wanted. No, the best course of action was to pretend Jason Cain wasn't in my house at all.

I walked back toward my office and resheathed the knife, slipping it away into my desk and out of sight. The desire to keep it on me at all times over the next twenty-four hours was relentless. But impractical. So, in the drawer it went.

I slumped down in my chair and shifted my mouse to bring up the design I was working on. I stared at it mutely for several long seconds, then decided to scrap the entire thing and start all over again. It's not often I cross off a design and bin it this late in the game. All that effort. All those hours. For what? But for some strange reason I decided Mrs Montgomery-Smith would like a little more than my signature designs. I was thinking alternate, sharp and definitely hot.

God knows I needed something to occupy my mind for the next few hours. Anything to make me stop picturing Jason with that sexy glint to his eyes and hunger in his stance.

Seven hours later I'd created what I humbly think is my most impressive piece of work to date. It was captivating; sensual with a kick. Not many people could live with this style; bold prints mixed with striking stripes. Complementary colour combinations that almost, but not quite, clashed with contrasting patterns and designs. One word could sum it up: Edgy. It certainly matched my current mood.

But despite how different it was from my normal designs, I loved it. And for a moment I just stared at it, thinking where the hell had this come from? I mean, I try new things out all the time. I keep abreast of current fads and the latest fashions in the market, it's my job. It's what my clients expect. But I had never taken a step in a completely different direction before; a setter, not a follower, of the latest trend.

Mrs Montgomery-Smith could easily dismiss it with one highly opinionated glance. But it was too good for that. I *knew* it. This was something altogether special. And it had just popped into my head unexpectedly, on a day that had taken a decidedly disastrous turn.

Which made me realise belatedly that I probably wouldn't have had this epiphany if Jason Cain hadn't walked through my door.

Oh good Lord. Jason Cain is my muse?

I made a strangled sound from the back of my throat and shook my head vehemently. *That* was out of the question completely. A coincidence, nothing more.

"You should take a break," Jason said from over my shoulder. Surprising me for more than one reason.

I hadn't realised he'd walked into my office and was looking at my design on the laptop screen. But that wasn't the entire reason for my shock. He sounded like he cared. Until he continued talking, that is.

"You've been at this for seven hours now. It's time for food and I'm starved."

I swung around to glare up at him. He just raised his eyebrows in a quasi-challenge which we both knew I wouldn't accept.

"Besides," he added, signature smirk gracing his lips at last. "You've started making strange noises to yourself, next you'll be holding a conversation all on your own."

"Rather like you are right now," I shot back, turning to my laptop to hit print. I always kept hard-copies of my designs, in case the client asked for them.

Hot breath washed over my shoulder and across my cheek. Jason's voice was a seductive murmur in my ear.

"Kate, when have you ever ignored me?"

The cocky, self-assured bastard. I purposely didn't answer. He just laughed out loud and moved toward the door.

"By the way," he said over his shoulder, "I like Italian dinners and red wine. Be a doll and fix me up."

"I'll bloody well fix you up," I muttered under my breath, hearing a distinct chuckling sound from further in the house.

I concentrated on writing an email to Mr and Mrs Montgomery-Smith and attaching my design file to it. It took all of two minutes. Not nearly long enough for me to settle my heartbeat and steady my nerves. I shut-down my laptop not feeling the usual sense of relief at meeting an impossible deadline and finishing an exceptional project outline. I should have been ecstatic. I would normally be opening a bottle of wine in celebration. Now I was determined to cook Chinese and slap tap water on the table.

But that would be immature. And would fall right into Jason's god-complex trap. I needed to behave the way my mother had raised me, and not let the man see how he affected me at all.

I straightened my blouse, dusted off my dress pants and walked out of the office, flipping the light switch off as I left. The TV was on low as I entered the living area. Jason was sprawled on the couch as though he belonged there. My eyes took in the length of him, every... single... inch. I closed my lids and sucked in a long breath of air, then forced myself to ignore the Adonis reclining on my settee and crossed the open-plan space into the kitchen itself.

I heard the early news programme start up in the background. It did not surprise me that Jason Cain would keep abreast of current affairs. As I began pulling ingredients out of the pantry and fridge I couldn't help feeling how nice it was to have someone else in my home for once. I'd been working so hard on building my client base, making a name for myself in the cut-throat arena that is interior design, that I had neglected my social life.

Occasionally Gen would come over to watch a movie, or I'd have a few pre-dinner drinks with old girlfriends before we hit the town, but admittedly they had become less frequent. And a man in my lounge, while I prepared a meal in the kitchen, was unheard of. It was just a shame that this ideal picture of domesticity included a man like Jason Cain.

The sound of my home line ringing cut into my thoughts and interrupted my food preparation. I walked the short distance to the phone and lifted the handset, offering my usual greeting when the line connected.

"Katie Anscombe."

"Hey, sis! How're you holding up?" Nick asked, concern etching his voice.

"Never better, darling," I replied, habit making the response automatic.

"Is that right?" he drawled down the line. "You haven't killed each other yet then?"

My eyes flicked up to the lounge in time to see Jason sauntering over towards me. I was momentarily stunned silent as he smoothly glided past without acknowledging my presence. I watched as he approached the vegetables I'd been halfway through chopping and for a moment I thought he was about to take over dinner preparation. But he bypassed the partially cut onions and peered into the pantry. I rolled my eyes as he pulled back, hand fisted around the neck of a bottle of Merlot. An expensive bottle of Merlot.

"No, not yet," I murmured into the phone. "But the temptation is definitely present."

The Merlot clug-clug-clugged into a wine glass, which was promptly pushed across the bench towards me and then the action repeated for his own glass. He then leaned back against the sink and took a sip, eyes locked on mine.

"Just remember he's there for a reason, sis," Nick was saying in my ear. "Don't damage my staff until the lock-down is over, OK?"

"Why *are* we in lock-down?" I asked, eyes still held prisoner by Jason's determined gaze. He leaned forward and pushed my untouched glass of wine a fraction closer. The message was clear. I ignored it.

"Just a little trouble with Declan King, nothing for you to worry about."

"You say that like King can be reasoned with," I pointed out, well aware of who Declan King was. I kept abreast of current affairs as well, and Declan King was Auckland's premier criminal.

"A misunderstanding, that's all." Nick explained breezily. Then ruined the casual effect he'd been aiming for by adding, "A small exchange of bullets in a back alley while I extricated Ben's target from King's clutches. King really took it entirely the wrong way."

I froze, white knuckled around the telephone handset, as an image of Nick being shot flicked through my head.

"It was nothing, Katie," he offered, maybe picking up on my

stunned silence. "All in a day's work," he added, making me suck in an angry breath of air.

"I wish you wouldn't treat me like a child, Nicholas," I murmured, then watched as Jason placed his glass on the bench with care and rounded the edge of divider to reach my side. He lifted up my glass with one hand, then lifted up my free hand with his other, and placed the two together.

My lips twitched, despite Nick's overly casual explanation of what could have been a dire event.

"Katie," Nick said on an exasperated sigh. "It was nothing, *really*. You don't need to get upset. Can't a big brother wash over the nastier side of his profession to his sister if he likes?"

"Bullets, Nick," I pointed out. But this was Nick, and bullets and my brother went hand in hand. I'd had to learn to deal with my fear early on. Now was no different.

My eyes were still on Jason while I spoke, watching as he returned to his glass of wine on the other side of the kitchen. He settled back against the cupboards and raised the glass in a toast, waiting for me to mirror the move.

I shook my head in bemusement, for a brief moment forgetting how dangerous my brother's chosen profession actually was, and lifted my wine in a salute then took a sip. It was nice. So I took another straight away, feeling the tension of Nick's admission ease with each progressive mouthful. Jason smiled. It wasn't a smirk, which was why I lost all train of thought for a moment and just stared.

"Katie? Are you even listening?" Nick asked, voice raised as though he'd been trying to get my attention for a while.

"Sorry, darling," I quipped. "I'm a little hungry, skipped lunch to work on a project. I think I might need to eat something before I pass out."

"Oh, OK. Just," Nick paused, clearly unsure how to phrase his next words. "Just don't get into anything with Cain, all right?"

"What do you mean?" I asked, a definite nervous edge to my tone.

"Katie. He's, fuck, how do I put this? Well, he's a good employee and I don't want to lose him, but he's also, um, he's a..."

"Nick, for God's sake spit it out!" I demanded, getting frustrated with my brother and realising belatedly that I'd taken three more sips of my wine. The glass was now half empty.

"He's a player," Nick blurted, as though trying to get the words out before he changed his mind.

"Why on earth would you tell me this?" I asked incredulously, downing another large sip of wine. I grimaced and placed the glass back on the bench, only to watch as Jason refilled it in the blink of an eye.

"You think I haven't noticed how he looks at you, Katie?" Nick surprised me by saying, his voice low, almost a snarl. "He thinks he hides it." Hides what? "But we all see it. A man like him and a woman like you..." He stopped talking to suck in a breath of air.

My heart skipped a beat. Just what the hell was Nick saying? Had Jason actually looked at me with interest before today? Was he really attracted to me? Or was it just my lust addled brain making something out of nothing? Oh, God. If Nick had seen Jason looking at me in some manner, what had he seen me do in return? A blush stole up my cheeks at that thought. Had others seen my desire too?

"It's just that we've got to know him a bit over the past few months," Nick added finally, "and well, it's clear he is not ready to settle down." Oh dear Lord.

"Nick," I said, and there was no denying I was getting uncomfortable now. "This is highly inappropriate." For crying out loud, the topic of conversation was standing across the room from me watching my every reaction and probably hearing every word Nick had said as well. This was so embarrassing. What if Jason hadn't been looking at me the way Nick thought he'd seen?

Oh God, I'd give anything for this conversation to be back on gun shooting ground. How much did Nick think he knew? How much was true? But Jason had been blasé around me, so how had Nick seen differently? I wanted to believe what I think Nick was saying, but I just wasn't sure.

"Katie," Nick said softly. "You're not his type." Oh. Well, there went my stupid, romantic hopes up in flames. "So maybe this is all a waste of time, but from the stream of blonde busty bimbos he's trotted out before us I'd say the guy has a way with the ladies. I'd hate for him to take advantage of your current predicament and enclosed living quarters, and make a move on you just because he's got an itch to scratch."

Well, that was saying it straight. And blonde busty bimbos? I was not blonde nor was I a bimbo. And, regrettably, busty was not an adjective you'd use to describe my chest. I sighed.

"All right, warning heeded. I'm going back to preparing dinner. Take care of yourself, Nick."

"Katie," Nick said in a pleading tone of voice. "I didn't mean to upset you."

"I'm not upset," I immediately replied and watched Jason still the movement of his glass. It hung suspended in front of his lips as he cocked his head to the side slightly and studied me closely.

I took another large sip of wine to stifle my chagrin.

"All right," Nick sighed. "Just be careful. OK?"

I closed my eyes slowly and lowered my head. Nick meant well, but he failed to register that I was a big girl now. Twenty-nine years old and all grown up. I didn't require this needless interference and direction of my life. But Nick and Dominic both thought I was still the little sister with pigtails and a grazed knee, who needed a lollipop to stop the tears and the crap beaten out of the kid who'd pulled on my hair and made me trip over.

"I'll be fine, Nick," I promised, then made myself say the words he wanted to hear. "Love you." It's not that I didn't love him, I most certainly did. But right now I wanted to throttle him.

"Love you too, sis," he whispered and rang off.

I returned the handset to its cradle and then lifted my eyes to

Jason. He held my gaze for several seconds then flicked a look over the half prepared meal.

"How long until we eat?" he asked bluntly.

Ah, this was familiar territory. Thank you, Lord.

"Half an hour," I replied pushing past him to finish off the onion and get to work on the meat.

Jason just stood there, watching me work, sipping on his wine and burning me simply with his presence. I thought he might say something consoling about my over bearing and over protective sibling. I thought he might comment on my culinary skills, he seemed to be watching me like a hawk right then. I even considered he might just lighten the oppressive air since the phone call and defend himself against Nick's claims.

But he did none of those things. For several minutes he just watched me and when he finally decided to break the unbearable silence it was to say, "I'll open another bottle of wine then."

I shook my head in disbelief.

"Is that wise?" I asked archly. Hardly the actions of a dedicated bodyguard.

"Oh, I don't know, Kate," he said in that drawl of his, when he's winding up for a cheap shot. I bristled, but kept my focus on the sauce I was stirring on top of the stove.

His hot breath against the bare skin at the nape of my neck was the only warning I got that he'd moved. I jumped slightly, unable to prevent my reaction to the nearness of him.

He chuckled, then purred, "You seem to need something to make you relax."

His hands came down on my shoulders and I just about squeaked in utter surprise. He began to to knead my muscles, his fingers firm and persistent in their pursuit of my body's capitulation. I couldn't have relaxed now if my life depended on it. This was so intimate, so close.

So nice.

My head rolled back on my neck, an uncontrolled movement,

completely involuntary. If he kept this up I'd moan or make some equally embarrassing noise to let him know how much he was getting to me. I should have moved out of his reach. I should have bit back, slapped his hands away. But *no*, I just stood there and let him massage my shoulders for a good two minutes. The sauce bubbling away making steam rise up from the stove and the aroma of tomatoes and basil wafting through the air.

He moved closer all of a sudden. The heat from his chest washing down my spine. His fingers and hot palms never stopped rubbing, kneading, almost stroking. I think I might have made a purr.

His cheek brushed against mine as he leaned over my shoulder, his larger frame completely engulfing my own. The sink was in front of me, his body was behind, and his hands on my shoulders made escape to the sides impossible right then. Not that my mind would have considered that a viable option. No, my mind had packed up shop and my hormones had moved right on in.

I leaned back into him, appalled at myself for showing this blatant sensual response.

"Mmm," he murmured in my ear, his face and nose nuzzling my hair. "Maybe I will spice things up a bit with a brunette for once."

I jerked still at his words. He'd definitely heard everything Nick had said on the phone. And he was angry. I would be too, if someone pigeon holed me like my brother just did him. It would have been easy to let him continue this little game; to torment me because he was lashing out. That was Jason; a trained killer. That didn't just mean he could take someone's life with his bare hands, it also meant he could destroy them with words as well.

But as much as the man infuriated me, I wasn't going to let him do something he'd regret. Nick's warning to me was still forefront in my mind. But rather than heeding his advice and protecting myself, I felt compelled to protect Jason instead.

"Don't let him make you do this, Jason," I said softly. I felt his body stiffen. "I know we walk in different worlds. I know you despise all that I appear to be. But that doesn't mean I don't respect who you are. Nick doesn't know you, he thinks he does. And likewise, you don't know the real me."

I turned to face him then, he'd taken a step back, utterly stunned at my speech. I don't know if the words meant anything or not, but his breathing was quick and the pulse at the bottom of his neck fluttered with increased speed. Whatever I'd said had done *something*.

I held his gaze for several long seconds and then turned back to the stove to serve up the meal. By the time I had our plates ready, Jason had returned to his earlier self. Wine glass in hand, steady look in his eyes. I placed the laden plates on the table, organised cutlery and napkins and then took a seat.

I'd already begun my meal before he finally sat himself down in the chair opposite me. I took a sip of wine and lifted my gaze to his face. He was still watching me, a strange puzzlement to his features that hadn't been there before.

"You are a complex woman, Kate," he said, picking up his fork at last and taking a bite of his meal.

I relaxed, realising the moment had passed and Jason was once again the cool, calm, collected soldier I knew so well.

Then he murmured, wine glass to his lips, "But you're wrong."

Wrong about what? That he doesn't know the real me? Or that he despises all that I appear to be?

CHAPTER 3

HAVE I BEEN ON HIS TOO?

Jason offered to stack the dishwasher and because I still felt so off kilter around him, I agreed. Slinking into the lounge and surfing channels on the TV. I finally settled on a wildlife documentary. It seemed the safest route to take. I didn't think he'd appreciate home makeover shows, and I couldn't quite stomach a crime story. Nature seemed, well, *natural*.

Until the lion caught the gazelle and the zebras started mating.

I must have made a sound of disgust. It wasn't so much because of the scene playing out in full colour on my larger than life TV screen, but more because I'd clearly chosen poorly. Couldn't it have been about the eating habits of flamingoes or something?

"Not a horse fan, Kate?" Jason asked as he slid into the armchair off to my side. I forced myself not to stare at the small expanse of naked rock hard abdomen that peeked out from under his t-shirt. It was difficult, but I managed.

"Equid," I replied distractedly.

"What?"

"Zebras are part of the equidae family. So are horses. But they are technically not a horse."

He huffed out a laugh. "Is that so?" he asked, but he clearly wasn't interested in an answer.

I flicked a gaze towards his face to see if I could determine what he was thinking from his expression. His eyes were on the zebras. Head cocked to the side as he watched them do their thing. Unlike most wild animals, it seemed to go on for much longer than necessary.

"I can see why you'd watch this," he muttered eventually. "I wouldn't," he added. "But, yeah, I can get why you would."

"Excuse me?" I asked, a little taken back. Why would he think zebras mating would be my thing?

He flicked deep chocolate brown eyes to me, that smirk in residence again. Then waved an arm loosely at the screen. The zebras had thankfully completed their moment of abandonment, but the narrator had not finished dissecting every single move.

He held my gaze for an extended period of time, then said, voice low, "It's clean." What? "Don't have to get your hands dirty. Voyeuristic even," he added, then turned back to the TV.

What the hell?

"Er, you're not making any sense, Jason," I pointed out.

"OK," he said, shifting in his seat so he could face me.

I didn't like the change of position, the fact that I now had his undivided attention. Any attention from Jason set my blood boiling, but to have the weight of his complete concentration and gaze on me was almost too much.

"Zebras aren't the real issue. But I guess, as a metaphor, they'd suit you."

He'd completely lost me. It must have shown on my face.

"You watch a lot of TV?" he asked, apropos nothing.

"Some," I admitted. It was a good way to switch off from designs and the day to day drudgery of life. A distraction that required little effort.

"I thought so," he said in a superior way that made my hackles rise. "You don't go out much, do you, Kate? Not many drinks with friends or dates with handsome men."

Oh, and now I was feeling rather uncomfortable. Jason Cain psychoanalysing me. This was *so* wrong.

"Some," I murmured, aware I was repeating myself, but for an entirely different reason.

He nodded. Sanctimonious man.

"Haven't seen you with a boyfriend. Not once. Not at any of Gen and Dom's gatherings."

"Is there a point to all of this, Jason?" I asked, starting to get a little miffed with the line of conversation.

"You asked," he pointed out with a shrug. "You watch life, Kate. You don't dive right in. You sit back where it's safe, where you won't get mud on your designer shoes or a tear in your expensive silk skirt. You're a spectator, not a participant."

His hand flew back to point at the TV screen.

"I bet half of what you know is from television or books. Have you ever seen a zebra in the wild?"

"Have you?" I shot back, noticing my arms had crossed over my chest as though I could defend myself with that move alone. I forcefully unravelled them and rested my clasped hands in my lap.

"Did a safari in Africa when I was nineteen," he said casually.

I felt about two inches tall. Jason *had* seen and done a lot of things, I was sure. What had I done? A few European and North American holidays with my parents. The obligatory overseas experience, or OE, for young Kiwis to London for a year. But that was about it. The rest of my life had been in Auckland. I attended university here. I started my business and career here. I bought my first home here.

I suddenly wanted to be anywhere else than in this room with this man, who judged.

"I'm not sure I understand your point, Jason," I said standing up from my seat. "But I am sure I don't care to work it out right now. I'm going to bed. The spare room is made up, you can sleep there."

I managed two steps towards the exit before he replied.

"First, I'll stay awake. Out here. No point protecting you if I'm asleep. But don't let my discomfort worry you, Kate. You just get your precious beauty sleep and I'll keep us safe."

My fists clenched and I turned to glare at him. What I wouldn't give for a throwing knife right now. His lips twitched at the edges.

"Second," he added, resting back in the armchair as though my obvious anger was the height of entertainment for him. "My point is simple. You're too wound up. You need to relax. Live a little. Taste life. Take a risk."

I arched an eyebrow at him.

"Is that so?" I asked, mimicking his earlier words and tone. "And you would be the expert on living life and risk taking, I suppose."

He shrugged, an infuriating movement that made me fume.

"I've lived a little. I could show you how."

"What?" I spluttered, forgetting to clench my fists, but instead somehow finding them resting at my sides ineffectually.

His slight lip twitch turned into a sexy smirk.

"Yeah. I reckon I could teach you to loosen up."

I felt like the ground was falling out from beneath my feet, the terrain shifting. One step in the wrong direction and I'd lose my footing. Jason looked like he was searching for something, no, that's not entirely right. He was hunting for something. And I had the distinct impression I was his prey of choice.

God, the man made my head spin, in more ways than I cared to admit. Part of me hated him. Part of me was drawn to him. And part of me wanted to rise to the challenge I could see in his eyes, and shock the living daylights out of the arrogant prick.

The question was, which part would win right now? Did I go there? Did I carry on this ridiculous conversation and risk further embarrassment? Not to mention increased blood pressure.

Obviously my higher reasoning was defunct. Or I just wanted that challenge.

"And how would you achieve that, Cain?"

"Well," he drawled, rising up from his chair in one smooth move. A glide of muscles and limbs, and a heart palpating show of sensual agility. "It would mean getting dirty. Probably a little sweaty."

I swallowed, unable to take my eyes off the amused chocolate brown of his. He chuckled. The enticing jerk. And then took a step towards me. I took one back automatically.

Shaking his head he chastised, "No, no, no, Kate. If you want to taste life, you have to face it. None of this running away. Meet it head on, grasp it. Can you do that?"

I froze, was this actually happening?

He took a further step and there was nothing I could do to make myself move away. I hated that he did this to me, stripped me of everything and left a wanton mess in its place. But I was addicted to that sensation he stirred deep inside, a pull low in my belly, a rush of wetness to my core. No man had ever elicited such differing emotions in me before. No man, but Jason Cain.

"Good," he almost whispered, his voice lowered to such a degree that it sounded too intimate.

He took another step and came to rest right before me, my head had to tip back to keep eye contact with him.

"So," he murmured. "Dirty and sweaty." I forced my eyes to remain open and not give in to the delicious image he created. "And most importantly, Kate. I'd want to hear you." Oh, God. "No holds barred." The urge to clamp my thighs together was almost too great. "Let down that wall." I was drowning, gulping for much needed air. He reached up and tugged on my ponytail until the tie came loose and the strands fell about my shoulders. And I just let him.

I just let him.

His eyes darkened, heading toward that chestnut colour he usually has when he's angry. He didn't appear angry right now - oh no, angry was *not* what I'd describe Jason in this second - but then I'd never seen him like this before, so had nothing to go on. I was guessing that darker colour came out when any emotion swelled. Right now, I couldn't tell if that emotion was a good one or not. It felt good, but Nick had said Jason was a player. Was he simply playing me now?

"Jason," I began, in an effort to sound level headed and in control.

"Yeah?" he murmured, eyes scanning my hair as he ran a few strands between his fingertips, distractedly.

This was such dangerous ground. Exciting and exhilarating. Oh dear God, was it exhilarating. But I wasn't sure that I could trust it. Nick's warning rang out in my head and I simply could not ignore that. By shutting this down though, I *would* confirm everything Jason thought I was. A spectator in life, not a participant.

But I couldn't risk the fallout if this was all just a game to him. I was *not* going to put myself there.

And besides, who the hell was he to tell me what I am or am not?

"I'm going to bed," I said, voice only slightly shaky. "If you want a *cold* shower, there's towels in the cupboard under the sink."

I didn't wait for a reply, but swung on my heels and walked as casually as I could out of the lounge. I couldn't get to my bedroom fast enough, but I made myself walk slowly. Heel, toe. Heel, toe. Heel, toe. The click of the door to my sanctuary was the signal that I could finally breathe.

I sank back against the closed door and sucked in air; a drowning victim given a second chance at life. Oh good heavens. The man was a stick of dynamite away from an explosion. My heart was racing, my respirations were way too fast. My body ached in all the most delicious places and my skin tingled.

I had never felt so much at once before.

A bubble of laughter sprang up my throat, but I resolutely forced the sound back down before Mr Perceptive out there could notice. He was right though. I did watch life. Oh, I had my place in it, one I'd carved out meticulously. One I didn't risk. But in all the years I'd been making a name for myself, building up my business, finding a niche, I hadn't once felt what I felt just now.

Jason Cain pushed every button I had... and then some I didn't even know I'd been missing.

I stared across the room in a numb haze, trying to align this new Jason I'd just been introduced to, with the Jason I'd known for several months now. Had I missed what Nick and maybe others had seen? Had I been so distracted by my attraction for him, that I hadn't seen his own for me?

I'd assumed Jason was indifferent, because that's what Jason had made sure I'd see. But Nick said he looked at me a certain way. What way? Dear God, I wanted to know. Was I crazy to want him to feel the same way? Hell, I'd be crazy not to want him to feel the same way.

I banged my head back softly against the closed door, not loud enough for him to hear, but enough to clear my head. And then tried to remember every single time I'd crossed paths with Captain Jason Cain. Unsurprisingly, each had been etched into my brain and could be recalled with crystal clarity.

That first time I'd been caught entirely off guard and Jason had endeavoured to keep me that way ever since. I'd turned up at Dom's house to check on his new woman at the time - Genevieve - and Jason was there. I'd been attempting to lighten the mood, as Gen had been involved with a dangerous and nasty ex-boyfriend receiving injuries to both her physical and emotional self. I'd joked in the usual Katie Anscombe way. It meant nothing, it was all a ruse designed to make people smile. But it had made me look like a flighty socialite without substance.

Jason had shown his disdain immediately. That scowl I've come to know so very well gracing his handsome face. I'd taken one look at him and felt my world alter. One of those strange, inexplicable, but entirely real moments. I literally took one look at the man and I knew my life had changed. I wanted him, from that instant. Despite his unfriendly greeting, despite his obvious judgement of my behaviour. I took one look and decided he was the man I wanted in my life.

Why? Was it simply a case of opposites attract? He didn't faun all over me, he was strong, potent, in command of his world. God, it gives me goosebumps even now. I can't adequately explain it, but one look at Jason Cain and I wanted to have his babies.

That bubble of laughter rose up my throat again, and this time I couldn't stop it escaping. At least I kept a lid on the volume. This was insane. I'm an accomplished, independent woman. But all of that was stripped away when presented with a male who met every criteria my subconscious had for a mate.

Just like that animal programme on TV, we are all subject to evolution in the end. To the procreation of our kind. When stripped of everything else we are just animals. And I had it bad for the alpha of all animals. Twenty-nine years old and my biological clock was obviously ticking.

I knew how that first encounter had gone, I've played it over and over in my head. But had I missed something? Had I only looked at it from my perspective because he'd bowled me off my feet? I replayed the scene over in my head, trying to remain objective. It was hard. My life had changed that day, the significance of meeting Jason had altered who I thought I was.

But over lunch he had watched me, his eyes never straying to his plate or the others at the table, until things heated up and he had to defend his sister. The entire time the ASI guys chatted, and Dom kept a proprietary hand on Genevieve's knee, Jason had been glaring at me. I thought it was because he found my presence annoying. The socialite sister tagging along and claiming the men's attention, when urgent matters were needed to be discussed instead.

Oh my God. He'd been unable to look away. I'd forgotten that. He'd been as drawn to me as I had to him.

I quickly scanned through my memories for other events when we'd crossed paths. Most of the time it had been at Dom and Gen's barbecues, which were held only fortnightly. Other than that, I'd bumped into him three times at Sweet Seduction, and once outside of ASI.

My head jerked up, from where I'd been staring blindly at the carpet. Every single time we'd seen each other he'd looked at me as much as I'd looked at him. If he was really not attracted to me, wouldn't he have just ignored my presence altogether?

A smile stretched my lips. *"Kate, when have you ever ignored me?"* I hadn't. But then neither had he ignored me.

Oh Lord, was I insane to think this? Was I reading too much into a few casual glances? No, they hadn't been casual in the slightest. Nick was right, Jason did look at me a certain way.

Images flicked through my head in quick, beautiful succession. Dom's house, across the patio where the barbecue sits. Our eyes connecting for longer than necessary. Sweet Seduction, picking up a takeaway coffee and turning to see him sitting in the corner with Adam, eyes on my behind. Outside ASI, crashing into him as he exited the front door, his arms grabbing my shoulders to stop me falling, his eyes locked on my breasts as I sucked in a surprised breath of air.

Jason Cain was attracted to me, and he hid it about as well as I think I hid my attraction for him.

Oh good Lord, this was madness. For months he had occupied my mind. Have I been on his too?

CHAPTER 4

EVEN OBSERVANT, CALCULATING, INTELLIGENT EX-SOLDIERS, WHO WERE TWO STEPS AHEAD OF ME, COULDN'T READ MINDS

I CHANGED INTO MY SILK PYJAMAS AFTER COMING TO THAT mind blowing realisation. Climbing between the sheets, I wondered if I could sleep at all. My heart was beating an unfathomable rhythm inside my chest, my palms were sweaty with excitement and nerves. My head was reeling from the memories I had replayed and the different slant I now could interpret in them.

I wasn't an idiot though. Just because I could see that Jason had been hiding his attraction to me for all this time, didn't mean he'd suddenly change tomorrow and pursue me with open honesty and blatant lust. He might have propositioned me tonight, in an offhand way, but that was probably more of a knee-jerk reaction, a defence mechanism he relied on, when dealing with a challenging opponent. At least, I'd like to think I'm a challenge.

But I knew that what made Jason a mystery I couldn't stop craving to figure out, was also what made Jason refuse to acknowledge his attraction for me. Something held him back, and just because I'd seen through his ruse, didn't mean he'd show his true colours now.

I sighed, rolled over onto my side and tried to get some sleep.

Impossible. I knew Jason was just outside my room, in the lounge, lying out on the settee. Or knowing Jason, he'd done a circuit of the property as soon as my door had closed, just to make sure the place was secure. He was a tightly coiled spring, always alert and ready to strike or move to defend. You never knew when the spring would snap. You just knew that he could at any second.

It was that tight control, I think, that attracted me the most. Everything Jason did was planned, executed in an exacting manner. He didn't do rash, or spontaneous. He taunted me with my need to watch and not get involved in life. But Jason controlled everything. If he'd decided to proposition me, it wouldn't have been an off the cuff remark.

I sat bolt upright in bed. My heart thundering, my breaths trying to catch up. Jason did come on to me, didn't he? *"Yeah. I reckon I could teach you to loosen up."* How long had he wanted to do that? *"Dirty and sweaty. And most importantly, Kate. I'd want to hear you. No holds barred. Let down that wall."* Yes, that was a come on. Wasn't it?

I shook my head. This was ridiculous, I was making myself exhausted trying to work Jason out. But, what else could 'dirty and sweaty' mean? If not a come on, then what? Just a tease. A play to get me to react.

And here I was back at Nick's warning, making my heartbeat settle and my breath leave me in a defeated rush. I flopped back down on my bed and stared blindly at the ceiling. Enough! I needed to sleep, and then tomorrow this would all make some sort of sick sense.

Several minutes of clearing my mind, slowing my heart rate and relaxing my frame, just like my yoga instructor advised, and I managed to fall asleep. Thankfully it was sound enough that I didn't wake until morning, when reality came crashing back in.

The smell of bacon frying and coffee percolating permeated the air. My bedroom door was still shut, so the scents had managed to waft beneath the door frame to make it to my bed. It was clearly strong coffee and bacon wasn't a smell I was overly used to at this hour of the day.

I blinked sleep away, then attempted to push all memories of last night from my head. Going around in circles again this morning would not solve a thing. The only thing I should be concerning myself with right now, was the fact that Jason was in my kitchen cooking breakfast.

Was he cooking it for me?

I growled low in the back of my throat and pushed myself out of bed. I was such a lost cause.

Hurrying through my morning routine, I told myself the pace with which I washed, then brushed my teeth was merely because I wanted to be a good host, not at all because I wanted to see Jason. In my kitchen. Making breakfast like he belonged there.

Oh damn, I did have it bad.

And he was a player. Nick had said.

I sighed, straightened my blouse, checked my skirt and forced myself out of my bedroom and down the hall.

Jason stood at the stove humming a tune I couldn't quite recognise. I'll repeat that. He was humming a tune. Cheerfully. I couldn't align this softened and carefree image of Jason Cain with the soldier I had come to know. A small part of me wept for joy. Now *this* Jason, I could really like.

I hadn't made a sound. I'm sure of that. But somehow he knew I was there.

"You going to pour the juice, or just watch me cater to your every need?" He didn't even bother to turn around when he said that. Just kept on flipping bacon strips in the frying pan.

I walked haltingly over to the fridge and pulled out the bottle of OJ.

"Of course," he continued, still not acknowledging me with the courtesy of a glance, "I offered to see to your needs last night, but you turned me down."

I snorted at his cheek.

"Clearly the offer wasn't tempting enough then, was it?" I was rather proud of that comeback.

"Kate, Kate, Kate," he drawled in that now infuriating, but familiar way of his. "You wouldn't know a good offer if it came up and spanked you on the arse."

I bristled. How dare he?

"Or maybe I can recognise a player when I see one." Anger and embarrassment had made me say it, but I regretted the words as soon as they left my lips. God, Jason just pushed all my buttons. I admit some good and some, like now, infuriating.

Jason turned around giving me the full force of his chestnut glare.

"What would know of players, Kate?"

"I don't like games, Jason," I said, my voice softer than I had intended. It gave too much away.

"Games are what make life worth living, Kate. But then, I shouldn't expect you to know that, seeing as you barely participate in life as it is."

My hands found my hips and I returned his glare with equal fervour.

"Just because I don't care for your type of games, Cain, does not mean I don't know how to have fun." It was a fudge, a distraction at best. Something to make him focus on anything else but my inability to take risks. I didn't want Jason to think of me as a wall flower. I'd never thought of myself that way before.

He turned back to the stove and flicked the switch to cool the element, even took the time to shift the pan away from the heat. Safety first. Captain Jason Cain was in the room. His attention was soon back on me however.

"And how do you have fun, Kate Anscombe?" he asked, muscled arms crossed over his big chest.

Oh dear. He'd put me on the spot now.

"I, ah, I go out?" The words were said with a rising inflection on the end, as though I was unsure of my answer and was seeking confirmation from him.

He huffed out a sound of amusement.

"Yeah. And where do you go?"

"Bars. Clubs. I've been around." Oh boy.

He chuckled and shook his head.

"And when you go to these bars and clubs is it with men? Or women?"

"My girlfriends. But we, ah, we meet men all the time." God, could he tell I was making this up? Sure, I've been chatted up in bars before, but I don't make a habit of trawling for men when I'm out.

I guess that was his point. My eyes flicked over his face, trying to see where he was going with this. Just a tease? Or was it real? An attempt to get me to step out of my comfort zone.

"Have you kissed a stranger before?" he asked. "When you're out with your girlfriends meeting men?"

I couldn't tell if this was a game to him, or not. If it was, he hid that fact well. He was enjoying this, that much was obvious. He was also aware I was well out of my depth. For a second I doubted my attraction to him, what was it I saw in this man? Good looks and a fine body? He was attractive, in a bad-boy, know-you'd-enjoy-every-second-with-him way. So, maybe I was going through a rebellious stage. Maybe I had finally decided to be a teenager at the age of twenty-nine.

Jason Cain was everything my mother would warn me away from. But despite the casual ease with which he could tear a person down. Despite his lethal ability to find a person's weakness and exploit it. There was more to Jason. Sometimes I couldn't quite see it, but I *knew* it existed still. Don't ask me how, I just did. And *that* was the man I was attracted to. Confident, sexy, alluring physique or not. It was the man beneath the hard and deathly façade that called to me.

"My kisses are not given away freely, Jason. One has to work to earn them."

He paused, as though considering my statement as some sort of pearl of wisdom. Then nodded sagely, as if I'd said something he agreed wholeheartedly with. Me not giving my kisses away freely? I smothered the snort that wanted loose. And decided I'd test a theory.

"Did you sleep well?" I asked, to get the ball rolling. I wasn't the world's best flirt, I had to work up to it.

"Didn't sleep," he replied, his attention back on the breakfast cooking. "Told you that last night."

"Yes," I agreed, leaning my hip against the counter-top off to his side. His eyes darted over towards me, then purposefully returned to the stove. "You said a lot of things last night, Jason," I added.

"Did any of it sink in?" he asked casually, as he started to plate up the food.

I paused, taking my time replying. "I put it all down to testosterone, to be honest. You forget, I grew up with two older brothers. I'm not as much of a pushover as you seem to think."

"I don't think you're a pushover, Kate. I think you're too scared to taste life."

I laughed, I wasn't sure if it sounded natural enough, but it was out now. I had to forge on. "You think you know me, Jason. You haven't got a clue."

I moved to the table and took a seat, as if the conversation was boring me. My heart rocketed within my chest, I was struggling to keep my breathing level and slow. Perspiration had started to coat my upper lip. I brushed at it while his back was still turned, and then picked up my glass of orange juice with a trembling hand.

I was playing with fire, and I knew it.

"Strange thing being in the Army," he said, as he slid a plate of fried tomatoes, scrambled eggs and toast before me. "You learn to read people. Your life can depend on reading a person right. I don't claim to be as good as those profilers, but survival out there means you hone skills a civilian wouldn't necessarily think to use."

He hesitated while he retrieved his own plate of food and then sat down, and without offering another word began to shovel eggs on his fork. I stared at him, waiting for more, but acutely aware I wasn't going to get it.

He did this on purpose. Evasive, oblique replies. He knew they wound me up. Everything *was* a game to Jason. Even me. I forced myself not to push for further explanation - it's what he expected - and focused on my food.

It was good. Too good. A girl could get used to this. Which only maddened me more. Damn this man for turning up uninvited and complicating my life. Damn me for letting him affect me so.

We might have been attracted to each other, but that didn't mean we embraced it. I huffed out a near silent laugh, which sounded like a soft snort.

"What's so funny, Kate? Picturing me with one of your knives thrust between my ribs?"

Yeah, he knew he wound me up, all right.

"Not everything is a battle to be fought to the death, Jason."

"No, you see, that's where you're wrong, Kate. Life's a battle, every damn day. And if you don't take it seriously, you die."

The snort was definitely audible that time.

"I'm not one of your soldiers," I pointed out. "My life isn't that cut-throat."

"No, you're not a soldier," he agreed, giving me a slow and appreciative once over. "But, I'd bet your life is cut-throat."

I shook my head, placed my fork down on the side of my plate, and opened my mouth to reply. Jason beat me to it, waving his fork in the air to emphasise his words.

"Take this design job you're on," he said. "What would you do to close it?"

I blinked. What did he think I'd do?

"Would you flirt?" he asked, voice lowering slightly. "Wear a short skirt and show off those beautiful long legs?" He thought I had long legs? "Wear a tight top to emphasise those pert little tits?" Yeah, that's right. Long legs, but small breasts. That's really how he saw me.

I folded my arms across said breasts, watching as his eyes followed the movement, his lips tipping up in that infuriating smug smile.

"You're doing it now, Kate," he said huskily.

What?

"I am not!"

"Bringing my attention to your tits. Next you'll be bending over at the waist to pick something up and offering me that fuckable arse."

I growled. "You are so crass."

He chuckled. "It's a tits and arse world, baby. You gotta be prepared."

I stared at him, unsure how this conversation had taken such a... disturbing turn. So much for my flirting skills.

"My point," Jason said with meaning, "is your world is just as cut-throat as mine, and you'd do whatever is necessary to survive."

"By flashing my legs and breasts?" I offered, incredulously.

"Well, do you?"

"No!"

"Really? Be honest. Look at what you're wearing."

I glanced down at my ensemble. A deep red blouse and slim-line cream skirt. My heart plummeted. The blouse was fitted, the neck-line not exactly slutty, but low enough to show off my meagre assets to their best advantage. The skirt was above knee, and sitting here it had risen further, to mid thigh. I was also wearing heels, that I knew made my calf muscles look damn good from behind.

I wasn't even seeing a client today. I'd done this because Jason Cain was in my house. It was armour, my armour. With dawning mortification I realised he was right. I did dress for the battlefield, albeit a battlefield of potential contracts and button pushing ex-soldiers. It might not have been a fight to the death, but it was a fight.

At the moment I was fighting to throw Jason off balance, and therefore survive the next few hours in his presence without losing my head. Or heart.

Jason leaned back in his chair and let his eyes flow over my outfit. They rested on my legs for an extended period of time. Without raising them to my face, he said, "There's nothing wrong with using what you've been given to get what you want."

Chocolate eyes flicked up to mine.

"You just gotta be sure you really want it," he added.

I was losing this round, and the Anscombe in me was disappointed and irritated that I'd let Jason have any ground at all.

No, my life wasn't cut-throat, but with Jason in it, it was definitely a battle to be won. I held his gaze for several seconds, unwilling to back down, and then swiped my plate up off the table and headed to the sink. My back to the table and Jason, I leaned down and emptied what was left on my plate into the rubbish bin.

Jason started laughing behind me. I swung back and arched a brow, the emptied plate still in my hand.

"This is a bad idea," he muttered, shaking his head.

"What is?" I demanded, not liking the way he was looking at me. I couldn't decide if it was appreciative or not.

"You don't even know you're doing it, do you?" he murmured.

"Doing what?" I asked, placing the plate on the bench so I could give him my full attention. When I turned back around he was standing right there. I hadn't heard him move, not the scrape of his chair or the sound of his rubber soled shoes on the wooden floor.

I pressed my back into the bench, unable to retreat further. Then cursed myself mentally for trying to back up at all. I straightened my shoulders and raised my chin. Receiving that smirk of his for my efforts.

"Life is what we make of it, Kate," he whispered, his eyes searching my face as though looking for something there.

"Very Zen of you, Jason."

He shrugged, then took a step back and it felt like all the warmth in my body had left with him. This physical attraction was getting too intense. It was ruling my every thought now.

I struggled to think of something to level the playing field with, to distance myself from what his proximity did to my pulse. But I was rattled, no witty words sprang to mind. There was much more to Jason than I had realised. Oh, I'd suspected, but never truly seen. He was observant, calculating, intelligent and two steps ahead of me.

Nothing he'd said this morning didn't ring true. Rather than deter me, it made him even more fascinating to my eyes.

I was in so deep and I didn't know how I'd actually got there. But the real question? Was Jason in deep with me too?

"And what do you do to close a deal, Jason?" I asked, my eyes flicking over his face to see his reaction to my words.

He smiled, it wasn't a smirk. It was impressed, I think. He knew I'd been floundering, and he was surprised and pleased that I'd found my voice at last.

"Whatever I have to do, Kate," he replied. "Whatever it takes." I could believe that.

"Then maybe we're more alike than you realise," I pointed out, pushing past him to gather his plate from the table. He watched my every move.

"Maybe," he agreed, voice soft. My eyes automatically drawn to his. The tone of his voice sounding so intimate. I wondered briefly what that tone would sound like when whispered in my ear. "Or maybe opposites attract," he added, making all thoughts of whispered words of nothing in my ear vanish.

What the hell did that mean? Was he just admitting outright that he was attracted to me?

I think my mouth might have been hanging open slightly as I watched him walk toward the doorway into the lounge. He turned and looked over his shoulder at me, lips twitching at my shocked stance.

"Just one more thing, Kate," he said, breaking into my mental stall. "By the time this lock-down is lifted, I *will* have earned one of your kisses."

Oh, good Lord. I sucked in a breath of air, realised it was the first I'd inhaled for several seconds and forced myself to say, "In your dreams, Cain." The only thing that came to mind.

His smirk spread into a full blown smile.

"Oh, don't worry about my dreams, Kate. Worry more about *yours*."

My heart fell, but thankfully he was no longer looking at me to see my reaction, having turned already to walk out of the room.

Did he know what it was I dreamt about? Could he tell from just looking at me? Jason Cain had a front row seat to my dreams, but only in my mind, because I placed him there. There was no way in hell the real Jason could be aware I dreamt of him. Even observant, calculating, intelligent ex-soldiers, who were two steps ahead of me, couldn't read minds.

Could they?

CHAPTER 5

STAY WITH ME

My turn to deal with the dishes, while Jason touched base with Eric at ASI. The lock-down was still in effect, with no end in sight as yet. I wasn't sure how I felt about that. Having Jason in my home, in my presence, for more than just a few minutes was taxing. Exhilarating, but exhausting at the same time. I felt like I had to maintain my mental and emotional guard. Which was ironic, considering he was my physical guard right now.

I had no idea how to fill in the hours that stretched out before us today. The only answer was to throw myself into work. I switched my laptop on and checked my emails first. There'd been a read-receipt from Mr and Mrs Montgomery-Smith, but no return email. I stared at the receipt message on the screen for several moments, then plucked up the courage to do what needed to be done to close the sale. Determinedly ignoring thoughts of Jason's lesson about cut-throat worlds and closing deals.

I dialled Mrs Montgomery-Smith's cellphone. She was definitely the one who wore the pants in the relationship, my being hired to redecorate their house would be on her say-so and no one else's.

"Katie," she purred down the line when the call connected. "I am so pleased you called."

Well, that was a turn up for the books. The last time I spoke to her over the phone she told me in no uncertain terms that her time was precious and not to waste it.

"Good morning, Mrs Montgomery-Smith," I chirped, Anscombe Interiors persona in full swing. "I trust you are having a pleasant start to your day?" I said with bubbly enthusiasm. For some reason my clients responded to that.

"Fantastic!" she exclaimed, sounding more like a fervent teenager than a thirty something year old woman. "I love your design. Did you have help with it?"

I gritted my teeth. Jason Cain muse-type help or not, I did not appreciate my work being questioned.

"No, Mrs Montgomery-Smith, the design is 100% Anscombe Interiors."

"Yes, yes. But have you hired someone new? This is so different from your website portfolio."

Ah. I guess she had a point. I cursed my initial reaction, knowing my imbalanced response to anything Jason Cain related could very well lose me this sale.

"You know fashion, Mrs Montgomery-Smith," I said in an appeasing tone. "One must stay abreast of it, or fall behind the crowd. You led me to believe you were a trendsetter, I took that on board and created something that would surely impress the most discerning of your peers."

Never count yourself among their kind, even if you had been since birth. To Morgan Montgomery-Smith I was a designer first, and a socialite second - if at all. Just because my name was well known in the circles she ran in, due to my father and his father's social position in this city, did not mean, in this circumstance, I could draw on that claim to fame. Not that I would anyway. My father raised me better than that.

"Well, you have surprised us, Katie," Mrs Montgomery-Smith said in that forced purr. "Malcolm even showed your design to one of his friends."

I perked up at the mention of Mr Montgomery-Smith regaling his colleagues with my design. If they were anything like the Montgomery-Smiths, then they would be forced to redecorate their house in order to keep up with the Joneses - or Montgomery-Smiths as the case may be. Word of mouth was a powerful business leveller.

"Be sure to thank Mr Montgomery-Smith for me," I murmured, with the appropriate level of modesty.

"Indeed. His friend was very impressed and is eager to see your final work. In fact, I told him you would have the sitting room finished in no time, and we would throw a small dinner party in order for him to get a feel for the room and your work. I think you should be paying me a commission, Katie," she chuckled, as if her compliment wasn't at all forced. "So, when can I book the caterers?"

I stifled my own responding, but no doubt slightly sarcastic, chuckle. She was like a steam roller once she got going.

"Once the contract is signed it should take no longer than a fortnight to complete," I said, flicking through the hard-copy of the proposal I had sent her, to ensure I had my time-line correct.

The Montgomery-Smith's sitting room was almost large enough to host a ball. It wasn't a job I could do on the fly in a couple of days. And the type of materials I'd used were exclusive, but thankfully I had exemplary artists at my disposal who I knew worked swiftly, and all of the furnishings I had selected were from hours and hours of previous sourcing. I kept a large private portfolio of fabric samples and the like, to call on at times like this. In addition, the Montgomery-Smiths didn't require new furniture, only decorations and fittings. So, two weeks was an acceptably short time-frame.

"Oh, that long?" She sounded disappointed.

"You want the very best, don't you, Mrs Montgomery-Smith?" I pushed gently.

"Of course. Only the best. I'll sign the contract you emailed and have it delivered later today. Should I expect you at our house this afternoon?"

I flicked a glance over my shoulder to find Jason unexpectedly leaning casually against the door frame. I blinked in surprise. I'd been thinking of him, wondering how long the lock-down was going to continue for, but I certainly hadn't anticipated seeing him in my office, watching me. How long had he been standing there?

He raised his eyebrows at me and cocked his head, but otherwise didn't make a move to leave.

"I'm currently obligated to another project, Mrs Montgomery-Smith," I advised, forcing myself back on task and thinking the excuse up off the cuff. "I expect that to be completed by the end of the week, however," I added. "Shall we say Monday as a start date?"

"Oh, all right. If it has to be Monday then what else can I say?"

"It will make for a clean start," I offered. "And a chance for you to think up any extras you wish to include by then." I don't often encourage my clients to create more work for me, but this woman needed a distraction. Thankfully she took the bait.

"Oh lovely. You are so accommodating, Katie." Yes, that's me. "I'll let Malcolm know and I'll expect you at nine on Monday morning."

"Excellent," I replied, just as the phone clicked indicating the call had been disconnected her end.

I looked at the handset and then shrugged, placing it back in its cradle on my desk.

"The new job?" Jason asked. I nodded, typing in a few notes on the Montgomery-Smith's file, turning the flag from blue - a quote and proposal in progress - to orange - a verbal agreement to a contract reached. It was only when I had the signed contract in my hand that the file would go red.

It would be the only red file I currently have. I worked hard, but I was not always busy.

"And you didn't even have to break a nail to achieve it," Jason added.

I saved my work and turned slowly in my chair to glare at him.

"Can't find anything to amuse yourself with, Jason?" I asked a little pointedly.

"Oh, I'm sure I could think of something," he murmured. "And seeing as your hard day's work is done, how about we start with your knives."

"Excuse me?" I asked.

"Come on, ninja warrior princess. Show me your blades. You've got to have more than that one in your drawer."

My eyes darted to the drawer in question. How had he known the knife was there? My fingers itched to check it was still in its resting place, undisturbed by my unwanted guest. Then it occurred to me, he would have searched my house after I went to bed. Logic told me it was so he knew where possible weapons were should he need them - or should they be used against him. But my sense of privacy baulked at that explanation.

"Didn't find my stash when you snooped?" I pressed.

"I'm guessing they're in your bedroom," he replied casually, not denying the fact he'd snooped at all. "Couldn't search in there without you thinking I was making a move."

"Didn't stop you from making a move at dinner," I snapped.

"Kate," he said on a bark of laughter. "You have no idea how I make my moves."

"And I have no desire for you to regale me."

"Oh?" he breathed, and in less time than it took for me to gasp, he was standing before me, leaning over my body where I sat in my desk chair. "Are you sure about that?"

I held his gaze, refusing to show how much his proximity meant to me, what it did to me. How my skin tingled and my heart rate escalated. And suddenly oxygen seemed way too sparse in this tiny room.

"I don't need you to regale me, Jason," I breathed, my voice sounding husky and deep. Damn! "I can guess. It would involve a gauche pick-up line and some sleazy smooth moves."

His lips spread into an amused smile. "Smooth moves. Is that what you think I do, Kate?"

"I have no idea what you do, Jason. I don't pay attention."

He laughed outright at that. "Oh, Kate. You are a hopeless liar." He shook his head, still smiling. "But I'll put you out of your misery." Please don't. I frowned at him instead of voicing that. "I'm a straight up guy."

He didn't say anything else. My frown deepened with obvious confusion.

"I just ask," he explained.

"Ask?" I replied, not getting it.

"Yeah," he nodded. "If you know what you want, then you should just get on with asking for it. *I ask.*"

That didn't make any sense at all. But rather than show my confusion further, I said, "And that works for you?"

"Sure it does. Want an example?"

I blinked up at him. He hadn't moved an inch away.

"Er, OK? Why not?" I said with as much nonchalance as I could manage. I was anything but calm right then.

He moved closer, so close I could feel his hot breath across my cheeks. So close I knew if I leaned forward a mere inch my lips would touch his. So close I could see the striations of sienna and umber in his eyes; little flecks that seemed to dance in the light of the room.

"Kiss me, Kate."

"That's not a question," I whispered.

"Isn't it?"

"No, it's an instruction," I managed to croak.

"Oh, then I guess I'm more of a take what I want kind of guy," he pointed out, just as his mouth moved the necessary distance to reach mine.

I pulled back before we could connect.

"I wouldn't kiss you if you were the last man on earth," I said through numb lips. How had we gotten here so quickly? From minutes ago at breakfast to this.

I was beginning to think, that when Jason Cain made his mind up, nothing could hold him back. He'd decided something over our morning meal. He'd decided he wanted that kiss.

He smiled. It was clearly amused... again. Jason could do amused grins with such casual ease.

"I told you already, Kate. You're a hopeless liar."

"I am not," I said with as much conviction as I could muster, pushing my chair away from his looming form and slipping out from under him. I strode across the office and shuffled some files distractedly, all the while aware of his attention on my back.

By the time several minutes passed and he hadn't said a further word, I was starting to feel like an idiot. I sucked up whatever courage I had left in me and turned back to face Jason. He was leaning against my desk, smile in full force on his stubbled cheeks.

Captivating. One look, and nothing else existed in that room but him.

"You done escaping life, Kate?" he asked, voice deep and for some reason mesmerizing. "Or do you want to taste it?"

Oh my Lord.

"You can't be serious?" I whispered.

"Deadly," he replied. Quite an appropriate term for a man like him.

I sucked in a fortifying breath. "I'm still not going to kiss you," I announced. My desperation to remain on an even footing with this man making a *complete* fool of me.

He could tell.

I took an embarrassing step backwards towards the door. In imitation of the gazelle caught in the lion's sights on the wildlife programme last night.

His smile turned rapacious.

He licked his lips slowly, pushed off from the desk and took one large legged stride across the small space of my office to come chest to chest with me.

Why had I not even attempted to retreat further?

I knew why.

And so did Jason.

Every interaction we'd shared since meeting flashed through my mind, followed by every conversation we'd had since the lock-down began. We'd been fighting this, we'd been battling the attraction. It hadn't been cut-throat, but it had been a combat of sorts. For Jason, his reasons to fight that attraction were mixed up in what made him... him. For me, it was more simple. I was a spectator not a participant.

For one brief, clarifying moment I knew this was the point of no return.

Spectator or participant?

He paused, giving me one last chance to run. But when I showed no sign of withdrawing, in a smooth glide of muscles and limbs, he hauled me hard against his chest.

Big. Solid. Hot. I was already lost.

The first touch of his lips against mine felt divine. *Literally god-sent.* My body trembled, my hands automatically reached up to wrap fingers in his still too short hair and around the nape of his neck, and then his tongue swept the inside of my mouth.

Game over.

"*Kate.*" He breathed my name against my lips like a benediction. "Oh God, Kate," he murmured, deepening the kiss further.

It felt surreal, a dream come true.

This couldn't possibly be happening. We fought, we bickered. We made each other mad. But right now, he seemed as lost as I to the moment. The second our lips touched all reasoning left us. Not that much had remained beforehand. But I couldn't have fought this if my life depended on it. And he obviously had no desire to stop what was happening either.

His shirt hit the floor.

My blouse followed.

Several more feet covered, out of the office and down the hallway.

My bra was discarded next.

His naked hand wrapped feverishly around a breast, fingers seeking contact.

The door to my bedroom passed.

His belt buckle came undone and various ASI paraphernalia hit the floor with a thud, along with his jeans.

My skirt puddled in a pool of delicate fabric next to them.

The bed met the back of my knees.

His boxers fell around his boots. They got rapidly toed off.

My lace underwear flew across the room to land on top of a lamp shade.

My back hit the bedspread, his front hit my chest.

And not once did we stop kissing. Not even as he ran roughened fingertips across my trembling skin. Or palmed my breast firmly, tweaking a nipple between his thumb and forefinger. Not even as he urgently whispered against my lips, "Protection?"

I mumbled something about being on the pill, but my words were lost to his lips and tongue so swiftly, that it was hard to tell if he'd deciphered them at all. And still we kept kissing. Not stopping as he shifted his weight to cover me, to control me. Large palm enveloping both my wrists, pushing them purposefully into the pillow at my head. One warm hand wrapped around my thigh as he pulled my leg out to allow him a better position at my apex.

Then with one erotic sounding groan he thrust himself inside. Filling me up, stealing my breath, and all sense and any ability to speak. I moaned, as he began to move with a speed that seemed impossible. I wasn't sure if he was still angry with me or the situation, and his pace and fervent movements were a by-product of that. Or if, like me, he just could not get enough of the person before him.

It didn't matter, it was too late to analyse this. It was a thunderous storm rolling out between us, uncontrollable, unstoppable. Inescapable. Maybe it had always been inevitable that he would end up in my bed and I would welcome him with open arms. Maybe this was fate. I didn't care. He felt so good. So right. He matched every move of mine as though coordinated. Where I was soft, he was firm. He moulded to my body as though he was made for me.

We met in a fluid movement of flesh on flesh. Slick skin against evermore slick skin. It was delicious. He used every available inch of the bed, rolling us, thrusting so firmly that we hopped across the covers with each pound inside. It was invigorating, shocking yet exciting. Every single touch he made sent adrenaline coursing through me. But his dedication to the task was what surprised me the most. He sought every single gasp from my lips as though it was gold. Every single writhe he hunted down with single minded determination. Each moan was doggedly pursued. Each orgasm, and there were more than one, was fervently chased with a level of passion I could not have guessed existed in this world.

He was exactly how I had imagined he would be. The moment was hard, fast, powerful. Everything Jason Cain had always appeared to be; *hard, fast and powerful*. And I greedily took every single thing he offered.

We both came together in the end spectacularly. Neither able to contain our responses in that moment, to hide our reaction to this incredibly intense coupling. We lay panting, still wrapped up in each other's arms, still floating on a blissful cloud of release.

And then he started laughing. A delicious rumbling sound from deep inside his chest.

"That was entirely unexpected," he murmured, laying a soft kiss against my neck. "But not at all unwelcome."

I didn't know what to say to that. I suddenly felt very awkward. It had happened so quickly. An out of control explosion of lust. I was embarrassed to admit all thought had left me. In the heat of the moment I had forgotten every warning Nick had said, every logical reason that had existed proving this was a very bad idea.

My body had just acted. My response was ingrained; an animalistic reaction to his advances. Similar to those blasted zebras last night on TV. I hadn't acted at all like the Katie Anscombe everyone knows. I'd lived a little. I'd tasted life. I'd taken a risk.

Jason had drawn that from me, even when I had been so sure that he never, *ever* could. I felt shocked, totally astounded, stupefied by what I had let transpire. And consequently scared out of my wits for what would happen next. A line had been crossed, *so recklessly*. And now he would throw it in my face, be the player Nick said he was.

But he didn't pull away.

His hand was idly stroking down my side, over my hip and back up my stomach. His eyes were hungrily soaking up every inch of my naked skin. Devouring every curve and dip. His fingers felt hot and slightly rough. His breath was still uneven, but it had nothing to do with the exercise we'd just had. Instead it was entirely because of me... lying before him, available to his touch.

His deep chocolate brown eyes came up to hold my gaze.

"What are you thinking, Kate?" he asked softly. Such an unexpected show of consideration from him.

I licked my lips, my eyes darting all over his face to see if I had missed something. If the smirk was about to make a return or chestnut was creeping into the edges of his eyes. But they weren't. This was a new Jason. A sated and content Jason.

I had no idea how to handle this man. It frightened me. Because this Jason was the manifestation of the Jason I knew existed under the hardened façade. This was *my* Jason. And now I had him, I wasn't sure what to do with him.

"OK," he said, his lips tipping up in a beguiling smile. "I'll tell you what I'm thinking then," he murmured, his face nuzzling into the curve of my neck. "Time for round two," he whispered, huskily.

I let out a ridiculous surprised squeal as he rolled me on top of his body, positioning me exactly where he wanted me to be. Then without warning he slowly sank himself inside my entrance. Just an inch.

"Am I going too fast for you, Kate?" he asked, working his way in inch by inch further. "Or do you want it faster?"

Oh boy. I was having trouble keeping up with him as it was.

He rolled us over suddenly, so he was again on top, then swirled his hips in a circle, making me catch my breath.

"Stay with me," he whispered, and I knew the words meant more than he was letting on.

I stared up at him, his face so open, so perfect and carefree...

And I just nodded, a smile gracing my lips, finally accepting that I had crossed that forbidden and dangerous line... and that it was *all good*.

CHAPTER 6

THE START OF SOMETHING BETWEEN US

"So, do you keep them in the bedside drawer or the dresser?" Jason asked, his hot breath tickling the hair on my neck.

He was draped around my back, his hips framing my rear, his arm wrapped possessively around my stomach, hand firmly clasping my breast. The position made me smile. Jason was doing absolutely everything I thought he would do. I knew he was a dominant man; a male in charge of the world he walked within. Be that in his job, in his home-life, or with his women. Not that I thought too often about his 'women,' I tried not to. But although Nick had only just pointed out the blonde busty bimbos to me, it hadn't in fact been a surprise. Jason Cain was an extremely virile man.

"What do I keep hidden?" I asked, trailing a finger down his forearm, watching as goosebumps rose up in its wake.

It was utterly surreal to be touching him like this. How many times had I dreamt about this exact moment? How many times had I fantasied about how we would behave after sex? Awkward? Distant? Dismissive? Jason's actions around me in the past had never given me much hope, even if my heart longed for it. My mind, however, had been realistic, so this... *comfortable closeness* was entirely unexpected.

But, oh so wanted.

"Your knives, Kate," he murmured. "I'm still trying to picture where they would be. In between your Victoria's Secret underwear? Or maybe, stacked in organised piles beside your Kombatan Training Manual?"

I ignored the obvious questions there and asked instead, "How did you know I studied Kombatan?"

He shrugged, laid a kiss against my bare shoulder and squeezed my breast once. "A guess," was all he said and by the sounds of it, all he was going to say.

I pushed the puzzle aside. Jason could be obtuse when he wanted to.

So, I went back to the rest of his statements instead.

"Where would you prefer to see them, Jason? In between satin and lace, or cared for appropriately, as my trainer would advise? Blades oiled, sheathed and placed in a way that meant easy access and no possibility of damage while stored."

His nose nuzzled my hair at the back of my neck as he thought of an answer. He hadn't stopped touching me, discovering me, since we'd finished our slower second round of sex. I wondered if he felt like we had so much time to make up for. Jason had been a satellite fixture in my life for several months now, but from the moment I laid eyes on him, I wanted more. Had he?

"Hmm," he murmured, shifting his body even closer at my back, as though the small amount of space created with his explorations was unwanted. "Now, what would I like to see?"

He paused, ran a hand seductively down my side to my hip and then dug his fingertips into the flesh there. Almost like he was marking me, from the strength with which he fondled my skin. Everything he did was proprietary. I hadn't quite expected such ownership from him so early on.

Well, I hadn't dared to think of much past the initial 'moment' at all.

"The Kate I know would follow her instructor's directions," he pointed out, letting his breath wash over my skin; hot, slightly sticky, entirely too erotic. He pulled his face back and watched my skin pebble from the effect. Then added, "I wouldn't be surprised if your knives were stacked appropriately, sheathed and oiled and within easy grasp. The soldier in me would appreciate that."

Yes, I could imagine Captain Jason Cain kept his weapons well maintained and equally well stored.

"But," he continued, his hand suddenly stroking slowly around the front of my lower abdomen, and then edging closer to the curls at the top of my thighs. I bit my lip from moaning at the obvious direction his eager fingers were heading, trying in vain to listen to his next words. "Don't get me wrong," he said, as his finger slipped through my folds, seeking entrance, seeking *me*. "The man in me admires a woman who can defend herself. It is a turn-on."

His one finger was joined by a second as he slowly, languidly thrust them both in and back out, repeating the action with infinite patience, as though he had all the time in the world to make me wetter and wetter and wetter still.

His forearm shifted sideways, making me spread the thigh on top out further, allowing him better access. He rocked his hips, readjusting himself at my back and making me aware of his current aroused state, then pressed his erection in between my butt cheeks, broad tip down, rubbing at the back of my folds with each dip forward. His shaft slid up and down that rear channel with a determined motion that made my heart skip. With his fingers occupying my core I wasn't entirely sure where he thought he was going to place that enlarged organ.

"Now," he said, voice deeper than before, sexily husky, not even trying to hide his turned-on state. "For you Kate, I'd want to see something more than a level head and an abide-by-the-rules character trait." He would?

His lips trailed across my shoulder, up to the soft flesh on my neck where he proceeded to suck and nibble, making me writhe under his touch, arch my back and give him a firm surface to rub back against. His erection came dangerously close to pressing in where no one had ever been before. But for the life of me I couldn't seem to stop my reaction to him. His fingers were deftly seeking my complete surrender, I was losing all perception, my mind closing down to the world outside this room, outside this bed, outside of *him*. He could have suggested anything right then and I wouldn't have faltered.

He was a dangerous, dangerous man.

He moaned against the length of my sweat soaked neck, thrust a little more firmly between my butt cheeks and said in a decidedly raspy voice, "I'd want you to push the limits." He was losing me. What were we talking about? "I'd want you to surprise me. To never be predictable. To be everything I know you are deep down inside. To let go of your boundaries, to live, to taste. *To risk.*"

I made a strangled sound that was entirely too sensual. I'd meant to question what he was getting at, but forming words was no longer possible right then.

His fingers still swirled and pumped and tweaked and rubbed deliciously. His lips and teeth grazed and soothed and trailed over my skin. His hard arousal made itself known with each purposeful thrust between my butt cheeks. And the heat of his chest branded my back, seared through my skin, and left an indelible impression on my body from behind.

Then his free hand came around one of my cheeks; hot, roughened skin with each touch, yet gentle in the way he stroked, kneaded, fondled, until his thumb pressed into my rear.

"Do you have any lubrication?" he asked, slowly working his way inside, just a little, just his thumbnail, just enough to make my heart rate sky rocket and my mind stutter to a complete and utter halt.

I liked a little variety in my love making, but I had never taken the plunge where my butt was concerned.

"Ah," I managed to squeak out, my body tensing slightly at the knowledge that Jason very much wanted to go *there*.

Maybe I could do it. I'm not sure. It was unexpected and I'd never considered doing anything like that with any other man. On the flip side, I did find myself a little panicked at the unfamiliar sensation of longing this new arousal brought out in me. It was new and a little overwhelming. No man had ever created that reaction in me before. I was intrigued though, and excited, as well as being entirely turned on by his desire to do something a little naughty, a little forbidden.

He'd said he wanted me to surprise him. He had no idea what I was capable of desiring. No idea what I fantasied about when alone. If he knew the things I imagined, the things I pictured doing with him, *to him*, I was sure he'd be utterly astonished.

No man had ever seen the real Katie Anscombe either.

"Kate," he almost chastised, his voice firm and commanding, but still layered with a hint of understanding, of compassion. He must have thought my hesitation was due to fear, not a calculated thought pattern leading to lust-filled fantasies becoming reality. "Have you ever tried it?"

I shook my head no, feeling a blush roll up my skin; a blazing sensation of heat over my cheeks. I may have had sweat soaked images of him and me doing all sorts of passionate things inside my head for the past few months, but the realisation that they were only fantasies, not based on reality or experience, was a little unnerving.

"Do you want to?" he asked, not stopping his movements with his fingers in the front of my body, but slowing down his pursuit between my butt cheeks.

I felt like a weight was somehow hidden in that question. I was pleased he asked, although embarrassed that he had to. But there was something in his tone. A challenge. Could I live life? Would I?

I can dream, but can I do?

"I'm not sure," I finally admitted, still unable to take a full breath, despite the way I was reacting to his touch. Both at the front and behind. My ridiculous safe-road-only mind was saying no, but I my body was having other ideas. I rocked back against him, seeking his thrusting fingers, and equally searching for more pressure behind.

A low chuckle worked its way up his chest.

"Kate," he breathed. "There'll be time to introduce you to that. And I *will* introduce you to it. I will taste all of you. Every... single... part of you." His fingers thrust in time to each word, his thumb pressing harder on each syllable, but not quite breaching fully just yet.

If my heart had tripped before, it just quit beating now. Because it was obvious, from his words, from his tone, from everything this man was showing me right now, that this was not a one time event. I felt strangely numb from that realisation. Not unfeeling, no, there was just too much I was feeling for my body to comprehend.

Jason Cain had started something today that he had every intention of continuing. His statement did not mean he'd introduce me to new experiences this afternoon, or this evening. It was clear he was referring to days, maybe weeks, ahead. My body did a full shiver. He growled. Removed his thumb and fingers, grasped my hips on either side to pull my butt back further and shifted his erection to my wet folds, sliding inside in one deep, possessive plunge.

The movement was so smooth, so calculated, yet also so completely at the edge of his control, that for a moment I thought he was doing what he had set out to do. But the moment I felt the stretch where his fingers had been fondling before, my body completely relaxed and opened up for him, taking every long, thick inch of him inside.

"Oh, Kate," he husked behind me, starting up a steady rocking of his hips, thrusting in and out with long, wet glides. "Fuck, I'd take you any way I could get you. Whatever you chose to give."

Oh dear God, I could get used to that. I could get used to this man in my life. In my bed.

"Let me hear you," he demanded, shifting our bodies from our side until I was on all fours before him and he was pounding deep inside. His thighs slapped against mine, his fingers dug into my hips as he pulled me back on to him at each thrust forward. "Come for me, baby. Let go. Feel me filling you up, taking you somewhere beautiful."

I moaned at his words as much as his forceful movements. Jason Cain seemed to never do anything in half measures. All or nothing. From his command of my body right down to his wicked, yet captivating words.

"Take me with you, Kate," he rasped, not faltering in his pace as he leaned his chest down on my back and began to run slick fingers over my sensitive nub between my legs. "Oh, yeah, Kate," he groaned against the sweat moistened skin on my back. His tongue came out and lapped up my spine eagerly.

It was such an erotic movement and right then, when my body was firing off nerve endings and my brain was firing off synapses, I just came apart at his touch, at his words. I cried out an inarticulate sound. It might have been his name, or it could have been a simple scream of release. But neither mattered, it came from deep inside and was loud and long, and exactly what Jason desired.

"Oh God yeah, Kate! Like that."

Several more hard and fast thrusts and then he simply exploded, his body shuddering behind me, his fingers gripping my hips tightly, almost unforgivingly, as his release shot hot and long inside. It seemed to go on forever as his thrusts became more languid and his breathing became more ragged, until finally he collapsed us both down on the rumpled sheets, spent.

"Now, that's the Kate I want to see," he said between deep breaths in and out. I was equally breathless, maybe more so than him, because I couldn't form words at all and he seemed to still be able to speak.

His hot breathy lips laid a kiss against my skin at my neck, as he rolled us to our sides so I wasn't crushed beneath him.

"Fuck," he exclaimed softly in amongst my hair. "That last one might have done me in for a while. I think you've milked every last drop out of me."

I couldn't help but laugh a little at that.

"You think it's funny, huh?" he whispered, pulling me closer still.

The fact he couldn't get enough skin on skin contact was so unexpected. I hadn't, in all my wildest dreams, thought Jason Cain would be a cuddler.

"For that, Ms Anscombe," he said, effecting a commanding tone, one I would have expected from Jason Cain, Captain in the SAS, "You get to make me lunch."

What? I threw an incredulous look over my shoulder and watched the light dance playfully in his eyes. Chocolate, but not just the soft, deep and dark chocolate I'd seen before. This one was more complex. Multiple tans and mahoganies and siennas competing with each other. How had I ever thought his eyes were just plain brown?

His face softened further, the smirk I was used to seeing touched the edges of his lips, but wasn't quite all there was to marvel at either. With the complex shades in his eyes and the softness to his whole façade, this was a Jason I hadn't yet met. He kept surprising me. He wanted me to be the one who kept him on his toes. But I had no hope in hell of keeping up with Jason. He was an enigma, multi-layered. A mystery I was desperate to solve.

There was more to him than I had ever thought possible. And I liked it. I liked it a lot.

I turned over completely to face him and reached up a hand to run fingers down his cheek, over his roughened stubble, to finish in a smooth glide across his kiss plumped lips. He flicked out his tongue quickly, licking my finger and then sucking it into his mouth in an obviously sensual move.

I rolled my eyes and let a huff of air out at the same time.

"What?" he said overly innocently, eyebrows raised, mock incredulity on his face. When I just kept staring at him, not providing a verbal response, he leaned forward and kissed me lightly on the lips - short, abrupt, very Jason Cain. "Get in the kitchen and cook me my lunch, woman," he ordered, making me roll off the bed with an exaggerated sigh.

"So demanding," I complained, half heartedly. I *was* hungry after all.

"This is only the beginning, Kate." He spoke softly, from his now sitting position on the side of the bed.

I flicked a glance over my shoulder as I slipped a satin kimono robe on and took a step towards the door to the room. There was more to those words than the obvious. Of course they sent a thrill through my body. The implied meaning; the start of something between us, making my body shiver in delight.

But there was darkness there, something Jason was trying hard, but in the end, futilely, to hide. I hesitated on the threshold while he held my gaze. A steady, challenging look in his eyes.

And like I have done so many times in the past, I refused to take up the challenge that he offered, refused to take the risk and destroy the moment we had just shared.

As I turned back to exit the room I swear I saw disappointment cross his handsome face.

And it left a heavy weight inside my heart.

CHAPTER 7

IT WAS ONLY FAIR, AFTER ALL

LUNCH WAS GOING TO BE A CASUAL AFFAIR. I COULD HAVE GONE all out and cooked a quiche, but aside from that taking too long, it would have set a precedent. One I was sure Jason would have gladly taken advantage of. Just because he demanded I *cook* him his lunch, did not mean I had to jump at his command. He may have expected his soldiers to follow his directions to the letter, but he didn't take his soldiers to bed.

I was hungry, so refusing to make something for lunch would be ridiculous, but that didn't mean I was going to do exactly as he instructed. So I hauled out fresh bread and meats and salad ingredients and laid them all on the table, and was just in the process of placing condiments alongside everything else when he walked in the room. No shirt, just jeans and ASI belt essentials, and a the most glorious tanned, well defined chest and arms.

I expected Jason to have scars, even a blemish would have made him seem more real. But his skin was smooth and unmarked, perfect. With an upper body like that, he should go around shirtless every day.

"Like what you see?" he drawled, reaching into the fridge for some ginger beers. His muscles rippled with the action, I wondered if he was doing it on purpose or not.

It was hard to tell with Jason. He made everything seem like a simple movement to effect a certain action, but Nick's words of warning still hung menacingly in my mind. Could Jason be so shrewd?

Still, no use lying to the man about this.

"Very much. In fact I'd like to declare a rule. You must never wear a shirt when in my house."

His eyebrows rose slowly up his forehead, bottle of ginger beer halfway to his lips.

"Is that so," he murmured. "Well, if you get a rule, I get one too."

My heart skipped several beats and my breath stalled in my throat. I swallowed and forced myself to stop fussing with the utensils on the table and stare into his eyes.

"What would that be?" I asked in my best attempt to sound in control. I'm unsure if it worked, his smirk may have been there since I started talking. Or not.

"You never wear underwear when in my home."

There was a lot in that short sentence to get hung up on. Of course my oversexed brain skipped the whole going commando issue and fixated on the *when in my home* part of the statement. As if Jason had every intention of taking this, whatever it was we had going on here, to the next level.

"You say that like you expect me to be in your home." And there, I said it. And here he was thinking I couldn't take risks.

"Kate," he admonished, placing his bottle of drink down on the bench beside him. The purposeful movement made me still. I felt a little like I'd been sighted by a predator who was preparing for their next hunt. "I see no point denying that I want you. Here. In my apartment. In the car. *On* the car. Wherever I can get you, I want you. And since we've got that out of the way, then I have no hesitation in admitting I want you ready for me, available to me, in my home. I want to know when you cross my kitchen and stand at my dining table, that all I have to do is bend you over the surface and sink myself inside."

Oh dear Lord I was getting wet again. The image he created was entirely too good. I hadn't been to the loft since he moved in. It used to be Genevieve's though, so I know the layout, I know her furniture, her long table is still there. I can picture it all, down to the colour of the stain on the surface, the shape of the edge of the table top, the height it sits at. I can picture everything. I can feel everything.

I closed my eyes slowly, leaned back against my table for much needed support and breathed through the sensations his words created.

"You like that, don't you?" he whispered.

His words came from directly in front of my face. I didn't open my eyes. I couldn't yet. I was still in his loft, spread across his table, being taken by him; no holds barred.

"Does it make you hot, Kate?" I nodded in answer, unable to voice a word right then. My eyelids still closed, heat washing up my cheeks. "Turn around," he demanded in a gruff voice.

I jumped slightly at the instruction, my eyes flicked open to peer into his. Chestnut stared back back me, dark and rich and filled with wicked thoughts.

"This is me, Kate," he said, still whispering, as though any increase in volume could shatter the moment.

I blinked up at him, unsure what he was getting at. He saw my confusion. A smattering of regret crossed his features. There one second and gone so quickly the next, I was unsure if I actually saw it. Then the Jason Cain smirk came out in full force.

"I'm hungry," he said, moving past me and throwing himself into a chair. "Worked up an appetite."

I'd missed something. Something vital to understanding Jason, to understanding what we could be. I'd missed it. And a part of me new that there was no way to undo the damage from the failure to grasp what Jason had been trying to convey. Granted he'd been his usual obtuse self, but the gravity of what had been missed, left a weight in my stomach and a heart that was filled with only empty air.

Lunch was a non-event after that. Oh, we ate, but pretty much in silence. Afterwards Jason checked in with Eric at ASI while I cleared the table and tidied the kitchen. I took more care than I needed to, ending up disinfecting my entire kitchen bench, shifting appliances and cleaning behind recipe books; something I only do about twice a year.

It wasn't until I was returning all my cookbooks alphabetically to their rightful places that I registered I had an audience. My head twisted to look over my shoulder and my eyes captured the amused ones of Jason's.

"You're hiding," he pointed out. It wasn't accusatory, just a statement of fact. I shrugged in reply.

He stared at me for a long drawn out moment.

"You scare too easily," he added, and this statement felt like it had been hurled right at my face.

We stared at each other for several seconds longer and then both of us jumped a mile in the air when a knock sounded out on my front door.

"Jesus," Jason swore, his hand going automatically to his hip and the holstered weapon there. He shook his head, looking disgusted and angry. I was thinking he was disgusted and angry at himself for lowering his guard, for not hearing a visitor approach the house. For being too wrapped up in psychoanalysing me.

He took a few steps into the lounge to peer out of the front window.

"Who is it?" I asked, from my vantage point at the dining room threshold. I knew from experience with Nick that at times like this I did *not* offer to open the door.

"Courier," Jason shot back over his shoulder, checking I wasn't coming closer, I think. "You expecting a delivery?"

I nodded. It would be the signed contract from Mrs Montgomery-Smith. "Yes, some documents from a client."

Jason nodded, gave me a glare that obviously meant 'don't move,' and headed to the front door. I watched from my vantage point further back in the lounge as he pulled his gun from its holster and held it at his side hidden, while he reached forward with his free hand to open the front door. I'd already catalogued how close a hidden knife was. It would take me two seconds to be armed. I decided that time-frame was acceptable, given the chance of this being anything other than the contract delivery was slim.

Jason greeted the courier driver, signed the electronic receipt machine with his non-dominant hand making it seem natural, while his gun hand held the weapon ready but out of sight behind the half opened door. Then he took the envelope and watched as the courier walked back to his van sitting on the street. Once he was sure things were as they should be, he shut and locked the door, and turned back to me.

He did not look happy.

"Tell me how Nicholas Anscombe's sister could be so stupid?" He'd spoken slowly, articulating each word as though it pained him.

My head shot back on my shoulders feeling like he'd slapped me.

He didn't wait for an answer. "Didn't it occur to you that in a lock-down *everything* is locked-down? Including anything coming in, as well as out?"

Oh.

"The whole premise of a lock-down is that those being protected remain cut-off from any potential harm. To do this *everything* is cut-off, because how can we tell what will be harmful and what won't? Do you think King would not stoop to using a courier" - he held the envelope above his head then and shook it for emphasis - "to exact his revenge?"

I bit my lip, entirely flustered and embarrassed and unable or willing to think of an excuse. He was right. I should have known better, and Nick would be ropeable right now if he knew what I had allowed to happen. I should have had Mrs Montgomery-Smith send the contract to my postal box address. I could have then picked it up tomorrow when the lock-down would no doubt be lifted. I felt like a fool, and Jason's glaring attitude only made me feel worse.

"It was a mistake," I whispered, unable to find my usual volume right then.

"A mistake that could have cost you your life," he pointed out, not quite finished with the reprimand it seemed.

I nodded, accepting the telling off as it was deserved and then walked over to hold out my hand for the envelope. I stood there with my arm suspended between us and waited for Jason to calm down and give me the delivery. He stared at my hand, as though it was a grenade about to go off.

"You are not opening this," he ground out.

"It's just a contract," I explained, still holding my hand out. "I need it."

His head shot up to look at my face. "You need a hell of a lot more than this!" he practically yelled.

"What does that mean?" I demanded, my fists now going to my hips. At least I wasn't holding a useless hand out in the air anymore.

Jason took a step toward me, bringing his chest up to mine. The envelope got held behind his back, making me want to reach for it like a child in the school yard. I had a momentary flash of me jumping up and down trying to reach for something he held behind his back, while he taunted me. It was entirely ridiculous, but when I'm nervous my mind wanders, and I can picture almost anything in my head.

"Fuck, Kate!" Jason growled, right in my face as his free hand came up and grasped my ponytail, holding my head still so I could look at him and nowhere else... like say, behind his back where I wanted to start reaching. "You think this is a game? Is everything a game to you? How old are you, twelve?"

Oh, he did not just say that.

Jason had a lot of different things on his belt, much like Nick does and all of the other operatives at ASI do. Taser, stun gun, cellphone, pistol. And a knife. In a sheath, but still, how many times have I unsheathed a knife in training? How many times has my trainer made his students unsheathe knives from different angles, in different circumstances, for any number of different reasons? It was one thing to know how to handle a knife when it was in your hand, but you couldn't use it unless you held it. Disarming an opponent and using their weapon against them was part of the advanced training I'd received only last year.

I licked my lips purposely, hoping Jason would catch the movement and I could use his distraction to unsheathe the knife at his waist. For a moment I thought he'd ignore it, too angry to contemplate a 'seductive' move like that. In my frustration I began nibbling on my bottom lip instead, and for some reason that's what did it. His gaze darted down, his hold on my hair loosened marginally and then he licked his own lips. Just once. I didn't even get to see the colour change in his eyes, I had his knife unsheathed and held against the side of his torso in the next second. The very sharp tip digging in ever so slightly.

His eyes darted up to mine and held them. Neither of us moved. I had no intention of using the knife, it was a message, nothing more. Just what message I was sending to the man assigned to protect me, I don't know. But he'd made me mad with that last statement. Twelve, indeed.

"You going to gut me, Kate?" His words from yesterday, said in a level and calm voice.

"No," I replied instantly. No way did I want to slice him, but he would know I wasn't a pushover when this was all said and done.

"Then why the knife in my side?" he asked, casually.

"Because you wouldn't have expected it."

He sucked in a breath, his eyes darting all over my face; cheeks, jaw, lips, nose, hairline, eyes, back to lips.

"You are an intriguing woman, Kate Anscombe," he said, his voice lower than before. "But you have no idea what you're playing with."

I wasn't afraid of the implied threat. It was all Jason. Words used as weapons, designed to throw me off balance.

It wasn't working. Well at least not the way he intended. I found him utterly kissable when he got all growly like a bear.

"What am I playing with, Jason?" I said, leaning forward until my lips were a mere inch away from his. The knife was held steady at his side.

He blinked slowly. The moment seemed to hang thick and heavy between us. Then the sound of the envelope hitting the floor broke the spell and his free hand came up to cup my chin firmly. His fingers dug into skin down either side of my jaw, not so much that I wanted to complain, but in a way that let me know he meant all business.

"You deserved a good spanking for letting a courier come to that door," he said out of nowhere. "But I was prepared to let it slide. Everyone's entitled to one mistake and you'd accepted that it *was* your mistake. But this," he said pulling on my ponytail slightly. My head jerked at the motion, the movement clearly saying despite the knife tip at his side, he was the one in control. "Pulling a knife on me again, *my* knife. My hand is itching to spank your bare arse."

The grip on my chin vanished and in the next second his hand was firmly cupping my butt cheek. He rubbed the naked flesh beneath my robe slowly. The heat from his palm scorched my skin. Then he pulled me closer, groin to groin, hand still stroking softly. A shiver rolled down my body uninvited. He began to smirk.

"Drop the knife, Kate," he instructed huskily. His hand still rubbing in a motion that sent pools of delight to my core, despite the message he was conveying with that simple action.

My breathing was ragged, my heart rate making it difficult to think or hear; the blood thundering through my veins. Even my knife hand had begun to shake. I was better than this normally. My trainer said I had the steadiest hands in his class. But I had never faced off against someone like Jason Cain in the dojo.

"Kate," he growled, "Last warning, drop the damn knife."

"Or what?" I whispered and watched his eyes flare, the pupils enlarging slightly as darker chestnut flashed out from deep chocolate brown.

The ludicrous thing is we both knew he could disarm me easily. He'd done it once already, and I hadn't even been able to figure out how, let alone break down his moves to study it for next time. He could do exactly the same thing again and have me disarmed, but I knew Jason had more than one method of getting me to drop that knife. So did he. So why didn't he do it? Why this intense stand-off, this exciting, invigorating challenge?

His fingers dug into my butt cheek, he made a low growling sound like an animal, that for some bizarre reason made me even wetter. His grip loosened, his hand rubbed a gentle circle once, twice. And even though I knew what was about to happen, anticipated it, even *wanted* it, I still jumped and squeaked out loud when his hot, large palm came down hard on my cheek. The smart making me moan, which was only interrupted by the clinking of the blade as it hit the hardwood floor at our feet.

"Fuck," Jason groaned, his hand back to smoothly stroking my butt, soothing the sting. "What the fuck are you doing to me?"

I could feel his erection pressed into my stomach, I could see his chest rising and falling in such an uncontrolled ragged rate. A vein bulged in his neck, the blood pumping furiously through it. He was turned on in more ways than I had ever imagined a man to be.

We were in the middle of my lounge, I don't know how we got here. I'd crossed the space to take the now forgotten envelope from his hand, he'd met me halfway to tell me off. But it didn't matter, we were here now and the couch was off to the side... waiting.

I pulled back out of his grasp, somehow he let me. I saw a momentary flash of loss cross his face, but I didn't hesitate. I turned around, placing my back to the beast willingly. And then lowered my chest over the edge of the couch.

"Holy fuck," he breathed out behind me, no doubt seeing my butt on display as my robe had risen up against the settee back and now bunched around my waist. "You're killing me, Kate," he moaned, one hot hand smoothly gliding over my sensitive butt cheek. The other pushing the hem of my robe up higher, displaying more of my body for him to see.

I was acting on autopilot. I'd never behaved like this before. But Jason brought something out in me, something fierce and alive and very much desired.

I heard his zip getting lowered, the sound of his jeans hitting the floor, then one knee pushed between my thighs and widened my stance, making my swollen folds more visible, more accessible to his touch and sight. His long finger ran through the wet channel there, making his whole body shudder at my back and a small moan escape my lips.

"You are so fucking beautiful," he breathed out behind me, dipping two fingers inside.

I wanted him, all of him, not just his fingers, so I arched my back further and pressed onto his hand begging for more.

His fist in my hair pulled my head back. It was firm and definitely controlled, but it didn't hurt.

"You're not in charge of this," he warned. "You gave that up when you displayed yourself for my taking." He paused, then demanded, "Do you understand?"

I nodded, making my hair pull where he held it tightly.

"I want noise, Kate. Lots of it. I want to hear you when I take you, when I make you mine."

I nodded again, no way was I arguing with that idea right now. I was *so* turned on.

"Fuck," he breathed out again, as though to himself. His hand still running smooth circles over my butt cheek. Then without warning, he impaled himself to the hilt in one swift plunge.

I made a sound, it obviously wasn't enough for him, because he pulled me upright by my hair. It was much rougher than I was used to, but right in that moment I don't think either of us were complaining at all.

"Was that good for you, baby?"

"Yes," I moaned as he rocked back and forward, his thrusts determined and controlled; hard and fast, and timed to match my panting breaths.

"Are you sure, 'cause I can't hear you," he growled in my ear. "Let go, Kate. I'll catch you."

"Jason," was all I managed as an unexpected orgasm struck from nowhere. I knew I'd been turned on, I knew I'd been more aroused than I had ever been in my life, but the force with which I was pummelled by the ecstasy the orgasm created was breath stealing. All I managed after saying his name was one long, loud scream.

"Yes," he said on an expelled breath of hot air at my neck. "Yes," he moaned as his own release shattered his control and made his movements no longer measured and determined, but frantic and a little bit insane.

We were both breathing too hard as he pushed my body forward gently to lean us over the back of the couch. His lips laid a trail of delicate kisses against the skin at the nape of my neck, his sweat mixed with mine through the back of my silk robe, making it cling to my frame between our feverish bodies.

We lay there for several unbelievably dizzy seconds, blood pounding through my body sending endorphins tingling through my frame. A lazy smile graced my lips. I don't think I could have been happier. I'd heard of the different types of sex people could have. Jealous sex. Revenge sex. Make-Up sex. But nothing beat the passion of mid-argument sex.

I could so get used to this.

Jason let out a long sigh, pulling a bit of his weight off my body slightly. He brushed my straggly hair off my face, where it had come loose from my ponytail.

"You are a surprise, Kate," he whispered softly. But when I went to turn around and face him, he pushed his body back into mine to hold me in place. "But I will still spank your fine butt if you do anything as reckless as you did today again."

A shiver raced down my spine. It had nothing to do with fear, but everything to do with delightful anticipation.

"Fuck," he breathed again at my back. "That fucking turns you on, doesn't it?"

I didn't answer. Let him await our next argument with as much heightened anticipation as me.

It was only fair, after all.

CHAPTER 8

KATE, KATE, KATE

I DID GET TO REVIEW THE CONTRACT EVENTUALLY. BUT ONLY after Jason opened it away from me and begrudgingly handed it over, once he knew it wasn't a bomb or something, with another reminder of how angry he was that it was here at all. I just smiled sweetly and once the forms were in my hand waltzed off to my office to red flag the file. I should have started work on the project. There's a lot I could do over the phone or via email, but even though the Monday start date I'd given Mrs Montgomery-Smith was a misdirection, I didn't see the point in slaving away until then.

Not with Jason Cain in my house.

I came out of the office to find him sprawled across the settee. The settee he'd just had his decidedly wicked way with me on. My turn to smirk. He caught the smile on my face and chuckled, then patted the seat next to him in invitation.

"I'm sure we can use this thing for what it's actually designed to do," he said, surfing channels as he spoke.

"Bah," I scoffed. "What fun is that?" I slipped into the seat beside him as his head turned to look me in the face.

"You are a naughty girl, Ms Anscombe. But I must admit to

needing a little recovery time. Shall we watch a movie and then you can tell me all of your fantasies in great detail. We've got the whole night ahead of us, after all."

"We have? What did Eric say?" I asked.

Jason settled on the movie channel and placed the remote on the armrest, then lifted his arm next to me in a clear sign he wanted me to get closer. I was momentarily caught off guard. I don't know why. He'd cuddled after sex in bed, why not now? But it was an image I'd failed to imagine in my head, so no matter how much it was wanted, it still surprised.

I snuggled in though, no way was I missing an opportunity to touch his body.

"Ben is in Wellington helping the police bring down their mob boss. Once that's all handled, then Nick will have something to keep King happy with back here."

"Declan King wants this other guy out of the picture?" I asked, piecing it all together.

"Yeah, that's about the upshot of it all. Once McLaren is contained, King has free rein of the North Island. Nick will make sure he realises it's because of ASI."

"A favour to win a reprieve."

"Yep. Nick's good at that sort of thing."

I was pleased to hear Jason speak so highly of my brother. There was obvious respect there, even if they'd been at each other's throats when Jason first came to town to help out his sister, Gen. Obviously both men had developed a healthy working relationship. It boded well for any personal relationship Jason and I would have in the future.

And just like that I was on uncertain ground.

Jason didn't notice, turning his attention to the movie which had just begun screening. Eventually, I cleared my mind of all the discordant thoughts tumbling through it, and settled in to watch as well.

It was altogether too pleasant an experience, watching a comedy on TV with Jason at my side. We heated up a frozen pizza when we got hungry, found a second movie as the afternoon turned into night, and through it all he held me close, making sure I was sprawled across the couch and resting my cheek against his chest, while his arm wrapped around me protectively, comfortingly. It was a feeling, a beautiful sensation, I could easily get used to. I could already tell a part of me had fallen for this man in more ways than I cared to interpret.

I mean, I'd always been attracted to him, from the first moment we met, despite his rude greeting and less than enthusiastic response to my presence at Dominic's house. I had been confused at his instant obvious dislike of me, but intrigued nonetheless. I'd never been one of those girls who went for the rugged bad boy image. I liked my men strong, sure, but not dismissive.

So why had I been dreaming about Jason Cain? And why did this moment, surreal as it was, feel so very much wanted and right?

Because, if I was honest, for the first time in my life a man didn't treat me the way I expected, the way I had come to regard as my right. Those who met me within my family social setting treated me as the daughter of a well respected man. They showed the correct amount of consideration, never over stepping the mark. It was boring, and although some were very agreeable, none ever made my stomach flip or my heart beat out of my chest.

And then there were those who I met through work, who showed respect of my professional accomplishments, the right amount of admiration for my skills and what I had achieved, and treated me with courtesy, showering me with dinners and events that matched the level of esteem I had earned. Again, they were often enjoyable encounters, but they rarely led to a second date.

I had experienced one safe 'tryst' after another. Some had managed to get closer than others, even making it to my bed. But none were anything more than what I expected. No surprises. No risks. No life.

Jason had been correct, I realised. I did just float through my world without trying too hard, without putting myself out there in the hopes that I'd find something special, something that made my world spin, rather than just pass by.

It was an uncomfortable epiphany. But my troubled thoughts were interrupted by Jason's cellphone. The ringtone was a standard old school phone bell-type trill, which cut through the closing credits of the movie with a jarring-like quality.

Jason withdrew his arm from around me and picked his phone up from the side table where he'd had it resting. He still had things on around his waist, but he'd manoeuvred them all to the other side, including his gun and the knife I'd threatened him with. I was certain it wasn't so much to keep them out of my reach, but to make it comfortable for me when I lay against him. That made my heart speed up for some reason.

"Cain," he announced into the phone, not giving away the fact he was lounging on my settee with my body pressed hard up against his. He sounded professional and one hundred percent on the job.

"Good to know," he added, after whoever was on the other end had said their piece. "Hear from you in the morning then," he concluded and swiped the screen to end the call.

He returned the phone to the table and turned to look at me. I waited patiently for him to convey whatever message the caller had left.

"Eric," he explained. "McLaren's been arrested. Nick's got an early morning breakfast meeting scheduled with King tomorrow. We're still on lock-down until Nick gives the OK."

"Oh," I said softly. My mind racing to catch up with my hormones, which were already on board with one more night in Jason's arms. "So...?" I began.

"So," he finished for me. Then added with a wicked gleam in his eyes. "I'm not sleeping on the couch again tonight."

"I thought you didn't sleep," I pointed out, my heart pumping in my chest.

"I didn't last night. King could have made a move. He's unlikely to tonight with McLaren out of the way, but the lock-down's in effect until we can be certain he's appeased." He waited a beat, then said, "Not that I plan on doing much sleeping tonight either, but for entirely different reasons."

His voice had lowered on those last words sending a thrill of desire and anticipation through me.

"I thought you needed time to recover," I pointed out, playing devil's advocate in the steady and hungry looking gaze he had on me.

"I'm young and fit, Kate," Jason pointed out.

I didn't say anything in reply, I was too busy concentrating on breathing. If I lost track of that, I'd probably pass out. His hand slowly came up and brushed my hair off my face, then reached behind my head to slip the hair tie out. He ran his fingers through the strands distractedly for several seconds. I wasn't sure what the faraway look in his eyes meant. Was he having second thoughts? He was definitely thinking something through though. Some question or puzzle he needed to work out. I don't know if he solved it, but he came to a conclusion in the end, which brought his eyes back to mine.

He held my gaze for a moment and then said, "I'm going to ask you do something and I don't want you to think too much about it. I just want you to go with it. To let go of everything you believe you need to think about, and just do it. OK?"

I sucked in a shaky breath and just stared at him. What on earth could he ask me that he didn't want me to think about? What did it mean?

"I don't understand," I finally admitted.

"You don't need to," he shot back, a little more firmly than before. "You just need to trust me. To let me handle everything so you can simply enjoy."

And now my heart had reached an epic speed inside my chest, it almost ached with the pace it was keeping. My throat was dry and even though I couldn't breathe properly, what I was sucking in scraped over the roughness in my neck and made me want to lick my lips and swallow futilely to ease the sensation. I knew it would only make me cough, and right now I couldn't allow that sort of distraction. Jason was all my mind would let me deal with.

"O..OK," I stuttered instead, watching his lips tip up on the edges in a small smile. It wasn't so much as amused, I don't think, more like it was resigned. He wasn't making any sense at all.

"OK," he said softly though, still running a hand through my hair. "Go in to your bedroom, Kate," he instructed. "Strip out of the robe and lie down on top of the bed on your back."

What?

"Wait for me. Don't touch yourself. Don't move. I will come to you. Understand?"

No. Absolutely not.

He waited patiently for me to answer. His eyes never leaving mine. Like before, I felt as though there was more to the question than the word *understand* implied. A weight to his query that meant something I was still not getting. Admittedly, I was confused. Why would he want me to strip naked and lie on the bed? And wait? And what was he thinking saying I couldn't touch myself? As if I'd do that with him in the next room and at any moment walking in on me on the bed.

"Kate," he pushed. "Don't think. Just do."

Oh. Right. OK. I nodded my head slowly, still holding his intense gaze.

"I..I'll go then?" I suggested.

"Don't touch yourself," he repeated, for some reason thinking that command was the most important of all.

I frowned at him, but got up off the couch, suddenly on shaky legs, and walked back-stiff out of the room. I almost shut the door to my bedroom - I mean, I was about to strip bare - but he hadn't told me to do that. So I didn't. I also forced myself not to think, and just slipped my silky robe off my shoulders and let it glide to the floor. The feel of the delicate fabric floating across my skin sent a shiver down my spine.

My eyes closed and I had to breathe through my nose to stop my body shuddering. For crying out loud, it was just a piece of material.

I glanced back over my shoulder, but Jason hadn't followed me into the hall. I could hear him channel surfing again. My frown deepened. I stood there for at least a full minute, listening to the channels on the TV changing mid sentence, again and again and again. He wasn't coming. At least he wasn't leaving that settee just yet.

I shook my head and returned my eyes to the bed. A soft glow of light came in from the hallway, but I hadn't switched any illumination on in my room. Jason hadn't told me to, and I was guessing this game - it seemed like a game and if I thought of it as a game it kind of made sense - was all about me following instructions clearly. No deviation, hence the repeated *"Don't touch yourself"* command.

I huffed a breath of air out and climbed onto the bed. My knees felt cushioned by the duvet cover, my hands automatically curled into the soft, thick fabric beneath them. I stilled on all fours on top of my bed, unsure what to make of the fact that *everything* felt... more. More texture. More sensation. Just more.

I continued my crawl up the bed, not wanting to be unprepared when Jason came in the room. And being prepared meant having carried out his instructions... to the letter. I rolled over onto my back and let out a slow, shaky breath as my skin came in contact with the cool surface of the linen. My butt wiggled involuntarily, as though trying to make a cavity in the bedspread to cradle itself within. But it was more than that, I couldn't quite grasp it yet, but my body wanted something else my mind wasn't prepared to acknowledge just yet.

Although I could still hear the distorted sound of the changing channels on the TV from out in the lounge, in my room everything seemed unnaturally quiet. The lack of any ambient noise around me made me hyper-aware of my breathing; how it sawed out of my chest as though I'd just run a marathon, when all I'd done was walk from the living area to my bed.

I tried to settle my respirations, all the while trying to slow down my heart rate, but my mind kept getting distracted by the scratch of the material beneath my skin. My fingers gripped the duvet cover, scrunching it up, and then flattening out, seeking friction, sensation, a positive response to a need I couldn't quite grasp.

Minutes passed. My breathing became more controlled, but my heart rate was a lost cause. And my need to move was excruciating. Jason told me not to think, to just do. But my mind had stalled on his last instruction: *"Don't touch yourself."*

I let a long, slow breath out through pursed lips. I felt so vulnerable lying here in the semi dark, completely nude. *Waiting.* And I felt rebellious because of it. How dare he order me around and expect me to do exactly as he demanded.

I lifted my head and peered out into the hall. Still no Jason, but the TV was flicking through its channels every few seconds. How would he even know if I disobeyed him?

I don't know why touching myself seemed to be the only form of disobedience I could conjure up. Surely getting up off the bed made more sense. Even getting dressed, turning on the light. Taking a bloody cold shower would do. But I dismissed all of those notions as inadequate. He wanted me to obey that last command. Why else did he repeat it?

And, if I was brutally honest with myself - and there was no one here to see the blush that came at these next thoughts anyway - I was entirely too turned on. Who gets turned on by this sort of thing?

Obviously me.

I licked my lips, took one more quick glance out of the doorway, still seeing nothing there and hearing the TV channel surfing, so I slowly began to stroke a hot hand down my chest, pausing slightly at my breasts. My back rose, pressing my already rock hard nipples into my palms and I closed my eyes as my hands squeezed the flesh tight.

Oh, dear Lord that felt good.

My eyes sprang open to make sure Jason hadn't appeared or heard the small whimper that escaped my lips. But the TV would have been too loud and was still alternating channels, the abrupt interruption to sentences making it obvious he was still surfing out there.

I smiled at my defiance of his instructions. Captain Jason Cain was not in charge of me.

One hand travelled on reluctantly from my nipple, but there was a more urgent area needing my attention. Eyelids closed again, I let a long sigh out of my mouth, turning my head to the side as my fingers found their goal. My body shivered, then followed that up with a jerk as I started rolling my clit beneath my fingertip.

I could still hear the channels changing from down the hallway, so I didn't bother to open my eyes and check the room again. I just concentrated on what my fingers were doing, on the wetness beginning to coat their tips, on the swelling and throbbing that had taken up residence between my thighs.

This was so wicked and because Jason had forbidden it, so decidedly naughty. *But oh so nice.*

A finger dipped inside, and I wished it was Jason's. Or better yet, his hard shaft. I pumped the single digit three times, then needing *more* I withdrew it and replaced it with two instead. I could have rolled over to my bedside drawer and retrieved my vibrator, but that seemed like too much of a deviation from Jason's instructions and I wasn't sure how much time I actually had left.

Needing to finish this, needing to get the release my body craved, I worked harder, blocking out everything else except what my hand and fingers were doing, and the building tension inside.

Half of me expected to be interrupted, for Jason to burst in and demand I stop. To pull my hand aside and and replace my fingers with his. It was an image that just made my body tingle with ever-more urgent desire. I *wanted* him to catch me. Oh dear God I wanted him to take over. To punish me for my disobedience, to carry out the threat of spanking me like he'd promised.

This was why we were doing this, wasn't it? This game of cat and mouse.

I think I knew he was there, even though I didn't open my eyes, couldn't hear anything else but my laboured breathing and the TV out in the lounge. But my mind chose to ignore that sensation of being watched and finish what I - no what *he* - had started.

I came apart in a dizzying array of colours behind my lids. So unexpected considering the dimness of the room. I gasped, bit my lip, and then had to bury my face in the pillow beneath my cheek to stifle the cry that escaped my throat. I don't know if it was the imagined fantasy of having Jason watch me, or the fact that if he did catch me I'd be in for some trouble, no doubt. Or just the whole scenario he'd created. But the orgasm was one of the best self-induced I'd ever had.

Of course, despite his body not being the stimulant to bring me to climax, he had certainly been involved in the event. So, could it still be called self-induced?

I panted through the aftermath and slowly came back to the room. It was still dim, only a small amount of light from out in the hallway reaching the bedspread where I lay covered in a thin layer of perspiration: breathless, boneless, replete. But there was enough light to see a figure sitting in the armchair at the end of my bed. Elbows on his spread knees, his threaded fingers up to his chin as he leaned forward... watching. A more perfect position to observe my actions did not exist. Jason would have had front row seats to what I was doing, to my reaction to every stroke, every plunge of my fingers inside.

My eyes met his, he held perfectly still and stared back at me.

Then said, in that deep, rough voice that meant he was turned on, "Kate, Kate, Kate. What am I going to do with you?"

CHAPTER 9

A MAN WHO PUSHED MY LIMITS IN MORE WAYS THAN JUST ONE

"Ah," I spluttered, shifting to a half sitting position on top of the covers, to better face the devil at the end of my bed.

I was suddenly unsure if I'd done the right thing. He looked immobile sitting there in the armchair across the room. Sure, I could see an obvious bulge in his jeans, but he wasn't acting on it. He was simply staring at me, with a soft shake of his head, as though disappointed somehow. I bit my lip, confused, then quashed that snivelling reaction and lifted my chin in defiance. Something crossed his face, flashed in his eyes. I refused to kowtow to it,

"This is what you expected to happen, isn't it?" I queried, making sure my voice was strong and level. Not a quaver in sight.

"No," he replied succinctly and my heart fell. "How can there be trust between us if you don't follow my directives?" he added.

Oh. I quickly redirected my thoughts from that unhappy revelation.

"So, what happens now?" I couldn't believe I was still anticipating a spanking for my actions. Not just anticipating it, but wanting it with every fibre of my being. Something of that desire must have shown on my face because Jason chuckled. It was a relief to hear him make a cheerful, if not slightly wicked, sound.

"You want me to punish you, don't you, Kate?" I held his gaze. "And just for that, I won't"

Disappointment washed through me, quickly followed by belated relief. Ah, there's my self-preservation at last.

He rose from his seat and started walking languidly toward the side of the bed, his fingers undoing the top button of his jeans with casual ease. My heart did a little happy-happy-joy-joy dance inside. *Finally!*

"Did it occur to you," he said, as his jeans met the floor and he toed them and his boxers off. His stiff erection met my hungry eyes as he came to rest at the side of the bed. He didn't come closer, just started stroking himself before me, letting me get my visual fill of all of him. Every single long, thick splendid inch of him under his well practised strokes. "That to have delayed your gratification until I arrived would have been better? Phenomenal even."

My eyes darted up to his, but quickly returned to what he was doing next to the bed. I'm not going to apologise for that, there was no way I could pull my gaze away from this spectacular vision for long.

"Kate," he chastised, making me lift my eyes reluctantly back to his face. "Eyes up here," he ordered and I gave him an incredulous glare in return.

He smirked, but didn't say anything more until he was sure I wasn't going to look away. It was hard not to, the man was gloriously naked before me, palming his erection and stroking it teasingly knowing exactly what the action was doing to my pulse. I kept my gaze resolutely on his face, even though he'd stepped closer and I could hear the soft sound of him pleasuring himself inches away.

"For this to work we have to trust each other implicitly," he said softly. But the soft edge in his voice was a disguise. The real meaning was hidden in the depths and weight of each word.

Of course trust was a prerequisite for any relationship, and him saying that we needed it did send tendrils of delight through my frame. But there was more here. Just like every other time. He was trying to tell me something, in his Jason Cain obtuse way. It was beginning to get through. Maybe repetition really does work.

Still.

"What are you really saying, Jason?" I asked, holding his gaze.

"I think you know, Kate. You're a smart woman. The question is, the only question that counts, can you do it? Can you take the risk?"

For once I just wanted him to come out and say the words. Why couldn't he? Was he embarrassed by them? Unsure of how I would react? Jason was taking a risk of sorts revealing himself to me in this way, but the risk was tempered with reticence. If he didn't actually say the words themselves he could deny ever taking the risk in the first place, when he eventually crashed and burned.

But that wasn't the crux of my dilemma, was it? Could I be the woman he wanted me to be? Jason Cain was a dominant and he wanted a woman in his life who would fit the role. I'm not entirely sure how far this all went for Jason. Did he want a pure submissive in his bed? Or was there some give and take? He was giving me glimpses, but not enough to make an educated decision in the end.

My eyes trailed down his body. Over every curve and dip across his broad chest. I longed to reach out and touch him, to lay a wet trail across that perfectly tanned skin with my tongue. To work my way down his torso, teasing with nips and bites, then quickly following up with soothing kisses. Watch goosebumps appear in my wake and know I could make his skin tingle like he does mine.

I'd wanted Jason for so long. I'd dreamt of him offering himself to me in some way. But in none of those fantasies did it include this scenario. To give up complete control to him, in return for ecstasy in his bed. I wasn't at all in doubt that that's what I would receive. Jason had been going easy on me this past day, introducing me bit by bit to his world. Never so much as to make me run screaming, only enough to entice me further into his web.

The fact I was using a spider as an analogy to describe Jason Cain was not lost on me. In a way I did feel a little trapped. Because how could I turn away from this? How could I not reach for what I desired when it was offered, when I'd had a small delicious taste, even if it was offered with caveats in place.

I knew so little about a dominant and submissive relationship. And part of me believed that Jason wasn't a true dominant, in the very strictest sense of the word. How could he be, when he'd been so casual in sharing that role up until now.

Or maybe, I hadn't been in charge at any time at all. Maybe, he was that good at making me feel I was, when in fact he controlled everything.

"You're thinking too much, Kate," he whispered, reaching one hand forward to cup my chin and tilting my gaze back up to his face.

He'd stopped stroking himself, but his erection was still sitting proud and long and hard between us. Clear evidence of what I did to him. It sent a thrill through me knowing I turned him on to that degree. But could I do this?

Could I take the risk he was asking me to take?

"I'm not sure," I finally admitted. He deserved an honest reply. "I've never done anything like this before."

He nodded in understanding, then said, voice soft like a caress, "I'm not sure I could be any other way."

And there you have it. The stalemate. I clearly wasn't ready to take that leap of faith, to risk. And he clearly wasn't capable of moulding himself to anything other than who he was. I admired him for knowing himself so clearly, but I was a little angry that he couldn't explain as plainly to me exactly what he required. An oblique reference to dominance was not enough for me to go on. He expected me to fill in the blanks.

"Where does that leave us?" I finally asked, feeling my heart getting wearier.

"You haven't ruled it out completely," he said, still cupping my chin with one hand. "I can only assume you're afraid to take that next step."

I nodded, it was true. I still wanted him, I still ached for him. But I was... confused. Reticent like his admission was to me.

"Can you give me 'til the morning to give my answer?" I asked, stalling for more time with this man. Clinging with my fingertips if I had to.

He frowned slightly, I knew the hesitation for what it was. He was about to deny me that luxury. Jason Cain was not someone who gave an inch. He'd asked a question, I'd been unable to answer it immediately. To him the matter was as good as closed.

I couldn't have that. I needed more time. I wasn't sure of my answer, which meant my answer could still be a yes. I just needed more information, *more time.*

My hands gripped his hips and without giving him a chance to pull away my lips wrapped around his erection tightly. And I took as much of him as I could manage in my mouth, more than he expected, I think.

"Fuck," he breathed out. "Kate!" His hands automatically fisted in my hair, exactly the response I was after. "Oh, Kate. You are playing with fire, baby."

His hips started rocking, but I knew he was still holding back. That didn't bother me, it was enough for now that he wasn't stopping this at all. And the knowledge that he didn't want to scare me lifted my heart and replaced the weariness of before with brilliant light.

He groaned when I started playing with his sac, fondling the balls within firmly. Jason seemed like the kind of man who wanted to *feel.* He moaned, rocked harder, held my head still with his hands and started to really fall into the moment. Still holding a little back, but now more just a natural consideration than a calculated thought.

"Oh God," he breathed out above me. "Where did you learn that?" he asked in an almost pained whimper when I grazed the length of him with my teeth, then sucked hard on the way back up, adding a little tongue flourish at the tip.

I hummed my incoherent answer and received a loud and long moan from the back of his throat.

His movements were a little frantic now. His control was slipping. I think it surprised him more than it did me. Whatever I was doing was more than Jason Cain had bargained for and I took absolute delight in that fact. There was control here. Even though he held my head still with his grip in my hair, and he measured the distance he rocked into my mouth. Even though everything was done at his pace, at his direction. His reaction to my touch, my method of arousing him with my lips, to *me*, was something he had absolutely no control over in the end. It was all mine. My control over him.

And that realisation made me want to take that risk, because no matter how dominant Jason ended up being, I would always hold a measure of control over this man.

He pulled back creating a popping sound as the tip of his erection came free of my pursed lips.

"Oh, Kate," he breathed, following me down on the bed. His lips trailing over my collar bone, sucking on the sensitive flesh at the side of my neck, as his hand found one breast and began playing there. "My turn," he added, as he continued to move his large frame down the length of my body, soft kisses and nips making me squirm.

He spread my thighs, lifting one above his shoulder and then the other up as well. Then with one small smirk up at me he dipped his head between my legs and took his sweet time showing me exactly what the word payback means.

The first orgasm rocked through me making me gasp and shudder and cry out his name, but he wasn't nearly satisfied with that. He got up on all fours, commanded me to "stay still" and then reached into my bedside drawer.

And OK, so the blush that coated my cheeks wasn't as noticeable in the dim light of the room, but I could feel it, and I was sure he could feel it across my entire body, when he came back holding my vibrator in one hand.

"Thought you could hide this, huh?" he murmured, ducking his head again to between my thighs.

I whimpered in reply as he began to suck on my over sensitised clit, expecting him to slip the vibrator inside any moment. It didn't happen, and the longer he took the more I wanted it. His stimulation at my nub was welcomed, but because of the promise of what could happen, it wasn't enough.

"You want more, Kate?" he asked huskily against my thigh as he lay a delicate kiss on the skin there. "Here?" he asked, slipping the tip of the vibrator in between my folds, but not entering me yet. "Or 'round here?" he asked, as the vibrator slid through the dampness, coated in my free flowing juices, to end up between my butt cheeks at the other entrance.

"Jason," I warned, wanting and not wanting at the same time.

"It's OK," he purred, "Just a little, not far. Just at the edge. We'll start slowly, baby. Ease you into this."

This was it, his last attempt to get me to commit, to say the words. To take the risk.

I closed my eyes, felt him *everywhere*. And whispered in a husky voice that couldn't possibly be mine, "OK. I trust you."

He made a growling sound and dipped his head again, sucking and licking and making me writhe, and arch my back, and beg openly for more. He concentrated on my clit and the front of me for several delicious moments, adding a finger, then another and starting to pump to a rhythm he decided would work. It did work. An orgasm approached in lightning speed and just when I thought it would slam into me, knock me sideways, sweep me completely away, he switched on the vibrator, ran it through my soaking folds again and then pressed it into my butt an inch, no more.

Oh thank you God, fuck! I don't care to swear harshly, but this moment deserved the expletive, I will not lie. In fact for several long, drawn out, utterly ridiculously sensational seconds - or maybe minutes - *fuck* was on repeat in my head.

It wasn't until Jason turned the speed down on the vibrator, twisted it slowly and pulled it out, that I realised I'd said all those swear words aloud. I was not embarrassed. There was nothing right now that could embarrass me. I was beyond such superfluous emotion. I was in another dimension. I was further out than cloud nine.

"Kate," Jason whispered as he rose above me. "I know you're tired, and I'll let you sleep soon. But I need you, baby. Roll onto your stomach."

I followed his instruction without hesitation, somehow finding the strength to roll over at his command. He grunted his approval, then spread my legs tenderly, lifted my hips a fraction off the bedspread, not far, and then guided himself inside.

It didn't take long for me to join in on the moment, how could I not with Jason pumping behind me, and panting above me, and moaning in my ear?

"Play with yourself," he instructed, a little breathlessly. And again I did exactly as he demanded, slipping a hand between the bed and my stomach, finding my almost too swollen clit and rubbing back and forth. "That's it, Kate. That's exactly what I want."

He was telling me this was how the game - *his* game - was played, and that all it took was what I was doing. Acting, not thinking. Following his directive so I could let go and taste life. Live.

It wasn't much to ask, was it? And on that thought I came soundly, screaming his name into the covers as he continued to pump into me, each thrust eliciting a small grunt from between his lips. Just as he was about to come, he grabbed a handful of my hair and twisted my head gently, but firmly, to the side so he could find my lips.

His orgasm was breathed into my mouth on a long groan of bliss. His movements slowed, as his erection slowly deflated, until finally he slipped out and slid his big body down my side. I was almost asleep already. Then he simply lifted me off the bedspread, cradling me in his arms and slipped me between the sheets, following in behind to wrap me up in his embrace.

"You did good, Kate," he whispered, laying a kiss in amongst my sweaty hair. It clung to my face and forehead, but he gently pulled the strands away and tucked them behind my ears. "So good, baby," he added.

"Is that what you wanted?" I said on a yawn.

"Oh, Kate," he whispered. "You are more than I could ever have imagined you'd be. Sleep now, baby. I'm not going anywhere."

I didn't need to be told twice. The heat of his body enveloped me. The hardness of his chest as it framed my back, matched only by the comfort and safety of his muscled arms wrapped around me.

Sleep was indeed easy to embrace with him by my side. In my bed. I dreamt of reality, not a fantasy that couldn't possibly compare. And throughout it all, I lay entangled with Jason, a man who pushed my limits in more ways than just one.

He challenged me without even saying a word, but the greatest challenge of all, was going to provide the largest reward, I was sure.

CHAPTER 10

THIS IS ONLY THE BEGINNING, KATE

WHEN I WOKE IN THE MORNING TO HIS PHONE RINGING ON THE bedside table, Jason was still there. I'm not sure why that surprised me. My cheek was resting on his chest. My body flush against his side. My leg over his thigh and his large frame curled into mine as his arm draped down the curve of my spine, where it came to rest with his hand cupped possessively around my hip.

I could not have been more content.

He rolled over slightly to reach his phone, but before he answered it, returned us both to our former positions. With my ear so close to the speaker I could hear both sides of the conversation.

"Cain," Jason said into the device with his usual gruff abruptness. From the tone of his voice you wouldn't have known he was naked in bed with a woman, let alone naked in bed with the woman he was assigned to protect.

I wondered how the rest of ASI - and in particular my brothers - would react to Jason and I getting together while under a lock-down. It wasn't really any different from the way Dominic and Genevieve started their relationship. She'd been under ASI protection too. So had Eva, Nick's fiancée. Both women falling for their saviours when under incredible stress.

I can't say I was under incredible stress, but the situation had been an acute one. Still, an uneasy feeling settled in the pit of my stomach thinking about both Dominic and Nick's overprotective reactions. Maybe we'd have to fudge the truth a little on the time-line of getting together.

"Lock-down's been lifted, bro," Eric was saying on the other end of the line. "You'll be pleased to know all operatives are recalled to ASI HQ for a debrief."

I knew Eric would think it was a relief for me that Jason could now leave, but I felt strangely hurt that he thought Jason would feel the same relief at being able to get away from my company. Of course, all of that was irrelevant now. The situation had changed. Still, it felt discomforting that Eric was aware of Jason's former dislike of me. Had our whole love-hate relationship been so obvious?

"Good. I'll be there as soon as I can," Jason replied, swiping the phone to disconnect the call before Eric could even reply. Giving the impression he was keen to get going. Maybe Jason wanted to keep how and when we got together from the gossip mongers at ASI as well.

The phone landed on the bedside table with a soft thunk and then Jason was facing me again, his hand brushing my hair from my face.

"You heard that?" I nodded. "I should get going," he added, but didn't move an inch away.

A small smile curved the edges of my lips.

"You going to be at Gen and Dom's this afternoon?" he asked, appearing as if he had no intention of getting out of this bed for a debrief.

"Ah, the barbecue," I said, trying to work out the date. Every second Sunday Dominic and Genevieve held a barbecue at their house. It was the only home big enough to take all of ASI, Sweet Seduction, ADK -

Dominic's lawyers firm - and our combined extended family numbers. We were a big group now and Gen took great delight in rounding us all up each fortnight to relax and enjoy life. That was Genevieve, a real mother hen with a party attitude. "Yes, as always," I replied, except this time I wouldn't be watching Jason out of the corner of my eye. I'd be *with* Jason.

"Good," he said, giving a short nod of his head in approval. "Save a beer for me," he added.

All I could do was smile.

He smirked slightly, a wicked grin I was quickly getting used to.

"Now that that's sorted," he husked in my ear, as his hand started to stroke down my side making me shiver, "Go in the bathroom and turn on the shower." Another instruction. My heart rate sped up and a longing tugged low down in my belly. Wow, he only had to give a command in that soft, steady way and I was already wet. "Step under the spray and place your palms against the tiles. Spread your legs. Arch your back. And wait. I'll come to you." Pause. "Understand?"

I nodded, and without waiting for repeated instructions, slipped out from beneath his touch and from between the sheets, and walked straight into the attached bathroom. I heard Jason make that low growl of approval from the back of his throat as he rolled over onto his back in the bed. He was as turned on as me, and it seemed he got more aroused when I obeyed his directions immediately, without hesitation or argument.

For some inexplicable reason that made me moan, a soft sound from deep inside, leaving a flush in its wake as my body temperature rose to match the arousal within. If this was what it was going to be like, there was no question I'd made the right choice. I knew Jason would give me the best sex I had ever had, I knew it from the moment I saw him. From the moment I saw how he acted, how he spoke. The way he moved. Like a panther on the prowl, in charge of the world around him. Determined, focused. Powerful.

I'd known all of this just by watching, observing, the man. But to have it confirmed now was incredible. Fantastic. An utter turn on.

Jason brought out the sex craved woman in me. No matter how much he wanted my body, I wanted his even more.

I waited only long enough for the water to heat up and then I stepped inside, closing the sliding glass door behind me. I let the water spray over my feverish skin briefly, then wanting nothing more than to have Jason here with me moving things along, I placed my palms readily against the cool tiles, arched my back as instructed, and greedily spread my thighs.

Water trailed down my back, little droplets that spread like hungry fingers across my skin. The shower spray was forceful, I'd had all the plumbing replaced in my bungalow when I redecorated, so the water rebounded off the tiles on the floor haphazardly. Several drops even managed to make their way up my thighs to land delicately against the tender flesh at the apex.

It was a beautiful kind of torture. Any stimulation was wanted, but it was so soft and ethereal almost, that it taunted instead of simply touched. I lowered my head and concentrated on breathing, trying to stop myself from panting in need and hunger and anticipation. All the while praying that Jason hurried up.

I don't know how long it took for the sliding door at my back to open and a waft of cooler air to rush inside the stall before the heat of his body ran down my back and legs. He didn't touch me, just closed the door behind him and when I went to look over my shoulder, instructed in a hoarse whisper that didn't even sound like him, "Don't turn around. Eyes closed."

I knew, of course, it *was* him, but the moment took on a surreal element. His voice sounded different, spoken in a way and tone he hadn't used in my presence before. It was entirely intentional, I was sure. That coupled with not seeing who the person actually was who entered the shower behind me, made unusual images flash though my mind. It also made me hotter. Wetter. Hungrier for his touch.

He stood right at my back for several long drawn out moments, then one finger dipped directly inside, between my legs. He hadn't touched me elsewhere. He hadn't given me any warning. Just the solitary finger dipping in until he could reach no further.

Panting was the least of my worries now, I'd started to make a whimpering sound that I had absolutely no control over at all.

A second finger, on the same hand, found my clit and started to rub gentle circles, bringing a rush of blood to the area, making the nerve endings start to scream for release.

"Don't come," he ordered in the same voice of before. My whimpering got louder. "Not yet," he added, then withdrew the finger and returned with two instead.

He started a steady rhythm up; in, out, rub against my clit, in, out, rub against my clit. He repeated the action again and again and again. Seconds passed. Minutes. Maybe hours, I'm not sure, but the tension built to an inferno inside, making me buck and writhe and moan loudly. I knew now that he liked to hear me, but in the closed confines of the shower stall, with the spray from the water dampening the noise, it sounded so erotic. Almost like an adult movie soundtrack. And it was coming from *me*.

"I have to..." I started to plead.

"You will not," he interrupted with finality.

"Jason," I begged and felt a hand wrap around the wet strands of my hair pulling my head back. Lips began trailing over the exposed flesh of my neck, then when he found a soft spot, sucked hard.

Oh good grief. I was coming apart. I couldn't contain it any longer. Every nerve had fizzled and zapped between my legs, low down in my groin. Every ounce of my concentration had been between my legs, on what he was doing to me there. But to suddenly have such powerful sensations at the other end of my body, up by my head, made the nerves splutter and spark and threaten to explode. Confusion reigned for several bliss-filled moments, and then clarity came crashing back in on a wave that was about to wash me away despite his directive not to come.

How the hell did he know to do that?

Just at the last moment, he either took pity on me, or could simply tell that I was not going to be able to deny my body any longer, because he rasped into my ear, "Now, Kate!"

My scream of release was deafening in the relatively small shower stall. My legs buckled, unable to hold my weight up anymore, but Jason wrapped an arm around my waist and held me upright, while he continued to kiss my neck and stroke my core, eking out the last of sanity, making me groan in delight, which quickly got mixed with a growl of approval from him.

Light flashed and faltered behind my lids. Thoughts and words came in broken sentences inside my mind. My body shook and shuddered, wetness that had nothing to do with the water from the shower trailed down between my thighs, coating his fingers and hand slick. He cupped me between my legs, no longer making any effort to stimulate me, well aware that for now I was at my limit, but the warmth and intimacy of his hand holding me there sent a secondary round of shivers and quivers throughout my body.

Jason was breathing as hard as me. His chest and stomach draped over my back, while his arm still supported me and his erection pressed firmly from behind.

"Baby," he finally murmured. "Are you all right?" His hand had slipped out from between my thighs and now rested against the tiles in front and to the side of my face, taking both our weight I think.

I just nodded, still too breathless and mindless to be able to say a thing. He held me like that for so long. Not asking for anything in return, just giving me time to come to terms with what I'd experienced. It had almost been shocking, that level, that intensity, of release. I had never enjoyed something so... well, the only words I can describe it are rather trite, but appropriate. It had been earth shattering, world altering. I could never go back to 'boring', never go back to my vibrator alone on my bed, ever again.

Jason had changed me. And I think he knew it. That's why he didn't say or do anything for several minutes. Just held me, breathed with me, let me accept what he'd shown me, what he'd given me, until I was ready to move on.

At some point I must have taken my own weight, because he pulled back slightly and reached for the shampoo. Then with infinite care he started to wash my hair, making sure to keep the suds out of my eyes when he rinsed it clean. He repeated the action with conditioner. Preening and grooming me like a mother would a precious child. His care and attention, his focus and steady pace, was so unexpected. A side of Jason I hadn't thought was there.

But he seemed lost in the moment, as though there wasn't anything more important than making sure I was taken care of. Everything he'd done was for me. His erection looked hard and straining, when he turned me toward him to rub liquid soap over my chest and arms. He must have needed relief himself, but his only concern was my well being. My comfort. Me.

He washed me with tender, but purposeful strokes. These were not to get me aroused as such, these were entirely for the task at hand. When he finally finished, I took the bottle of soap from his hand and returned the favour. The entire time his eyes, showing a deep chestnut colour laced with the familiar chocolate brown, never left my face. Neither of us spoke. What was there to say? The moment was special, intimate in a non-sexual way. Precisely what we both needed, I think.

By the time I'd touched every inch of his rather well defined and incredibly sexy body, I was turned on again. There was no point denying it. And now his erection looked angry and definitely needing some attention of the sexual kind.

I poured soap into the cupped palm of my hand, lifted my eyes to his briefly, then wrapped my hand around the thick circumference of his shaft.

He made a strangled sound, his body jerking and shuddering as his hand came out and slapped the tiles to the side of us hard. As if it was an involuntary movement, like a reflex action when the nurse taps your knee with that little hammer. I was surprised he hadn't anticipated that was where I'd be touching next. I'd covered every other inch of his glorious body, his erection was the last place left.

But he confirmed his shock by saying, in the sexiest, roughest voice he'd used yet, "Kate. This is not about me."

My eyes lifted to his, my hand still gently stroking, the spray of the water washing the soap away.

"Do you want me to stop?" I asked. He swallowed thickly, then reached out with one hand to cup his palm around the side of my neck.

His thumb stroked the skin across my collar bone in time to my hand stroking him. Then, still holding my gaze, he shifted his hand to my shoulder and gently, but firmly, guided me to my knees in front of him.

I got the impression he couldn't say no, even though he wanted to. He obviously wanted to give me this moment in the shower, for my enjoyment alone. But the offer to help him find his own release was too great for him to ignore. With a pained look on his face, which had nothing to do with his urgent need for relief, he watched as I licked the last residue of soap off his erection and palmed his sac beneath.

Then in typical Jason Cain style, he demanded, "Lace your hands behind your back."

My eyes lifted to him and he must have seen the question on my face, *he didn't want me to touch him with my fingers?*

"Don't think," he added. "Just do."

I followed his instruction, unsure how I would keep my balance, let alone how I would be able to stop myself from reaching for him. I couldn't imagine that this was going to be comfortable, but if this is what he wanted, then I'd give it to him. He'd just blown my world, it was the least I could do.

Once my hands were secured behind my back I got back to work, using just my lips, teeth and tongue on his arousal. Within seconds his fingers were entangled in my hair, guiding me, controlling my movements, where without my hands on his body, I could not.

"That's it," he breathed, throwing his head back against the tiles behind him, eyes closed in bliss. He kept hold of my head and slowly rocked his hips back and forward. The sight of him thrusting himself toward my mouth was so incredibly sexy. Losing himself in between my lips. Taking what he needed to find his own release.

But it didn't take me long to realise I was equally lost to the experience. Not being able to touch him, I was forced to concentrate on the sensations I felt on my lips. The taste of him, mixed with soap, on my tongue. The fine line he made me walk with the depth in which he entered me. It was a slow sensual slide down a seductive slope, and before too long I was moaning and shifting on my knees trying to find some form of relief to the urgent pressure that had accumulated deep down inside.

"Oh, Kate," he groaned above me, making my eyes, which had closed, flick open to look up at his face. "You have no idea how sexy you are kneeling there. How much I like the idea that me getting off in you, gets you off too."

Oh my Lord. I pleaded with my eyes for him to ease the build up of tension in my body.

"You want to come, baby?" he asked, huskily.

I nodded against him, making him suck in a breath at the movement it created in my mouth; teeth grazing.

"You need me to make you feel good?" he asked, breathless and eyes a little wild. "Or do you want to do it yourself?"

He was giving me options. How is that a dominant? I think Jason played by his own rules. He was still very much in charge, because I hadn't just sought my own release, I'd waited for him to offer a solution. But he still gave me a form of control. How did I want to come? With him inside me, or him thrusting into my mouth while I played with myself?

I pulled back, at the same time he pulled back, allowing me to reply.

"I want you inside me." I breathed the words out like they were as essential as air.

He cupped my cheek, holding my gaze as I looked up at him from where I still knelt.

"You please me, Kate," he said softly. Then turned the taps off, opened up the sliding door to the shower and reached down to lift me to my feet.

Within seconds he'd towelled us both off, then he grasped my hand and led me back into the bedroom. The sheets were still in disarray, having not been made since we got up. His cellphone was beeping on the bedside table, obviously we'd missed a call, maybe more than one. He ignored it all, helped me to lie back on the bed and then crawled on top of me.

"I'm close to the edge, baby," he murmured, wasting no time guiding himself inside. "As much as I want to fuck you every way possible, missionary has its benefits."

I smiled up at his serious face, I had no problems with missionary style. It *had* always been the quickest way for me to get off.

He started slowly, even though I could see the strain in his muscles as he held himself above my chest. Even though I could see a vein pulsing erratically on the side of his neck. Even though he panted with each slow glide inside, and sucked in air like he was drowning with every smooth retreat.

His eyes closed, his head dipped down, as he breathed my name, *"Kate"*.

Not surprisingly, it didn't take long at all for me to come. His pace picked up as I moaned and writhed beneath him. His cellphone rang, but we were both too far gone to even care that someone somewhere was trying to enter our world. And as soon as my orgasm waned he roared his triumphant release, collapsing onto my body, his lips finding mine as he continued to pound into me, lengthening his moment as long as he could.

Finally we stopped all motion, sweaty again despite having just exited the shower. Jason stayed draped over my body like a welcoming blanket, still inside me, still connected. He lifted his head, brushed my hair back to reveal my eyes, and just... stared.

"This is only the beginning, Kate," he finally murmured.

It was a promise.

The world was waiting for us, evidenced by yet another call on his phone, no doubt Eric wanting to know why the GPS on Jason's car hadn't moved from my driveway yet. But the world was irrelevant right now.

I took hold of his words and clasped them tight.

I'd taken the risk...

And Jason Cain had caught me with open arms.

CHAPTER 11

I AM SPEECHLESS

BUT, REALITY CAN BE A SHIFTING TYPE OF SAND. FLEETING. Changing. Never what you think it actually is...

Jason failed to appear at Dominic's and Genevieve's barbecue that afternoon.

He never phoned, nor did he return my half dozen calls.

He dropped off the face of the earth. Or at least he did for me.

I have no words to describe the feeling his sudden absence created. The gaping hole he carved out by not being there.

I had given all of me. And he had seemed to accept it whole-heartedly.

But now he was gone. As though he'd never stepped foot in my life so intimately, so irrevocably, before. As though he hadn't changed the very make-up of *me*.

I am speechless. There are no words.

I am...

Speechless.

CHAPTER 12

BUT I AM

TWO WEEKS LATER

IT WASN'T MEANT TO HAVE HURT THIS MUCH. I HAD LET HIM into my heart for just one day.

One day.

And now I was shattered, *destroyed*, broken into a million different sharp edged pieces. Because of Jason Cain.

I hated him. I truly did. And there's not many people Katie Anscombe hates. Ask my brothers. I'm a love and let live kind of girl. But Jason had asked me to live life by letting him in. Now I was desperately in love with the man, but conversely broken hearted by his careless and cruel actions, as well.

How could he have been so callous? How could I have fallen for the game, for his player ways?

I shook my head in disgust at myself. Thankfully, I am not a pushover, otherwise the past two weeks would have been a complete disaster. As it is, my passion for decorating was severely challenged. It's just a good thing that my proposal - a proposal that I have refused to further acknowledge as coming about because of any so called muse - covered all the basics. All I had do was purchase the necessary items, implement the design and fluff the final sitting room for the

Montgomery-Smiths. It was a success, but I'd be happy if I never laid eyes on the wretched place again.

Unfortunately, Mrs Montgomery-Smith had other ideas.

I sighed as I pushed the doors open to Sweet Seduction. I hadn't been inside Gen's coffee/chocolatier/music store all week. It became too hard. I kept expecting to see *him* there. I kept wondering if he was watching the security camera footage at ASI. I kept having to remind myself that Jason had simply used me and moved on, and wasn't in the slightest bit interested in what I was doing now. So, that's why I was forcing myself to drop in and touch base with my future sister-in-law.

Jason's sister.

And *that* was not the best thought to have when I was trying to act normal around everyone.

The sounds of coffee beans grinding competed with the almost too loud voice of Pink coming out of the speakers. *Lets Get This Party Started* seeming incongruous with the late afternoon shopping crowd on a Friday in High Street. But then, Genevieve and her best friend Kelly were always up for a party, no matter the time of day.

I walked with purpose, head held high, smile on my face, towards the counter. Intending to get my sisterly duties over with, before I had to schmooze with clients at the Montgomery-Smith's sitting room extravaganza. It was going to be a very long day indeed.

Dom and Gen were holding another barbecue on Sunday, and I needed to make my excuses now, before she roped me into providing a salad or something essential to the feast in Gen's mind. I always found it difficult to say no to Genevieve's enthusiasm, so it was best I got in my apologies before she got in her request.

Kelly was the one to notice me first. Her blonde curly locks bobbing up and down as she greeted me with a huge smile and happy blue eyes. I must have shown some of the discomfort I felt at being around genuinely happy people on my face, because her smile fell slightly and she cocked her head to the side. Then before I could correct myself, she said something out of the corner of her mouth to Gen, whose gaze lifted to me as I came to rest at the counter.

"Hello, darlings," I said in my best Katie Anscombe Prior To Jason Cain Ruining My World impersonation.

"What's wrong?" Genevieve asked without missing a beat.

Oh fudge. I was so mucking this up.

"Why nothing's wrong, silly," I replied. "Unless you call the boring event I have to attend tonight and the fact I can't make your barbecue on Sunday something to be worried about."

Ah, that was smooth, Katie. Very well done.

"Oh," Gen said, not believing my distraction for a minute.

Then she must have registered my actual words, as a frown passed over her porcelain cream face creating shadows. She took an abrupt step away from the coffee machine, to come closer to me. I forced myself not to take a step back. That would have looked suspicious.

"You have to come on Sunday," she said, in a voice that meant all business.

"I wish I could, darling, but something's come up." I was prepared for this, so I already had a false emergency made up. "One of my clients has had a disastrous event with a room I designed for them, and Sunday afternoon is the only time I can straighten things out before the shop in question has to open on Monday.

"You can't do it tomorrow?" she asked, frown still in place.

"No," I said with a shake of my head to send the message home. "Can't gain access until Sunday afternoon." I too added a frown to let her know I was disappointed.

"But, Katie," she pleaded, really putting the Genevieve Cain convincing, yet still somehow sweet, whine into the words. "Dom and I have an announcement." The last was said on a whisper, as she leaned across the counter towards me.

My heart flopped. Dominic was already marrying Gen. They'd set a date. Everything was planned and under way. Any announcement they had wouldn't be around their impending nuptials. I had an idea of what it could be, and it would be something important to Genevieve and Dom. Something I *should* be present for. But if her sister-in-law should be there, then her brother definitely should. And it was a risk - Ha! - my heart just couldn't take.

The sadness I felt at turning her down was evident on my face. She looked shocked. But it was more for the fact that I would pass up an important moment in their lives for work, than the notion that I was sad over it.

"I'm sorry," I mumbled, feeling entirely rotten about the deception and about letting Genevieve, someone I loved, down.

"Oh, OK then," she said with a small voice. "I guess we can just tell you on Monday maybe. After everyone else knows."

Oh, boy. Did she sound so woeful at that idea.

"Darling," I said, cajolingly. "I'm sure you won't even miss me. You'll be too excited with whatever reaction you receive to your good news."

It was obvious I'd guessed what the announcement was about, and Genevieve's beaming smile confirmed I was right and she knew it. She didn't say the words, clearly she and Dom had decided they wouldn't mention their surprise until Sunday. But I think she was pleased I'd cottoned on.

"Congratulations," I whispered, reaching over and squeezing her hand.

"When is it going to be your turn, Katie?" she asked innocently, as her carefree words sliced like a knife through my heart. "Even Jason has been talking about settling down and having... Well, you know."

Oh, and now the knife was twisting. I couldn't find my voice.

"I don't know who he's got in his life," Gen continued, oblivious to the blood pouring out of my chest and pooling on the ground, "but for the past two weeks he's been acting really weird, secretive even. Dom and I think he'll be bringing her on Sunday to the barbecue. I just hope she's not his usual blonde bimbo with big tits." She giggled at her apt description of Jason's *usual* type.

I needed to sit down. My legs were shaking, and not in a good way. I could feel that the colour had drained from my face. It hurt.

Everything hurt.

I dug deep. I needed to get out of here and clear my head. "Well, I'm sure whoever she is, you'll love her. As much as he does."

Those last words were said on a croak. Even Genevieve couldn't miss that. I cleared my throat, winced at the dryness there and asked, "Can I get a skinny cappuccino to go?"

Gen looked at me strangely for a second and then offered a small smile and set to work grinding the beans and tamping them into the portafilter. I pretended to be interested in the chocolates on display in the glass front case. When she handed me the black with hot pink writing cup, I pointed at a particularly cute packaged selection of chocolates, in an effort to get her attention off my pale and washed out face.

"I think my client would love that gift box, darling. Can I get that as well, please?" I was sure Mrs Montgomery-Smith wouldn't care less, but my mother had always taught me to come bearing gifts.

When she handed me my change back, she asked, concern lacing every word, "Katie, is everything all right?"

"Of course, darling," I replied instantly. "Just been a busy few weeks, that's all."

I placed the change in my purse, picked up the gift box of chocolates and finally lifted my gaze to Gen, offering a smile. It faltered at the worry that met me in her eyes.

"Katie," she said softly, leaning forward slightly to offer her next words. "You know you can talk to me about anything, don't you?"

My lips twitched in a parody of a smile. I was trying, I really was. But the idea of talking to Genevieve, about what had happened with Jason, was ludicrous.

"I'm OK, Gen," I said evenly. The use of her nickname, and not my signature moniker for everyone, making her pull back as though I'd hit her in the face.

"Oh, Katie," she whispered, her words getting lost in the noise of the busy café. I glanced around and noticed she had an ever growing queue, so took a relieved step back.

"I'll let you get back to work," I murmured. "Good luck for Sunday," was said over my shoulder, as I practically ran from the store.

I'd made it to my car parked on Chancery Street when my cellphone rang. A quick glance at the caller ID and I swore. Thankfully under my breath, as there were people nearby.

Dominic. Genevieve had ratted me out.

I beeped the locks on my car and opened the door, before I swiped the screen to answer. This conversation would require an element of privacy. I slipped into the driver's seat, placing the chocolates and my handbag on the one beside me and said into the phone, "Darling! I hear congratulations are in order."

The door swung shut just as Dom coughed down the line.

"She told you," he said in a deep and smooth voice. The one he used when he was trying to hide his reaction to something. Being a lawyer he was good at that. Maybe I should take lessons from him. I certainly needed some practice at hiding my emotions right now.

"I guessed, Dom. You must be thrilled." For the first time, in I don't know how long, I felt happy. Talking to my big brother about something so joyous as this.

"We were going to announce it together on Sunday, but Genevieve said you can't come. I guess it makes sense you're the first to know. You always did have a way of ferreting information out of us when we were kids."

"Ferreting! Pfft! I just know you two and I know how much you're in love. A baby is the next step."

"Well, usually the wedding comes first, but, well, you know how the best laid plans can go." He almost sounded tongue-tied, something Dominic never was.

I laughed softly. "I'm pleased for you, Dom. This is wonderful news."

"It is, isn't it?" he murmured. "And we would have loved to have had you with us when we told the world."

"Well, I promise not to breathe a word of it. Until you get a chance to make the official announcement, of course. Then I can't be held responsible for my enthusiasm at becoming an aunt."

He chuckled, practically a full blown laugh for him. "You sound good, Katie." It was said with a mixture of surprise and calculation. Dominic never said anything without having a valid reason to.

"I am," I lied with gusto. "Business is booming. I have an event tonight which I am sure will drum up more work. I'm really making a name for myself."

"And boyfriends?" Cutting to the chase. It wasn't the lawyer in him, it was all Anscombe male. Nick and my father had the same uncanny ability to see through a ruse and pick out the important thread that could unravel it.

"No one special." I lied again. In a way.

"Well," Dom said, clearly not wanting to get too far down the my-little-sister-is-actively-having-sexual-relations line of conversation. "If you have any problems, you know some dickhead causing you issues, just let us know." *Us* being him and Nick, of course. "We'll teach any imbecile who hurts our sister a lesson gladly."

"Gee," I said, letting mock sarcasm coat my voice. "Just what I always wanted, big brothers beating up my boyfriends when they tell me my butt's too big."

"Katie!" Dominic chastised. It was entirely too gentle to mean anything. "You don't have a butt." And he wasn't meaning that in the you-don't-have-a-big-enough-butt-to-mention way, he said it because to him, I was not an object to sexualise in *any* way. Brothers!

Of course, I wasn't letting him off that easily. "I don't have boobs either."

Silence. "Well, OK," he said slightly flustered. I stifled my giggle. At least I'd deflected the conversation off the real issue. "Take care and enjoy yourself tonight."

"You enjoy Sunday too, Dom. Thanks for calling." And that there was my mistake. Reminding him that he'd called me. For a reason.

"Are you sure you're OK, Katie? Genevieve said..." He paused, obviously not wanting to repeat exactly what Genevieve had said about my behaviour or performance in her store just now. "She said you looked out of sorts." I wondered what *out of sorts* was a euphemism for.

"I'm fine, Dom. Just overworked. That's all." Silence again. He didn't believe me. Was I that bad a liar? "Anyway, I've got to go, I'm running late for this thing."

"Thing?" he asked, amused and clearly ignoring my efforts to cut the conversation off at the pass.

"Event. Schmooze-fest. A client is throwing a little party to show off the room I just designed for her and has invited several of her friends to meet me. She seems to think they'd all be interested in hiring my services."

"That's great news," Dom said enthusiastically.

"Yes, well, I'm not sure I want to do similar designs as the one I created for her." I shouldn't have admitted that. I should have just got out while I was ahead.

"Why ever not?" Dominic asked, incredulously. "Business is business, Katie. You can't pay the bills if you don't have the contracts lined up."

"I know, Dom. I'm not entirely new to this sort of thing."

"So, why don't you want to do this design again? Why miss opportunities when they are presented to you just because you need to change things up a bit."

I bristled. I was not a flighty person.

"That's not it at all."

"Then what is it?"

"I just don't think the design will work elsewhere."

"That's nonsense," he retorted. "You once told me a design can be manipulated for any environment, as long as one of the individual elements within the design has a commonality with the final location."

Oh dear. I had said that.

"Sometimes you have to go with your gut," I replied weakly.

"That is the worst argument you have ever given me, Katie. I'm disappointed."

I lowered my head to rest it on my steering wheel. Great. Being told off by my lawyer brother because I'm not debating an issue to the best of my abilities. I said this day was going to be long. I just didn't realise how tediously long it would be.

"Dom," I said on a sigh.

"It's all right. You've said enough. I understand you don't want to talk about this, but we're worried about you, Katie. And it's obvious that something is not perfect in my sister's world."

"Dom," I whispered. "I'm too old to have my big brothers fight all my battles for me. There comes a time when I just have to stand on my own two feet."

Silence again. Dom was very good at that. I refused to fill it, as it was his most powerful weapon.

Finally, he relented.

"OK. I'm here if you need me. *We're* here if you need us."

I didn't say anything, my voice was lost, just swiped the screen to end the call.

I stared blankly out of the car windscreen, replaying the entire afternoon. From walking into Sweet Seduction - my coffee was now stone cold - to Genevieve's worried expression and then Dominic's brotherly phone call. But the biggest *blip* in my mind right then was their news. The announcement that they'd be making on Sunday at the barbecue.

It *was* great news. Dom would make a brilliant father. They both deserved it so very much. I was happy for them. So very happy for them.

My tears plopped heavily onto my lap, leaving isolated spots in the fabric. The more they fell, the heavier they felt... on my legs... in my heart. I shouldn't have been crying. I had no right to feel this desolate at such fantastic news. There was no reason for me to be so bereft. So sad.

But I am.

My cellphone broke the silence, but failed to still my weeping.

Nick. Brother number two checking up on me. Was it Dominic or Genevieve who phoned him? Maybe someone was watching the Sweet Seduction security cameras at ASI, after all. I was going to have to avoid visiting Gen's shop for a little while. I think I was going to have to avoid everyone for a while. I couldn't afford for them to see me this way.

Broken.

I started the car, wiping at my face to clear my vision, and pulled away from the kerb, checking the clock on the dash to make sure I had enough time to make myself presentable before I attended Mrs Montgomery-Smith's soiree.

There were still too many hours left in this day.

CHAPTER 13

IT WAS THE BEST I COULD HOPE FOR

I WAS BORED OUT OF MY TREE. AND MY CHEEKS HAD STARTED TO hurt from all the fake smiling. They almost, but not quite, over shadowed the pain in the centre of my chest. I sucked in a deep breath to try to still the roll of my stomach at that thought and took a tiny sip of my cocktail drink. I was in no fit state of mind to get drunk. That could wait until I made it home, but in front of these people... Not a chance.

"How long have you been decorating?" the woman beside me asked. I think she'd been introduced as Mrs Clarkson, but I had never met her at any of my parents' charity events, and my mind was clearly not retaining superfluous information right now.

"I graduated from university eight years ago. I started my business not long after that." I attempted to put a little cheer in my voice, but I was unsure if she noticed.

"You've made a name for yourself in a short amount of time, dear. Well done!" The 'well done' was said in that oh-my-how-did-you-do-it condescending voice people use when they don't truly believe what they're saying.

"Yes, quite," I replied, swallowing the cringe at what my mother would say to that retort.

"Katie is the next best thing," Mrs Montgomery-Smith added, as she approached from the other side of the room.

The sitting room I had completed for the Montgomery-Smiths *was* extraordinary. The design could easily be called my pièce de résistance. The one project that would be at the front of every portfolio I put together from here on in. And the reason why all these stuffy people were here tonight clamouring for a slice of my attention.

I sucked in a shaky breath at how terribly ungrateful I was being. This was not me. Not the Katie Anscombe I normally strove to be. Jason had changed me in more ways than I cared to acknowledge right now. But I would not let his... heartless behaviour affect my future employment.

I pasted a smile back on my face and re-entered civilised conversation.

"It is such a thrill to be here, Mrs Montgomery-Smith," I said with enthusiasm. "I am so grateful for this evening and your continued support."

"Oh *pish*, Katie. You deserve it." And I think she actually meant it, too. My smile turned genuine. Look past the peacock that she is, and there was actually someone nice underneath. She may have driven me a little crazy during our professional entanglement, but her heart had always been in the right place.

And then she ruined my mental appraisal by say, "Oh, there's Henry and Alexandria! I must tell them all about the swimming pool we want to put in."

I started chuckling, realising I was thankfully alone again, as she trotted across the sitting room to greet two new arrivals to the event. I took a bigger sip of my drink and breathed freely for the first time that night. Apart from the newly arrived Henry and Alexandria, I had done the rounds, spoken to everyone present; wowed and schmoozed as expected. They had my contact details and had all been dazzled by my skills. All in all a successful, if not mind-numbingly boring, night.

I couldn't exactly leave yet, being as I was the quasi-guest du jour, but excluding Henry and Alexandria, I didn't have to impress anyone else. Maybe I could fade into the background and be lost in amongst the artwork until it was time to go home. I'm sure, despite them all being here to meet the designer who created this 'masterpiece', that no one would miss me.

I took a furtive look around, and then slipped out of the main part of the room and headed toward the darker, shadowy end. The Montgomery-Smith's sitting room was enormous, split up into three areas. The main event tonight was being hosted in what Mrs Montgomery-Smith called her parlour, or where she would entertain guests after dinner. At one end was a more informal sitting area, with a small selection of books and comfortable chairs. Towards the other end, where I was slinking away to now, were French doors that opened up on to the terrace, and several hand picked, well placed objets d'art. It was all for show, no seating to be had here. Simply an opportunity for the Montgomery-Smiths to show off their prized possessions.

And because of that, no one would be hiding here with me.

A cool breeze came in from the terrace. It wasn't exactly warm out, but even with my thin blouse on, I wouldn't freeze to death. I'd chosen to wear a slim line silk skirt that stopped just below my knees; a very professional and appropriate-for-this-evening looking outfit with a hint of bling, as the deep red silk in the skirt caught the lights and tended to shimmer in them. The top I had on was black, with intricate matching red silk flowers embroidered into it. It had long sleeves, the cuffs hanging over my wrists delicately, but even though the material would provide some warmth, it wasn't much. The sleeves were sheer, my pale skin visible through the loose weave. The blouse also had a lower than strictly acceptable neckline, but the length of the sleeves made up for the flash of décolletage. And anyway, let's not forget I am by no means busty.

I paused on the threshold of the terrace. I hadn't intended to go outside, but remain hidden amongst the art, in the shadows. But the stars were out and a full moon beckoned in the night sky, pulling me forward like an ocean wave. As soon as I stepped out onto the stone patio, I realised I was not the only one who was seeking a refuge tonight.

A spicy and strangely alluring smelling tobacco wafted on the air, but one quick glance around and I couldn't even see the smoke, let alone see the person who was wielding it. I stood frozen for a second trying to decide if I should go forward and be undoubtedly discovered, or head back inside, and probably be thought a fool. The smoker, whoever they were, may be hidden to my eyes right now, but I was haloed in a soft muted glow from the sitting room. I stood out like a sore thumb.

Shaking my head at myself, I prayed they would leave me alone, as I took the necessary steps to fully emerge under the moon. Surely they could see I was escaping.

I stopped beside a statue of Venus and stared unseeing up at the stars. I should have really been mingling. As Dom had said, it was an opportunity not to be missed. But I'd well and truly done my dash tonight. I was all faked out. This was the real me. Alone. Sad. A little bit teary eyed, truth be told.

I'd grown up in this environment, my parents on occasion having to attend events such as these and dragging their children along. But although my parents might have been part of this world, they were not entrenched in it. Thankfully. But several people here had mentioned my father in passing, or a charity event my mother had planned. I may not have known them, but they knew me - or at least my parents.

Jason wouldn't fit in this world. He'd look at these people and have less patience than me with their pomp and circumstance, their never ending need to be on top, to be seen. In some ways Jason and I were two completely different people. Even his sister was more able to slip into Dominic's life, than Jason would ever have been able to slip into mine.

Maybe he did me a favour. Maybe he knew this already and was saving us both further regret down the line.

I sighed. It was louder and longer than I had intended. Epiphanies can do that to you.

The smell of the tobacco grew stronger until it was obvious the smoker of the exotic smelling cigarette had approached. I turned my head slightly to see a tall man leaning against the stone railing several feet away. Watching me. He took a slow drag on his cigarette and blew the smoke out gradually, dark eyes on my face.

I blinked at him, unsure if I should greet the man or just ignore his presence altogether. He took another pull on the cigarette and waited for me to say something. I found his silence amusing for some reason. A small smile graced my lips. If he was part of this crowd he was blatantly disobeying the rules of etiquette. I turned back to look at the stars and he let a low chuckle out.

"You don't much care for this sort of thing, do you?" he asked, in a smooth voice like velvet.

"I'm not the only one escaping," I pointed out.

"Ah," he said in reply. I heard the click of a lighter and saw the flare of a flame out of the corner of my eye. He was lighting another cigarette. "Care to join me?" he asked, holding out a slim metal case that held more cigarettes inside.

"I don't smoke," I answered with a shake of my head. My body had turned slightly to look at him and I hadn't even realised.

"Neither do I, officially," he quipped, taking a purposeful drag on his cigarette. "And I'm not escaping, I've just arrived."

I stared at him for a second longer than I should have. He wasn't familiar to me, I think I would have remembered him if I had met him before. He was tall, but not as tall as Jason's six foot three. He was also much slimmer than Jason's soldier's physique. And at this point, I decided Jason Cain was not going to be the standard by which I compared all other men. I discarded all images of Jason from my mind and concentrated on the strange man beside me.

He had slightly wavy brown hair, combed back in a careless fashion. When he leant forward to flick ash off his cigarette, his hair flopped over his forehead, obscuring eyes, the colour of which

I couldn't decipher in the current lighting available. He was dressed in a fine suit, one I am sure would have cost a fortune and matched the extravagance of his highly polished Italian leather shoes. He had gold cuff links on his wrists, the glint of a large round faced watch flashed from beneath the edge of his shirt sleeve.

I felt a sudden disappointment settle in my stomach. Then frowned at my reaction. Had I wanted this man to be something other than those stiffs inside Mrs Montgomery-Smith's sitting room? How utterly ridiculous. I was in no place to entertain a distraction.

Or was I?

My eyes flicked back over to the tall man, who was still watching me keenly. I held his gaze, not wilting under his perusal.

"Why the need to escape?" he asked, softly.

"It's been a long night," I offered, looking back over the Montgomery-Smith's garden. Only dark shadows met my eyes.

He nodded in either understanding or agreement.

"I thought I'd drop in, see what all the fuss is about, and make a hasty retreat afterwards," he suddenly admitted. "Malcolm said I might like their new look." Malcolm being Mr Montgomery-Smith and their new look, I guess, being my design. The stranger didn't seem enthralled with Malcolm's assessment though.

"Are you in the market for an interior designer?" I asked, not really interested in the answer but still stuck in wine and dine mode, it seemed.

"A decorator," he corrected, but there was a teasing note in his voice. My eyes flicked over to his, he was no longer smoking. His hands were thrust deep in his trouser pockets, a boyish grin on his face. "That's what they really are, isn't it? Someone who decorates a room."

"Ah," I said, mimicking his earlier nonchalance. I turned back to the stars, effectively dismissing him. "And what is it you do exactly?" I asked the night sky.

His voice came from right beside me when he spoke, I managed not to jump. "I provide the *decorators* with fine art in order to dazzle their clients."

My face swung around to look at him again. If he was an art dealer of renown I would have met him already.

This close I could see his eyes were hazel, hints of green in amongst the brown. They were unremarkable, despite their tonal colours.

"Where is your store?" I asked, finally believing at least something good could come of this tedious night. A new art dealer on my books would be a coup. Especially if he was a recent addition to town. Being the first to support a fledgling business could establish strong ties. And give me the edge over opposition.

"Parnell. I plan on opening in ten days time, but I can't find a decorator who can work on such a short time-frame." He smiled. It was beguiling, I suppose, but my mind was elsewhere.

I didn't have any contracts lined up following Mr and Mrs Montgomery-Smith's. And although I'd received countless compliments this evening, no one had hinted at a desire to redecorate their homes. Oh, they had talked the talk, but none had actually come out and said they were in the market. They'd snaffled up my business cards with pristine white toothed smiles, but none had asked so much as for a quote.

"Interior designer," I corrected absent-mindedly.

"Interior designer," he murmured in reply. Then, "You wouldn't happen to know of one, would you?"

My gaze flicked back toward the French doors and the darkened end of the sitting room I had designed.

"Have you even looked at the Montgomery-Smith's new sitting room?" I asked.

"I don't need to," he replied. "I know exactly what I want already."

"Ah," I said with understanding. "Then in answer to your question, I am not aware of a *decorator* who would suit your needs." I turned away to look out over the black garden, people like this man were hard to work for; their minds already made up and incapable of direction from a designer. My skills would be wasted here.

"Ms Anscombe," the stranger said, with obvious amusement in his tone. "Do I look like the sort of man who wouldn't have done his homework?"

I bit back the sigh before it escaped. I wasn't sure if liked this man or found him infuriating. One minute he amused, the next he offended. And it was clear he'd had an ulterior motive all along. I was a little sick and tired of men disrupting my life. But then, Mrs Montgomery-Smith hadn't been a walk in the park either.

And Dominic was right. I couldn't pay the bills without signed contracts lined up. And I most definitely needed something right now to keep me busy, to keep my mind occupied.

Did it matter if this man was eccentric in his behaviour and interactions with those he employs? He was clearly well off, part of the social stratosphere that I was raised within, and that the Montgomery-Smiths revelled in. And it is there that the money is to be made.

"Are you trying to gain my services, Mr...?" I asked, leaving the question open for his name.

"Tremayne," he replied smoothly, offering me a hand to shake. "Richard Tremayne. And yes, Ms Anscombe, I want you designing my new store. But I want it completed by Monday week. Can you achieve that?"

Even though the question was direct, there was still a hint of levity in his tone. He'd intended for his words to be frank, but they'd fallen short of commanding. And I'd had a taste of commanding when done correctly, and as much as I didn't want to think of Jason again, it always led back to him in the end.

Everything led back to him.

But, I needed to focus. Richard Tremayne was wealthy, probably successful, and wanted to hire me, nothing more. I had to remember that and forget about strong minded men in my bed. This was work. I was in no position in my recovery of the Jason Debacle, to be thinking in any other terms except professionally.

I'd throw myself into my business, ignoring the ache that seemed to fill me up inside, and with time things would get better. Then, maybe, I could consider another man in my bed. Commanding or not.

"I would need to see your premises to determine what time-frame would be achievable," I said, turning fully to face him at last.

His smile was slow and languid in coming. He thought he had me already. Clearly he hadn't dealt with an Anscombe yet.

He reached into his jacket pocket and pulled out a business card, then handed it over between two long manicured fingers.

"Nine am tomorrow, Ms Anscombe. I'll bring the coffee."

I took his card and retrieved one of mine from my pocket in return.

"No need," he said, jovially. "I already have one. As well as your latest catalogue. Like I said," he took a step backward, intending to leave, I think, "I do my homework. You're exactly what I want."

He offered a nod of his head and then spun on his heels and walked down the steps into the night. I'm not sure if he'd even stepped foot inside the Montgomery-Smith's house, let alone greeted them. But within seconds he'd disappeared in amongst the dark shadows of their back yard.

What a strange man.

I glanced down at his business card, tilting it to get a better view in the dim light from the house. Gold embossed flowing print displayed his name and contact details, including a phone number, website, physical address and his business' title: *Tremayne Arts*.

I flicked it over in my hand, wondering if he would be as difficult to deal with as Mrs Montgomery-Smith. Then, dismissing that as irrelevant, slipped the card into my pocket.

It had been a very long day and night, but maybe, at least, I would have something to show for it. And a pressure filled job to occupy my mind.

At this point, it was the best I could hope for.

CHAPTER 14

IT'S A DATE

My bedside phone ringing woke me. I'd set my alarm for seven thirty, leaving me enough time to get up and face the day. A day that included a possible new client. I was still a little unsure about Richard Tremayne, but a job was a job. And I was not above admitting I needed all the financial assistance I could get. Let alone the distraction a contract would provide.

I picked the handset up and mumbled out, "Katie Anscombe," flicking a glance at the clock to see it was just after seven. Who phones at this hour?

"Katie," Gen's excited voice said over the line. "I spent all evening yesterday phoning everyone. So, you don't have to worry about a thing. I've sorted it. Can you bring a pasta salad?"

I blinked, rubbed a hand over my sleep encrusted eyes and tried to sit up.

"Darling, you're going to have to be more specific. What have you sorted?"

I fluffed a few pillows behind my back and settled in for a Genevieve Cain runaway mouth moment. If I had coffee, I'd be set.

"Well, you know, chickie. The barbecue."

"The barbecue? Genevieve, I told you I can't make it this weekend."

"No, you said you couldn't make it Sunday night. So, I changed it to tonight instead." *Oh.* "Dom and I really want you there with us. But you're going to have to act all surprised. No one would appreciate you knowing ahead of time. Gotta keep it fair, you know?"

No I didn't know, and I really didn't want to face this. Damn. She'd changed the barbecue to this evening, because I couldn't make tomorrow's date. I felt tears prickling behind my eyes, I blinked my lids rapidly, trying to still their onslaught. I'd done enough crying, thank you very much. But this, *this*, was too much. Lovely, sweet Genevieve going to all that trouble to fit in with me.

Sure, she wanted *everyone* there for her and Dom's big moment, but it still filled my bitter heart with warmth. And then the thought of having to face Jason again froze it solid.

"Oh, Genevieve," I said on a breath of air. Then corrected myself. "That's sounds brilliant." I forced a little joy into my words.

"Everyone thought I was being crazy, changing the date by one day," Gen was saying, but I found myself slinking further and further beneath the covers, gripping the handset in a white knuckled clasp, and blanking out slightly on her actual words. "But I think they've got used to my uniqueness by now. I didn't tell them it was because you couldn't make it, just in case they were pee'd off or something. But I made them all promise to be here by six. I've started getting a bit tired in the evenings, so it's a little earlier than usual. Hope you don't mind. Kelly just said she'd hit the town afterwards, if Dom and I kicked everyone out for an early night in bed. I laughed at that, couldn't exactly tell her I'd be asleep by nine, no hanky panky for me."

There was a grumble in the background, which had to have come from Dom. Either bemused at Gen's forthrightness, or contradicting her about the whole no hanky panky thing.

"I know, honey," Gen said, voice slightly muffled as she held the phone away, "but it's Katie, I can't say that. You flipped when she saw your naked butt, how the hell do you think she'd respond to you suggesting I just lie back and think of Britain and you'd do all the..."

The phone was abruptly pulled from Gen's hand, by the sound of the scrabbling in the background. There was a grunt, followed by a giggle and then Dominic's voice down the line.

"Six o'clock tonight, Katie. Bring a pasta salad. And no excuses. You will be there."

"Dom," I attempted.

"No excuses. We need to see you. OK?" The last was said more softly. He was worried.

"OK," I replied, meekly.

There was a pause, then a sigh his end.

"Good. See you tonight, sis." The line went dead.

I returned the handset to its cradle and curled up under the covers again. I spent the next few minutes refusing to cry, then mercifully, my alarm went off and the day of distraction could finally begin.

Tremayne Arts was on The Strand, just below Parnell Rise. It had a pleasant façade and maybe half a dozen parking spaces out front. A boon for this part of Auckland City. As the business wasn't yet open to the public, there were plenty of spots available for me to park in. I pulled up next to a shiny Lexus, which I was guessing belonged to Tremayne.

Picking up my satchel, which included all the necessary equipment I'd need if I chose to take this contract on, I slipped out of my car and after locking it, headed over to the front doors. I didn't need to knock, Tremayne opened it when I was still a few feet away. He'd been watching for me. I felt a little jolt of surprise shoot through me at that thought. I wasn't late, so he shouldn't have been pacing at the doors for my arrival, but an almost creepy feeling slithered down my spine.

Nick, in all his brotherly over protectiveness, had instilled in me a wary observant quality. It wasn't something I found at all natural, but over the course of the past few years his constant reminders of trusting your first impressions and never ignoring that initial reaction to a situation, has made me more circumspect. I don't think I would have even considered Tremayne's behaviour unusual in the past, but Nicky had a way of getting through my resistance. Making Tremayne's intense demeanour and obvious heightened anticipation of my arrival cause me to startle slightly.

I forced myself to calm and not show the small amount of alarm I had felt. Smiling at Tremayne, I offered a greeting.

"Good morning, Mr Tremayne."

"Please, call me Richard. And may I call you Catherine?" he asked, holding the door open for me to walk through, but not stepping back enough for me to slip past without brushing his sleeve.

"Of course," I murmured, ducking my head as I stepped into a large open planned space.

The natural lighting streaming through the large exposed windows along the front of the building made long shadows appear in haphazard stripes across bare concrete floors. It was a complete blank canvas. No flooring or lighting in place. No wall breaks or designated areas existing. Just a huge square room, with offices and amenities along the back wall. Nothing else.

For the first time since arriving I felt a much more welcomed feeling settle inside my stomach. Excitement. The exuberant thrill of creating something out of almost nothing. *What I could do to this space.*

"Ten days, you said?" I asked distractedly, scanning the height of the walls, taking further steps inside to look at everything from different angles. I had a dozen different ideas streaming through my mind already. Some of them running away and becoming behemoths in seconds. All of which I needed to rein in as the man had said he already new what he wanted. No doubt anything I suggested would be dismissed. He may not have been a dominant person, but he knew how to get what he wanted, I was sure.

"Yes," he murmured, making me flick a glance over in his direction. He was leaning against a wall, legs crossed casually at the ankles, watching me keenly. "I'm on a tight schedule."

I returned my attention to the room itself. Something about his continued appraisal of me left me unnerved. I wasn't sure if it was entirely bad, this sensation of unease. Which sounds paradoxical. But sometimes that jittery feeling you get when something disturbs you can be because of something good. At this point, I couldn't tell if I liked his obviously male regard, or not.

"You said you already know what you want. I gather that means you have a theme or design in mind already?" I asked, still scanning the space, estimating distances and the potential that existed. Already choosing the central piece of furniture that would make this showroom shine; an almost completely circular shaped settee I'd spotted in one of my furniture supplier's storerooms last month. It would be perfect as a focus point, not to mention a suitable spot to sit back and relax, while you gazed at artwork around the space.

"Not at all," he replied, surprising me enough to stop what I was doing and devote my attention to him. "What I meant to say is, I know *who* I want. To create the design, of course."

"Oh." It slipped out. I couldn't deny I felt flattered. In a professional manner, of course.

"I've seen much of your work, Catherine. I like it. I especially like the modernity and unexpectedness of Malcolm's sitting room." So, he had been inside the Montgomery Smith's room. Just not last night. "I could imagine something along those lines here. Can't you?"

I returned my gaze to the blank room before me and forced myself to overlay an image of the Montgomery-Smith's design in this space. My heart fell. Because he was right. This could be a grand room, it could really make a statement. And as much as I didn't want to revisit a design that had been created at such a pivotal part of my life, at a moment in time I cared to forget, I knew I might have to.

But, most art showrooms tend to be bland, to allow the art to speak for itself. If you detracted from the pieces for sale, then you sold your product short. If I created anything here, it would have to be a version of the Montgomery-Smith's to produce ambience and awe, toned down to a degree where necessary, to complement the art.

"What type of artwork do you sell, Mr Tremayne?" I asked, my mind moving a mile a minute now.

"Richard, Catherine," he reminded me. "Please call me Richard. I have every intention of us becoming fast friends throughout this process. And friends call each other by their given names. Am I correct?"

My friends called me Katie, not Catherine. Even my parents called me Katie. Jason, of course, called me Kate. For some reason, neither of those nicknames felt suitable for this man. I was nowhere near ready to hear him call me anything other than Catherine. Catherine was almost someone else in my mind.

I just offered a nod in agreement, not wanting to get too bogged down by semantics.

"As for the artwork, everything you saw at Malcolm's house, I sourced for him."

Ah, and there went that idea that it couldn't coexist with the Montgomery-Smith's design. I had worked the final look around their artwork. It was made to measure.

Which meant, this job could go an awful lot easier than I had first thought.

I walked over to the far wall and looked inside the offices. They were finished to a professional standard, so was the kitchen and bathroom area.

"I gather you're satisfied with these," I said, nodding my head toward each room.

"Yes, they'll do."

"So, that leaves this wonderful space." I'd opened my arms up and waved to indicate the vast empty room we were in. Richard's smile at my choice of words and action was genuine. He was pleased I could see the potential.

"Yes," he murmured. "What's the verdict? Can you make something of it?"

I peeled my eyes off the room and turned my gaze to him. He'd stepped away from the wall and now stood, hands in trouser pockets making him seem approachable, even handsome.

"Yes, I could make something of this." I'd kept my voice level, professional. But inside I was eager to get started. I'd already fallen for the project, there was no way I'd turn down this job now. "Do you have any specific requirements? Areas set aside for different artwork? A piece that requires special treatment and placing?"

"I can give you a catalogue with all the pieces I currently have and we can work through what should have priority and not. I know what sells, but I'd like your interpretation of what should go where. It will be your design. Fully. I'll just provide the pieces as your muse."

I sucked in a small breath at his words. The design I'd create would be based on the Montgomery-Smith's, and we all know how I managed to come up with that. In that instant, I had a sudden urge to flee. But I scolded my ridiculous lovelorn heart and told myself this was business. A job. A contract that would pay the bills.

"All right," I said with a nod of my head; more for me, than him. "I can't provide a quote until I've seen the pieces and we're agreed on a display plan. Once I have those items locked down, the design can be created in forty-eight to seventy-two hours."

The fact that I would be mimicking a completed design and already had focal furniture picked out in my mind, knowing they were available at my suppliers and easily covered to suit the finished look, made the time-frame required to complete the project a fraction of what I would normally require.

"I'd need at least ten days to achieve the finished product," I added, "so it would be advisable if I could see the catalogue of your stock today and we arrange a time to discuss your needs as soon as possible." I was ready to get this started. To throw myself into something that would take utter focus and block out everything else.

"I can give you a catalogue to take away this morning, and as for arranging a time to discuss my... needs, may I suggest dinner tonight."

He must have seen the wariness and reluctance on my face, because he quickly added, "A business dinner, if you will."

I hesitated, trying to think of a way out. Then the obvious flashed through my mind. The barbecue. I already had plans that I couldn't possibly put off. I mean, Genevieve had changed the date to fit in with me. I couldn't, in all good conscience, deny her wishes now. Even if every fabric of my being wanted to avoid her and Dom's house, in the hopes of not having to see Jason.

The bottom line was: Hurt Genevieve to save face or have dinner with this strange man? I couldn't wound Genevieve, even to avoid pain myself. I'm not that kind of person. So, the decision was easy in the end, despite the angst it brought with it.

"I'm so sorry," I said, trying to convey honesty in my words. "But I have plans tonight I can't get out of. Perhaps we can meet tomorrow?"

Richard held my gaze for quite some time, his face blank, but there was depth behind his eyes. Shadows of something I couldn't decipher. Was he determining what argument to give? Deciding whether to push me or not? I couldn't tell, and then the mystery of his profound gaze passed. I felt like I'd witnessed something intriguing. Something that gave me hope that there was more to Richard Tremayne than I had thought. But with his eyes returning to a more lazy look, the intense feeling I had been seeking, vanished.

I wasn't sure what to make of my reaction to a simple look in someone's eyes. It was as though I was searching for something, something vitally important, but had found only a hint, a possibility, and no more. The disappointment in not finding what I wanted was more prevalent than I expected. Just what had I hoped he would do?

"That's unfortunate," Richard said, with a small smile. "I'm out of the city tomorrow on business. It will have to wait until Monday."

I frowned, realising the time-line for this project had just become more urgent. The sooner we had his pieces locked-down in the overall plan, the sooner I could design the final look. Without knowing that pre-requisite I could only do so much tomorrow. It would probably take at least until Thursday or Friday now, to finalise a design. I couldn't even offer a sufficiently accurate quote until I had some idea of his requirements. Without pinning down his signature pieces of art, the ten day time-frame would be impossible to achieve.

Richard didn't wait for my reply, just wandered off to the office at the back of the room and returned moments later with his catalogue.

"You can, at least, start with this today, I presume?" he asked in an arched tone that made me believe he was disappointed in my refusal to attend dinner this evening and therefore the consequent delay it caused.

I didn't particularly like letting people down, but Genevieve was family. I was committed to the barbecue, but that didn't mean I couldn't work around it. Gen had said she tired easily, perhaps I could get away from their house early enough for a late meeting.

"My appointment this evening is quite early," I began, taking the catalogue from Richard's hand. He stilled all motion, holding on to his side of the booklet, while I clasped mine. His eyes lifted hopefully to mine. He seemed genuinely interested in getting this project started. It made me feel more inclined to make this suggestion. "Perhaps we could meet for a drink afterwards?"

His mouth spread into that lazy smile and he released the catalogue at last.

"I think that would be a splendid idea, Catherine. What time?"

Ah, and now to guess how long Gen would want festivities to continue. Does getting tired mean bed by eight, nine or ten?

Perhaps the truth would be best. Richard's reaction to my suggestion seemed genuinely happy. For the first time I felt relaxed in his company.

"I have this family thing I have to attend," I admitted. "It starts at six, but I'm unsure how long it will go for. Can I phone you when it's over and we'll arrange to meet then?"

"How about I come with you, then we can skip out as soon as your obligations are met?"

His proposal was given in such an offhand way I was momentarily stunned into thinking it was appropriate. Then reality returned and I formed the words in my mind to deny him such a liberty. Family gatherings were no place for a business acquaintance to attend. How would Genevieve feel announcing her news with a stranger in the room?

He must have seen my reticence, because he took a step closer, dipped his face to peer into my eyes and said, voice low, "I was hoping we could be more than just colleagues, Catherine. I know we'll be discussing the design this evening, but I had intended to get to know you a little better as well. And for you to get to know me better, too. I would like to accompany you as your date."

Silence met his announcement. Date? I couldn't do a date. No way could I date. And him? I just met him. Even if I was in the market to date, I'm not sure he'd be who I'd pick. The whole time I'd been in his presence I'd been searching for something. Something powerful, something that I craved. And I hadn't found it. Not yet.

My eyes flicked over his face. Strong lines met my gaze, a soft smattering of stubble, that roughened up his look a little, graced his cheeks. The shadow adding character and depth I hadn't noticed before. And his eyes were a lovely colour. Browns and greens, a hint of autumnal golds.

"What are you afraid of?" he whispered, his voice sounding intimate despite the size and emptiness of the room we stood in. "Would your family be surprised if you turn up with a date?"

Yes. But that wasn't the real reason why I baulked at this idea. Apart from being unsure how I felt about this man, Jason would be there. I couldn't turn up at Dominic's and Genevieve's with another man. Not yet. It wouldn't be right.

But then, no one else knew what Jason and I had experienced together. Jason was acting as if I didn't exist, let alone as if we'd shared something so very special, so very personal, together. And let's face it, Gen was sure he'd be bringing one of his blonde busty bimbos to the event.

Oh, dear Lord. I couldn't face that and hold my head up high. I couldn't swallow the humiliation.

Then, did I have to be the jilted lover?

My gaze swept over Richard again. He was still close, but not overstepping the mark. In fact he hadn't overstepped the mark once since I'd met him. Sure he was a little eccentric. But he was also often amusing, handsome and part of my world. My reluctance to accept any advances he'd made had all been because of Jason.

Damn! I would not let Jason Cain make a fool of me.

"I'm sure my family would be delighted if I brought a date," I said, a little breathlessly. Not because I was excited, but because I was a little scared.

I'd said the words, now I just had to live with them.

"Brilliant. Shall I pick you up at five-thirty?"

"It's a date."

CHAPTER 15

AND THE BROTHERS GRIM AND GRIMMER?

JASON

GENNY WAS ACTING EVEN MORE BLONDE THAN USUAL. FORGETTING *where she put things, smiling to herself at strange moments, singing fucking stupid shit songs all the fucking time. If I didn't know any better I'd say she was in love.*

Oh, wait. That crazy train had already pulled into the Genevieve Cain station.

And there was the prick now who had tamed my sister. Talking to the Olds as though he didn't have anything better to do than make happy with the in-laws.

Prick.

Ah, fuck it! I knew this was going to be a mistake. Coming here, tonight. Being around those two love-birds. Avoiding the stink-eye from Nick.

And... seeing Kate again. Let's be honest, that's the real reason why I was angrier than a drill sergeant during peace time on a sunny day.

Kate, Kate, Kate.

I sucked in a much needed gulp of air in the hopes it would blast the fuck out of the hole in my chest. If I wasn't careful, I'd turn into a pansy.

"What's your problem, Cain?" Nick, the second prick, asked, as he snatched a beer off the table at my side.

That was going to be my beer. I was guarding them for later. I gave him a glower as he twisted the cap off and chucked it in the bin. The beautiful hiss and aroma of barley and hops filled the space between us; the only thing that stopped me from growling out loud.

Nothing beats the calming influence of beer.

"Not got a problem," I replied, taking a sip from my own near-empty bottle.

"Then why the sour puss face?" he demanded, leaning against the bar as though he was settling in for a convo.

I so did not need another conversation with this dude. One heart to heart was enough, thanks. I think I'd pass on any more 'friendly' advice he might have to give.

"Bored," I offered as answer, then finished off my drink.

I had another bottle open and to my lips before he had a comeback. Maybe I'd just get pissed tonight, that way I could avoid everyone.

"Fuck, Cain," Nick exclaimed, loud enough for Genny to notice. I gave him a purposeful scowl. He flicked his gaze over to where my sister stood talking to Kels, and offered a smile and nod to let her know all's well. Even Nick didn't want to piss her off today.

Nick turned his attention back to me and leaned in, lowering his voice so we couldn't be overheard.

"You've been a bear with a sore head for weeks now. What's crawled up your arse?"

"Is it affecting my performance?" I asked, bristling.

Nick was a fair boss, but he ran a tight ship. I was used to falling into line where my job was concerned. It rankled with me that I may have let my personal... issues, roll over into my professional world.

"Not yet," Nick said ominously. "But since the lock-down you've been closed off. I keep expecting you to turn up in camouflage with a bag full of M4 Carbines and knock us all off."

My eyebrows rose on that delightfully whacked image.

"Fuck, I'm not unstable, Nick. Just..."

"Just what?"

"Maybe I just need to get laid," I said, the first thing that came to mind in order to distract him.

"So, where is your bimbo tonight? You going solo for a reason? Hoping to see some action here?" The last was said with a decided edge to his tone. A don't-fuck-with-me-fucktard edge.

And we were back at the heart to heart part of the night I would have liked to have avoided.

I held his frosty gaze, hoping mine was equally as chilling. Hell, I was going for freeze his fucking balls off with the glare I had going on. He didn't back down. That was why I respected the prick. But, shit, if he brought Kate up now, I would so fucking lose it.

"I did what you asked. I won't go back on my word."

"You better fucking not," he ground out, then abruptly did a one eighty and smiled all charming-like as Eva approached, a smirk gracing her lips.

"Hey, cowboy. Whacha doin' hiding over here?" She offered a pleasant enough smile to me, but turned a come-here-big-boy grin on Nick. He was so fucking lost. Pussy.

"Getting you a beer, angel. Got side tracked by Jase." He pulled a beer out of my stash and twisted the cap off for her. She took a sip with her hand wrapped around his on the bottle.

I almost gagged.

"Don't mind me," I grumbled, as they goo-goo eyed each other. Just fucking shoot me now.

"We won't," Nick replied, not taking his eyes off his woman.

"Good to see ya, Jason," Eva said, pulling Nick away to do God-I-don't-want-to-imagine-what.

I ran a hand over my face and sucked back another mouthful of beer. This was going to be a very long night.

"Hey, big bro," Gen's sweet voice broke the silence that had enveloped me in my little shitty hole. "Guarding the beer stash, I see." She knew me well.

"Best seat in the house, sis."

"You OK?" Oh fuck, not her too.

"Never better."

"You don't look OK."

I gave her a pointed look. "I'm hungry. When's the barbie being lit?"

She flicked a glance around the room, taking in all the happy-happy-fucking-joy-joy people milling about.

"Just waiting on Katie, then we can get started."

"Why not heat it up now? I'll man it if you want." Any reason not to be sitting in the room when Kate arrived, I'd grab.

Fucking chicken-shit.

"Are you sure you're OK?" What? "You look kinda pained. It can't all be about your stomach."

"Genny, I'm fine. Fucking leave it, all right." And that was a bad move, because Dominic was within ear shot.

"Ease off, arsehole." Yeah. Bad move. "You treat Genevieve with some respect."

"Jesus, Dom. She's my fucking sister. We've talked like this since we could form words."

"I don't particularly give a shit. She's my wife now." Well almost, but I didn't care to correct him, he was in lawyer mode. "I'll not have you upsetting her with your anger management issues."

Anger management. Well, fuck. I guess he had a point.

Another hand rubbed over my face.

"Sorry, Gen," I managed. Dom grunted, about as much approval as I'd get. Gen just bit her bottom lip, looking unconvinced. "Not sleeping well," I offered, in way of explanation. Just because it was the God's honest truth didn't hurt either.

"Oh, Jase," she said, reaching out to place a delicate hand on my shoulder. "Is there something I can do?"

Talk Nick 'round. Tell him I'm not a bad influence on his sister. Convince him I am worthy of her time. That she needs me as much as I need her. That I won't drag her down with me and ruin her life, that I'll treasure her above all else. Worship her.

Fuck.

"Oh, Jase," Gen repeated on a whisper.

And just when I thought it couldn't get any worse, what with fucking blurry vision making me look like a pansy, she arrived.

Her lilting voice echoed out of the hallway like a fresh breeze blowing away days of stifling grit and dust. My chest constricted painfully and I tried uselessly to suck in a breath. Fuck, that shit hurt.

"Hello, darling!" she was saying, and a small smile curved my lips at her familiar greeting. "What a beautiful evening for a barbecue."

It was now.

I heard Dominic grumble a few words out and then my world collapsed. Well, it was fucking teetering on a precipice for the past fortnight, all it would have taken was a stiff breeze to push me over. Or a fresh one.

"This is my friend Richard. I hope you don't mind me bringing him along, we're having drinks later."

Oh, fuck no. No, no, no, fucking no.

I stood up, making the beer bottles rattle in the ice bucket from the speed with which I bounded out of my seat. Gen had to take an alarmed step back. I automatically reached out and wrapped a hand around her upper arm to stop her tipping over sideways. But I wasn't concentrating on anything other than what Kate had just said. Those fucking awful God-dammed words.

My friend. What friend? I'd never heard her mention a guy by the name of Richard before.

Fuck, you douche, you spend one fucking weekend with her and you think you know the woman? Grow some fucking brain cells.

"Ow!" Genny cried, trying to pry her arm from my claw-like grip.

I glanced down at the bruise starting to form around my fingertips, and made an awkward yelping sound, flinging her arm away as though it burned.

"Jason!" she exclaimed. But didn't stop there. No, this was my sister, it would be too much to expect her to curb her tongue. "What the fuck's got into you? Have you lost your mind?" Yes, quite possibly.

"That friggin' hurt, you moron! I'm going to have a bruise now. Won't be able to wear tank tops for a while. And I just bought a really cute one."

"What is going to bruise?" Dominic, entering my nightmare.

"Jason just squeezed my arm like he was having an epileptic fit, or something. What do they call it, petite mal? You know, when the patient locks up but doesn't shake all over."

"Let me see," he murmured, giving me a fuck-you glare while he stepped up to check on Gen's rapidly bluing upper arm. Ah, fuck.

My hand rubbed over my face and when I lowered it she was there. In the room, watching the entire scene play out, spotlit by the lack of conversation in the house right then. I couldn't look away. It was like I was being sucked into a vortex. A pulling, drawing sensation that I had no hope of fighting, no desire to avoid. I wanted to sink deep down into those beautiful pools of blue. I wanted to die there, if I could.

And oh God, she was gorgeous. Even more so than I remembered. Absolutely fucking spectacular.

But then Nick stepped between my view of heaven and me. Another fuck-you glare from an Anscombe brother and then he turned his attention to Kate. And the dickhead with her.

Who the fuck are you?

"Hey, sis. Who's this?" Nick asked.

Kate gasped at her brother's question. Or maybe at being interrupted mid shock and awe staring match with me. I don't know. But it was pained, in a way that sliced through my heart and fucking tore the shit out of it.

"This," she cleared her throat, then tried again. I wanted to reach for her. Soothe her. Let her know everything was all right. But it wasn't, was it? Nick had seen to that. "This is Richard Tremayne. I'm designing his art studio for him."

One look at the wanker beside her and I could tell he didn't want to be considered just a business acquaintance. A grin spread my lips, it was definitely on the evil side of the divide.

He thrust his hand forward for Nick to shake and said, voice a little louder than necessary, "We've just started seeing each other. Tonight's our first date, in fact."

I'm not sure how I got there, I don't remember taking the necessary steps. But the look of mortification on Kate's face at this twat's announcement made the distance covered to reach their side non-existent. I slipped my fisted hands into my jeans pockets and stared the motherfucker down.

"Gonna introduce us, Kate?" I asked in my most insincere voice. I couldn't give a fuck who he was. I wanted nothing more than to clock this intruder and carry Kate off like a fucking caveman after the event. I could even picture it. Every single glorious detail. It involved lots of blood, his blood. And Kate gripping my arse as she hung upside down over my shoulder.

"Jason Cain," Kate said, voice only slightly shaking, "this is Richard Tremayne."

Ah, but my Kate did what I asked without question, didn't she? Was it wrong of me to feel the tightening of my balls at that?

"Pleased to meet you," the fuck-knuckle said, holding his hand out for me to shake. I stared at it, not removing my clenched fists from my pockets. If I removed them, there would be blood.

His hand slowly lowered and a look of unease crossed his face. That's right. I'm the one you should fear, arsehole.

"Ah, well," Nick was saying, sending me what-the-fuck looks in between each word. "This is Dom and Gen's house, but.." he looked around and noticed that the hosts had disappeared. I tried not to feel bad about that, it was probably because I'd upset Gen. "They seem to have vanished. So grab a beer and welcome to the madness." A definite glare directed at me on those last words.

"Great," Tremayne said through gritted teeth, eyes on the threat, not even glancing at Nick. Heh. "Would you like a beer, Catherine?"

My eyebrows rose on that. Who the fuck calls Kate, Catherine. I snorted. I didn't mean to, but come on! The fucktard was definitely not on the in. A smile spread across my lips. Kate rolled her eyes.

And just like that, I was lost. I have no idea what the imposter was *doing. Hopefully grabbing a beer. He could have my last post. Good luck with that, beer guard was not as easy as it sounds.*

"Can I have a word with you, Kate?" *I emphasised her name. Her correct name.*

"I..." *she started.*

"In the kitchen," *I added, expecting nothing less than absolute obedience. She lifted her chin. Feisty. My cock swelled. Then, thank you God for all that is good in this world, nodded her head in agreement.*

Oh fuck, what I could show this woman.

"OK," *she said, flicking her gaze over my shoulder.* "We'll just be a minute."

"Is everything all right?" *Imposter, imposing again.*

"It will be," *I threw over my shoulder, then forced myself not to reach for Kate's hand, just stormed from the room.*

She'd follow.

Fuck, I hoped she'd follow.

My path was blocked by Nick out in the hall.

"What the fuck are you playing at, Cain?"

"Just gonna talk, Anscombe," *I ground out, arms ready at my sides.* "Nothing in your directive about not talking to her."

Nick's eyes darted over my shoulder, but I didn't need the movement to know Kate was there. I could feel her. Like sunshine on my back. Like the warmth of a fire after a cold and wet day.

"Nick?" *she asked, tentatively.* "What's the matter?"

Nick gave me one last murderous glare and then smiled at Kate.

"I don't think you should abandon your date, Katie. You can catch up with Jason at another time." *His eyes hardened when they returned to me.* "And you! You and I have an agreement. Don't fuck it up."

We did have an agreement. I said I'd stay away from her. I fucking cracked like a rookie soldier caught across the enemy line. I'd walked away from her on cloud nine, fucking humming a fucking tune, and by the time I'd made it to ASI I'd started to doubt. Me. Kate. My need for control. I mean, fuck! I'd been fighting the attraction for months, one weekend with her in my arms was not going to put an end to the doubts, was it?

And Nick, the prick, saw through me as soon as I walked in the office. Even before the debrief, he pulled me aside and screwed with my head. Not that he wasn't pointing out exactly all the fucked up shit that goes through my mind on a daily basis. Not that he didn't see right through the façade and recognise a man on the very edge.

But I allowed my fear that Kate wasn't the sort of woman who could handle my demands to rule my decision. I let Nick feed that fear until I was so unsure, but so desperate to not harm her further, that I agreed.

I was fucking mental. But not anymore. I saw the way she looked at me when she walked in that room. I saw the way she couldn't pull her gaze away; like me, stuck still by an invisible magnetic force. And I saw the way she tried to soften the blow when the fuck-wank imposter implied they were dating. She did that for me.

It was one thing for Nick to pull the brother card, to push my fucked up buttons and tell me I was a time bomb waiting to go off. Without Kate before me, I could see things his way.

With Kate here, nothing else fucking mattered anymore.

"I lied," I finally growled, almost spitting the words in Nick's face.

In the next second Nick had his fist around my t-shirt and my back against the wall.

"Hey, boss, take it easy," Eric piped up, appearing from fucking nowhere. "It's a barbecue. Let's all chill."

Not gonna happen.

I pushed back and slammed Nick into the wall on the other side. A picture in a fancy arse frame fell to the floor and the glass cracked.

"Whoa there, e hoa. Calm down. This is Dom's house and he ain't gonna like you trashin' it." And now the big Māori was charging into the fray.

Eric wrapped an arm around Nick, who was trying to swing a fist at my face, while Ben hauled my arse backwards, as though I didn't weigh over a hundred and twenty kilos. And then Koki and Adam *arrived, helping Kate take a step out of the blast range. And the cherry on top? Dominic storming down the hallway, fire in his eyes and a whole lot of hurt promised in his clenched fists.*

He was so going to back Nick, no doubt about it. My time was running out. I'd be turfed out on the street in a minute. Way to fuck up Gen's big event. Because, sure as shit, it was meant to be something special and her fucked in the head PTSD soldier brother couldn't even behave in a civilised fashion.

Well, if the shoe fits.

"This is only the beginning, Kate," I said, directing the words to her and no one else.

"I think this is the end for you tonight," Dom shot back, indicating the door with a nod of his head.

I held Kate's gaze. She looked shocked. Surprised as all hell. Speechless.

But then she said, voice firm and unwavering, "Just go, Jason. Before you make even more of a mess of things."

Ouch. I deserved that.

But OK, I like a challenge when I'm given one. This was, by no means, over.

Kate was going to be mine. She just needed a little convincing.

And the brothers grim and grimmer?

Yeah, they could just go fuck themselves.

With a purposeful look at Nick, as I wrenched my arms free of my supposed captors and took a step towards the front door, I said with as much force as I could muster...

"I fucking quit!"

See how that affects our agreement.

CHAPTER 16

COULD THIS DAY GET ANY WORSE?

KATIE

WHAT JUST HAPPENED?

Jason stormed off down the hallway and banged through the now opened door.

Gone.

My head was shaking back and forth, I think my body was trembling as well. I felt a little light headed actually. As though all blood had left my face.

"Katie, are you all right?" Dom asked. He probably shouldn't have, because it drew my attention to him first. So he was the one to receive my anger.

"Did you just throw Jason out?" Never mind that I assisted. I had no choice, Dom and Nick had seen to that.

"Yes," he replied, without apology.

"What?" Genevieve shrieked from the other end of the hall. None of us had seen her arrive. "Where's my brother gone?"

Oh boy.

"Sweetheart," Dominic said, a *whole* lot of apology in that word. "It was for the best."

Gen stared at him, mortified, for several long seconds. We all waited. I think everyone knew what was going to happen, but with Gen there's just no preventing it. It's a knee jerk reaction and now she's pregnant, I can imagine it'll get a lot worse.

"Dom," she cried in a pitifully small voice, and then the tears started falling. My heart ached for her, she'd worked so hard to plan this evening and it had all gone to hell.

Dominic was beside her in a second, so keen to reach her before she crumbled that he pushed Eric out of the way roughly, making him fall into the wall and another photo frame to tumble. Ben made an angry sound at the damage, Dom muttered some sort of excuses, pulling Genevieve away to have more privacy and then, for some reason, all eyes turned to me.

Nick was the one who spoke.

"Do you have something to tell me, Katie?"

"What do you mean?" I shot back, sounding completely guilty.

"Is there something going on between you and Jason Cain?"

"That's none of your business," I replied, eyeing Eric, Koki, Adam and Ben. There were a lot of unnecessary people in on this conversation.

Nick didn't seem to care about that right now. He was fuming. I couldn't tell if he was angry at me or Jason, though.

"He's the wrong man for you," Nick said, and from his tone he meant every single word.

My mouth fell open in shock. I could *not* believe my imbecile brother would say that. What on earth made him think it had anything to do with him, or that I would listen to his ridiculous over-protective ideas about who I should and shouldn't date. Of course, Jason and I weren't dating. I had no idea what we were doing, but he had said this was only the beginning.

Like he had at my house. Which made me feel all sorts of warm and wonderful when I shouldn't have been feeling anything but anger, facing off against my brother and his posse of men.

I lifted my chin defiantly.

"You don't know what you're talking about, Nick."

He sighed. "Katie, I know more than you do. You're just going to have to trust me. Stay away from him. OK?" No, it was not OK. "Anyway, you've got a date tonight, what the fuck are you doing entertaining Cain?"

"It's not how it seems," I defended Richard's presence, and by extension the way it made me look like a hussy.

"How about you concentrate on the man in there," Nick said pointing purposefully back at the lounge where Richard had been left, "and forget all about Jason. He's wrong for you, Katie," he semi repeated.

"Nick," I started, really getting annoyed now, but then surprisingly Eric, of all people, butted in.

"Sweetheart, Nick's got this right."

"Yeah," Ben added, on a sigh. "He has, Kat."

"And the rest of you?" I demanded, arms crossed over my chest, eyebrows arched.

Various nods of agreement from Koki and Adam. An awkward silence followed. It lasted a very long time, because, for the life of me, I just didn't know what to say. How to defend Jason against something I wasn't even privy to. I could ask, what exactly made Nick think this, and I wanted to. I even opened my mouth to say the words, but Nick just raised his hand to stall me.

"You just have to trust me, Katie. When have I ever put you wrong?"

I blinked at him, wanting to argue the point, but there didn't seem to be much chance of winning that right now. Nick was determined, he'd said his piece, he meant every word. I'd have to get him on his own and pick away at his resolve in order to get any answers now. He was too strong willed to break his silence in front of his men.

"I don't think I can be around any of you right now," I said. The truth. And it seemed to be a slap in the face, each one of them grimacing at my words and tone. "Please give my apologies to Genevieve and Dominic."

"Katie!" Nick attempted to stop me mid spin away. I ignored him and walked stiffly back into the lounge.

Richard was in conversation with Brook, one of Nick's men, and my parents. Making an impression, if the smiles and avid conversation was anything to go by. I'd hoped he'd been cornered by one of the Sweet Seduction gang, then escape would be easier. But getting my parents to understand our early departure was going to take some doing.

I sucked in a deep breath, tried to still my anger-filled rapid heartbeat, and crossed the space to stand beside him. His smile down at me was genuine. It did absolutely nothing to my heart rate. Didn't speed it up. Didn't make it trip. Nothing.

I offered a wan smile in return and his lips dipped slightly, a frown attempting to come out.

Well, no time like the present to announce our imminent departure.

"I'm afraid we have another appointment," I said, aiming my words at my parents, but avoiding eye contact with my father. Guilt was gnawing at my conscience already. "We have to leave, unfortunately. Genevieve and Dominic are aware." A slight exaggeration of the truth, but Dom would figure it out soon enough.

I could feel Richard tense beside me, now alerted to the fact that something drastic had happened while I was out of the room. I hated dragging him into this, but my ticket out of here was him. I'd make my apologies once we were well away.

Of course getting well away was never going to be easy.

"Katie, don't you think you should have some dinner before you go?" Mama suggested softly.

I checked my watch to make my point. "I'm sorry, but we have to leave." My eyes flicked to Richard's, pleading for him to back me up.

"Yes," he said, jumping in to save me with smooth grace. "My fault, actually. I made our reservations earlier than Catherine had planned, and we can't change them now or we'd lose our table."

"Where are you dining?" Papa asked, voice steady, but I could tell he saw through the ruse. I'd heard that tone many times before, but usually when he confronted one of my brothers, not me.

"Kermedec's," Richard replied without hesitation, naming one of the top restaurants on Viaduct Quay.

"Oh, how nice," my mother voiced. "I guess you can't stay then."

"You can reschedule, surely?" Papa suggested, eyeing me thoughtfully. "A family barbecue should take precedent over dinner out."

"Papa," I said, having to meet his eyes for the first time. He had that look on his face. Concern edged in disappointment. I would always be his little girl, always be a worry of some sort or other to him. But I was also letting him down tonight, leaving an event before it was socially acceptable. *Family* barbecue or not.

"Go if you have to, Katie," he said, dismissing me with a slight turn of his back.

My mother frowned, well aware that I'd somehow upset my father, but also embarrassed by *both* our behaviours right now.

"It was lovely meeting you, Richard," Mama said, picking up the reins my father had dropped and carrying on with Anscombe integrity. "I do hope we get an opportunity to see you again. For longer, perhaps."

"I too would like that, Mrs Anscombe." Richard nodded his head towards my mother, offered a smile to Brook, who had remained quiet throughout this little battle of wills, and shook my father's hand. At least Papa had remembered himself at the last moment.

I kissed Mama on the cheek and went to follow Richard, who had taken a step away, towards the exit.

"Katie," my father called, before I had a chance to catch up to a rapidly retreating Richard. "Is everything all right?"

I almost sighed aloud. Everyone seemed to be asking me that question, but I don't think they really wanted to know the answer. Katie Anscombe was *always* all right.

And in that vein, I said, "Of course, darling. Splendid."

Papa's face fell, just briefly, then he caught himself and frowned instead. I didn't stay long enough to see the disappointment.

Richard was waiting for me at the door, he helped me into my coat and we slipped out without another confrontation. He didn't say anything as we walked down the front path to his Lexus, or as he opened the door for me to slip in. He still hadn't said a word by the time he had joined me and started the car. It wasn't until we were several meters down the road that he spoke.

"Do you wish to talk about it?"

I smiled over at him. "Not really. But thank you for the rescue."

"It was a rescue attempt, then?"

"I'd say it was a success, not just an attempt. Wouldn't you?"

"That's not my point, and you know it. You required an escape from your brother's house," he said purposefully.

I didn't feel at all comfortable talking to him about this. Yes, technically, he was my date. But he was also a client and I didn't know him well. Besides, what would I say? I'm in love with my eldest brother's soon-to-be brother-in-law, and my other brother's employee, who happens to think there is a reason that Jason is *wrong for me*. What a mess.

"I think we have more pressing matters to discuss, Richard. You're heading off tomorrow and we need to finalise your featured pieces. If we get this sorted and you agree to my quote, I could have a design finalised by Tuesday morning."

"You don't need to quote, I've already committed to you being my designer. I'll pay whatever you suggest."

"That's highly unusual," I said, surprised at his lack of business acumen.

"I'm not really in a position to negotiate, Catherine. I need this completed in ten days time. It's a finite time-line, and as such, I am at your discretion. I'll even sign a contract this evening, to get the ball rolling. Could you have the design completed by tomorrow night?"

I blinked at him, stunned. Not so much at the speed with which he wanted things progressing, he'd made no bones about that, but that he'd simply sign a binding contract without a quote in place. I couldn't make a number up off the cuff. It would take some calculation. I could give him a ball park figure maybe, once we'd agreed on the final pieces to be featured. But it would have to be extremely elevated, in order to protect myself. I'm not in the business of ripping off my clients, but I am also not in the business of setting myself up for a loss.

Richard would have to look after himself, I couldn't and wouldn't do it for him. But this left an uneasy feeling in the pit of my stomach.

Still. A job is a job. "Yes, I believe I could have a design finalised by Sunday night." My heart stuttered at the impossibly short timeframe I'd just verbally committed myself to. But it was a much more favourable sensation than the ache that had been there for way too long. I grasped the adrenaline rush, pushing all other unwanted emotions away.

Anything I could do to replace that anguish and confusion I would.

"Brilliant," he replied, with genuine enthusiasm. "The other reason why I don't want to wait for a quote is, I would also like security included in the final finished product. And I expect it would be difficult for you to estimate a costing on that."

"Security?" I asked, confused. "Richard, I'm an interior designer, not a security consultant."

"But your brother runs a security firm," he pointed out. "Surely you have worked with him on properties before."

I had worked with Anscombe Securities and Investigations before, or at least the securities division. Which included mainly Eric, who was their security guru and also the consultant ASI used to install security systems on those properties they were contracted to protect. Many of my clients had asked if I could suggest a reputable security and alarm company, and of course, I had pointed them in Nick's direction. Richard's suggestion wasn't that unusual. But he clearly wanted me to deal with them, rather than do so himself.

"Usually my clients converse directly with ASI themselves," I decided to admit.

"Yes, yes, but I really don't have the time and as we've established, I must have the showroom open in ten days time. I very much desire for you to do this for me. As a favour, if you like. I will also be more than happy to compensate you for your time and effort. And really, how bad can it be dealing with your brother?"

He had no idea. Especially now. But then, I could make sure that all my communications went through Eric and not Nick. Even if Eric was of the same opinion as my brother and his men. And none of those boys could resist an opportunity to push their point of view. Oh Lord, what was I going to do?

"I'm afraid I would have to charge significantly for this, Richard," I tentatively said. If I was going to put myself through this, then damn it, I would make it worth my while. "It is highly unusual, and could interfere significantly with the time I need in order to meet your deadline."

"Of course, I understand and would expect nothing less. You don't seem to be the sort of business woman who would sell herself short. And to be honest, Catherine, you *would* be doing me a favour. I just don't have the time myself and after talking to Brook, was that his name? It all fell into place. How much of a coincidence is it that my designer has inside access to a top notch security firm? This would kill two birds with one stone for me. I could not be happier. So, please, my dear, charge away."

Something about this made me feel uncertain. Maybe it was just the unexpectedness of it. The new territory it would make me traverse. Not to mention the fact that I would dearly like to have nothing to do with Nick and his men right now. But whatever the reason was, it would be rather irrelevant in the end. This could well end up as a very lucrative deal for me. And truthfully, all I would be doing would be liaising with ASI on Richard's behalf.

"All right, then," I said, with a smile. "We'll finalise the pieces tonight, have you sign a contract, and I'll take care of the rest."

"Ah, Catherine, you are a dream come true," Richard said, as we pulled up outside a wine bar in Mission Bay.

The rest of the evening went uneventfully. We sipped delicious wine in a softly lit and cosy atmosphere, and managed to pin down exactly what pieces Richard wanted on display and roughly where they would go. The how would be left up to me, but I'd worked with artwork my entire career. I knew exactly the right way to make a piece shine.

By the end of our *date* I was eager to get on with the project. Even the notion of incorporating security measures into my time wasn't a hardship any longer. The passion for design had surpassed all other slightly negative emotions and I was floating on a joyous cloud of anticipation. I even thought I might get a few sketches down before I headed to bed, despite it being well after midnight when the Lexus pulled up at my front gate.

In order to have Richard sign a contract, I had to invite him inside. Which was a little unnerving, what with the late hour and the few glasses of wine I'd had. But he waited in the lounge for me to retrieve the papers, not bothering to sit in a comfy chair. And signed the documents with only a brief scanning before committing ink to paper. I'd used a generic contract, and quickly incorporated a few caveats about pricing and the security consulting I would be required to do. Other than that, it was fairly vague. Just a commitment on both our parts. For me; the completion of the project in a given time-frame, and for Richard; payment of the final price up to a certain maximum limit. I'd been generous in the baseline quote, but he hadn't even blinked an eyelash when he read it.

After the deed was done, he stood upright, lazy smile in full swing... and then looked at his watch.

"It's getting rather late and I have an early start. Will you forgive me if I don't stay for a nightcap." I hadn't offered him one, but was immensely relieved with his need to leave straight away.

"Not at all," I replied, walking to the doorway and opening it up to the night air.

He stopped on the threshold, turned back and looked at me keenly. The security lights had come on as soon as the door opened and he was backlit by brilliant white.

"I enjoyed tonight," he murmured, his lids lowering slightly with his voice. I held my breath, hoping he'd just depart and not attempt anything uncomfortable for both of us.

But if wishes could be horses....

He leaned forward, his hands coming up and lightly grasping my upper arms to stop any backward movement I might have endeavoured, and kissed me on the lips.

It was pleasant, his lips soft and warm. But that was all, really. Other than an uncomfortable feeling that grew as I didn't allow him to deepen the moment. He pulled back slightly irritated, I think. At least he looked put-out when my reluctant eyes met his.

"Good night, Catherine," he said formally. "Please phone me when the design is ready to be viewed."

And with that he spun on his heels and disappeared into the night.

I let a much relieved breath of air out and shut the door behind me. I was really unsure of what I was doing. Perhaps this was a huge mistake. Business and pleasure never mixed well, and especially not in my current frame of mind.

After gathering myself sufficiently, I took a step away from the door, intending to switch the lights off in the lounge and head to my office and jot some ideas down. No more than that one step away and a soft knock interrupted my plans. I spun back around and glared at the closed door, thinking, as my stomach fell, that Richard must have changed his mind.

I wasn't sure if I was up to fending off his advances. Everything was just so messed up, the night had been a roller coaster, I really didn't think I had any fight left in me.

My hand shook as I turned the knob on the door and swung it open. My eyes bulged, a gasp left my lips, as my chest ached for more reasons than just the sudden increase in speed of my heart.

"Did you even check the peep-hole?" Jason demanded, in his signature telling-off attitude, arms crossed over broad chest, scowl in place.

Oh, good Lord. Could this day get any worse?

CHAPTER 17

IT WAS A PROMISE I FERVENTLY HOPED HE COULD KEEP

"What are you doing here?" I managed to say, unoriginally.

"We need to talk," he replied, then promptly pushed past me, without waiting for an invitation, and walked into the lounge.

He glanced around, as though he was looking for something, but obviously didn't find it. Or maybe he did, because his shoulders relaxed and he took a seat on the couch. He lifted tired looking chocolate brown eyes up to mine.

My heart clenched. It hurt. For a moment I couldn't tell if it was remembered pain at what he had done, or the sight of him looking so uncertain, so defeated, so lost. I didn't want to feel anything for him, but I'd be a rotten liar if I said that I wasn't aching to soothe away his pains.

I forced myself to fold my arms over my chest defiantly, and stay standing, glaring back at the man who had broken my heart. God, I was certain I couldn't do this. It was tearing me apart.

"Kate," he said, and oh damn! His voice cracked on my name.

I couldn't do this. I started shaking my head back and forth.

"Baby," he said, getting to his feet and crossing the space to stand before me. "Shhh," he added, making me realise I'd started to whimper aloud.

He didn't touch me, just hovered, that uncertain look carved into his face. I sucked in a deep breath and told myself to harden up. Taking a few much needed steps away. Space. I needed space to deal with this.

"Why are you here?" I asked, once I'd placed half the room between us.

He looked blank for a second, adrift, but he was standing right there. I'd *never* seen Jason Cain this way before. A shadow of the man he'd once been. A haunted, vague representation of the omnipresent person he'd always appeared to be.

OK. So, something was definitely off. I studied him for a brief moment, waiting to see if his usual take-no-prisoners attitude fell back into place. It didn't. And the longer it took, the harder it was not to reach out to him. To offer comfort, to reassure.

But, I couldn't. I *wouldn't*.

"What's going on, Jason?" I asked, keeping my voice level, not soft.

He shook his head, sucked in a deep breath, and then ran his palm over his face. In that same move he'd made at Dom and Gen's tonight. A move I'd never seen Captain Jason Cain effect.

I was beginning to feel entirely too uncomfortable, Jason's out of character behaviour throwing me for a loop.

"I..." he started, then looked around the room for inspiration. "I came to tell you..." He stopped mid-sentence again. Sucked in another breath, while my heart silently folded. "I owe you an explanation," he finally managed to get out.

Yes, he did. But I wasn't sure I was ready to hear it, even with him acting so bizarrely. Hadn't my heart taken enough of a battering for one lifetime? Must it take even more?

"I don't know, Jason," I said, my voice softening without my permission. "Two weeks," was all I could manage to say.

His hand came up and rubbed across his chest, above his heart. I don't think he knew he was doing it. And oh, dear God. No. *This* Jason would break me, if I let him.

"You should go," I whispered.

"You won't hear me out?" he asked, sounding a little more like the Jason I knew. His stunned reaction making his voice strengthen in surprise.

"I can't do this," I said under my breath, then headed toward the front door. I opened it, and waited for him to move.

For a surreal suspended moment in time I watched him assess the situation, take in my rigid stance by the open door, the obvious message I was relaying. And I thought he'd cave. I thought he'd do what I asked and leave. And a part of me, I hadn't even realise existed, baulked at that idea.

I was angry with him. Hurt by what he had done. But I did not want to see Jason Cain leave with his tail between his legs. That was not the Jason I knew.

He walked slowly towards me, his eyes locked on mine. My heart thundered, my fists clenched, and I willed my eyes not well with threatening tears.

Where are you, Jason? Come back.

What the hell had happened to make this man lose so much of himself in just two short weeks?

And I knew, right then, that if he stopped, that if he showed me even a hint of the old Jason, I would listen. Because he was battling something deep inside himself right now, and if he had the courage to stand against it, to fight for what he used to be, then the least I could do was hear him out.

But he made it to the door without a word. He even took a step outside. My heart fell, my shoulders sagged, and I realised it was over. He'd fucked up, I'd been hurt too much to allow him any purchase back in. This was it.

And I didn't want it to be, even though it hurt still. Even though I was petrified of being hurt more. I did not want this to be the end.

This was not how Jason and I parted.

Was it?

I lifted my eyes to his, as he'd stopped on my doorstep and turned around. That pull I'd always felt was still there. That desire to lean closer, to inhale more deeply, to reach out and touch. It hadn't been drowned in amongst the pain, it was still as strong as ever.

Oh, damn.

"I was in the Army for fifteen years," he said from out of nowhere. "Ten of those in the SAS. Eight as Captain of my squad." He stopped talking to take a breath, his eyes staring down the hallway behind me, faraway. Then, "It was a big part of my life."

I wasn't sure what to be relieved about the most. The fact that he hadn't given up, or the fact that he was opening up about his time in the military. A time I knew had left an indelible mark.

I'd known this. Not the details, mind you, but the depth of connection Jason had to the New Zealand Army. I'd also known how hard it was for him to be dismissed. All because he was defending his sister against a gun-toting lunatic ex. But he'd fired a weapon, whilst not on orders from his superiors, and killed a civilian. Warranted or not, the Army had let him go.

Jason has had difficulty accepting this, I think. It's only a guess, evidenced by his behaviour since then. And now he didn't even work for Nick in private security. Now he had no job. No anchor to keep him safe.

My throat constricted with the overriding empathy I felt at those thoughts.

"It's not an excuse," he continued. "I just thought you should know that." I blinked at him, his eyes were shadowed, much like his face was now. Much like, I was beginning to realise, his heart was, too.

He was suffering and despite what he'd done, all I wanted to do was ease his pain.

When I didn't urge him to leave, but just stood there, openly watching him, waiting for more, he went on.

"I know you've cottoned on to what sort of man I am, Kate," he said, leaning forward to rest his hands on either side of the door frame, by my head. "You do, don't you?" he queried, as if he doubted his previous statement.

"You're a dominant," I said softly, but surprisingly without any embarrassment. It was who Jason was and I'd obviously accepted it.

He nodded, a look of relief flashing across his face.

"I'm not a sadist. I'm not into whips and paddles, hot wax or nipple clamps. It's not like that. I don't derive pleasure out of someone's pain. I just... I just need the control. I need to be in control." He ducked his head, breathing deeply, then whispered in a voice that cracked a fissure right through my heart, "It's intensified since I left the Army." The admission cost him something. He didn't raise his head again after that.

I stood there, unable to move for the moment. Not necessarily stunned, because I wasn't. I'd almost expected this. But a part of me ached for Jason. For what he must have seen and done as an elite soldier in the special forces. Of the person he must have become because of it. And now, the person he had be to exist without it.

He was lost. In more ways than I had realised.

I closed my eyes slowly at that knowledge. The knowledge that explained so very much. I still felt anger at him for walking away from me without a backward glance. I still felt fear that even letting him in this far would cause me more pain. But I think, maybe, there was a burgeoning sensation of understanding, or at least, acknowledgement that Jason was a messed up man, and he regretted what had happened as much as me. That it may have been a mistake, brought on by whatever made Jason who he now was.

I opened my eyes and looked across the small space between us. Jason's head had come up enough for him to view me through his lashes. Pain etched a picture in his eyes, across his firm jaw, through his rigid stance. I held his gaze and didn't turn away from him.

"I want to tell you what I've seen." He spoke slowly, as though he was carefully choosing each word. "What it's done to me. But..." he sucked in a deep breath, ran that hand over his face again, then abruptly pulled back from his position resting on the door frame. "It doesn't excuse my behaviour with you," he admitted, eyes alight with turmoil and, I think, *fear*. It wasn't what he was originally going to say, I could tell by his tone. It wasn't a deflection as such, I think it was more to do with the fact that he simply wasn't ready to talk about his experiences yet.

I hoped one day he would be ready. And then I wondered if I was.

Although my chest hurt and my eyes burned with unshed tears, all on his behalf, I was not going to easily forget the past fortnight. It had been my hell on earth. And all because of him. I wanted to be the better person, and let him off the hook with compassion and understanding. But there was a part of me that still smarted. God, that was still broken, by what he had done.

"Two weeks, Jason," I semi-repeated, voice soft. Even if I felt compelled to address this with him, I still had no real desire to hurt him with my words either. It was such a conflicting place to be. Angry at being hurt so badly. Heartbroken not only for me, but now, more so for him. And finally, I simply missed him and wanted to believe he missed me.

So short a time he was entwined in my heart and life. And now I felt like that was a part of me I'd never have back again.

"I'm sorry, Kate," he said slowly, with meaning, making eye contact throughout each word. "I'm so sorry," he added, shifting forward on the stoop until I could feel his breath wash across my lips. "I never meant to hurt you," he continued, chest rising and falling too rapidly. Matching mine.

I couldn't move. His apology was heartfelt, I could tell. But the defeat and broken look I'd seen in his face, nearly brought me to my knees. For a moment I battled with these new emotions, as they warred with those I'd felt for the past two weeks. How did you get over that? How did I move on from here? Do I move on with him?

"Jason," I said, sorrow coating every syllable of his name. He closed his eyes and dipped his head. "You hurt me, Jason," I whispered. "You broke me," I managed to get out, but the words were almost unintelligible.

He must have heard them, because a hitched sound escaped his lips. He leaned forward slowly, hesitantly, breathing erratically... then finally touched me, by nestling his face into the curve of my neck.

Tortured bliss. Oh, dear God, he was close to crumbling apart, and I was right there with him.

"I'm so sorry, baby. I made a mistake. A fucked in the head mistake. But even as I made it, I knew it was wrong." He was rambling now, desperate to get the confession out. His lips feathering against my sensitive skin, as he hurriedly murmured each word. "I knew it wasn't what I wanted to do," he continued. The only part of his body touching mine was his mouth and breath. Oh, I longed for more. And I also wanted the strength to turn away. He'd hurt me, but then he'd been hurting too. "But I was confused and uncertain," he went on, "and Nick saw through it all and twisted my thoughts further."

What? Nick? My brother? What on earth did he have to do with this?

I didn't get a chance to voice those stunningly important words, because Jason was on a roll of confession here and he wasn't even stopping to suck in breaths.

"But it's not just that, Kate. I *let* him. Fuck, baby, I let him pull me away from you. I don't deserve you, Kate. You're too good for me and even now I don't know if you can handle the demands I'll want to make. But I can't stop it. I want you so badly. I want every inch of you. I want your body. I want your heart. Fuck, baby, I want your very soul."

And with that my heart shattered, and through some miracle started to mend again. How could I not be affected by that raw and honest admission? How could I turn away now? His whole body was heaving with barely controlled emotions, his lips were desperately brushing soothing kisses against the skin on my neck. I felt his pain, as though it was mine. I felt his desperation, as though it was mine. I felt his regret, as though, it too, was mine. I felt it all, and it humbled me, scared me, and gave me hope.

But, Nick? I couldn't get my head around it, even as a part of me replayed all of Nick's words at the barbecue in my mind.

"He's the wrong man for you. Katie, I know more than you do. You're just going to have to trust me. Stay away from him. OK?"

Nick knew what Jason had suffered. Nick knew how affected Jason was by his time in the Army. Nick knew everything that Jason couldn't yet voice to me. And he'd determined that I couldn't handle someone as broken as Jason Cain. Nick, *my brother*, had decided to end our burgeoning relationship before it had a real chance of starting. He interfered. He *fucked* not only with me, but with Jason.

I was immobile with rage. A solid form of disbelieving mass standing statue still in the warm embrace of a pleading man. A man who, in such a short amount of time, meant everything to me.

Jason finally realised I wasn't melting under his touch, that I wasn't encouraging him further. That I hadn't offered him forgiveness. He pulled back, until there was once again space between us, enough for the cool night air to start to chill me. And he looked crushed.

Broken.

Without conscious thought I lifted the fingers of one of my hands to his face. Caressed one digit slowly down his cheek, then cupped his jaw, locking his gaze on my own.

For a moment neither of us said anything, just stared at the other, waiting for something... momentous to occur. I felt like I was standing on the edge of a precipice, staring across a darkened abyss to the light on the other side. I could choose to go back, to avoid the chance of falling over the side and sinking into the bleak, black chasm. Or I could take a gamble on the light I could clearly see across the other side, in this man's eyes. Take the risk, breach the divide, and walk in sunshine.

I'd taken a risk once, and fallen off the edge into the abyss.

I stared at him, seeing the man I'd fallen for before I fell, and the broken man that had been left afterwards. I wanted to reach for that sunshine on the other side of the abyss, and it was a lovely thought, but reality is not made up of fantastical analogies. Besides, there was more to it than just forgiveness. Jason was a tortured man, moulded from his experiences. Encounters that I could probably never imagine in my worst nightmares. Did I truly think I could help him? Did I truly believe I could be the woman he needed me to be, in order for him to live life?

I stared into those beautiful, yet haunting, chocolate brown eyes, and saw my own fear and doubts reflected there. Neither of us were one hundred percent certain about this. But the longing that intertwined and overrode the apprehension matched my own. He wanted me and I realised, I still wanted him.

I searched his eyes for anything else, anything that would indicate he could hurt me again like he did two weeks ago. Maybe there was something wrong with *me* to even be contemplating this after what he'd done. But he was messed up, and I couldn't let go. Should I allow my pride and fear to rule my heart? Or should I let my heart guide my way? I was scared of being hurt again, but I was more fearful of not living life, of missing a chance I may never get again. Of letting him walk away. I am what I am, and what I am is in love with this broken man.

The longer I looked, the less fear and uncertainty I saw in his eyes, on his face. And the more desire and determination took their place. A small smile spread my lips. A little of the old Jason Cain I'd come to love seeping back in. There was hope. And if there was hope...

Still, I can be stubborn.

"If you ever hurt me like that again, Jason, I will walk away," I said, voice steady, but low, my intention to do as I said in every syllable that left my lips.

"Kate," he whispered, and so much was conveyed in that one word from his lips. So much relief and joy and sorrow at what had transpired. And hope for what could now come.

"What now?" I asked, because despite - well at least I think - letting him back in, I didn't know what the next step was. This had been so monumental, such an enormous hurdle to overcome. I wasn't yet one hundred percent recovered. In all honesty, I hadn't yet fully forgiven him.

Oh, I understood my brother's duplicity in what had transpired. I understood Jason's messed up psyche had allowed Nick to steer him down that path. But it had hurt, damn it! You don't just get over something like that, simply because you understand and the person has apologised.

This would take time, and right now, I really didn't know what happens next.

"We take this one day at a time," Jason said softly, receiving a relieved nod of my head from me. "But if you think I'm going home to my flat tonight and leaving you alone to mull this over and change your mind, then think again."

And Captain Jason Cain was back.

Thank God.

I offered a smile, it might have reached my eyes, I'm not sure. Then Jason slipped his hand into mine, held my gaze for a suspended moment, and walked past me back into the house. The front door clicked shut behind us, he paused to lock it, then the lights in the lounge were extinguished, and he guided me down the hall.

His touch was sure, but gently, when he undressed me. I was momentarily surprised he helped me slip my nightdress on when he was done. But the relief was also apparent. He stripped down to his boxers, then with eyes still holding mine captive, helped me slide under the covers of the bed.

The bedside lamp was switched off, as he pulled me into the circle of his arms and laid a soft kiss in amongst my hair.

He knew I was still in pain, and he didn't push me. He simply held me, offering the odd kiss to my temple, wrapping me up in his large, safe arms, and waiting for me to fall asleep.

I wasn't sure what was next, but for now I'd take this, willingly.

Jason had hurt me, but there'd been a reason why. A messed up, screwed up, brother interfering reason why. But a reason why nonetheless.

And as much as I'd been hurt, so had Jason. But he'd fought for me, against Nick. Against my fears and rejection. Jason had fought to get back to me.

God, I hoped I could let him back in. I really hoped that I could be everything he needed me to be. Because I was in love with this broken man, and I knew loving him would never be easy.

As I finally drifted off to restless sleep, I heard him murmur, "I'll make it up to you, I promise."

It was a promise I fervently hoped he could keep.

CHAPTER 18

AND I MEANT IT

I DIDN'T WANT TO WAKE UP. I DIDN'T WANT MY MIND TO LIFT from the delightful fog of dreamland and discover Jason wasn't in my bed. Hadn't been here at all. That everything that had happened in the middle of the night was just a fantasy. And reality was the hell I'd lived in for two whole weeks.

I must have moaned in distress, because the bed shifted beside me and a hot body wrapped around my frame, pulling me close, tucking me beneath his, burying his face in the curve of my neck.

"What's wrong?" Jason asked, and if I could have found my voice right then I would have shouted to the world, *"Nothing's wrong. You're here"*.

Instead all I could manage was to cling to him as my body shook with relief and the release of pent up angst.

"Baby," Jason murmured, his voice still thick with sleep. I must have woken him. "It's OK. Everything's OK," he whispered, stroking my side, laying kisses between the words on my skin, holding me tight. Then hitting the nail on the head with, "I'm not going anywhere."

A sound escaped my lips, it was painful. Both to my constricted throat and to my recovering lovelorn heart.

"Kate," Jason murmured softly into my hair. "I'm so sorry," he added. "Can you forgive me?"

I concentrated on breathing for a while, on swallowing past my aching throat, until I could finally voice an answer.

"I've already forgiven you, Jason." And it was the truth.

His whole body jerked, then abruptly relaxed, moulding into mine. "Then what's the matter?" he asked, sounding tentative and confused.

"It's forgetting that I'm having trouble with now," I admitted. "I thought you wouldn't be here when I opened my eyes."

His arms tightened around me and he lay a soft kiss on my temple.

"I'm done fighting this," he whispered. "I'm done letting anyone else fight it either. I'm telling you now, if someone tries to get in our way again, I will bulldoze them. I will trample them into the ground and to hell with the consequences. Why the fuck do you think I quit ASI?"

I sat up slightly to look down at him, to get a better idea of what he was feeling by the expression on his face. I thought he'd resigned because he was angry, a knee jerk reaction to Nick interfering in our lives. Was there more to it than that?

He reached up and pushed my hair back off my face so he could see my eyes. His hand cupped the side of my head as he gazed up intently at me. Everything Jason did was intense. And I loved it. And I'd missed it. *Never again.*

"He can't hold my job over my head anymore," he explained and my stomach plummeted.

"Tell me," I demanded, mind hardening but my voice belying that emotion with the way it quaked. "Did Nick threaten you with your position at ASI to get you to comply?"

Jason stared at me for so long that I thought he'd decided not to answer. But he must have seen the conviction, the need to know, on my face. He let a long sigh out, something flickering in his eyes. I couldn't tell exactly what it meant, but he did choose to answer honestly, so I assumed it was the decision to not hold anything more back.

"He was trying to protect you." My whole body stiffened, Jason noticed and started soothing me with gentle strokes up and down my arm with the palm of his hand. "I was a mess, Kate. I knew I didn't want to walk away from you, but my mind wasn't making any sense. Nick saw my hesitation and made things pretty clear, helped me to sort it all out in my head."

"He screwed with you!" I almost shouted back. Nick took advantage of Jason's mental state and confusion, and made him do what *he* thought was for the best. I was so angry with my brother, I could hardly draw a breath of air.

"Calm down, baby," Jason murmured. "It's not entirely his fault, now is it? I let him," he added, the words carrying the weight of his guilt and regret. "I fucking let him," he muttered, his eyes drifting away and agony taking up residence on his face.

The anger at Nick I had felt only moments before was replaced with heartache. Jason was a very messed up man. I could see the pain, of caving to Nick, clearly in his features. The disgust at himself, at the weakness he'd shown. Jason fought for control in everything he did. I wondered how he had survived the Army, where as a soldier you had to follow commands or die. Where was the control in that?

It didn't make any sense in my mind. He had thrived in the military, a place where he couldn't exert his demands like he did the rest of his life. How had that worked? And is that why he kowtowed to Nick's demands? Because Nick was his superior and it was ingrained in him to follow his superior's commands without hesitation?

I couldn't contain the questions any longer. I had to figure out at least this part of Jason Cain.

"Why the Army?" I asked, receiving a raised eyebrow at what he thought was a sudden topic change. "I mean," I added, licking my lips to try and moisten my suddenly dry throat. Was it wise to bring this up? Could I cause more damage by taking him back there? "You had to follow commands in the Army," I explained. "You wouldn't have been in charge."

His face relaxed slightly, he didn't exactly smile, but my statement must have made some sense.

"There is a form of control in structure," he said softly. "I knew what was expected of me, what was expected of my men." He paused, his brow furrowing slightly as he thought his next sentence through. "I felt less in control when I left the armed forces, than I had ever felt while following commands."

Structure and control. They went hand in hand for Jason, and he needed them both. ASI would have provided him that structure, Nick liked his business running 'just so'.

"Is that why," I asked tentatively, "Nick was able to influence your decision when he demanded you leave me alone? Because you were expected to follow his directives?"

I held my breath, as his steely chestnut coloured eyes drilled into mine.

"*I* let it happen, Kate. Don't try to make me into something I am not. Nick *was* my boss, I followed his lead, but ASI is not the Army. I could have fought back. I could have argued the point with him. Fuck! I could have been a fucking man and done what I wanted to do from the very start."

He was angry now. With me, for trying to make sense of why he left. For trying to blame Nick instead of him. Jason felt guilt at what he had allowed to happen, at the weakness that he had displayed. He wanted to carry the blame alone, because he saw himself as culpable.

And, he was right, to a certain degree. He could have thrown down the gauntlet and stuck to his beliefs. He could have been a 'man' and stood up to Nick in order to keep being with me. He didn't, so therefore he carried some blame.

But, and dear God help me to make him see this, *he is only human*. And a human who has seen and done more than most. And who, if my guess is right, has suffered psychologically because of it.

Jason is entitled to make the odd mistake. Yes, I would have preferred it was a different mistake than the one that broke my heart. But he's trying to correct his mistake now. He's apologised wholeheartedly for hurting me.

I would not be who my parents raised, who I have strived to be my entire life, if I couldn't forgive this fractured man.

I moved until I was kneeling before him. He'd sat upright in bed when he'd released that last tirade. I was now eye level with him, face to face, nothing in between.

"Jason Cain," I said, making sure I had his full attention. "You did me harm," I started, voice soft, but the words cutting. I watched as he flinched. "I have forgiven you," I added, meaning every word, but he didn't relax his stiffened stance. "But I have not forgiven my brother for taking advantage of your mental state and for harming me further." He started frowning. Unsure how to take my words, I think.

I reached over and clasped his hand, entwining my fingers in his.

"There's something about you, Jason," I said, looking down at where my body met his through our touch. "Something that has called to me from the moment I first laid eyes on you. I didn't want there to be. You didn't make it easy." My eyes flicked back up to his. "But it's there and you feel it too. I know you didn't want to walk away," I whispered, as his eyes held mine and I felt myself falling... *falling*. He could do that; make me fall when I shouldn't. "And I also know, that were you not the man you are today, the product of your experiences, you wouldn't have done what Nick suggested so readily."

"Kate," Jason interrupted, preparing to argue the point, to deny that he had suffered in the past, and still did, and that was the cause of his actions. But I wasn't finished.

"You broke me, Jason," I said, reaching over and placing a finger across his lips to still his protests. I felt his whole body shake at my words, at their meaning and truth.

I wasn't saying this to be cruel, to fight back and cause him pain.

There was a point to this madness. There was a reason why we'd been through what we had.

"But Jason, don't you see?" I said, leaning forward, to keep his focus on me, on my eyes and nowhere else. "*You* were already broken," I whispered. "How could you not make a human mistake, when you are so very, very human yourself? We both are, and we've got the scars to prove it. But baby," I said, using his nickname for me and watching the dawning awe grace his face as I did, "you've already started healing my break. Please, let me do the same for you."

We stared at each other, inches apart, but still too far away. I wanted to crawl into his lap, to wrap my arms around his neck, to cover him in kisses. To make everything better through my touch and love. But I needed him to hear my words, to accept this as truth. He is only human. And humans are messed up, *fucked up*, basket cases at the best of times. Including me.

"Jason," I said. "Let it go. Let me in. Accept my forgiveness and allow me my anger at Nick. It *is* warranted. The blame of what happened is not yours alone to carry."

He looked at me for a long time, his fingers grazing over my knuckles in the hand he still clasped with his. His eyes moved across my face, taking in every inch of it, while he processed what I'd just said. Then he sighed, offered me a small nod, and pulled on my arm until my lips met his. The kiss was soft and careful, so full of beautiful acceptance that I felt tears sting the backs of my eyes.

"What are you going to do to him?" Jason asked, as he shifted me until I was straddling his lap, my knees either side of his stretched out thighs, my groin flush against his. It was intimate, but not sexual. Neither of us had quite reached that stage after everything we'd faced up to since he'd come back. Still, there was nowhere else I wanted to be, and no amount of space I wanted between us.

"I need to confront him. I won't be happy until I've given him a piece of my mind."

"Will you be armed?" he asked, casually. Too casually. "I only ask, because I'd like to be there if you draw a knife on Nick. I've gotta admit to wanting him to bleed. Just a little."

I chuckled, resting my head down on his shoulder, my breath fanning across his neck as my face curved towards his.

"He doesn't know I've been practising Kombatan. It would be a good way to gain the advantage right off the bat," I said, feeling a lightness begin to enter the room, enter our words. Our hearts.

Jason's body shook with the rumble of laughter through his chest. "Today?" he asked, clearly wanting me to slice into my brother sooner rather than later.

I hesitated. Ah, fudge. I didn't have time to confront Nick today. I had an art studio design to complete on a ridiculously tight time-frame. The only reason I'd accepted this contract was because I could use elements and materials from Mrs Montgomery-Smith's sitting room to hasten the finished product. I usually allowed myself three times as long to complete a design than I had Richard's. But the money was not to be sneezed at.

Which reminded me I had professional reasons to visit ASI, so no doubt about it, this week was going to be jam packed.

"I can't," I explained, laying a soft kiss against Jason's neck and pushing back upright. "I have to finish this blasted concept drawing for Richard's art studio by this evening. I'm going to have to lock myself away in my office all day. I'll have to plan on visiting Nick tomorrow," I added, but I don't think Jason was listening to the rest of my statement, he'd stalled somewhere back near the beginning.

"That fucktard you brought to Gen and Dom's?" Fucktard? I worked to keep my grin contained. Jason was jealous. This was just too good to ignore.

"Yes, he's paying me a fortune to get his showroom ready for opening night in ten," I looked at my watch to check the date, "make that, eight days time. So, I'm going to be very busy for the next week or so. He's a demanding man." I threw that last in to get a reaction. Finally feeling like we were getting back to level ground.

There was still lingering pain and fear, but with every further second with this man, I felt it slipping away. I felt the break that had split me near in two, begin to mend. This was where I was meant to be, and the pain in getting here just made it that much more sweet.

Of course, I hadn't anticipated the reaction I'd actually get to my teasing. My body was thrown through the air and even before it settled on the rebounding mattress, Jason's frame was pressing into me on top. His thigh spreading my legs and rubbing seductively, his hand entangled in my hair and tilting my head to the side, his other holding my chin to ensure my gaze never left the serious look on his face.

Oh, blissful heaven. This was why I'd chosen to take another risk. No one made me feel like Jason did.

"When are you seeing him again?" he demanded, chestnut staring me down.

"He's away on business for the next few days, we're corresponding via email and phone." My answer was swift and honest. I wasn't so sure that pushing Jason's buttons had been an entirely good idea, despite the return to familiar and much wanted - no, *needed* - ground.

He nodded, pleased with my response or the speed of it, I couldn't tell which. "Then I guess I'll have to help you get this design out of the way." His tone made me think he'd meant to say, *out of your life for good.*

"And how are you going to help me, Jason?" I asked, the smile I'd fought earlier starting to show at the edges of my lips. His eyes darted down to watch the movement.

"Oh, I don't know, Kate. Filling your mind up with better things than a fancy arse room full of art, maybe. Making you focus on something else other than that twat's *design.*"

"That's not actually helping me get the project out of the way. I've signed a contract, I have to complete it," I pointed out, enjoying this jealous side of Jason he was suddenly showing a little too much.

"Baby," he said with a wink. "I'm gonna be your muse."

My breath left me in a rush and he began to frown, seeing my stunned reaction. Jason had been my muse once before already. A muse that allowed me to create a masterpiece which was going to bring me more business, I was sure. But, how did he know? Was I that obvious?

"How?" I managed to get out, but no more.

"How what, Kate? What have I said wrong?"

"How did you know?" I finally asked, but he was obviously still confused, because he just kept frowning down at me, his hand in my hair gently caressing my scalp, the other stroking my side tenderly. Even in confusion Jason soothed me.

"How did you know you're my muse?" It must have been the way I said it. I hadn't been precise in my words, incapable of being completely coherent. I hadn't been specific, told him he had been my muse once before and when. But he must have understood my meaning, because the frown disappeared and the sun came out from behind the clouds.

"Kate, Kate, Kate. Now how exactly did I inspire you?" he murmured, as his body sunk further into mine, until his hips were between my thighs and I could tell he'd moved on to the better part of our conversation. "I want details," he whispered, rocking his hips slowly against me, making me suck in faster and faster breaths. "I want times," he added. "I want to know that you affect me as much as I affect you. And that it's all good, baby."

He leaned down and slanted his lips across mine. Once. Twice. Then on the third time he groaned and deepened the connection until I was writhing and moaning and digging my fingers into his back. Begging for more.

He pulled back, panting. "Tell me," he instructed. "Tell me and I promise you, I'll give you inspiration that will blow your beautiful mind."

"Jason," I murmured, letting my eyes show how much affect he had over me. "I think you've been my muse since you barged into my life," I said, then added, "But since you've slipped into my bed you've set everything on fire."

"Fire, baby?" he murmured, nuzzling his lips into my neck,

trailing kisses around to my throat. "I like that," he whispered, nipping and sucking, working his way down over my chest to my breasts. "I want to be your inspiration, your muse," he said, voice low and gruff.

He latched onto to a taut nipple through my nightdress, and worked it and me to a frenzy until I was pressing back up into his groin with fervent need. Rocking against each thrust of his hips, desperate for him to take this to the next level.

"Because, Kate," he said, pulling back to blow hot breath across moistened skin through the damp material. I shivered. Then offered a full body shudder when he added in a husk, "You're my saviour. The one person who makes it all so much easier. The one person I can't live without anymore."

He threw his attention into my neglected breast and nipple, allowing me a moment to get lost in the sensations and his admission just now.

I was his saviour. His anchor. I liked that. I wanted that. I needed him to have that.

"Baby," he groaned, quickly removing his boxer shorts, then lifting my thigh high, once he'd settled back in place, to allow himself better access. And then with a slow thrust forward of his hips, he sank to the hilt deep inside my core. I gasped and he moaned an erotic sound above me. "I love you," he added, the words spilling from his lips with such ease.

Oh my Lord, I hadn't expected that. I had not expected Jason Cain to open up his heart to that degree. He was a messed up, slightly broken man, who needed to control his environment or float away into the darkness that threatened each day.

But somehow he'd found the strength to say those words, to put it out there. To strip himself naked and stand before me; a man in love. To let go of his past. And to let me in.

"Jason," I said on a breath filled with such delicious emotions, as he diligently sought my own form of release.

"Let go, baby," he demanded in a thick voice. "Just let go."

So I did. On his command, but very much willingly. I gave in to the sensations he was creating, and gave in to my heart.

"I love you too," I managed to cry, as an orgasm swamped me; rolls and rolls of wave upon wave of rapture washing over my frame from head to toe. Shuddering through my nerve endings, firing off shocks of electricity through my skin, throughout my body, through my head and heart. I felt alive and present, but also conversely floating on a cloud of true ecstasy, that wasn't just confined to my flesh anymore.

No, what I felt was all consuming. It involved every single part of me, every cell. My body. Heart. Mind. And soul.

"Kate!" Jason cried out on his own release. "Oh, Kate," he said after several hard thrusts had segued into slow steady rocks of his hips. "Oh, baby," he murmured, cradling me in his arms, as the last of our orgasms waned.

He kissed the side of my neck, where his face was buried. Our breaths slowing, but our hearts still beating equally as fast as each other's.

"I'm never letting you go," Jason murmured, his whole body relaxing into mine.

"I won't let you," I replied, stroking a hand down his sweat soaked back.

And I meant it. We'd found our way back to each other. The pain he'd caused was healing. And if he broke again, I would be *his* reason to heal.

I would be his anchor. Just as he was my muse. And always would be.

CHAPTER 19

AND I KNEW THERE WAS MORE TO THAT QUESTION THAN THE WORDS LET ON

Jason was making breakfast. He said it was the only meal of the day he was any good at. I didn't complain, not when my mind was already replaying the events of this morning and somehow turning those erotic sensual images into a design that would steal people's breaths when they walked into Tremayne Arts.

I was twisting the Montgomery-Smith's final look, using the same materials in different colours to obtain a faster finished product - sourcing furnishings took time, I was short on that - and lifting the whole concept drawing to another level completely. I couldn't even stop myself from going directly to my office after I'd showered and dressed. I bypassed the kitchen and a barely dressed Jason so I could put pencil to paper and sketch a few of my more luxurious ideas before they fled my mind.

By the time Jason found me, tray of food and steaming mugs of coffee in hand, I'd rough drawn three different areas of the final concept. I was on a roll, and Jason must have picked up on that. He simply placed the tray down on a side table, passed me my coffee and a slice of toast, and then sat down to eat his own while he watched.

I nibbled on the bread, interspersed my flurried pencil drawing with a sip of caffeine, but never stopped pouring my thoughts onto the sketchpad in front of me. By the time Jason cleared the tray - having been hand fed some fresh fruit and yoghurt, but too busy to contemplate anything else - I'd finished my initial concept art in two hours flat.

I sat back and stared at the array of images spread across my desk; amused, dumbfounded and totally ecstatic.

"You know," I said, not looking over my shoulder, but knowing Jason was standing just there, "for a muse, you rock."

He laughed out loud at that, a deep, freeing sound from right inside his chest. I turned in my seat to look at him, as he leaned against the door frame, smile in full force.

"You finished already?" he asked, surprise lacing every word.

"Just the concepts. I now have to polish them, transfer them to my laptop and make them look professional, then make a detailed list of furnishings I'll use, including a floor plan and structural guide for the builders. *Then* I'll be finished."

"Oh," Jason said, stepping into the room properly and coming to stand behind my desk. "So a little longer then?"

I huffed out a breath. "I'll be working late," I pointed out. "I probably won't break for lunch and dinner will have to be an at-the-desk affair." I turned fully in my chair to face him, he took the necessary steps to bring himself between my legs, still standing over me, but his hands already twining my hair around his fingers, as his eyes devoured my face.

"I should let you get on with it then," he murmured, not making any move away. "I need to go for a run and check on things at the flat anyway. How about I bring back dinner at about six?"

I glanced back at my desk reluctantly, his hands in my hair were just too nice.

"Make it eight," I suggested, bringing my eyes back to his. "And the next week will be pretty high pressure. I need to contact the builders I use and get ASI on board."

"ASI?" Jason asked, interrupting my train of thoughts.

I nodded. "Yes, Richard wants security for the store and suggested I liaise with ASI as he doesn't have the time."

"Is that normal? Do interior designers handle that side of things directly?"

"Yes and no," I replied. It was a little unusual, but often a designer was handed a comprehensive brief, that included amenities such as that. I just hadn't heard of it happening much in New Zealand. Perhaps it was more common overseas. "It's new to me though," I admitted. "I'm charging my client an arm and a leg for the service though, so that's got to count for something."

Jason smiled down at me with determined approval, his movements in my hair stilling. "From now on he is *always* 'your client'. Not Richard. Not anymore."

I frowned at him. "Will you demand this of all my clients?"

"No," he said swiftly. "Just the ones who try to make out they're your date." Ah. "Understand, Kate?" he asked, tightening his hands in my hair. The message was clear; his tone of voice mixed with that short, sharp command. This was Jason the Dominant. He'd finally brought him out into the light for me to see.

A frisson of excitement swept through me; *this* was what I craved, what I feared I'd lost. Jason's demands and my capitulation. There was no denying I thrived on this.

And thankfully maybe because he'd only ever demand what I could give - it wasn't something I felt the need to fight over. Richard *was* my client and although I'd handled the situation less than perfectly, I had no desire to give the man any more false ideas.

"I understand, Jason," I said, feeling his body relax. Feeling his hands start up a soft, soothing motion in my hair against my head. A massage that alleviated any tension the topic had caused. It was an easy enough thing to give him. And, if I looked at his demand neutrally, it wasn't an unreasonable request at all.

"Kate," he murmured. "You are perfect for me, do you know that?"

I smiled up at him, but he wasn't done.

"Not many women would accept such a bald faced directive without bristling at the imposition it caused, or the tone it was delivered in." He looked thoughtful for a moment. Then added with a long drawn out sigh, "I crave the control, but I'd crumble if you couldn't handle my demands."

He was such a contradiction. Demanding, controlling, but fearful of each command that slipped through his lips, as though he didn't truly want to be this way. He needed it, I'd even say it ruled him, this desire to control his world. But it conversely threatened to tear him apart. The fear that I would walk away because it was restricting, too limiting, too one sided.

What he didn't realise was, the Jason who turned me on, who I was irrevocably attracted to, was the man who made the demands, who asked in that abrupt way of his, "Understand?" It sent a thrill through my body no other man had ever managed to elicit. It made me wet with wanting. Craving his firm hand and forceful instructions. I lived to hear his next demand. I hungered for his next directive. I *loved* it when he showed his true colours.

"Don't for a minute believe I want you any other way, Jason Cain," I said, standing up from my chair to bring me closer to his body. "The second you stop being you, is the moment you should fear most."

He looked down at me, his hands loose at his sides as they'd fallen from my hair when I shifted to stand. He held my gaze for several seconds, then sucked in a short sharp breath.

"Do you want more?" he asked, voice low. Could I handle more?

"Is there more?" I asked instead.

"Kate, I would have you stripped before me for our pleasure in an instant, if I thought you'd accept my proposition."

"What do you mean?" I asked, my heart leaping into my throat excitedly. Aroused by something I didn't yet completely comprehend.

"We talked about rules, remember?" I blinked up at him, trying to remember any rules. "You wanted me shirtless when in your house." I flicked my gaze over his naked chest. He'd followed my rule to the letter. "I said I'd want you without underwear in mine."

Oh. I nodded.

He leaned in, hot breath fanning my lips, as he whispered, "I'm extending my rule." I swallowed, seeing the lust build in his eyes. "You wear skirts when you're with me." Oh, OK. I could do that. "No matter where we are. Inside our homes. In the car. Out on the street. At Gen and Dom's Sunday barbecues."

I nodded. A part of me, on a base level, wanting nothing more than the eroticism that notion brought with it. The easy access of a skirt, not trousers.

"That's not the end of the rule," he pointed out. "But I like your enthusiasm." His grin was infectious. I smiled back up at him and he chuckled. "Kate," he said, bringing his lips within skimming distance of mine. "I want you to never wear panties when you're with me either."

My eyes searched his face for the joke. There wasn't one.

"A skirt and no underwear?" I said, stunned. But remarkably feeling incredibly turned on. A small surprised breath of air left me.

He nodded, neck stiff making the nod short and sharp. He was on edge again, waiting for my surrender. Unsure if I'd go for such a blatantly sexual command while in public.

"Anywhere, as long as I'm with you?" I asked, needing complete clarification. But well aware my body had provided the answer already.

"If you're not with me you're fully clothed, but as soon as we're together, baby, you lose the knickers. Understand?"

I licked my lips, a nervous and equally excited reflex action. His eyes darted down to the movement and he made that growling sound at the back of his throat. Seeing my capitulation in my body's physical reaction to his demands.

"I'm with you now, Kate," he pointed out. I immediately dropped my gaze to the jeans I'd put on that morning, making me in breach of his rules. "I'll give you a countdown from three," he whispered, voice so low and seductive it was hard to decipher the words. "Then I'm stripping you naked for the rest of the day. Bare arse naked. You'll sit at your desk naked. You'll eat dinner naked. You'll email your client your design while naked. You'll answer the phone naked. Then you'll present yourself to me at the end of the day... naked. Understand?"

"A countdown from three," I said with a nod, feeling aroused, excited, frantic with need, and about to combust all at once.

Oh, I was so on board with Jason's naughty rules.

"Three!" he said loudly, stepping back and allowing room to move.

I took a step away from my chair toward the door.

"Here, Kate. Remedy your transgression here. Now."

My transgression? Oh, he was pushing things. But then I saw his smile, amusement and laughter dancing behind the grin. He was loving this, and the relaxed way he beamed at me, waiting for me to fight back or run, seemed to lighten the moment and turn the whole event into a seductive game.

He wanted me to fix things here, strip out of my jeans and underwear in front of him, just as much as he wanted me to say no and deny his command. And in all honesty? I was having a hell of a time deciding which option would be more fun. Doing a seductive little striptease to make his blood boil and hopefully bring the man to his knees. Or standing my ground, ensuring he'd carry through with his punishment; stripping me naked and making me stay that way for the rest of the day.

"Two!"

I jumped. I needed to make a decision. It was one thing to *willingly* allow a particular path to be taken, but to not commit myself to the final outcome seemed like I had relinquished all control.

And that there let me know just how Jason Cain worked. He was still the one calling the shots, but within his demands he'd allowed me some power. Only some, because to outright deny would be impossible, he would still get his way in the end. But if I didn't like these controlling games he played, then I shouldn't be here with the man, should I?

Just as well I loved them then, isn't it?

I undid my top jeans button and within moments had my knickers and jeans down my legs, as my butt went up in the air, pushing the garments to my ankles.

"Stop!" he instructed, when I went to lift a foot out of one trouser leg and straighten up.

He began a slow walk around me, my head still down, my bare arse poking skywards, as he came to rest at my back. He stood there for several long seconds, not touching, just taking his fill of my current displayed state

"You're beautiful," he rasped. Yeah, he was going to be on his knees before too much longer, I could tell.

"Can I move?" I asked, when he continued to just look at me.

"Spread your legs as far as your jeans will allow," he said, suddenly. I followed his command hoping it would mean he'd finally touch me. I was ahead on my design for now, a little recreational distraction could be allowed in the limited time-frame I was working with. "Rest your head down on the chair." My desk chair was ideally placed to support my upper body, but leave my rear still higher and on open display. "Play with yourself," he husked behind me, as I heard the soft, muted sound of the buttons on his fly coming undone.

I whimpered, but raised a hand to between my thighs and started rubbing a finger across my nub, coating it in the slick moisture that had already gathered there.

"Use your fingers to spread your folds apart," he murmured, the sound of his palm stroking his erection the only other noise in the room right then. I did as he asked, feeling cool air coat my sensitive centre. "Dip two fingers inside," he commanded, his own breaths and movements picking up speed.

I slowly sunk the digits inside, then took the liberty of pumping them several times in sync with the sound of his own stroking. I moaned at the image I had in my mind of him at my back, pleasuring himself as he watched me doing the same.

"Fuck!" he moaned behind me. "You're glistening and swelling. Are you close, baby?"

"Yes," I managed on a whisper.

"What do you need, Kate?" he asked.

"You," I wasn't ashamed to reply.

"Put you thumb on your clit and start rubbing." He wasn't giving me him just yet, he was making me wait, making me work for it. I followed his command without conscious thought, moaning loudly as I felt the tension building.

I had two of my fingers inside, pumping a steady rhythm, while the thumb of the same hand rubbed circles over top of my sensitive clit. My other hand held me steady, wrapped around the chair seat for support.

"Bring your other hand around to your rear," he said, panting through the words.

"Jason," I said on an embarrassing whine. "Are you going to touch me?"

His free hand wrapped around my hip, holding me steady so I could lift my hand away from the chair to my rear. I'd got his touch, but nowhere near where I wanted it.

"Keep playing with yourself," he directed, his fingers tightening at my hip. There'd be little bruises there tomorrow. I loved the image that thought brought with it. "Your other hand," he panted out behind me. I could feel his fervent motion, back and forth in rapid succession, as he stroked himself closer to his own release. "Lift it up so I can suck on a finger, baby."

It was a little awkward, but I rose the hand at my back up and he bent down to lick and suck my index finger into his mouth, his tongue swirling around the sides and then cool air coating it as he pulled back.

"Place it at your entrance," he rasped. I must have hesitated. "Do it, don't think."

My hand came down haltingly to my butt cheek, finding its way to my rear entrance, where he'd played before, pressing the vibrator in and allowing the vibrations to send me into overdrive. I could feel the puckered rosette there spasming already. I'd never paid any attention to this part of my body before, but Jason made me aware of so much more than I'd ever seen, ever knew, existed. He opened up my mind, my body. Hell, he'd opened up my heart and soul as well.

"Good, Kate. Now rest it there, just on the entrance. Use a little pressure."

"Jason," I warned, not believing for a minute that I could do what he had done.

"Trust me, baby. You're gonna like it. I know I am."

I breathed out at his words, hearing his arousal in them, knowing he was being turned on watching me bent over before him, pleasuring myself and about to breach my own forbidden void.

"Press that fingertip in," he demanded, his tone firmer, commanding; Captain Jason Cain in charge of the room.

It felt illicit, it felt naughty, but surprisingly it felt exceptionally good. I moaned as my butt spasmed around the tip of my finger, hungrily trying to pull it further in, while an orgasm thundered towards me. Each pump of my fingers and rub of my thumb in front, combined with the unusual, but highly erotic sensation of my finger imitating the movements at my rear, sending me closer to the edge by the second.

A delicious pressure built that I couldn't fight, a wonderful sensation of impending release making my body jerk and my desire for more increase.

"You coming, baby?" he asked. "Or do you want me there too."

Where? Coming with me or replacing my finger with something of his? His own finger? Or his cock?

And, oh dear God, I've never used that word before, but the moment deserved it. I bucked, let out a groan and then came apart around my fingers and thumb, feeling his hand move from my hip to clasp my own at my rear and his finger press above mine, pushing it a little further in.

He pumped my finger in time with my orgasm, and while I screamed at the effect it all had on me, I felt his release burst hot and wet over my butt cheek.

"Oh fuck, Kate!" he groaned above me, more and more of his seed spilling out onto my hot flesh.

He eventually slowed both our movements down; his own stroking of his shaft above my butt cheek and my finger just inside my rear. Easing everything, eking out our orgasms, savouring the moment with me for as long as we could. Finally he helped me withdraw my finger, and then with an arm around my waist he brought me upright again, flush against his hot, naked chest. His release would be soaking through his jeans, as they hadn't fallen completely to the floor. He'd obviously just undone the fly to gain access to his erection, and no more. But he didn't seem to care about the mess he was creating, he just held me close, let me gain my balance and kissed the side of my neck, down onto my shoulder.

"You OK, baby?" he asked.

"Ah-huh," I replied with a sated nod of my head.

He chuckled, the rumble reaching me through my back directly from his chest.

"You liked that?" he added.

"Yes," I managed to say on an exhale.

"Next time you get me."

I stiffened. Him, finger? Or him, *him*? I still couldn't say the word unless in the throes of passion.

He noticed my reaction, of course.

"Yes, Kate. All of me. Just like I get all of you. Do you want all of me, baby?" he asked, nuzzling behind my ear.

And I knew there was more to that question than the words let on. *Did I want all of him?* Mind, body, heart and soul. *And* him taking me in that way; where my finger had just been, his hand guiding me, and where I realised I'd liked it more than I had imagined I ever possibly could.

I was beginning to see, that with Jason, I could like a lot of things, I had never possibly believed before.

"Yes, Jason," I said, feeling him inhale a deep breath at my back, "I want all of you."

"Baby, you got me. You have so fucking got me. I am lost."

CHAPTER 20

YES, MY BROTHER RAN A TIGHT SHIP

THE FINISHED DESIGN WENT THROUGH TO TREMAYNE BY ELEVEN that night. Jason had allowed me time to complete it; going for his run and checking on his flat. He even turned up with dinner at eight, having left me alone for the rest of the day. After making sure I was sufficiently clean and pampered following our office encounter.

He'd behaved himself in the shower too, just ran liquid soap on a loafer all over my body, bringing the skin tingling to life under his so very careful touch.

I had missed him afterwards, but I'd been able to throw all my energy and creativeness into the project, completing, for the second time in a row, an out of the world design I could truly be proud of.

I'd also worn a skirt without underwear for the rest of the day, getting used to the sensation ahead of time, so that when Jason returned it was almost natural. So natural, in fact, that I'd forgotten I wasn't wearing anything under the above knee skirt I had on, until Jason's hand ran up my thigh when we sat down to dinner, and began to leisurely bring me to orgasm as we ate.

The dessert he'd bought was a non-event after that. I slipped under the table and sucked and nipped and stroked my thanks in return. Then when he had collapsed to his knees, exactly where I wanted him, I reluctantly had to head back into my office to finish the design. Jason watched TV, checking on me with a late cup of tea as the evening progressed, and then curving an arm around my shoulders, when I'd shouted my joy at completing the first part of the contract on time, and leading me into the bedroom. Where he proceeded to instruct me to strip naked and climb between the sheets.

Miraculously we had slept and not done anything else. A sense of comfort had swiftly replaced the pain and fear of the past two weeks. I was so very thankful, but I was exhausted and tomorrow was going to be another jam packed day. I liked working under pressure, but this project time-frame took the cake for pressure, that was for sure. It was ridiculously short, I had to ask myself again and again why I had agreed to it in the first place.

Unfortunately, the truth lay in the same place as the truth about why Jason walked away from me. I had been a broken woman when Tremayne cornered me, just as Jason had been a broken man when Nick cornered him. We all make mistakes, and mine had been accepting an impossible deadline for a design project I should have known would be beyond reasonable to achieve.

Still, I'd signed the contract for it and there was no going back now.

Monday loomed and my schedule included confronting Nick, signing up ASI for security at Tremayne Arts, scheduling my builders to start work on the premises, and making a start on sourcing the furnishings. It was a big ask.

Jason knew immediately that there was no time to spare, as I was running around like a headless chicken, taking a bite of toast off the plate of breakfast he'd prepared, and carrying out conversations with my builders over the phone glued to my ear, pencilling them in for a four o'clock appointment at the showroom to go over plans.

I still hadn't heard from Tremayne, so I was getting slightly ahead of myself. But if the builders didn't start tomorrow, which meant they needed to know the brief today, then the deadline could be compromised. Just as I finished the call with my foreman, my cellphone chirped and buzzed and whirred. The generic ringtone I have set for my clients' numbers sounding out across the room. The screen said 'Richard', and as I reached for the phone I watched Jason cross his arms and stare at me hard.

I kept my gaze averted. Did he expect me to change the name on my phone from Richard to 'the client'?

"Katie Anscombe," I said into the device.

"Catherine, I love it! You are a genius, my dear."

"Thank you, Richard," I answered automatically, receiving a loud thud of Jason's hand as his fist hit the kitchen table's surface. My eyes flicked up to his and he mouthed, *Tremayne*. I guess, as in, 'Mr Tremayne' from now on. I rolled my eyes at him and returned my attention to my phone.

Richard had been talking and I'd missed half of it.

"That corner will make the Mark Hill sculpture stand out. You've excelled yourself. It's as if you were made to represent these pieces. I have every intention of using your services in the other locations I have planned."

Other locations? Just how many places did this man want art rooms at?

His voice lowered, turning a little husky on the edges. "In fact, I think you and I could work so well together, Catherine. We're from the same worlds, we understand each other. You've designed something right out of my head. I couldn't have expressed my wishes as well as you have conveyed my vision."

Oh, heck. I had no answer suitable to all of that. My eyes flicked up to Jason's angry chestnut coloured ones and I let a little breath out trying to release the tension in my shoulders.

"It's been an interesting process, Richard," I said, getting startled by the abrupt scraping of Jason's chair as he pushed himself away from the table. He started loudly clearing the dishes, making as much noise as he could manage in the background. I bit my lip to stop from grinning. He really was such child at times. "But I don't want to give you false hope. This will be my last art room design."

What I meant was, it would be my last design for him. It was too awkward now, I couldn't work for Richard Tremayne after this rushed, complicated, and entirely uncomfortable project. It wasn't fair to anyone, and I am not the sort of person to make life more difficult for myself, if I can manage.

"Really? Have you not enjoyed designing the studio?" Tremayne asked, putting me right on the spot.

Jason had also stopped making noise and was now just leaning his jeans clad butt against the bench. Arms crossed over shirtless chest as he watched me intently.

Oh, damn. What to say?

"I'm afraid the time-frame has been cause for concern," I offered as an excuse.

"Then we'll make sure you have more time in the future."

I frowned, but aside from saying it was him I was trying to avoid, I just didn't have an adequate answer. For the sake of Jason's pleasure, I couldn't be that rude to client, wanted or not.

"Well, it's my decision, Richard. Let's just leave it at that."

There was a long pause on the phone, the silence somehow threatening. I shook my head, unable to figure out why I felt intimidated by his lack of conversation right then. I couldn't explain it, but a type of menace hung over the line. Which thankfully snapped when he spoke again in an even and steady voice.

"I'll be out of town for the rest of the week, so I've arranged for keys to be delivered to your home for the shop. Please go ahead as planned, and if you would be so kind as to let the security firm in to do their necessary installations, I would be grateful."

So formal. Not even saying the name of my brother's firm. It was as if he was distancing himself from it all. But I could hardly complain. A week to just get on with the job without interruption and interference from the client; a designer's dream come true.

"You can be sure I'll have it all ready for you when you return," I said cheerily. "Where are you...?"

"I'm sure you will." He cut off my sentence mid-question. "That is why I hired you, after all."

"All right," I said, a little uncertainly. "Thank..."

Again he interrupted. "Contact me if you have any problems, otherwise I'll be in touch on Friday to arrange for the pieces to be delivered. You'll be ready by then, I assume?"

I blinked. He was shortening the deadline. Well, not really, I could still work around the pieces, but I'd have to make sure Nick's side of the job was completed by the time the artwork arrived. And Nick wasn't even aware of his part in this project yet.

I felt panic begin to engulf me, which was instantly assuaged by Jason's reassuring touch on my shoulders as he began to gently rub. I sucked in much needed air.

"You won't be back to see to the pieces' delivery?" I asked, feeling a little better with Jason's continued soft touch.

And then having it blown apart at Tremayne's next words.

"By Friday, yes. But I did make it perfectly clear I was working to a strict deadline before we signed a contract and that you would be handling much of the final presentation on your own, Ms Anscombe. I sincerely hope you are not reneging on your part of our agreement. I wouldn't want to have to bring my lawyers in at such an early time in the process."

My mouth fell open at the abrupt and drastic change in Richard Tremayne's tone. It was like he was a different man, all because I had challenged him on details. Oh, and said I didn't want to do another art room design after he'd admitted he wanted to work with me again doing the same.

I frowned. Jason squeezed my shoulders offering support.

"That won't be necessary, Mr Tremayne," I answered, in my most professional Katie Anscombe voice. Jason lay a kiss in amongst my hair on my use of Richard's surname. Or maybe, just to let me know I wasn't alone. It's a little hard to tell with him sometimes.

"Excellent," Tremayne said. "We'll be in touch, then." The line went dead.

I gingerly placed the cellphone back on the table, utterly stunned. What a creep he had turned out to be.

"What a fuck-knuckle," Jason announced. I was thinking his assessment was more accurate than mine.

I nodded. "An absolute fuck-knuckle," I murmured.

"Baby, those words don't suit you," Jason pointed out. "Not that I'm gonna complain too much. If you want to call him a fuck-knuckle instead of *Richard*," he said 'Richard' in a falsetto voice, imitating me, "I'll back you all the way."

"Thanks," I muttered, getting up from my chair and swiping up my phone angrily.

I needed to put Richard Multiple-Personality *Fuck-Knuckle* Tremayne behind me and concentrate on the next task... Nick.

I sighed, as I slipped my cellphone into my satchel. Oh, good Lord, give me strength.

In the end Jason decided it was best if he didn't witness my confrontation with Nick. Maybe he thought he'd not be able to hold back. In fact, I had thought pretty much the same myself. It was not going to be pretty. Nick had a temper on him and even though I was his beloved little sister, he never held back with me when irate. I was picking things were going to get quite tense, and throwing Jason's dominant personality into the mix would only escalate things.

I did, however, leave my knife in my satchel. Even if I was fuming at my brother's interference, I still had absolutely no intention of pulling a blade on him to get my way.

Carmel greeted me with her usual gruff smile when I walked off the lift on ASI's floor. Nick's receptionist/office manager had always scared me slightly, what with the grandma persona she openly portrayed and the dragon alter ego that reared its head when she deemed it necessary. The contrast was frightening. Her eyes flicked over me from head to toe. I was wearing a silk blouse in a muted, soft crimson colour, with a tan fitted skirt that met my knees.

I wasn't wearing underwear as I had just left Jason and not had the chance to correct myself. At Carmel's shrewd gaze I resolved to rectify that mistake as soon as I walked through the door beside her desk.

"You look different, Katie," she announced, her hand pulling free from under her desk, where it had been resting on the shotgun I knew was hidden there. Is it any wonder the woman set me on edge?

"Rushed off my feet, Carmel," I replied, hoping that would suffice as an explanation for whatever she saw was *different* about me today.

"No, that's not it," she answered, cocking her head as she released the lock on the door into ASI's inner sanctum. "Did you get yourself some?"

The last was said as I pushed the door open and came face to face with Adam Savill on his way out. One of Nick's men. Adam's slow sexy smile at Carmel's words met my eyes, his own gaze running the length of my outfit making me think I had a sign on my head that screamed, *Look, no underwear! Aren't I a naughty girl!*

"Katie," he drawled. "Have I missed my chance?"

"Darling," I replied, flicking him a sexy smirk, "who said you ever had one to begin with?"

His hand came up to his chest in mock surprise and pain. "Katie, it's like you've all grown up. Are those actual claws I see on your fingers?"

My eyes held his deep blue ones, as a part of me I never knew existed came out to play. "All the better to scratch a back with, darling."

He blinked, I think a little stunned. The Katie everyone knew never would have bantered in such a openly sexual manner before. But then, the Katie everyone knew had never realised her true sexual nature before. I offered a broad grin to Adam, then trotted off directly to Nick's office. No one had said he wasn't in, so I took that to mean he was expecting me. Nick probably knew the minute I left home. Hell, he had the ability to see where I was at any given time, considering my car had GPS tracking installed by ASI and monitored by Eric in the control room.

Which made me wonder if Jason had removed his tracking device yet. I pushed the uneasy feeling aside that Nick was aware of more than I would have liked, and knocked on his closed door, glancing up and staring resolutely at the security camera above my head. Within a few seconds the door clicked and I pushed my way inside.

He was alone, which was an enormous relief. I couldn't really face having witnesses to this conversation. It had been bad enough at Dom's house, with Eric, Koki, Adam and Ben in attendance. If Eva had been here I would have been forced to tame my words.

She wasn't, so I didn't hold back.

"How dare you!" I spat, covering the small space in rapid, angry steps to stand across from him at his desk.

He leaned back in his chair, steepled his fingers in front of him as his elbows rested on the armrests, and then held my gaze, an impassive expression on his face.

"You ignored everything I warned you about," he replied in a steady unaffected voice.

He knew. Jason hadn't removed his GPS tracking device and Nick knew his SUV had been parked at my house on and off for the past day.

"You had no right, Nick," I said through quick breaths. I needed to calm down. My fists were clenched and my respirations had escalated.

"You're my sister. I was trying to protect you," he pointed out in a reasonable tone that only infuriated me further.

"By interfering in my life as though I was a child who didn't know any better."

"Not a child," he argued softly. "But definitely an innocent. Someone who the likes of Jason Cain could destroy without a second thought."

"You don't know him," I said, exasperated.

"And you think you do? Katie," he said, a note of irritation working its way into his tone at last, "you have no idea who this man is, what he has done. You have no way of knowing how close to the edge he has become. He's unstable. One spark and he..."

"Stop!" I demanded, shaking my head as I held my hand up in emphasis. "Just stop!"

I was trembling, my nails cutting little crescent moons into my palms. The sting not even registering through the haze of red before my eyes. I panted through a couple of deep breaths, trying to get my temper under control. If I had been holding a knife I would have thrown it already. I stared at my brother, a man I had always held the utmost respect for, and realised we didn't really know each other, at all.

I sucked in one more deep breath.

"It's irrelevant," I announced, trying to move us on from the stalemate we'd clearly come to. Needing to address the far safer topic of business instead. But Nick wasn't finished, which shouldn't have surprised me. Nick had never met an argument he couldn't win. It wasn't in his nature.

"Katie, I'm not the only one worried. Dom's concerned as well."

I ground my teeth. "Oh, don't bring Dominic into this, Nicky. You're the one that pushed Jason until he resigned. You're the one who..."

"It was his decision to leave, I didn't make him," Nick interrupted.

"What a bloody lie! You held his job over his head like a guillotine, in an effort to get him to leave me alone."

He looked shocked, and for the first time since I walked in here, worried. He didn't think Jason would have told me that, he didn't think Jason was capable of opening up to that degree. He thought Jason was beyond repair. He didn't know Jason at all.

I pushed my case a little further.

"I'm twenty-nine years old, Nick. I am not a child anymore. I am more than capable of defending myself. I don't need you or Dominic to fight my battles. I..."

"Katie, *that's* a lie and you know it!" Interrupting me again. "I may have taught you to hold a gun, but you can hardly defend yourself against those enemies I may accrue through my profession. It's my responsibility to look out for you. I have to!"

He was getting distraught, but although I'd been referring to my *romantic* battles, not my physical ones, I realised I needed to address this with him too. I would always welcome Nick's defence if ASI brought danger to my door, but I was not weak. Not entirely defence-less. Not anymore.

I leaned over his desk, holding his gaze, while I slipped his letter opener into my palm, weighing its balance surreptitiously in my hand. Then while his attention was still focused on me, I swung around and flung the projectile directly at the camera lens above his door. Shattering the glass on impact, the slim blade twanging as it rocked back and forth, embedded deep within the device. A direct hit, without even having to try.

I turned back and found Nick standing flicking intense ice-blue eyes between my target and me. He was in shock, stunned silent. A little horrified even.

"Do you think I'm defenceless now, big brother?" I asked, lowering myself into the chair across from his desk as though nothing had happened.

By the time I was sitting; legs crossed at the knees, skirt flattened of all creases, his door had banged open and two of his men had stormed in. I flicked my gaze over my shoulder and found Eric, who had probably witnessed the destruction from the other end of the camera lens, and Brook, here to make sure no one needed medical attention.

Yes, my brother ran a tight ship. It was just a shame he didn't realise how perfect Jason Cain was for his operation.

And how perfect Jason Cain was for me.

CHAPTER 21

I WAS HIS ANCHOR AND HE WAS MY MUSE

"Holy fucking hell!" Brook exclaimed. "Did you throw that?" He directed his question at Nick.

Eric huffed out a laugh, shaking his head. "No," he said with obvious relish, "that would be the *other* Anscombe in the room."

Brook's gaze moved to me.

"Wow!" he mouthed. "Awesome," he added, with a devilish grin. "Can you do it again?"

"Brook," Nick warned. "It was a fluke."

My jaw gaped open incredulously.

"You pig!" I gritted between my teeth, reaching inside my handbag to finger my blade in readiness.

"If you pull that knife out, Katie," Nick said softly, menacingly, "Brook will have you disarmed and on the floor in a second."

"I will?" Brook asked, clearly wanting to poke the bear right now. Nick flicked him an annoyed look.

"How did you know I had a knife in here?" I asked.

"I didn't, it could have been mace," he pointed out, making me suck in an aggravated breath of air.

Silence reigned for several long and uncomfortable moments.

"Leave us," Nick finally said to Brook and Eric, but his frosty gaze never left my face.

The men obeyed his command, but not before each of them threw a sympathetic glance towards me. I straightened my shoulders and glared back at Nick.

Once the door clicked shut behind them, Nick let out a long sigh.

"That was impressive. How long have you been training?"

"Three years," I said, still sitting stiffly in my chair.

"Eskrima?"

"Some, mainly Kombatan."

"Kombatan. Good choice." He leaned forward resting his elbows on his desk and his head in his hands. "Where did I go wrong, Katie?" he whispered. "I'm good at judging character, and Jason is one messed up fuck."

I let a little laugh out, it wasn't amused. More like relieved. Nick wasn't a bully at heart. He'd been genuinely trying to protect me. But one thing I did admire about my brother, was his ability to look at things from a different angle, if you gave him enough reason to try.

"He has some issues," I conceded, and now it was Nick's turn to offer a laugh.

"Some, huh?"

"Nick. I love him."

His eyes came up to search my face and when he saw the conviction there he only muttered a near-silent, "Fuck!"

He sank back into his chair in an almost defeated movement.

"Dom's not gonna like this," he pointed out.

"It's not Dom's position to pass comment," I said with meaning.

"You're our little sister," Nick reiterated.

"Not so little anymore," I replied, nodding my head to the still embedded letter opener.

Nick started chuckling, which soon became a full bodied laugh. "Eva's so going to whip my ass over this." I raised an eyebrow in query. He just sighed, but didn't offer any further explanation. I could only hope that his fiancée had already called him out on his over protectiveness. She wasn't the sort of woman who appreciated being told what to do, if it didn't suit.

"Are you going to ask Jason back to work?" I demanded.

"No." He shook his head to confirm his answer, just in case I didn't get the firm tone in his reply.

"Why not?" He could be stubborn sometimes and I just didn't have the patience for it today.

"Because he wouldn't accept my offer," Nick replied, holding my gaze. "If Jason wants back, he can come and ask. But it's the only way he'd consider working for me again. On his terms, when he's ready. Not before."

He was right. Jason wouldn't take kindly to an offer of peace or a hand-out. But I really wasn't sure if he was OK with working for Nick again. And I have to admit, I wasn't sure I was happy for him to either. Nick had overstepped the mark by a country mile. Both with me and Jason. It was going to take a long to time to forget this.

"There's another reason why I'm here," I said, feeling it was time to finally move on from family disagreements.

"Yeah, and what's that, sis?"

"I need to hire your security services on behalf of a client I am contracted to. It's a time-limited project and he's requested that I oversee the security liaison as well as the design. I'm on a strict deadline, Nick," I admitted. "I might have bitten off more than I can chew."

"That's not like you, Katie," Nick replied, eyeing me curiously.

"I was not myself when I accepted the job." I flicked my gaze away, staring into the corner of the room to avoid his scrutiny. I shouldn't have bothered, he could see through me even if I was wearing a Mardis Gras mask on my face.

"OK, tell me what you need and where. I'll have Eric organise it."

I let a relieved breath of air out. For a moment there, when things had been on a knife's edge - pun intended - I wasn't sure if Nick would help me out in my self-induced bind. But he was my brother, and the bottom line would always be family first, even when we were mad at each other. Mama and Papa had taught us that.

"Tremayne Arts in The Strand. I've got the keys while the owner is out of town, so I can meet Eric there when he's free. My builders are scheduled for later today at four, so maybe we can synchronise watches."

"An art studio. They just want monitored alarms?"

"Yes. The artwork is fairly pricey."

"OK," Nick said, standing up from his desk and moving to a filing cabinet to withdraw some paperwork. "Take this to Eric and arrange a time to meet. He'll fill in the necessary caveats and then you can get your client to sign the paperwork, locking them in."

"Mr Tremayne won't be back until Friday, to organise the pieces being set up."

"I can't install security without a contract, Katie. You know that."

"The contract can between us, I'm acting on Tremayne's behalf. I have a contract with him that covers this. He's also paid a hefty deposit into my account this morning." I'd checked online before I left home. Richard, despite his disgruntlement with me earlier, had fulfilled his end of the agreement, by paying a percentage of my fee upfront. Leaving me feeling a hell of a lot more comfortable about the entire project, than I had at breakfast time.

Nick frowned at me for a moment. "I gotta say, it's a little unusual."

"This whole job has become a little unusual," I conceded, standing up from my chair.

"Are you concerned?" Nick asked, walking me to his door.

Was I? Not really, but there was just something unnerving about Richard Tremayne and the uniqueness of the project had not helped dissipate that reaction.

"Not enough to turn down the money I'm about to make, darling," I said, with a little Katie Anscombe cheer.

Nick shook his head at me. "Just watch yourself, OK?"

I gave him a glare for even attempting to offer that sort of advice right now.

"Hey!" he said, raising his hands in defence. "You're still my little sister, big girl undies on or not."

I cringed at the underwear reference, feeling decidedly breezy down there all of a sudden. But forced myself to smile sweetly as I escaped Nick's lair.

Eric clicked the control room door open as soon as I knocked and waved at the camera lens.

"Sweetheart," he called, as I walked in to find him on his own. The darkness of the room making the TV screens displaying various monitored areas under ASI care brighter than they needed to be. How he didn't get eye strain staring at all of those multiple LCD screens was beyond me.

"Darling, I have a job for you." I handed him the paperwork Nick had given me.

Eric glanced down at what was in his hand, his jet black hair shining from the light from the monitors.

"An alarm job? On one of your designs?"

"Yes, an art studio in Parnell. They require adequate security for one to one-point-five million dollars worth of art." I fidgeted slightly, my fingers playing with the edge of my blouse. Eric glanced down at the movement.

"What's the catch, sweetheart?"

"I need it completed by Friday this week."

He let a long low whistle out. "You don't muck about, do you?"

I smiled brightly back at him. "Darling, when I want something I just set out to get it."

"Katie," he replied on a laugh, "I only wish you wanted me."

"You know you'll always be my favourite, Eric," I said sweetly, buttering him up the best I could for my next request. "Can you do four this afternoon?"

He chuckled to himself, shaking his head as he placed the document on his desk amongst the clutter.

"For you, Katie, I would do anything."

And that was the God's honest truth. All of ASI would bend over backwards to help me out when I needed it. Eric may not have realised just what sort of time-bind I'd placed myself in, but he could read between the lines as well as the rest of them. If I asked, they all came running. It wasn't just Nick who wanted to protect me, but *all* of his men.

They were as much my family as my brothers. I left the ASI building feeling a lot happier than when I had arrived.

The rest of the day was taken up in sourcing soft furnishings and arranging paint colours, by the time four o'clock came around I was in a much better place, time-wise, than I had been that morning. A little over an hour and a half later, both the builders and Eric were briefed on what was required and had taken the necessary notes needed to be ready to start work tomorrow. Everyone unanimously estimated they'd need to be at Tremayne Arts by eight each morning and put in a full day's work, to have the studio ready to receive the precious pieces for display by Friday.

I locked up and sat in my car feeling elated that I had no doubt dodged a bullet on my impulsive acceptance of this job, and exhausted at the emotional investment I'd had to make to get this far. Not to mention the physical expenditure needed to organise so many different aspects in such a short amount of time. I was spent, but I still had one more thing to face before I could drive home and crash on the couch with a bar of Whittaker's Chocolate and a glass of Sauvignon Blanc.

The phone line rang six times before Richard Tremayne picked it up. The entire time it took for him to answer, I held my breath. I had no idea how the man would respond. And I didn't like the uncertainty one little bit. There was something to be said for predictability, for knowing ahead of time how things should be played out. I hadn't realised that Tremayne had thrown my normal routine for a loop. And until now, I wasn't aware that I did not handle surprises in my usually well ordered, or as Jason would say, structured, world.

A small smile graced my lips on that thought, just as Tremayne answered.

"Catherine, my dear. How has your day been?" Not an ounce of anger in his tone, at all.

I let a revealed breath of air out quietly, but couldn't help being stumped by this ambiguous man.

"Mr Tremayne, everything has gone swimmingly well."

"Please, we'd settled on first names, hadn't we? Now tell me, where are you at with the studio?"

I ignored the first name basis statement, it just wasn't worth the effort needed, and to be truthful, I didn't want to rock the boat. Keeping the client happy was still paramount in my mind. Despite Richard's shortcomings, he was foremost my client.

"The builders start on my plans tomorrow morning, along with the security installation. We're on target to receive your artwork on Friday."

"Ah, Catherine. I knew I could count on you. You know, I do owe you an apology," he said, chuckling slightly at his admission, as though his behaviour this morning on the phone was embarrassing to him. "You caught me at a bad moment, and I must admit the time pressures of this project have started to chip away at my usually relaxed demeanour. So, please, accept my humblest regret at my words earlier. Know that I am so grateful for all your work and cannot wait to see the finished product."

My eyebrows lifted. I hadn't expected an apology, he'd seemed pretty set in his disgruntlement this morning. And as Jason had said, he'd been a fuck-knuckle. But it simply wasn't in me to make an issue of this. He'd apologised, and as a professional I had to accept.

"Don't mention it, Richard." I forced a little merriment into my tone. "We're all working on a tight schedule which places us under undue strain. I completely understand."

"You are right, my dear. I don't know what I was thinking trying to get this business open on such a short lead-in time." Neither did I and I would have liked to ask what the hurry was, but he was already signing off. "I'll be in touch closer to Friday to organise the pieces and a viewing of the final look."

Once again, the phone went dead without a good-bye. Dominic could sometimes do that, too occupied by what was in front of him to bother with pleasantries over the phone. I was used to it, but it didn't mean I wasn't a little peeved at Tremayne. His ridiculous deadline was making all of our lives unbearable.

I sighed, placed my phone back inside my satchel and started the car. It had been a hellishly long day and I desperately wanted some pampering. As I drove the short distance from Parnell to Herne Bay where my home is, I wondered if I would be pampering myself, or whether a certain delectable soldier would make an appearance tonight. We hadn't arranged for a get together, I'd assumed we'd see each other, but as I negotiated rush hour traffic, I couldn't help second guessing my assumption.

What exactly did Jason Cain do in his down time? And considering he had a lot of it now, how stable was he going to be when I next saw him?

I was biting my lip contemplating all manner of outcomes when I turned into my street. Sitting directly outside my house was a black SUV. The elation at seeing Jason's vehicle parked on the street outside my home was magnificent. He was already here, and by the looks of it, as I parked my BMW behind his bigger car, not waiting outside, but rather, somehow, waiting inside.

The table lamps were on in the bay window at the front of the house, casting a welcoming muted glow across the sheer curtains. I could hear sultry music wafting through the door as I walked up the path; Robin Thicke's *"Tears On My Tuxedo"*. I wanted to hum along to the sweet words he was singing, but my voice was stolen as the door swung open and Jason leaned against the door frame. Faded jeans and shirtless.

I actually sighed. He grinned back and reached forward to take my satchel from my hand, ushering me inside the house. The smell of something delicious met my nose, which almost, but not quite, distracted me from the strong arms wrapping around my waist and soft lips pressing into my own. He tasted minty fresh and smelled like Jason. I moaned into his mouth.

"Welcome home," he whispered against my lips. "Hard day?"

It was so natural, to have him waiting, to have him ask how my day went, ask what I'd been doing. It was so natural, yet such a surprise I couldn't form words to answer him right then. I just stared up into beautiful chocolate pools and allowed myself to fall a little. Jason didn't push for me to talk, he just smirked, his signature smile, placed my satchel by the hall table and led me by the hand into the lounge.

The dining table was set across the way, complete with lit candles and chilled bottle of wine. I was betting it was a Sauvignon Blanc.

"I thought you said you were only good at breakfast?" I asked, stunned at the effort he'd gone to preparing a romantic dinner for two.

"Who said it's not Eggs Benedict," he shot back, striding over to the wine and starting to pour us both a glass. I enjoyed the glide of his hips as he walked away and the ripple of his muscles as he reached across the table.

"It doesn't smell like Eggs Benedict," I pointed out. It smelled divine. Beef of some sort, I was thinking, with an Indian twist.

"You're right. It's not," he admitted. "And I lied. I can cook breakfast and curry, but that's it."

I laughed as he handed me my glass.

"Here's to breakfast and curries, then!" I held the glass up for a toast.

Jason held my gaze for a moment, and murmured softly, "Here's to you letting me look after you when you've had a hard day at work."

I didn't know what to say to that, so I clinked glasses and drank to the toast.

"Have a seat, Kate," Jason ordered, in his usual way. I sat down where he indicated immediately, as he began to serve up our meal. He'd either timed it to perfection, or had been reheating it. It didn't smell burned, so it was clear he did know how to cook a curry. I felt my taste buds watering in anticipation.

After fussing away for a minute or so, he finally took his seat across from me at the table, his face cast in interesting shadows as the candle flickered between us.

"Eat," he encouraged with a nod of his head to my plate.

I took a mouthful and moaned at the succulent beef and star burst of flavours on my tongue. "This is incredible," I declared, hurrying for a second mouthful.

Jason smiled, leaned back in his chair, wine glass hanging from a relaxed hand, and watched me consume my meal for a while, then suddenly reached over the table to clasp my free hand in his. His thumb danced softly over my knuckles.

"I'm going to take good care of you, Kate," he declared. "Every day for the rest of our lives." I sucked in a breath at his words, but he wasn't finished. "Starting this week. I know you've got yourself worked up over this project and getting it finished on time, so let me look after you; morning and night. When you walk through that door you can leave it all behind you, and let me handle everything else."

"Are you asking me if you can move in, Jason?" I asked, trying to bring a little levity to the conversation with my tone and words. I failed. Jason was completely serious about this.

"I can't take care of you if I'm not here," he pointed out. "Let me look after you this week. While you've got this project on. Can you do that, baby?"

It wasn't really a question I had to think about, was it? I'd wanted him here from the moment I turned my car towards home. I'd longed to see him tonight, and that feeling wasn't about to disappear by the end of the week.

Besides, I think Jason needed this, as much as he desired it. And I don't believe that was all to do with the fact that he was now unemployed and twiddling his thumbs. I was his anchor and he was my muse.

But now, he was also my home.

"I can do that, Jason," I said softly. "I could do it for the rest of our lives," I openly admitted, placing my cards on the table and seeing where they fell.

"Kate, Kate, Kate," he husked, flashing me a purely satisfied male grin. "You were made for me."

Possibly. Probably. But Jason Cain was made for me also, and I hadn't even realised until I met him, that my life before had been incomplete.

CHAPTER 22

WEAR ME ALL DAY, BABY

THE NEXT THREE DAYS FLEW BY AND FRIDAY ARRIVED BEFORE I
even knew it.

It had been the most amazing week of my life.

I barely had time to think or to worry. My days were taken up
with Tremayne's studio refurbishment and all the necessary tasks
that involved; liaising with Eric and ASI, overseeing the progress the
builders made and ensuring they understood my brief and floor plan,
and organising the soft furnishings to be made and delivered in time
for decoration.

I'd used a modified version of the Montgomery-Smith's design,
taking aspects of the contrasting patterns I'd chosen for their sitting
room, but changing the colours to reflect a more neutral tone for the
purposes of showcasing the artwork on display, and not over shad-
owing it. One repetitive and unexpected colour was used to spark a
reaction; the concept was going to be my signature in each of my
designs from now on - at least for a time, anyway. By Thursday
evening there was only some minor decoration left to complete -
which I planned to do over the weekend - the project had otherwise
come together faultlessly, if not a little harried at the beginning.

The almost-finished look was spectacular and if Tremayne chose not to place his pieces in the spaces I'd created, the room on its own could be considered a work of art. I'd designed each area with the particular sculpture or painting that was to be displayed there in mind. No doubt as he turned his product over, new pieces would fit in equally as well, but I was going to offer a follow up service at a discounted price to entice further business. When he sold an item from his showroom floor, I could quickly modify the display to suit the next piece.

It was my version of up-selling. I was hoping Tremayne would go for it, even if I'd told him I wasn't going to work on studios again. I had to admit I enjoyed this. Despite the limiting and entirely ridiculous time-frame, and the unusual security request, it had ended up being an exciting and invigorating project.

But of course, that could have all been because of my morning and evenings that week.

I was woken each day to either an amorous Jason, or a freshly showered Jason after he'd had an extremely early morning run and returned to cook me breakfast. Twice he brought me my morning meal in bed, and then proceeded to feed me each piece of fruit languidly as he lay beside me in nothing but boxer shorts. Breakfast in bed always led to an amorous Jason and an invigorating start to my day.

Evenings were even better. I can't describe the feeling I had locking the door to a swiftly materialising masterpiece at Tremayne Arts each day, having shared an exhausting, but hilarious several hours in the company of Eric and my builders, whom I all adored. It was hard to imagine my day getting even better, but the moment I slipped into my car, waved good-bye to my contractors and headed towards Herne Bay, I knew what awaited me.

Jason.

And he wasn't just amorous, although that was perhaps one of my favourite character traits. He was also caring, loving, interested in my day, engaging, encouraging and humorous. I don't think I had smiled as much as I had this past week. My cheeks actually hurt. And a part of me, the part that had been damaged almost beyond repair, was scared that once the week ended, once Tremayne Arts was completed and the contract met, everything would disappear.

I tried not to think about it. I tried not to let my brain wander to darker thoughts. I'm not usually depressed in mind, but something had been changed in me when Jason walked out of my life. Something I was fearful of never being able to recover.

He didn't show any signs of wanting what we had to end. But I couldn't help thinking something had changed in Jason as well. And for the life of me, I wasn't sure if it was for the better. I liked Jason just the way he was; gruff, abrupt, short, sharp, demanding, sexy, powerful, controlled. Beautiful. To me he was... beautiful. And I was so lost to him now, that the thought of him changing from what I had come to love, and leaving me because of it, was debilitating.

When Friday morning dawned my heart, despite the accomplishments met and experiences I'd had this week, was heavy. My chest hurt, my eyes stung, and my throat felt tight with worry. It was stupid and perhaps unnecessary, but I had equated the end of this week with the end of my new found happiness. And even logic and reason failed to stop my battered mind from making more of my tortured thoughts than it should have.

"Baby, what's wrong?" Jason broke into my tumbling mental ramblings with those soft words.

I was getting dressed, after waking to Jason as he stepped out of the attached bathroom, recently showered from having his early morning run. I'd been staring into space, in front of my mirror, my make-up only half done. At his words, I resumed applying my mascara.

"Nothing, darling," I quipped, not making eye contact at all.

There was a strained pause, weighted with concern, from Jason. Then abruptly, "Let's get one thing straight, right now." My gaze met his in the mirror. He looked mad; his brows furrowed and chestnut glaring back at me from over my shoulder. "I am not your darling. I am not..."

He shook his head, his chest rising and falling quickly. He was so angry he couldn't even finish his sentence. I carefully placed my mascara tube down on the dresser and turned to face him fully.

"What do you mean?" I asked, trying to keep my voice steady, but the words wavered embarrassingly, and I had to blink rapidly to still the sudden tears. His reaction had confused and scared me.

The end of the week had come, but even that didn't make any sense.

He stared at me, a muscle jumping along his square jawline. He sucked in a deep breath and lifted his head to the ceiling, glaring at it instead of me, as though there would be answers written across the paintwork.

My hand came up and covered my mouth, in an effort to hold my frighteningly emotional response inside. I hadn't seen Jason like this for what felt like a very long time. Infuriated beyond reason.

His head came down and two tumultuous pools of brown locked on me, taking in my hand position and, no doubt, my entire trembling state.

"Do you love me, Kate?" he asked suddenly. My heart leapt and then faltered. "Answer me!"

"Y..yes," I stuttered. What was happening? Was he ending it? Was this his way of saying it wasn't going to work?

"You don't sound sure?"

Was I? Right now I was so confused by his reactions, by my fears, by everything, I had to think his question through. And that only made him madder.

His fists balled at his sides and I think if he had been closer to the wall he would have punched it.

I hated seeing him this distraught. I hated it.

"Jason," I said, standing and taking the steps necessary to bring me into his space. Why? Because I was feeling his anguish with him and it was impossible not to reach out and soothe some of that pain away.

"I love you more than my life," I managed to say, the words slipping out willingly, resolutely. Oh dear Lord, this man could ruin me.

His eyes flicked all over my face, searching.

"Is there anyone you love more than me?" he asked, voice pained and laced with trepidation.

But what a question. I couldn't wrap my mind around it; the desperate plea in every word, the almost childlike quality of it, said from the lips of a grown man. If I was confused before, then now I was confounded.

"Not the way I love you," I said on a whisper. His face darkened, so I hurried on. "I love my parents. My brothers. I love Genevieve and Eva. I love the Sweet Seduction gang and the ASI team, and those at ADK, all to some degree. But *none* of them I love the way I love you." I was rambling, unsure if what I was saying was what he wanted to hear. Desperate myself to end the confusion by removing the angst I saw in his features.

His shoulders relaxed, his face smoothed, but shadows still haunted his beautiful eyes. I let a slow breath out at seeing some release of tension in his frame. I was still confused though.

"Jason?" I asked, uncertainly, peering up into his face.

"You call all of them darling," he said in a deep, rough tone. I held his gaze as he looked down at me expectantly. I offered a small frown; 'darling' was my name for everyone, it was just a phrase, something I'd adopted to hide behind when the world expected me to behave a certain way.

Katie Anscombe was always happy and cheerful, evidenced by her familiar, yet conversely distancing, nickname for those people who threatened to see through the ruse.

Oh.

"You're not my darling," I said with dawning understanding.

"No," he said, jaw still twitching slightly with his contained fury which, as yet, had not dissipated. "Nor are you Katie to me." No I was Kate. Or 'baby' when he was feeling particularly friendly.

"Baby," I whispered, blinking up into his steady eyes. Chestnut still lingered there, but he released a breath of air out on a slow exhale, as though forcing himself to let the anger go. "You're my baby," I added, wanting the last of that ire to vanish completely. Wanting desperately for him to come back to me.

Was this how it would always be? He'd been so stable all week, so present and engaged. His usual demanding self, but a lightness gracing each command, each instruction, each directive that fell from his lips. But then, I had been elated and content. My growing apprehension had only reared itself fully this morning, having settled in my head and heart when I awoke. I'd been too busy this week; working, being pampered and loved, to have let the emotion have free reign until today.

And he had reacted to my doubts and fears, with his own.

Was Jason just as scared as I? Did he fear that this would be snatched away from his grasp at any moment and there wasn't a thing he could do to stop it? Did he feed off my emotions like I fed of his?

"What are we doing to each other?" I asked, more to myself than him. But of course, I'd said that aloud.

"What do you think we are doing to each other?"

"We're going to drive ourselves insane," I pointed out.

"No," he said with a shake of his head, his face softening, his arms reaching up and wrapping around my shoulders. "We're saving each other, Kate," he whispered into my hair. "You're saving me."

I gripped my arms around his back tightening the embrace, wanting to pull him closer, wanting to prove through my solid and persistent hug, that I would never let go. I couldn't, even if he tried to sever ties again, I would hunt him down and drag him back, all the while my heart would bleed because I'd feel his pain along with him.

And now I knew he felt mine along with me.

His head came down and soft lips met the flesh on the side of my neck. A caress full of more than just the sensation of skin on skin. It was laden with everything he felt, mirrored by me. Love. Hope. Fear. Need. Longing. I turned my face, my lips meeting his freshly shaven cheek, the smoothness sending a thrill throughout my body. Any contact with Jason was electrifying, but just then, with our hearts opened before us, the pain of possible rejection still fresh, I craved the physical connection as though he was my drug.

We moulded further together; seeking comfort, seeking reassurance, seeking love. His lips trailed over my jaw, while his hands roamed my body hungrily. Within seconds a fire had been lit and I wanted more.

"I need to be inside you, baby," Jason whispered roughly into my hair, his nose nuzzling the skin at my nape, his hands continuing to roam all over my body. "I need to reconnect. To make sure you're mine."

I think I understood what he was saying. Jason was a complex, broken man, a product of his experiences. But his reaction to my fears, his realisation that I had been scared it would all end, had affected him as much, if not more so, than me. And now he needed reassurance. And for Jason, that manifested physically.

I was completely on board with that method, had been from the moment he wrapped his arms around my body and laid his lips against my skin. And the fact that he hadn't simply ordered me to lie back on the bed and get ready, but voiced his intention in a way that explained rather than demanded, left me feeling strangely light-headed.

But Jason wasn't the only one requiring reassurance. I needed to know I had *my* Jason back.

"Then tell me what you want," I whispered back, pulling from his embrace and standing patiently before him. My gaze peeking out behind lowered lids, my hands clasped loosely in front of my body. I held my breath and waited.

Jason's naked chest rose and fell hypnotically as my eyes trailed appreciatively over his torso. He was dressed in his faded denim jeans, the buttons of the fly still undone, as he hadn't finished closing them when he'd spotted me in my trance. His erection was prominent behind the material, but also tantalising close to breaching the top of his boxer shorts. A shuddering breath escaped my lips at what I knew lay hidden beneath that waistband, within such short and easy reaching distance. My fingers flexed with the need to touch its silky length.

Jason watched my reaction intently, a small smirk playing on the edges of his lips, letting me know a little of my Jason had returned at last. But I was sure I wouldn't have him back completely until he sank himself deep inside of me, reminding me I was his.

"Turn around and face the wall," he instructed, his voice deliciously smooth and deep. My heart leapt for joy at the demand, my body responded immediately; tingles trailing out from nerve endings, pooling seductively at my core.

I swung away and faced the wall expectantly. My breathing now matching his in speed and raggedness, my breasts straining against the material of my blouse. I longed to rip the blasted thing off and feel his hands against my flesh.

"Place your palms flat against the wall, shoulder width apart, either side of your head," he whispered into my ear, hot breath making my shiver uncontrollable.

I complied without hesitating.

"Good girl," he purred. "Spread your legs." I did as he asked, arching my back hungrily. "I'm going to leave you clothed, so you feel every scrape of material against your hot skin, every little ounce of friction as though its my fingers skimming your sensitive flesh."

I whimpered, my head hanging forward as my breaths began to saw in and out of my mouth. It still surprised me, how turned on I got when he directed events like this. When his sexy, deep voice told me what was going to happen. Laid it all out there, prepared me in a delicious way, that could only be bettered by his touch.

"Are you ready for me, Kate?"

I moaned at the wash of breath that sent tendrils of bliss down my neck.

"Answer me."

"Yes," I whispered.

"Are you wet, baby?"

Oh, Lord yes I was wet. "Yes."

"I want to hear you, Kate. I want you to scream when I remind you that you're mine."

I was right, this was a reminder as much for him to reconnect, as it was for me to never forget I was his.

"Did you put panties on?" he asked, his finger laying a lazy trail over my butt cheeks. The fact that the thin material of the skirt hindered his access made me squirm with wanton need.

I shook my head.

"Louder!" he barked, making me jump right along with my heartbeat.

"No!" I shouted back.

"Good girl," he purred.

His hands skated down the outside of my thighs until his fingers reached the hem of my skirt. He gripped each side and then slowly, torturously lifted the edges up, scrunching the material in his fists as he raised my skirt higher and higher.

"You will not change out of this," he instructed. "I want everyone who sees you to see the creases I'm making, to know I took you like this, in your clothes, against the wall."

"How...?"

"How will they know it's like this, against the wall?" he finished my query for me, having read the thought right out of my mind. "Because they're men, Kate. And they all think about doing this very thing to you when you wear your tight little skirts. But they can't. And I want them to know it."

He was marking me. For some strange reason it made me smile. He must have seen the grin on my lips, because his cheek came to rest against mine as he husked, "You like that, don't you, baby? You like me staking my claim."

"Yes," I whispered, not needing him to force an answer from me. I was so gone for this man.

"Louder!"

"Yes!"

"I want to hear you scream, baby. I want your neighbours to hear you scream. Understand?"

"Yes, I understand!"

"Fuck," he breathed, his head resting down on my shoulder. "You make me crazy."

Ditto.

His hands released my skirt, leaving it scrunched up at my waist, and began slow circles over my butt cheeks. I wondered if he was going to do anything to my rear, and I realised I was eagerly antici-pating it, wanting it. I sucked in a breath at that erotic thought and pressed my butt back into him, encouraging him to do his worst. Or best.

"Baby," he groaned. "You want me there?"

I nodded, I couldn't voice my desire aloud. I half expected him to demand, *Louder*, but he just kept stroking my cheeks, and then suddenly smacked his palm against the right one, swiftly followed by the left.

I yelped at the unexpected sting and them moaned at the soothing rub of his hot palm.

"That's for even contemplating I would leave you again," he whis-pered huskily. "You and me, remember?"

I nodded. Then came the demand.

"Louder, Kate!" Smack, smack!

"Yes! I remember!"

"What do you remember, baby?" Smooth strokes of his palm. My skin felt feverish, stinging but tingling with delight. I was so wet now, my hips shifting in a futile effort to assuage the pressure pooling between my thighs. But I wouldn't dare move my legs. I couldn't, Jason was standing close enough to block my feet from moving. But we all know that's not the only reason why I wouldn't break his command to spread my legs.

Delayed gratification at his instruction. I thrived on this. I never knew it could be this way. I never imagined such rewards from such restrictions. Oh God, this was all I could ever desire in a man. Jason was all I could ever desire in a man.

"Answer me, baby. You're thinking too hard."

"You and me," I said, my voice decidedly husky. "Us, Jason. Always."

"Always, baby. And don't you forget."

The last was said as he guided himself to my entrance, managing to stroke through my wet folds and tease my clit, before sinking himself deep inside. I was momentarily disappointed that he hadn't taken me to that next level. I'd been ready and willing, but Jason was in command. And when he chose to take me that way, it would be because he designed it.

His hands came up and rested over mine on the wall, entwining our fingers as he started a steady rhythm.

"Push back onto me on every stroke," he instructed, voice thick with desire. My body arched and I fell into the rhythm he had established easily. "That's it, baby. You're so fucking beautiful."

His lips started trailing light kisses across what was exposed of my shoulder and up my neck, until he found a soft, sensitive spot of skin and began to suck. I bucked against him, the sensation at my core mingling deliciously with the new tingling at my neck. He was going to leave a mark, his mouth firm and unyielding, his suction bordering on painful. It was entirely intentional. Something that couldn't be missed, in case the wrinkled skirt was overlooked.

He pulled back panting. "Who do you belong to, Kate?"

"You!" I answered loudly without hesitation.

"Oh, fuck!" he shouted, approval at my words, and the loud and swift reply, evident. His hands untangled from my fingers and found my hips, as his speed increased and his pounding became punishing. But not the type of thrust designed to send a painful message home, this was all about a loss of control, what I did to him, what he did to me, wrapped up in the delicious sensation of his invasion of my body.

I moaned, it wasn't loud enough for him, because he rolled his hips in a circle, then thrust at exactly the right angle to hit my G-spot. I screamed at the sudden spike of lust, the wetness between my legs increasing in a rush, the sounds of our love making becoming more obvious with every glide forward and slide out of my moistened depths.

"Fuck, you're wet. Hear that, baby? That's what I do to you. And this..." He thrust hard and ground against me; letting me feel his length, how firm he was, how engorged, how he stretched me to my limits. "This is what you do to me, Kate. I'm fucking crazy for you, baby. I can't get enough."

"Jason," I moaned loudly, letting him know I was close. So close.

"Not yet!" he commanded, thrusting harder and faster, taking me in a way that only he could. It was all encompassing. It consumed me. It ruled me. It blasted any other thoughts or feelings right out of my world. All that existed was Jason's fervent pounding, his tight grip on my hips as he pulled me back onto his advancing shaft, again and again and again.

He moaned and I felt his erection swell further, letting me know he was about to burst with his release. I kept expecting him to tell me to come, he was so close, he liked us to come together. But he didn't and I wondered if he was going to seek his orgasm and deny me mine.

I was finding it harder and harder to follow his directive, the pressure so great I was whimpering and moaning and writhing beneath his onslaught and touch.

I felt one of his hands leave my hip and wrap around the base of his shaft. I wondered what he was doing. Stroking himself? Finishing off what our frantic coupling had started?

But he suddenly stilled all movement. His hips stopped thrusting, he stopped pulling me back and just held me firm at the one grip on my waist. And his hand on his shaft squeezed tight; cutting off any release he was about to have. He stayed like that for several long drawn out, heart pounding, breath rasping seconds.

And groaned an almost painful, "Fuuuuck!"

"Move!" I demanded and received a shockingly hard sting on my butt from the hand that had been left on my hip.

"Not yet," he ground out. "When we come, we come together. And Kate? I want you to feel how much you own me when I fill you full to the brim with my release."

I let a shaking breath out on a whimpered moan.

"Ready, baby?" he asked, voice shaking. How he was denying himself, I don't know. But with Jason there was always a reason.

"Yes," I managed to croak, my desperate need to orgasm evident in my tone.

"Now!" he ordered, thundering forward, both hands back on my hips, pulling me back hard with each punishing thrust forward, and grinding into me with a swirl of his pelvis once seated to the hilt.

He repeated this three times before I lost it. Before I fell tumbling head first over the edge and down into bliss. I screamed his name, moaning and bucking and screaming again and again, as he powered on, his movements possessing me, his body devouring me, his entire being owning me.

And then he found his own release and I swear the glass in the windows rattled at the roar he let out. Hot spurt after hot spurt filled me up, as he bucked and lost his rhythm, and simply ended up jerking and rocking into me on uncontrolled thrusts of his hips. It went on for what felt like a full minute, his release obvious in the heat and wetness that coated my walls, making them quiver and contract, squeezing even more and more out of the man. Milking every last drop.

"Fuck," he whispered, as his movements finally slowed, and his head came to rest in a sweaty weight on my shoulder. "Crazy for you," he added, his voice hoarse from crying out through his entire orgasm.

I shuddered beneath his frame, pressed flat against the wall now, and let an astounded laugh out on a breath of hot air.

"Do you understand now, Kate?" he asked, pulling back and brushing hair of my face tenderly. "That's how much you own me, baby. I am yours."

I sighed, feeling sated and sexy and wanted and... complete.

"And Kate?" Jason murmured, laying a soft kiss against my cheek. "Wear me all day, baby."

What? What did that mean?

He pulled back, slipping out of me in a smooth and wet glide, chuckling when I felt his release trickle down my leg.

Oh. That was him. On me. Overflowing and trailing down my leg unhindered by panties.

I groaned, and it wasn't all mortification at having him dry on my naked thighs. No, there was definitely a huge element of arousal in the thought that I would be at work, surrounded by colleagues, wearing Jason Cain.

Willingly. And with pride.

CHAPTER 23

I'D GLADLY DIE A THOUSAND BREATHLESS DEATHS

I was late. The carpark out the front of Tremayne Arts was full. Not a spare space for me to park my car. I had to park further down the street in a neighbouring business' carpark, hoping I wouldn't get towed or wheel clamped. As I walked back through those cars before the studio, I noted not only those of Eric's and my foreman's, but also several I didn't know and the sleek, dark Lexus of Tremayne's. Not to mention a rather large truck blocking the exit.

I sucked in a fortifying breath. It was not going to look good the designer turning up an hour late for the arrival of the showroom's pieces. And I was crumpled, my skirt creased, my hair a little ruffled, Jason still wantonly caking my upper thighs, making me moan at the erotic images that flooded my mind on that thought.

Lifting my head and straightening my shoulders I pushed through the front doors and into organised chaos. Jerry, my head builder was helping a half dozen men I didn't know unload the truck and unwrap artwork, under the careful direction of Tremayne. Eric was in the office, probably testing the alarm system, making sure it was ready for when we locked the doors tonight.

I walked directly towards Richard, meeting his curious eyes with a steady gaze of my own. *I would not blush. I would not blush.*

"Good morning," I chirped. Tremayne looked at his watch, but when his face came up to meet mine there was only a small smile, no outward sign of disappointment or anger at my tardiness.

"Good morning, Catherine. I thought it best we get started."

"My apologies. Car trouble." I don't think he believed my lie for a moment, but thankfully he didn't challenge me on it.

Eric, on the other hand, having no doubt overheard my excuse, didn't have any trouble voicing an opinion. A wolf whistle emanated from the door to the office.

"Looking good, Katie. Must be the morning air."

The blush was not to be denied. Tremayne cleared his throat at Eric's blatant disregard of professionalism. "If you could carry on here, Catherine, I'll get a briefing from your security man, so he can leave."

Yes, I was quite sure Tremayne wanted Eric off his premises after that little statement. I smiled sweetly and took the floor plan Richard had been using from his offered hand.

I didn't pay attention to what Tremayne and Eric were discussing. I thought it best to leave them to their male posturing. Eric had been clearly riling Tremayne up for some reason. Perhaps something had happened before I arrived to evoke that sort of response from ASI's tech guru. Eric was usually more circumspect than that.

By the time the pieces had been off loaded and only a few remained to be placed, Tremayne was alone in the office, peering at screens and tweaking buttons on the security panel. Clearly deep in concentration trying to come to terms with the highly technical system Eric had installed.

I glanced around for Nick's man, but couldn't see him. A quick flick of my eyes out of the front window showed his car had disappeared. I frowned at him not having said good-bye, but maybe

Tremayne had ordered him to leave without disturbing me. I think he was capable of behaving in that fashion.

The last sculpture was pushed into place with a resounding round of applause from Tremayne's removal men. They all said a short farewell to Richard, who just nodded his head distractedly, and then traipsed out of the door. I spun in a slow circle and took in the final - well near final, I still had some more minor tweaking to make over the weekend - effect.

"It looks stunning, Katie," Jerry said at my back.

I turned to look at my foreman. Jerry, obviously, contracted to many people to keep his business afloat, but we'd had a long time close working relationship. His craftsmanship and ability to realise my designs was faultless.

"Thank you, Jerry. You've outdone yourself again and at such short notice."

He smiled, a full beaming smile that cracked his slightly wrinkled, whisker covered face.

"You know we love working for you," he said. "Our side's all done, but if you spot anything I've missed, just give me a bell. I'll send your final invoice out on Monday."

"Excellent. I'll do what I can today, but by Monday my work, too, will be done."

We shook hands and he left the store, the bell on the doorway tinkling.

"We should celebrate," Tremayne said from over my shoulder. I hadn't realised he'd exited the office at last. "It looks brilliant."

I flicked my gaze over the room again, trying to see it from his eyes. I was pleased with what I saw.

"I have a few more small things to complete before it's done. I should really get on with them," I said.

"No, leave it for today, Catherine," Tremayne instructed. Following it up with, "I insist you accompany me to a late lunch. There'll be time enough over the weekend to polish things off, and unfortunately I have to fly away on business this evening, so I shan't see you again until Monday morning, when the store opens its doors."

Business out of town again. For a man hell bent on getting this project completed in such a short time-frame, he was determined not to be present for its execution. As a designer, I would normally be thrilled to be left to my own devices, but this contract had been high pressured, and his presence in the city would have alleviated some of that strain. I couldn't help feeling he liked to shirk his responsibilities. But then again, maybe he was just good at delegation.

I didn't particularly want to have a late lunch with him, considering our awkwardness of before. But had any other client suggested a celebratory meal so close to completion, I would have caved. Wining and dining is very much part of a self-employed interior designer's role.

I swallowed my discomfort and offered a small smile.

"Of course, a late lunch would be fine." I wasn't going to gush over it.

"Superb. We'll take my car."

"Thank you, but I'd rather meet you there. Where do you suggest?" I spoke with certainty, determined to cut all arguments off at the pass.

He hesitated, appearing a little flustered at my staunch refusal to share a vehicle. Maybe surprised I was making such a fuss. I couldn't tell with this man, but something still had me on edge. It could have just been his reaction to my turning down future work with him. Which made me realise I hadn't discussed my up-selling offer with him yet.

"How about Octave's on Parnell Road?" he suggested, naming an exclusive French cuisine eatery that was usually booked out well in advance.

"Splendid," I said, not doubting this man's ability to dine wherever he damn well liked, whenever he damn well pleased. "I have a proposal for you," I added, receiving the exact response I'd been hoping for.

"Oh, really?" he inquired. "How exciting." Well, maybe not the exact same response I had been hoping for, but at least he was no longer put out by my not sharing his car.

Octave's was typically busy when we arrived, but we were ushered to a private table upon arrival, the maître-d' almost appearing apologetic that the only available table was near the kitchen and not in the more favourable spots near the front of the restaurant instead. I half expected Tremayne to insist the poor man move other diners to accommodate us, by the way the maître-d' kept flicking concerned glances his way.

Thankfully, Richard didn't make an issue of it, just nodded his head and followed the little man to our table, pulling out my chair for me to sit down. To my utter surprise he placed both our orders before the man had a chance to escape.

"I hope you don't mind," he said flippantly, once the waiter had left, "but the Cassoulet is not to be missed."

I bit back my retort, thinking I didn't much like this version of Tremayne; bossy, entitled, overly privileged. He wasn't at all fazed by the maître-d's efforts to appease. He was completely at ease having someone bend over backwards to accommodate him. Where Jason could be demanding and dominant privately, Richard Tremayne seemed to publicly mimic, rather poorly I might add, Jason's behaviour. Failing to capture the masculine and extremely sexy mannerisms Jason portrayed, but instead coming across as more of a righteous bully.

He was the epitome of new money.

I wasn't comfortable with that realisation. But then, the only relationship I would be having with this man would be professional.

"So, tell me about your proposal, my dear," Tremayne encouraged.

I took a sip of the wine the waiter had poured before departing with our orders and offered my Katie Anscombe all-business smile. Then launched into my idea. By the time I finished, the meal had been served and Tremayne was resting his head, almost dreamily on his palm, elbow to table top, watching me intently.

"Well," I finished, "Would you be interested in an on going business arrangement such as that?"

"I would be interested in absolutely anything *on-going* with you, Catherine. I thought I made that perfectly clear."

"This would be purely business," I felt obliged to point out.

"Then I accept your proposal," he returned, making me relax into my seat with his lack of argument. I had expected more of a fight, especially when he'd mentioned, 'anything on-going with me'.

"Brilliant," I exclaimed, taking another sip of my drink. "I'll draft up a contract, then."

"I have another contract in mind," he murmured.

I blinked back at him as he leaned across the table towards me, making the whole exchange more intimate than it needed to be.

"You come and work for me exclusively." I sucked in an uncomfortable breath of air. "I have great plans, Catherine. I could offer you steady employment with vast rewards." The 'vast rewards' was said slowly, as though the words were rolling off his tongue. I leaned back in my chair, creating a modicum of distance between us. "It need only be for a limited time, but your reach, post our arrangement, would be immense. My studios will be across Australasia and with my name backing your designs, well, the sky is the limit, as they say."

He was cock sure of himself, I'd give him that. I hadn't even heard of the man before the Montgomery-Smith's soiree. I could hardly see *his name* having that much of an effect on my business reach. No, his intentions were to lock me into an agreement, which gave him exclusive rights to my time. I was thinking in an effort to persuade me of possible further *arrangements* we could make.

I cleared my throat before I replied. "I like variety, Mr Tremayne," I said, purposely using his surname to further distance myself from this conversation. "I appreciate the offer," I lied. "But my life is here in Auckland and I have no desire to reach beyond my current client base." All truth in that one.

He regarded me for a long moment, then reached forward and took a sip of his wine.

"And I cannot change your mind?" he asked, voice devoid of any emotion at all. It was a little creepy.

"No. I'm sorry," I added, feeling like I shouldn't be apologising, but unable to stop myself under his careful scrutiny.

"That is a shame, my dear," he announced, pulling his wallet from his breast pocket and throwing several large bills onto the table's surface. "I have a plane to catch," he suddenly announced, the previous conversation effectively dismissed.

I wasn't going to complain.

"I hope you have a successful business trip," I offered, standing from my chair, as he had already risen from his.

"Oh, I'm sure it will be more successful than today's," he said on a laboured sigh. This man was so dramatic. And changeable. Now he was cool, calm and remote, a far cry from the intimate and seductive he'd been going for before.

I wondered if he was mentally unstable. And not in the sexy, crazy way Jason was either.

"I'll see you on Monday for the opening?" he asked, placing a hand on the small of my back to guide me from the restaurant. I forced myself not to act on my fervent wish to shrug his unwanted touch off. I'd done enough damage today. I was just enormously relieved to have my car waiting for me out by the kerb.

"Yes, everything will be completed over the weekend, ready for your grand opening," I said, turning to face him on the footpath beside my car. His eyes lifted to my face.

"Take the rest of the afternoon off, Catherine," he instructed. "I've set the alarm on the studio and I'd like to leave it be until tomorrow. A test of the system, if you will."

The system didn't need testing, so his explanation seemed out of place.

"Very well, if that's what you'd like," I said, instead of questioning him on it. He was eccentric, his reasons were his own and wouldn't always make any sense.

"I do insist," he replied coolly. "You deserve an afternoon off." Changeable. My head was spinning keeping up with this man's mood swings.

He bid me farewell and wandered down the street to his own car, getting plenty of appreciative glances from the admiring females he passed. Why he was hung up on me, when he could clearly have any of the women on this street, was a mystery. But one I didn't really care to unravel.

I slipped into my car seat and pulled my cellphone eagerly from my satchel, thoughts of Richard Tremayne's unusual behaviour fleeing my mind in the wake of excitement that stole over me at my impending call. Jason answered on the first ring.

"Baby," he purred down the line, sounding equally as delicious over the phone as he did in person.

"I've been given the afternoon off," I said in way of greeting. "Do you have any plans?"

I could hear him suck in a slow breath of air and then let it out through pursed lips. He was thinking.

"My apartment. The code to the entrance is twenty-thirteen. The apartment door will be unlocked. Strip when you cross the threshold and wait for me on the edge of the bed. Understood?"

"Understood," I breathed down the line, already wet and wanting.

"And Kate?"

"Yes?"

"You may touch yourself."

Oh, OK. Hmm.

"Baby, you understand?"

Not really, but I'd play the game.

"I understand, Jason."

"Good girl." The line went dead.

I think I may have broken a few speed limits. I'm not sure, because I can't remember the relatively short drive from Parnell Road to Emily Place in the city centre. I miraculously found a park around the corner on Eden Crescent and practically ran the distance between that and Jason's apartment building's front door. My hand shook as I entered the entrance code on the keypad. The sound of my heels on the polished foyer floor couldn't block out the thundering of my pulse in my head. By the time I came to his floor, I was breathless.

And his door, to his apartment, was indeed unlocked.

I crossed the threshold and in one quick glance took in the entirety of his space. Kitchen, dining table, TV nook, French doors onto a balcony, huge raised bed off to the side, and even in through the open door to the boxed bathroom. He wasn't here.

This was the first time I'd been in Gen's old loft since she rented it out to her brother. The last time I was here was to help package up her personal belongings while she recuperated at Dominic's after surgery, having been shot by her ex-boyfriend. She never returned to the flat she'd lived in with her ex, and subleased it to Jason as soon as he was forced from the Army and accepted Nick's offer of employment.

Now the space belonged to a man. It still held that very industrial look; red brick walls, black exposed piping along the ceiling. But the place was slightly untidy and Jason's aftershave hung in the air. The bed unmade and the cover a utilitarian black. There were no cushions or throws on the couch to soften the image, and the vase Genevieve had always displayed on her dining room table was replaced with piles of sports magazines instead.

I smiled at the jumbled mess, feeling instantly at home in Jason's domain. And then began to strip my clothing, leaving a short trail from the door to the bed. Naked and entirely too exposed, considering the unfurnished French door windows, I perched on the edge of the large frame and sucked in much needed air.

Ten long minutes later I was beginning to get bored. After another ten, my foot was tapping and I'd started to hum an angry tune in my head to pass the time.

My cellphone chirped and whirred and buzzed in my

satchel across by the couch. I considered ignoring it, Jason had said 'perch on the end of the bed'. But the ringtone was Robin Thicke's *"Blurred Lines"* making me jump up and run towards it.

Jason.

"Hi," I said breathlessly down the line.

"You're not following my instructions," he purred back at me.

"What?" I demanded. "I'm naked and sitting on the edge of the bed like you said," I pointed out.

"What else did I say, Kate?"

Argh? Oh. "That I may touch myself," I mumbled.

"Louder."

I cleared my throat, glancing around the space and wondering how he knew I hadn't played with myself.

"That I may touch myself," I said, voice louder. "Are there cameras in this room?"

"Yes."

"You're watching me?"

"Yes."

Then I had a thought. "Is this monitored by ASI?"

"Baby," he chastised firmly. "You are mine." Oh, OK. So he'd cut the feed to ASI control, but he was watching the images himself. "So?" he demanded. "Are you going to do as I say, or do I have to punish you?"

"You're going to watch," I said, suddenly self-conscious.

Silence, then, "Place the phone on speaker next to you," he demanded softly, intimately. Ignoring my statement completely. But the instant his command left his mouth, my self-consciousness simply vanished.

Once I followed the instruction he added, "Move your hand to your right breast."

I immediately complied, feeling instantly aroused by his simple instruction, not having a hope in hell of denying him. Not wanting to, either.

"That's it," he encouraged. "Nipple between your thumb and finger. Pinch hard." I did. "Harder, Kate. I want to hear you."

I moaned and then gasped when I forced myself to pinch my nipple hard.

"Now flatten your hand and run it in light circles over the tip to soothe it. Imagine it's me."

I sighed at the image, pressing my breast up into my hand for further contact.

"Good girl. Now move back up the bed and lie down. Spread your thighs, baby. I want to see how wet you are."

"Where's the camera?" I asked.

"Don't worry about that, you just concentrate on the hand on your breast and know I'm getting hard watching this." I moaned, lying back on the cool rumpled surface of the sheets. "I'm stroking myself, Kate. I want to be buried balls deep in you right now, but I'm not even there. I'm miles away. I'm sitting in your office, in your house, watching you on your laptop screen."

"No," I moaned, wanting him with me, wanting him just outside the door, so he can barge in at the last second and bury himself 'balls deep' as he'd said.

"Yes, baby. So, you're going to have to make do without me, OK?"

Bastard. He laughed. Maybe I said that aloud?

"Reach up under the pillow to your left. Keep pinching your nipple," he commanded.

I stretched my body up his bed until I could slip my hand under his pillow, the smell of Jason drifting up off the disturbed sheets and wrapping around my frame. I sucked in a deeper breath of air and then stilled when my hand touched something solid.

"Pull it out, baby. I bought it just for you."

My hand withdrew, palm wrapped firmly around the cool cylindrical tapered shape of a vibrator. I surveyed it critically in the sunlight that filtered into the room. It had a variable speed adjustment at the base and a strange attachment consisting of two little prongs protruding halfway out of the unit angling up toward the tip.

"You can touch it with your other hand," Jason murmured. "Run your finger over the length, test the bunny ears."

"Bunny ears?" I asked, intrigued and slightly stunned at the same time. How on earth did this thing work?

"Can you picture it, Kate? When you slip that inside your wet, aching pussy, start the vibrations up and feel the ears as they stimulate your clit." Oh my Lord. "Or, you can be really adventurous, and turn it around, facing the other way. What do you think will get stimulated then, baby?"

Oh, dear. I wanted to try that.

"Save that until I'm with you." Jason interrupted my fervent visions. "Today is all about your clit. Lift your knees up and place your feet flat on the bed. Wider," he instructed when I automatically pulled my knees together to ease the ache that was now reaching untenable levels between my legs.

I whimpered when the cool air met my spreading folds.

"Not long now, baby," Jason encouraged, his breathing sounding laboured over the line. Images of him in my office stroking himself to me on the screen flooded my mind. I moaned. He was so going to pay for this torturous distance. "Turn the vibrator on," he husked down the line. "Place it at your entrance, but line the ears up, so when you sink it home your clit will beg for more."

Another moan as the vibrator started whirring and I gently placed it at my entrance, jerking slightly with the sudden cool sensation. The vibrations raced through my nerves, making me push the instrument harder without conscious thought. It was already halfway inside and I was writhing beneath it.

"Hungry, baby?" Jason whispered. "Want more?"

"Yes."

"Start thrusting, but pull the vibrator base upwards, so its tip is hitting the back of your pussy on each plunge inside."

I made the adjustment and found that the angle he'd chosen was for more than the sensation of being impaled against my back wall, but because the 'bunny ears' hit those bundle of nerves bang on. I cried out on the first connection, my hand pulling the vibrator back reflexively, but my body craving a repeat... and now!

"Three more times," Jason panted down the line. I wanted to sink the device deep and grind into it, but I forced myself to follow his command. "That good, baby?"

"Yes," I moaned.

"You want more?"

"Yes," I pleaded.

"You want me fucking you?"

Oh, dear God. Jason wasn't always quite so crass, but I could so do with him 'fucking' me right now.

"God, yes!" I said on a deep plunge of the vibrator.

"Fuck," Jason breathed. "You're going to make me come."

"I want you to come *in me*," I shot back, surprising myself with my bluntness.

Jason groaned, a long low sound down the line, his breaths now rapid, I could even hear the sound of his hand stroking his shaft. Then somehow he got himself under control and murmured, "I'm going to spank you for that, Kate. Behave!"

An almost hysterical chuckle left me.

"Keep the vibrator deep and ride it," Jason ordered, bringing my focus back to the here and now. "Tell me when you're close. We're coming together," he panted. "Even if I'm across the city, it's still you and me, baby. Understand?"

Ah, and here was Jason's lesson. He never did anything without just cause.

With a smile on my face I let the vibrator take me away. The device buried deep, as deep as I pictured Jason would be the moment I walked through my door at home to exact my revenge. And the ears gripped my little nub and stole all reason, blocking out all thought, and taking me somewhere no electronic device had ever done before.

"Jason," I managed, just as the orgasm was about to destroy me. "Oh God, Jason," I cried.

"I'm with you, baby," he called down the line, his voice husky and rasping, his moan matching mine in wretched bliss. "Let me hear you," he whispered through his own efforts. "Say it when you come."

Say what? His name? That we're together, that it's him and me, *us*, even though we're apart?

Or...

"I love you," I screamed, as the world fractured and my heart stilled, and I disappeared for a few seconds to somewhere else. Somewhere Jason took me, whether he was beside my body or down the other end of the line, watching me pleasure myself on a closed circuit security screen.

"Kate!" Jason cried out, joining me a moment later. "Oh God, Kate," he moaned. A few breathless seconds passing as he brought himself down, then he added, "You drive me crazy, baby."

I started giggling. That was rich, coming from him. Mr Crazy personified. My Mr Crazy.

I lay limp on the mattress trying to catch my breath, the vibrator switched off and discarded beside me. I'd be cleaning that up and bringing it with me, without a doubt.

"Kate," Jason whispered, breaking into the my plans for the rest of the night. "Come home, baby. I'm waiting."

I let an extremely happy breath out on those words. "OK," I said, rolling over onto my stomach and stretching like a well fed cat.

"You look beautiful," Jason murmured. "So fucking beautiful. You steal my breath."

I realised how appropriate his words were when my chest began a slow, deep ache. Because as soon as he'd spoken so tenderly, all breath had left me too.

We were both breathless because of the other. And I'd gladly die a thousand breathless deaths for one more moment with this crazy, slightly broken man.

CHAPTER 24

I KNEW THERE WAS A REASON WHY I LIKED THAT MAN

A BANGING ON MY FRONT DOOR WOKE US. I GROANED SOFTLY and Jason swore under his breath.

"Open up, it's the Police," sent us bolt upright in bed, wide awake.

"What the fuck?" Jason exclaimed, climbing out from under the sheets and searching for his jeans with jerking hand movements. He slipped them on without bothering with boxers first.

"Stay here," he grunted, running a hand through his hair and then scrubbing his face roughly awake. It was early. The clock beside the bed read six o'clock. We'd fallen asleep wrapped up in each other around two; those bunny ears had had a work out. But four hours was not nearly long enough to face policemen on the porch.

I lay back on the bed pulling the covers around me, but my ears were tuned to the sound of Jason opening the front door. My heart was pounding, adrenaline pumping through my veins, making it difficult to think, let alone listen. But still I strained to hear his greeting, conscious that early morning police visits did not normally bring good news. I wanted to get dressed and face it.

But then, I didn't want to move for fear of the why they were here.

"What is it?" Jason demanded.

"Is this the residence of Miss Catherine Anscombe?"

"Yes. What do you want?" Jason still demanding.

"We need to ask her a few questions. Preferably down at Central Police Station." Oh God. What was this about? If it was a death in the family, questions wouldn't be asked, would they? My body shook uncontrollably under the covers of the bed.

"What about?" Jason semi-repeated.

"A burglary at Tremayne Arts."

Oh my God. I sat upright in the bed again, then quickly threw my legs over the side and started hunting for some clothes.

"I'll just get her up, then," Jason murmured, but I was too busy trying to find clean underwear - Jason rule or not, one didn't go the Police Station without knickers on - so my concentration was shot.

"Are you Jason Cain?" the policeman asked, snapping me back into focus and making me pause with one leg in my underwear and one out.

"Yeah," Jason replied.

"This is for you. From Detective Pierce. He said you'd probably be here." I frowned and then heard the door click shut, presumably in the policeman's face.

I was standing in my panties and bra when Jason reached the doorway, looking down at a plain envelope in his hands.

"A burglary?" I said. Jason nodded, breaking the seal on the envelope and pulling a single sheet of paper out. "What does it say?"

"Nothing that could be good," he replied, handing the paper over to me.

I scanned the words, written in messy masculine scrawl.

Jason,

Whatever you do, don't accompany Katie to the Station. Await my or Dominic's call.

Ryan Pierce.

Detective Ryan Pierce was a police detective in the CIB; the

Criminal Investigations Bureau of the Auckland City Police. He was also good friends with Dominic and Nick, having gone to school with them both. What on earth was he trying to say in that none too helpful note?

I raised my eyebrows at a frowning Jason. He shook his head and took the paper from my outstretched hand.

"Get dressed, baby. You're going to have to go with the cops. I'll try phoning Dominic now and see what the fuck's happening. Otherwise, I'll follow behind in my car and wait for your call."

"Will you come into the Station?" I asked, pulling some tailored trousers out of my closet and slipping them on. The skirt rule was defunct today too, I needed to be fully clothed to face the Police.

"I trust Pierce," he said, reaching for his phone and scrolling through the numbers in his address book.

By the time I was fully and respectably dressed Jason had given up trying to reach either Dominic, my father, or Nick. All three not answering their cellphones. He could have tried Papa at home, but the Police had started banging on the front door again reminding us I had an escort waiting.

"I'll be right behind you. I won't be far away," Jason murmured, walking the short distance across the room to me and lifting his hands to cup my cheeks.

"Why do you think they need to talk to me?" I was just Tremayne's designer, he'd been the one to lock and secure the premises last night.

"I don't know, Kate," Jason said softly. "Maybe with Tremayne out of town they need you to look at the damage and assess what items have been taken."

That made sense, I should take my satchel with the floor plan and labelled pieces we put in place yesterday. "Do you think much would have been stolen?" My mind was whirling, trying to guess answers where there couldn't possibly be any yet.

"Baby," Jason murmured, "I just don't know."

I nodded, my face still cupped gently in big hands.

"Take a breath," he instructed. "Nice and slow." I did what he asked, feeling myself centre and calm down, just as he intended. "Good. Now, kiss me, Kate."

A small smile tipped my lips up and I leaned forward willingly to breach the short distance between us pressing my lips to his. Jason kept his hands on my cheeks and flicked his tongue along my bottom lip, sweeping inside when I moaned and opened my mouth. The kiss was slow and gentle, full of meaning; his love for me, his need for me, his desire to make me feel complete and sated. He was still trying to calm me down, even through a kiss.

We pulled apart, when the Police announced their presence again, and caught our breaths. Jason leant his head against my forehead and inhaled deeply.

"You know the drill, Kate. Make sure you have Dominic or your father representing you before they ask any questions."

The calmness he'd instilled, from that beautiful kiss, vanished. Of course, I'd been raised by a lawyer, I knew the drill as well as he did. Just because he'd reminded me didn't mean he thought I truly needed legal representation.

I nodded, took a deep breath in and then pulled out of his clasp. He looked a little pained at the separation. I could relate to that. No matter how much I told myself this was all routine and nothing to be alarmed about, it just didn't reach my rapidly beating heart. That unsettling feeling I'd had on and off throughout this entire Tremayne project was back with a vengeance, but I had no idea exactly what was triggering it. And keeping Jason close seemed the most natural thing to do in the face of such uncertainty.

"OK," I said resolutely, preparing myself for whatever lay ahead. "I'll grab my satchel and go."

"I'll see you soon. Understood?"

Understood. Even in this context the word felt so familiar that for the briefest of moments calmness invaded my mind.

"Understood," I whispered. Jason leaned forward and kissed me softly on the lips, then followed me to the front door.

My satchel was where he'd left it when I got home last night, having taken it from my grasp as I opened the door, and placed it by the hall table so my hands were free to molest him... at his instruction. I shook those rather delightful memories from my mind and faced the two uniformed officers outside. They looked impatient, so I thought it best to give them some Katie Anscombe cheer.

"Good morning, Officers," I said with a soft smile. "Sorry to keep you, but I'm afraid Jason had some trouble waking me up. Of course, I'd be happy to assist you in your inquiries. Shall we go?"

As suspected they both relaxed. My father had always advised to offer nothing worthy of argument, then watch as the wind is stolen from your opponent's sails. Too many people gave a defence when it wasn't even warranted. Getting out of this trip to the Police Station was not going to happen, therefore there was no point fighting it.

"Thank you, Miss Anscombe," one of the Uniforms replied. "Just this way," he indicated a marked Police car sitting behind my BMW.

We started heading down the footpath, one policeman in front of me, one behind.

"Kate!" Jason called, making all three of us turn to see him standing on the top step of my stoop, hands holding onto the porch overhang above his head, bare chest flexing in the early morning sun. He'd done it on purpose, bless him. My eyes automatically devouring every contour and inch, forgetting for a moment that I had more pressing issues to contend with right now. "I'll see you soon, baby," he said with a smirk.

I was smiling when I slipped into the rear of the squad car.

At six forty-five in the morning Central Police Station on Cook Street was humming. I'm not sure when morning shift change is for the boys in blue, but there seemed to be more than expected moving about the place. We entered through an internal door from an underground carpark, bypassing the public waiting area completely and emerging into the inner sanctum. Maybe that was why there seemed to be so many cops, we had come out in the bowels of the operation.

I was ushered directly through CIB - it had been labelled on the double doors in bronze coloured lettering - into what I assumed was an interview room and told to please wait. I *had* been offered a tea or coffee to drink, but declined. No one had confiscated my satchel or bothered to check whether I had concealed weapons inside. I felt decidedly uncomfortable when I realised I had left my Kombatan knife hidden in the lining. But consoled myself with the fact that had I been suspected of anything, I would have received a full body search, I'm sure.

It was a full quarter hour before the door to the room opened. Time enough for me to become nervous all over again. Deep voices in hushed conversation preceded the person who was entering, from the volume I couldn't tell who to expect. Not that I would have necessarily known them. But I was hoping it would be Detective Pierce or his partner, Detective Stone.

It was neither.

Dominic strode into the room, worry making fine lines crease his stoic face.

"Dom," I said on a breath of air, standing as soon as I saw him.

He shut the door behind him and came directly around the table I'd been sitting at, wrapping me up in his big arms. I sunk into his embrace for a moment, crushing his suit jacket, and then found my courage. Things couldn't possibly be that bad. "What's going on?" I demanded, pulling away and sitting down in my chair again, smoothing the material in my trouser legs; a nervous tick.

Dom sighed, he knew my tells, but took the seat opposite and leaned forward, elbows resting on the table's surface, hands clasped in front. His knuckles soon became white.

"It's not good, Katie." I shook my head at him, not understanding how it could be *not good*. Especially the 'not good' said in the way my brother had just said it; resigned and troubled.

"What's going on?" I repeated, my voice steady, my words sure, my heart and mind not.

"At some undetermined time this morning Tremayne Arts was burgled, the entire stock cleaned out. The alarm system did not pick up on a problem." Oh dear, how? "No one saw anyone suspicious in the vicinity at any time throughout the night. ASI was not aware that the building had been compromised, even though the front door had been left propped open." Propped open? What a ridiculous slip-up for any burglar to have made. "A *different* security firm noticed the breach when they did their scheduled drive-by for one of the neighbouring businesses. They advised the Police, who entered the building at five. The security camera tapes were missing, but the alarm system *was running*; it hadn't been deactivated." What? "Despite this, no recorded triggers had been sent to ASI control. They insist they had no idea something was wrong. The Police say the system could have been purposely installed incorrectly to effect this exact outcome."

I felt sick. There was no way in hell that Nick's firm would have done this. Why? For one and half million dollars worth of art? And so poorly? It was ridiculous. And although everything pointed to ASI, why would they set themselves up for this type of fall?

"Nick's been set up," I said, stunned at my conclusion.

Dominic just grunted, all the confirmation I needed. "What do you know about this Tremayne guy? Tell me everything."

I let a slow breath of air out. Richard Tremayne. There was just something not quite right about the man from the moment I met him. What was his game? What was the point of all of this? Insurance fraud? I wondered what sort of financial position Tremayne was actually in.

"He's... strange. I thought eccentric," I offered.

"You'll have to give me more than that, Katie."

OK then. From the beginning.

"I met him at the Montgomery-Smith's sitting room reveal party. I didn't see him inside their house, I met him on the terrace when I was getting a breath of fresh air."

"When was this?" Dom asked, pulling a pad and pen from his pocket to write my words down. Just like a cop, which made me think, where were the cops?

"Where's Pierce?" I asked quietly.

Dom's eyes flicked up to mine. "He's given me half an hour with you before the cameras start rolling and he walks in. Out of courtesy."

Oh. Bloody hell.

"Am I a suspect?"

"Not at this stage. More a witness to the events."

"A witness against ASI and Nick."

"Yes," he murmured.

"Why am I not a suspect?"

"Should you be? You designed his interior, your contract was for that."

Oh boy. I ran a nervous hand through my hair, flattening it into its ponytail.

"Katie?"

"Did Nick not mention I held the contract to liaise with ASI on security instalment at Tremayne Arts? Tremayne signed nothing directly with Nick."

"Jesus fucking Christ!" Dominic burst out. "No, he did not."

Nick was covering for me, giving me time, because it would come out in the wash eventually. He would have guessed that. I sighed.

"The job was unusual from the start," I murmured. "Tremayne had a ridiculously short time-frame in which to have the design and showroom completed. I only took the contract because he wanted a look and materials similar to the Montgomery-Smith's. Plus I had already several hard furnishings in mind that I hadn't yet used else-where, which meant I didn't need as long as usual to draft a concept, or even to acquire the finished decorations."

I wasn't going to mention I was distracted by a broken heart at the time and not of sound mind, and *that's* probably the main reason why

I took a job with such a short lead-in time. It wasn't really going to help my case, I didn't think.

"Go on," Dom encouraged, making notes here and there throughout my speech.

"From the start I found him changeable, one minute flirting, the next distant and demanding."

"Flirting?" Dominic interrupted. I couldn't tell if his shock was due to the fact I'm his sister and he wouldn't want *anyone* flirting with me, or that it was highly inappropriate for a client to flirt.

"Yes. He made it clear, and has repeatedly done so, that he wanted us to be more than just business acquiescences."

"How did you react?"

How did he think I reacted? "I turned him down, as politely as I could."

"How did he take that?"

"Again changeable. One minute politely resigned, the next petulant and then he'd try all over again to convince me to either start an exclusive contract with him, for his planned art rooms all over Australasia, or invite me to dine or share a drink."

Dom sat back in his chair looking contemplative. "Eric mentioned that Tremayne seemed unreasonably fixated on you. Gushing your praises to him on Friday when they went over the security system. So much so, that it even surprised Eric, and we all know how relaxed he normally is with that sort of thing." That sort of thing being flirtations.

"Did it surprise Eric so much that he was distracted?" I asked, my mouth ahead of my mind as I was just connecting the dots and coming up with Eric's unprofessional behaviour riling Tremayne up in the shop.

Dom's shrewd eyes flicked down to mine. "I think that could be assumed. What are you suggesting, Katie?"

"Someone falsely installed or changed that security system. And we both know Eric is the best in his field. He would not have made a mistake."

"So, he was distracted, and Tremayne did something to thwart the instalment. Very clever, sis. Not just a pretty face."

"Insurance fraud?" I asked my earlier theory.

"It is something Pierce and Stone have questioned. At this point, however, they have to be seen doing their jobs, hence the entire team from ASI being interviewed right now."

"They're all here?"

"The artwork was worth several million dollars. This is not small fry."

"Tremayne said it was estimated between one and one point five," I replied, stunned.

"Did he write that figure down?"

Oh. "No, just mentioned it in passing."

"It's insured for six million," Dominic advised, voice serious.

I sank back in my chair appalled. Why the hell did that man choose us for his misdeeds?

Just then a knock sounded on the door and Detective Ryan Pierce walked in. He looked calm and collected, but a muscle was jumping along his jawline, making his dark brown goatee beard quiver. He was not a happy camper and Ryan Pierce angry, was not something I wanted to ever witness again.

"Dom," he said with a nod of his head, then turned intense brown eyes on me. "Katie, you doing OK?"

I shrugged. "I'll be all right when this is all sorted, Ryan."

"I can imagine."

"My client will cooperate with any questions you may have," Dominic said in his lawyerly tone, getting up and moving himself around to my side of the table to take a seat.

Tension rode the air and I sucked in a breath, while my stomach plummeted at the change of atmosphere and what it would mean for me. Dominic wanted to establish a professional environment right off the bat, but from the look of Pierce, he wasn't impressed with the brush off.

"Katie's free to go," Ryan ground out, making both Dom and I jerk our heads back in surprise. "And for your information, Anscombe, I'm putting my neck on the chopping block over this."

My gaze swung between the two men, Dominic bristling from Pierce throwing his *professionalism* back in his face, and Ryan scowling from, I should think, the whole sordid affair.

"Thank you," Dom forced out between stiff lips.

"Yeah, well. For some reason a certain piece of evidence has been misplaced. It'll be found by five pm tomorrow, in amongst Harvey's car magazines on his desk."

Dom coughed, it was meant to be a laugh. I was just trying to think about what the evidence would have been. I was going with my contract, the one that outlined my liaising with ASI for the security instalment at Tremayne Arts.

"You've got until then to do what you can to clear Nick and the others," Pierce was saying, his eyes on me and not my brother.

But Dominic was the one to answer. "You think Katie can do something about this?" He sounded mildly incredulous.

Pierce swung his now tired looking eyes at Dom. "I think Katie has someone ideally suited on the outside of ASI who can."

He meant Jason. Who was no longer an employee of Nick's and therefore, as yet, not being pulled in for questioning.

Pierce turned towards the door to leave. "You've got fifteen minutes to get her out of the building, at which point the Captain will be back from his barber's appointment and if he sees her, he might just be reminded of her involvement in this case. Oh, and another thing," he added, not looking over his shoulder as he stood at the opened door, "we're concentrating on hard copy evidence from ASI as well as interviews today, by first thing tomorrow we'll be sending the technical forensic team in... if this case follows the path it's currently on."

With that he let the door click shut at his back. Dominic glanced down at his watch to check the time, I was guessing to see how long he had to get me out of the building before the Captain returned, and then started gathering his notepad and pen from the table's surface.

"Come on, let's get you out of here. Where's Jason?"

"Probably sitting in his SUV out the front of the building," I replied, following behind him.

Dom swung his head over his shoulder and smiled. It was a knowing smile, mixed with a huge dollop of relief.

"I knew there was a reason why I liked that man," he quipped, then strode through the open door.

Brothers!

CHAPTER 25

PFFT!

JASON JUMPED OUT OF THE DRIVER'S SIDE OF HIS CAR AS SOON AS he saw us walking through the front doors of Central Police Station. I was wrapped up in his arms before we'd made it across the street, his face nestled in the curve of my neck, his chest expanding on an obviously relieved inhale of air.

"Kate," he murmured, lips coasting over my skin. "Are you OK, baby?"

Dom cleared his throat. "Can we do this out of sight of the cops? Katie's got a reprieve, not a complete pardon."

Jason flashed the most threatening glare towards my brother, making Dom take a slow step back, well out of reach.

"Cain," he said evenly, "we need to bury the hatchet. For Katie," he added.

"He's right, baby," I said softly, placing a kiss on the edge of his firm jaw. His whole body melted at my touch and the use of our nickname for each other. It had been loud enough for Dom to hear, evidenced by another clearing of his throat, this time uncomfortable.

I think Jason liked that; making Dom uneasy, making him witness openly how much I belonged to him. Why did I do it? I know my crazy man.

"The car then," Jason conceded, leading us both back to his SUV. He opened the front passenger door for me and helped me inside, but left Dom to his own devices to slip into the rear. Jason rounded the hood and sat behind the steering wheel, he didn't start the vehicle up, just turned to face the back seat. "What happened?" he demanded.

Dom outlined the entire wretched business, by the end of it I was exhausted and nervously wringing my hands in my lap, picking up on Jason's anger, feeling the rage pouring off him in waves of heat.

"What do we know about this Tremayne guy?" he asked, hands clenched in fists on his thighs. I wished he'd reach over to soothe me, but Jason was in no mood to offer affection; he was fit to throw a fist, not entwine fingers in mine.

"Nothing," Dom admitted. "Harvey Stone admitted he's just popped up out of nowhere. No priors, no history. Zip. We only know what Katie's told us."

And that brought Jason's anger filled gaze back to me. I shrank back in my seat, not missed by him, and he sighed. Ran a hand over his face in frustration and then purposely reached out to clasp his fingers with mine. His thumb running over the skin of my knuckles was too quick to be considered soothing, but it was progress, nonetheless.

"Something Pierce said," Dom added speculatively, "just before we left. The tech forensic team won't be trawling through ASI's systems until tomorrow morning. He wouldn't have mentioned that if it hadn't have been helpful to our case."

"I'm not an employee anymore," Jason pointed out. "I wouldn't have access to their systems. Nick would have seen to that."

"I'm not sure. I'm going to head back in and have a few quiet words with my brother, if I hear of anything that could help, I'll phone." Dom opened up the door, ready to climb out. "In the meantime," he said looking back up at Jason, "if you've still got contacts in the Army, now would be a perfect moment to reinstate them."

Dom offered me a warm smile, which was shadowed by the concern obvious on his face, and then he slipped out of the car and crossed the street back towards the entrance to the Police Station. Silence followed his exit for some time, then Jason reached his free hand up to wrap around the nape of my neck softly.

"How are you really?" he asked.

"Scared," I admitted. "None of this makes any sense. If it is insurance fraud, why choose ASI and me to make it happen?"

"Easy target? Wrong place wrong time?" Jason suggested, but from the tone of his voice he didn't believe his words either.

"Tremayne sought me out," I mused. "He knew of me when he approached me at that party. I'm beginning to wonder if he even knew the Montgomery-Smiths at all. He never went inside, I never saw him with them. He cornered me on the terrace and then left."

Jason sat back and let a long controlled breath of air out. I realised why he was being so careful when he next spoke; eyes forward, staring out of the windscreen and not at me.

"Did you invite him to Gen and Dom's barbecue, or did he invite himself?"

His hand had stilled in mine, his body had tensed all over. He was still breathing, but I think that had more to do with his training than his emotional state.

Thankfully I could answer this question easily.

"He cornered me. Told me he had to fly away on business the next day and the time constraints of the project made it seem logical we meet that evening for drinks to discuss his requirements, in particular the pieces he wanted the design crafted around."

"You could have arranged to meet him after the barbecue," Jason all but accused.

"Yes," I admitted, feeling dreadful revisiting this. "I was not myself," I offered as an excuse.

His head turned on his neck, still resting back against the headrest, and sad eyes looked at me.

"Is that all?" he asked. What did he mean is that all? I was not myself because of him!

"That's quite enough, don't you think?" I spat back.

"Kate, do you know what I felt when I heard you at the door to Gen's house telling Dom you'd brought a friend? A friend called Richard?"

I swallowed painfully, my throat thick with emotion. I knew exactly what he felt, because I'd been immobile with fear that he'd have one of his blonde busty bimbos with him, and I'd have to see her fawning all over his body. A body I had claimed as mine for such a short period of time.

"It could have gone any number of ways," I pointed out, turning my head away to stare blindly out of the window.

"You think I wouldn't have been hurt?"

This was not all about him! "You left me, remember?! Not the other way around."

"It doesn't matter," he said dismissively, releasing his grip on my hand and starting the car.

"Of course it matters," I mumbled. "It mattered to me."

"What did?" he bit out, pulling the vehicle into mid morning traffic.

"If you'd brought one of your bimbos," I said softly. Silence met my entirely too honest admission. Then the car rolled to a stop around the corner in the first vacant carpark he could find.

He turned to me, a small smirk playing on his lips. "Is that why you caved to his suggestion? So you could wear him like armour when faced with a potential date on my arm?"

"Blonde busty bimbo," I said through gritted teeth. "Let's not call them something they were not."

He started chuckling. "Baby."

"Don't call me baby."

He laughed harder.

"It's not funny either. You're a playboy. Everyone knew it."

"Was," he whispered, the laughter stopping completely.

I frowned at him in confusion.

"I *was* a playboy, Kate, you're right. But none of them meant a thing. Nothing. And there were no *blonde busty bimbos* after I'd tasted you. There was no one, after you. How could there be? There's only one you."

I stared at him, my chest tight for lack of breath. My mind spinning trying to catch up on where this conversation had taken us. I let a slow breath of air out and then blinked a few times to clear my head.

"I brought Richard to the barbecue because I thought you'd have a woman with you and I couldn't face it," I whispered. "I'm not sure if it was coincidence, or if he took advantage of my state of mind to turn up and talk shop with Brook, making it look like chance. Instigating the entire evening, in order to scope out ASI and my connection to it, in order to put his master plan in place."

"There now, baby," Jason purred, reaching up and cupping my nape again, then leaning forward to lay a soft kiss on my forehead. "That wasn't too hard to admit, was it?" And he wasn't referring to my speculation on Tremayne.

"Jackass," I muttered, but my lips were twitching.

"Language, baby. It doesn't suit you." But he was smirking too. "So," he said, getting the car started and out in traffic again, "the fuck-knuckle could have planned this all along. You were a mark, a means to an end." His dancing eyes flicked towards mine. "A sex-kitten means to an end, but thankfully you've got taste and he didn't get far on that front."

Taste. I was smitten with someone else. A smitten sex-kitten. A bubble of laughter sprang up my throat. I coughed to clear it away.

"So what now?" I said, bringing myself, more than Jason, back on track. "We don't even know where Tremayne is. He didn't tell me where his business meeting was being held, if it was a business meeting at all."

"Exactly. He could still be in Auckland, or as I suspect, *is* out of town, providing himself a decent alibi. My guess though, is he'll come to us. How many people have their workplace burgled, over six million dollars worth of artwork stolen, and not return to the scene of the crime to liaise with the Police? If he wants to keep this charade up, he'll be back, if not already landed."

"But what then? He's here, the artwork's... where?"

"*That* is the more pressing matter," Jason admitted. "We'll get to Tremayne tonight, I should think. The artwork and the trail leading there is more important for now."

"Can you get anyone in the Army involved? Would that help us?"

"I doubt it, but I can make some calls. The Army has access to satellite imagery. If we can get coverage of Auckland from sun-up, we might find something of use."

"What about during the dark, when the shop was supposedly burgled?"

"That's going to require another source. Radar."

"Radar? As in radio waves to determine distance?"

"No, as in Auckland's underground radar. The one Nick uses to see what's hot and what's not in the underbelly of Auckland crime."

Oh. "And to use that...?"

"I need access to ASI."

Great. "Great," I said with defeat.

"Kate," Jason chastised. "Why do you think Pierce warned Dom about the tech forensic team?"

Oh. "Letting you know how long you had to use ASI's systems before you'd be caught."

"Exactly, baby. Your brother is not stupid. Either he already had my access cleared, due to some intel he'd heard on the radar. Or Pierce gave him sufficient unobserved time, after the arresting officers arrived at his door, to reinstate my clearance. Either way, Pierce knows that's what I'd have to use in order to get any leads. He's giving us time."

And the means to figure this out and get Nick and his team out of custody.

"Do we go to ASI now?"

Jason scoffed. "*We* are doing nothing. *You* are going home and waiting for my or Dom's call. *I* am going into ASI, stealthily. The place could still be under surveillance. The cops aren't stupid either, even if Pierce is making their jobs more complicated than usual."

"Now wait just a minute, Jason Cain," I started, turning in my seat and placing my hands on my hips.

"Ah-oh," Jason joked, shaking his head and keeping eyes forward, smirk in place.

"I am more than capable of helping. You might need a look-out."

"Pfft," was his reply.

"I'm good on a computer, I spend all day on one. I've watched Eric work. Are you good on a computer?"

"Of course! Do you think the Army just teaches us to disassemble a rifle and rub mud on our faces for camouflage? They're a little more technologically savvy than that, Kate."

My turn to *pfft*.

I received a glare for that comeback.

"I will be armed," I offered.

"No you won't be. Because you won't need to be. Because you won't even be in danger in the first place."

"It's ridiculous to do this alone, when you have resources at your command and..."

"You're not a resource," he interrupted, "even if you are at my command." Smirk.

I huffed in frustration. "I'm coming with."

"Kate," he warned.

"Jason," I imitated his growly tone.

He pulled the SUV to an abrupt stop, making me fall forward in my seat and have the seatbelt dig into my chest. I wheezed out a breath and looked out the window. We were home.

"Get out of the car," he growled.

"No," I replied, crossing my arms over my chest and glaring back.

"Woman! Don't make come around there and haul you out over my shoulder."

"It won't work."

"Three."

Oh God, he was giving me the countdown from three.

"Nah-uh," I replied ineloquently. I shook my head to emphasise my inarticulate response.

"Two," he ground out between clenched teeth.

"What? You're going to go all caveman on me and make a scene in the middle of the street?" What happens at one? We didn't get to one last time. One was still a mystery. Would I like one? I was thinking, right now, probably not.

"One!" he shouted, making me jerk as he opened his door and stormed around the hood of the car. I reached up and slowly lowered the lock at my window, my eyes meeting the furious chestnut of his.

We stared at each other for several seconds and then he smiled. It was slow and wicked.

"Zero," he mouthed. I didn't needed to hear the whispered words, I could make them out quite clearly through the closed window. His intent obvious and the hungry stare holding my gaze making me breathless.

He lifted up his hand, which had been out of sight at the side of his leg, and pressed the button on his remote access key chain. The door unlocked and he jerked it open.

"Easy or hard way, Kate?" he asked, still smiling that wicked smile.

Oh, hell. "Hard!" I bit back at him.

"Baby," he said shaking his head. "I was so hoping you'd say that."

My seatbelt came undone and he leaned in to grip my body, under my arms. I batted away his hands, wishing my satchel was closer, not in the back footwell of the car out of reach. Then remembered that Jason usually had a knife sheathed at his waist, so I started searching for that instead.

I don't know why I was fighting him. Adrenaline had gotten the better of me. The morning's events taking their toll and making all reason abandon my thought process. I just felt the need to fight back.

To argue this point with Jason. To not let him out of my sight for fear he'd never come back.

And not because he didn't want to. I knew he would always come back if he could. But if something happened to him, and God alone knows what was going on inside that mentally unstable mind of Tremayne's, he may not be *able* to come back. The thought of losing him now spurred me on, even as I was hauled from the vehicle screaming, and thrown over Jason's shoulder like a sack of spuds.

I started rifling through the various pouches and holsters dotted along Jason's belt. He realised what I was doing so landed a swift smarting slap to my butt cheek, making me yelp, lose focus long enough for him to get the front door open and get us inside, before I started struggling against his hold and flicking the safety latch on his knife loose.

My fingers wrapped around the hilt and then I was suddenly on my back on my bed, the springs making me rebound from the force with which Jason had thrown me, my hands losing their grip on the knife and making it tumble to the wooden floor with a clatter.

A loud click, followed by a second, filled the space between Jason's grunts and my screams. Then the cool sensation of metal at my wrist.

I stared at the handcuffs attaching me to the bedpost and turned a frosty glare on Jason, who was bending down to pick up the knife and with a smirk in my direction, sheathed it out of sight on his belt.

"Kate, Kate, Kate," he murmured. "Haven't had you tied up for my pleasure before."

"Come a little closer, *baby*, and I'll show how much pleasure I can give," I taunted.

He started laughing. "Feisty," he said with a shake of his head and then promptly sat down on the end of the bed, just out of kicking distance. I should know, I tried to land a foot to his privates.

"Argh!" I screamed, rattling the handcuffs. "Release me!"

"Not gonna happen, baby. You are your own worst enemy. Just

because you can flip a knife without getting a cut, does not mean you can run hell for leather into danger and I'd let you."

"You arrogant arsehole! You don't get a say in the matter!"

"Language! And I'd say my word is the only one that matters right now, wouldn't you?" he asked, flicking the handcuffs' key in his hand.

"Why are you doing this?" I asked on a defeated sigh.

"Because I love you, Kate," he replied without hesitation. "And I can't lose you again."

We stared at each other for longer than Nick and ASI had to spare. Then he stood up from the bed and went into the bathroom, returning with a glass of water and the waste-paper basket, which happened to be water tight.

Oh good grief, no. I was not peeing in that!

He placed the glass on the table next to the bed within my reach and the basket on the floor beside the bed.

I picked the water up and hurled it against the wall across the room. Glass shattered and liquid dripped onto the floor in a satisfying display of my rage.

Jason just stared at me, shocked.

"I can't lose you again either," I said, having now got his full attention.

I watched his chest rise and fall too quickly. I watched the chestnut in his eyes fade to warm, melted chocolate brown. And I watched as his shoulders fell and his face fell with them, and his heart was displayed openly on his sleeve.

"Kate," he pleaded.

"Together. You said it was you and me, always."

"Even when we're apart, baby," he reminded me. Damn! That argument wasn't going to cut it.

"Three years I've been training, Jason. I know how to defend myself." He stared at me, unmoved. "You wanted to see my knife collection," I offered my own little reminder. "Then let me show you how good I actually am."

"Do you really think me seeing your knives will change my mind?"

I answered honestly. "Yes. Yes I do." His eyes narrowed, but I could see the curiosity behind those captivating orbs. It was a piece of the puzzle he'd been trying to fit together, the little part of me that surprised him the most. Jason liked being surprised, but more than anything he liked a challenge. Figuring me out had been his biggest challenge yet.

"Just remember," he said, reaching over to release the handcuffs from my wrist, "I can have you back in these within minutes."

I rubbed my wrist and eyed him warily, then offered my best Katie Anscombe smile.

"Baby," I said with a smirk. My tone similar to when I used 'darling' on anyone else. Jason frowned. "It might be wise to remember that every blade I show you, I know exactly how to use."

He took a step back, his frown turning into that wicked smile he so often wore in my presence.

"Lead on, Ms Anscombe. Do your worst."

Oh, I wasn't planning on doing my worst. I was planning on appealing to the soldier in Jason, on enticing the 'Army' out of the man. I was planning on doing my *wickedest*, and going straight for his Achilles heel.

And he thought *I* needed the protection. *Pfft!*

CHAPTER 26

INTO THAT DARK ABYSS

It's not like I had a room decked out in rows and rows of gleaming, sharp knives. This wasn't a movie, but real life. Although, being an interior designer meant I did have access to competent builders and the ability to draw up architectural plans that made my little cubby of blades difficult to detect.

I stood up from the bed and rubbed my wrist again. I'd only been handcuffed for mere minutes, but it was enough to know that sort of bedroom play was not something I would tolerate easily. Jason watched me ease the faux ache in my wrists with keen eyes. I could only hope he'd come to the right conclusion and avoid metal restraints from now on.

Of course, if he were to use a fabric, such as velvet ribbons or silk scarves... I shook my head to clear those images. Being around Jason in any capacity played havoc on my imagination. But then, he'd opened a Pandora's Box when he introduced me to his alter ego. I wasn't sure if he realised that yet.

I walked past him into my wardrobe. The small bungalow I'd refurbished had included three moderate sized bedrooms when I purchased it. By the time I was through remodelling, it was made up of two, plus a small office, ensuite bathroom off the master and walk-in-wardrobe. A girl has to have her priorities straight. And once Kombatan became an important - and secretive - part of my lifestyle, a hidden panel, or cupboard, behind the floor to ceiling mirror at one end of the wardrobe.

I stepped up to the mirror, glanced over my shoulder to see Jason hovering right there, a curious and eager glint in his chocolate eyes, then turned back to see our reflections in the glass. I held his gaze over my shoulder for a moment, then reached up and pressed the right hand corner of the glass firmly with my thumb, making the mirror retract electronically in a smooth glide and soft hum of mechanics.

Behind it was revealed a dozen shelves laden with various sharp implements, each spotlit with LED lighting, all stacked in made-to-measure alcoves, to ensure no damaged while stored. I turned back to face Jason, whose eyes were scanning the entirety of the unit, cata-loguing and identifying each weapon, and waited.

"Ordered and stored appropriately," he finally murmured. I guess in reference to his earlier questions from weeks ago, "So, do you keep them in the bedside drawer or the dresser? In between your Victoria's Secret underwear? Or maybe, stacked in organised piles beside your Kombatan Training Manual?"

I wondered if he was disappointed. He'd said the soldier in him would be impressed if I cared for my blades as my instructor would have advised. But he'd also said that he wanted more from me. He wanted me to push the limits and surprise. I turned my attention back to the knives and tried to see them from Jason's point of view. I couldn't. I was too close to the blades on display. Each one having etched itself on my psyche. I couldn't be impartial when I looked at them, because they meant more than just weapons on display. They meant my independence and my security.

They were an extension of me.

Jason reached past me and ran a finger dangerously down one of the curved blades of an Ulak. I watched mesmerized at his movement. It was reverent and extremely respectful, even though he'd touched the blade which was a big no-no typically in knife wielding martial arts. When his finger finished its caress, he lifted the knife by its leather hilt, weighed it in his palm thoughtfully, then replaced it on the shelf next to its partner.

"Please tell me you know how to use that correctly?" he asked, his eyes finally flicking to mine.

I wasn't sure what they were saying. There was genuine concern for my safety in his gaze, but also something else, I think. Something even more important to me right then. Respect.

I nodded. "Yes. I can use any of these knives competently." My hand waved out in a motion from top to bottom, indicating the whole cabinet and its contents.

"Which are your preferred?" he asked. "Those you are most proficient with?"

My eyes scanned the shelves and instantly honed in on a Kukri. A Nepalese knife with an inward curved edge, not as obviously bowed as the Ulak. It was by no means an attractive blade, but it was well weighted, the hilt fitting my palm perfectly, the 40cm length enabling a certain distance in hand to hand combat. It was the knife I practised with most.

"Gurkha," Jason said, surprise lacing the word. He'd recognised the blade and knew it was the preferred weapon of all Gurkha armies. "I saw one used in Singapore," he said, distractedly.

"I didn't know there were Gurkhas in Singapore," I admitted. "I thought they were only found in Nepal or India."

Jason lifted his eyes to mine, removing his attention from the blade at last. "There's a Gurkha contingent in the Singapore Police Force. You can also find Kukri blades in the Royal Gurkha Rifles regiment in the British Army. It's a good knife, Kate. Good choice."

I let a slow breath of air out at Jason's approval and it seemed, acceptance. I hadn't realised how nervous I was showing him this side of me. It was like I was opening up a secret part of my soul and letting someone, whose opinion I cared about tremendously, take a peek

inside. It was an entirely revealing sensation, as though I was stripping naked before the man.

He might have realised, as his face softened with a look of understanding. Maybe it was similar to what he had gone through finally
admitting his dominant nature to me, facing up to my potential
ridicule or rejection, by showing me his deepest and darkest desires.
We had both stripped ourselves bare and thankfully not been found
wanting by the other.

"Can you use these accurately?" he asked, lifting up a SOG
Fusion throwing knife.

"Yes."

He hesitated, the knife balanced perfectly in his open palm. We
both stared at the matt black stainless steel blade. It was shorter than
the Kukri by almost twenty centimetres. But it was equally as unat-
tractive. I did own beautiful blades, but somehow I had gravitated
toward the utilitarian ones instead.

"If you come with me," he started. I interrupted immediately.

"*When* I come with you."

His amused eyes flicked up to mine. "*When* you come with me,"
he repeated, flipping the SOG over in his hand easily without even
looking at what he was doing, then replacing it on the shelf in its slot
next to its brothers, before going on. "You do as I say. No questions.
No arguments. Just do it. Understand?"

I held his now serious gaze and registered his determination and
his absolute conviction that this was an instruction I could not
disobey. I nodded.

"There can only be one person in charge, Kate," he pushed, as if
my nod wasn't quite enough to convince him I understood how
serious he was.

"I know," I said softly.

"I'm more experienced at this sort of thing," he pointed out. "This
is what I do. I can weigh up the risks of a given operation and determine the outcome from a chosen course better than you." I don't think

he was trying to be superior. He was simply being Captain Jason Cain.

"I understand, Jason," I said, evenly.

He sighed, ran a hand over his face and said, "If I ask you to leave. You leave. If I say duck, you throw yourself on the floor without blinking. If I say pull back, run, hide, *anything*. You do it. Understand?"

"Understood."

"I don't like this, Kate," he admitted, emotion making his words sound heavy and slightly thick.

"Together," I whispered.

"Baby." But he didn't say anything else, just stared at me for several long, weighty seconds.

I couldn't stand the tension anymore.

"What do think could possibly happen, Jason? Other than being arrested by the Police."

"I don't know, Kate. But that's when the shit usually hits the proverbial fan."

"He's an art dealer."

"A fucked in the head art dealer," Jason clarified further.

"Well, yes. He's unpredictable, but he won't be at ASI," I pointed out. "And I sure as hell won't be pulling a blade on a cop."

"You better bloody not," he shot back. Then sighed, flicked his gaze over the knives still illuminated and on display and then added, "Gear up. Time's not on our side. The longer it takes for us to get what we need from ASI, the more chance that we'll get caught. I'll phone a contact of mine in the SAS while you get armed, see if we can get surveillance images of the city from this morning."

It was a long shot and he knew it, but I was thinking he needed a distraction while I suited up and slipped my knives into place. Jason might have agreed with me being armed and accompanying him on this... what? Mission? God, I really didn't want to label this, it would make it more real. And although I was determined to be with Jason, to not let him out of my sight, I still needed to keep a certain distance from the reality of what we were doing. I'm no soldier, but I am a survivor. I survived two weeks with a broken heart and came out stronger because of it.

Hardly on the same level as a special forces military trained soldier, but in my world, it was something to be proud of. I was determined to make Jason - and my brothers, I suppose - proud of me too. Even if Jason still had his doubts about me going with him to ASI.

I slipped a Kukri blade into a sheath in the hollow of my back, then strapped myself into a harness that contained six SOG Fusion blades down my spine. A bit Lara Croft to be honest. When one blade was pulled, another fell into place replacing it. So each blade could be drawn from the same position, left and right sides of my hips, at my back. A made-to-measure jacket covered them all. From the front, I looked unarmed. From the back I had easy access to my knives, but you wouldn't know it.

I walked back into the bedroom to find Jason still on his cell-phone to his contact in the Army.

"OK, Horse. Just whatever you can find would be good. I'll send any pertinent information I gather from local intel that could help. But this is time sensitive, I need something, anything, to go on by tonight."

I couldn't hear this Horse person's reply, but he spoke for several seconds, before Jason finally answered with a half grunt, half chuckle.

"Yeah. I get that. But you would too if you were me." He hung up with a swipe of his thumb across the screen of the phone and pock-eted the device swiftly.

His eyes came up to mine, quickly flicking over my clothing, trying to see my blades. He wouldn't be able to, my trainer had supplied both the holsters and the fitted jacket. No point learning to wield a knife and not be able to successfully carry them in reality. He didn't do this for all of his trainees, but Johnson - my trainer - had been aware of why I was doing this, and who my brother was. Nick and ASI had a reputation around this city, even my trainer was aware of the sort of trouble that could land at my door.

"Would do what?" I queried.

His eyebrows rose at my question regarding his final words to Horse. For a moment I thought he wouldn't provide an answer, but his signature smirk graced the corners of his lips and he said, "Would risk my arse for a woman and her family."

Oh.

"Ready?" he asked, coming to his feet before me.

"Absolutely," I replied.

"Kate," he huffed out on a laugh. "I've told you before, baby. You're a crap liar."

I rolled my eyes and received a swat on my butt for my efforts as we left the room and headed toward the front door. He stopped me before my hand could turn the doorknob. His fingers digging into my shoulder blade until I turned to face him fully.

"One more thing," he whispered, and I sucked in a breath prepared for more reminders about how dangerous this could get, and how I needed to follow his instructions without hesitation.

But I didn't receive either of those threats. Just...

"So you don't forget what you mean to me," he murmured, before his face tipped forward and his lips melded to mine.

My hands were in his hair before I registered they had moved. My tongue was wrapped around his in a duel that was both delicious and dangerous. I craved more of the exquisite taste of this man, yet I knew if I gave in to that yearning we'd never make it out of that door in time to beat the tech forensic team to ASI. A battle of wills took up inside my heart and mind. Pull back and get this task over with, freeing Nick and solving the mystery of Tremayne. Or take, perhaps the last chance, to savour this man before me. To worship him with my touch. To sink into the bliss he so easily created.

I moaned as he pushed my back up against the closed door. My knives, sheathed protectively in their holsters, digging into my spine. Competing with the hardness of his chest and thighs that draped down my front. Making me demand more; fingers digging into his back, my breasts pressed up against him; tempting, teasing, taunting.

His hands slipped down my sides, over the curve of my hips. Fingertips brushing the edge of my SOG hilts under my jacket. But even that reminder of what awaited us didn't stop Jason. He grasped my rear, kneaded the flesh for a moment and then slid my back up the door making me wrap my thighs around his waist as he continued to devour me.

I felt his arousal. It matched my own. I could sense his need and hunger. Only equalled in my necessity and longing for him. He rocked his hips, moaned into my mouth and then swallowed my groan in response down. I was panting for breath, clutching his body and mentally willing him to strip me right there and sink inside my aching core.

Had I been following his rules, I think it would have been inevitable. Maybe it was for the best that I'd disobeyed him this morning. Albeit a refusal to dress in a skirt with no underwear for legitimate reasons. Because Jason didn't attempt to undo my trousers, he didn't make a move to escalate this to anything more intimate than what it already was. He just kissed me like we had run out of time, like the end of the world was here and we had to simply taste each other, because to do more right now was impossible.

There just wasn't enough time to sate that desire, to fulfil our fervent yearning for completion.

He pulled his lips away and rested his forehead against mine, breathing as raggedly as me. His chest was rising and falling hypnotically. His hot breath washed over my face erotically. His strong arms and thighs held me in situ, pinned to the door. His erection pressed firmly and snugly in place at my centre, pulsing with both our need and hunger.

"Kate," he murmured. "Do you see what I mean?"

I huffed out a breath of air in mild confusion and rampant frustration.

"What?" I asked, ineloquently, panting the word out and then sucking in much needed air.

He chuckled, pleased I was as affected as him, no doubt.

"Baby," he whispered, laying a soft kiss on my lips and then pulling his body away from mine completely.

My feet hit the floor on shaky legs as his warmth became only a memory. I struggled to find my balance, making his hands come up and gently cradle my upper arms to steady me. If he did this while we were sneaking into the ASI building I would be worse than useless. I guess that's why he got it out of the way before we left home.

"Kate," Jason said, bringing my dazed gaze back to him. He smirked, clearly enjoying my ridiculously uncontrolled response to his advances. "Do you see what I mean?" he repeated.

"I'm not sure I do, Jason," I admitted, now not only turned-on with no hope of release, but rapidly becoming confused with his repeated question.

"It's simple, Kate," he murmured, chocolate brown pools staring down at me. "You mean the very air I breathe. Without you I will be no more. With you, my world is complete."

I blinked up at him, a little shocked at his sincerity and the depth of emotion lacing his words.

"Baby," he added. "I can face anything with you in my life. You make the darkness recede and the light shine. So," he took a deep breath in, "if it comes down to it, you do whatever you have to do to stay safe. Even if you have to leave me behind."

What?

"Jason," I began, thinking he was making this entire episode out to me more precarious than it needed to be. Sure, Tremayne was probably crazy. Sure, the cops would arrest us and throw away the key if we were caught interfering in a police investigation. Sure, if we didn't figure this out and clear Nick's name an innocent man and his team may be charged with a false crime.

But, none of that leant itself to the level of concern and depth of fear Jason had gracing his handsome features right then.

For a moment I wondered if this was all causing some sort of flashback to when he was in the Army. If he was reading more into this than he should have, because of what he had suffered, and still suffered from, while in the SAS. I didn't have time to think that through to completion, because he cupped my cheeks, leaned down and stared me intently in the eyes and said...

"Understand?"

And whether Jason was losing touch with reality now or not, that one word was all I needed to hear to know I would do anything to ease this broken man's mind.

"Understood," I whispered back and prayed that whatever happened next would not tip Jason over the edge into that dark abyss that seemed to beckon my beloved man.

CHAPTER 27

THIS ISN'T WHAT WE THINK

ANSCOMBE SECURITIES AND INVESTIGATIONS WAS LIKE FORT Knox. I had been aware that Nick ensured his staff were safest when on site at ASI HQ. Surveillance cameras dotted the perimeter and even stood sentinel at differing locations across the street around the entirety of the block the building stood on. All of which could be viewed and directed by Eric in the control room inside. Of course, Eric was not in the control room, he was being questioned about a multimillion dollar burglary at Auckland Central Police Station downtown.

But there was more to contend with than the cameras.

Access was officially gained through the front entrance on street level, or from the garage beneath, up the monitored elevator which was only activated once the person attempting entry was visually approved by Eric in control, and then past a shotgun toting grandma, trained to assess threats and act appropriately with deadly force. And finally via an electronically key-coded titanium strength door. And then all the rooms inside were further controlled by key-code and security cameras.

Take out the cameras and you've gained access, might be a

reasonable thought. But all the cameras have secondary back-ups, housed in an isolated and military level secured CPU. As well as scanners available at strategic gateways, which should the cameras and their back-up fail-safes fall, could scan identification directly and send the images to control.

Getting in undetected was impossible. It was what we could do once in there that made all the difference. If Jason had received top level clearance from Nick then he could wipe evidence of our visit completely. If he only received a clearance level that allowed him suitable access to 'radar' then we would be videoed and recorded as having been inside the building. The security system could also accurately display what it is we did, if Jason's clearance wasn't high enough to cover our tracks.

I could only hope that Nick had thought of this, but considering his recent relationship with Jason, it was not a given that he would allow his ex-employee, who he considered was on the edge of sanity, full admission to ASI's inner workings, records and systems. I had faith Nick was wiser than that, but Jason did not.

"OK, this is how it's going to be," he said from the front seat of his SUV, which was parked several metres down Broadway in Newmarket, in line of sight of the front doors and garage entrance to ASI. The vehicle was out of the security cameras' range, but he handed me a pair of binoculars and a secured walkie-talkie, which obviously was meant to combat the distance our strategic parking had created. "You stay here and keep watch. I go in."

In itself the directive and his assessment made sense. But of course, my heart was unable to comprehend that.

"No," I said, trying to hand the binoculars and walkie-talkie back.

Both items got pushed back into my lap forcefully.

"What did I say, Kate?" Jason growled, one hand already on the door handle to the car, the other holding the items in my lap still, for fear I'd throw them back. Another good assessment.

"I should go with you," I offered, holding his irate glare.

He blinked once, sighed, then said, "OK. In the interest of moving this along as quickly as possible, so we can get our arses out of here before we're seen. How do you think coming with me will improve our chances of getting in and out undetected?"

"Well," I said, then couldn't think of a suitable argument to offer.

He was right of course. Me going with him wasn't strictly necessary to the successful outcome of this venture. But my heart was telling me he shouldn't be alone. What if he had a flashback in there? What if he needed me and I couldn't get inside to help him out?

I couldn't say any of this aloud. First, he'd deny he had any problems. He may even accuse me of being overprotective like Nick and Dom. And secondly, I wasn't entirely sure if he was having flashbacks. If he was, in fact, on the edge of sanity due to his experiences in the armed forces. I was only speculating, trying to understand his need for control and Nick's insistence that Jason was on the verge of something disastrous.

I didn't have an answer and my gut wasn't giving me any clues. I simply didn't know.

What it boiled down to was, did I trust him to get this done, or not?

I looked into his eyes and saw his desire to get this onerous task completed. I saw his concern for me. For my safety, for my hesitation to follow his command. I saw his strength of character, his ability to take charge and effect an outcome with a natural leader's grace. I saw his heart; the part of him that loves me beyond measure. The part of him that would do all of this for a man who had pushed his emotional buttons intentionally and held his job over his head in an effort to make Jason walk away from something he wanted above all else. Who had made Jason's imperfections public knowledge.

"Are you doing this for me?" I asked, trying to work out if that was why he'd risk arrest.

"Of course," he said, without hesitation. And then surprised me by adding, "And because Nick didn't do this. He's being accused of someone else's crime."

And that's all he needed say, to make me realise that Jason Cain was not the product of his broken pieces, he was the sum of all of him. His compassion, his strength, his control, his experiences, his heart. Jason might have a past that threatened *something* in him, but it didn't necessarily mean it threatened his mind, his sanity. His ability to act appropriately and assess a situation he was trained to handle correctly. His control.

This was what Jason was meant to do. This stealth and infiltration he was about to undertake was as much a part of him as his ability to love me. Jason was not perfect, parts of him were broken. But it was his imperfections that made him perfect to me.

"OK," I said, gathering up the binoculars and walkie-talkie. I placed the walkie-talkie next to me in the centre console, within easy reach, and lifted the binoculars to my eyes to scan the ASI building and see if there were any potential threats. "I'll let you know if I spot anything," I added.

He didn't move. My hand held the binoculars still before me, but I twisted my head to meet his gaze. He was smiling. That smile he only lets out, now and then, and which I think might just be all mine.

"Kate," he said in a low and delicious silky voice. "I love you."

"And I love you," I whispered, tears openly pooling in my eyes. He noticed.

"Don't just watch the building," he said after a short pause, changing the atmosphere in the car to one of business. "Watch the entire street as well. Even behind you. Every three minutes, you do a scan of your environment. Reassess threats. Just because I'm going in there does not mean you are safe."

I nodded, wishing we could skip forward an hour and bypass this adrenaline fuelling next sixty minutes.

"Good," he announced with a nod of his head, and then he was gone. Out the door, striding up the street, blending in with the Newmarket shoppers and almost disappearing from sight, if I hadn't been following his very fine arse so closely.

Twenty minutes later and I had disgustingly chewed several nails down to skin. Jason had confirmed he was inside ASI offices and had top level clearance - thank you Nicky - but had been silent ever since. I wanted to call out to him, but feared I'd distract him, or place him in harm's way for some reason. So I had bitten my nails, scanned my environment and found nothing out of place, and simply waited.

I hadn't realised I was an impatient person. But this angst was debilitating almost. It had me doing unnecessary things, like checking the volume on the walkie-talkie fifty times. I also considered that I could just phone Tremayne. Get in touch with the man to show my concern. Wouldn't he have expected me to call when I found out the showroom had been burgled? Wouldn't it make sense if I contacted him and surreptitiously drilled him for information?

Of course my ability to be surreptitious right now was debatable. Just ask the walkie-talkie. But the longer it took for Jason to provide an update, the closer I came to picking up my cellphone and just dialling Richard Tremayne, demanding to know why the bastard had implicated Nick and myself in this crime.

Instead I dialled Detective Pierce.

One would think, while I was performing look-out duties as my ex-military lover broke into a security firm under current investigation for a crime by the Police, that I wouldn't draw said Police's attention to me. Maybe it wasn't Jason's sanity that should have been in question, but mine.

"Ryan Pierce," came down the line after the ringing tone had sounded three times.

"Detective Pierce, this is Katie Anscombe."

"Katie?" Ryan said, sounding surprised to hear from me. I then heard shuffling of material, indistinct voices and the slamming of a door. Followed by an echoing silence that led me to believe Pierce had vacated an occupied room and was now alone. "How can I help?"

I smiled. Ryan was always so ready to offer a hand, even when he knew he shouldn't.

"Have you located Richard Tremayne yet?" I asked, and heard Pierce suck in a deep breath.

"Yes and no," he finally admitted, but didn't say more.

"Ryan," I said, in my most determined voice, "I don't have time to play guessing games. My brother is being accused of a crime he didn't commit and I've had a shit of a month. So please, what does 'yes and no' actually mean?"

"Shit of a month, huh?" Ryan mumbled. "All right, but Katie, you didn't hear this from me."

"Of course, darling."

"We touched base with him via phone to advise of the theft, he agreed to return to Auckland on the next available flight. We have him boarding in Queenstown and exiting the plane in Auckland, but since then, nothing."

"What time-frame are we talking about, Ryan?"

"The plane landed at ten this morning." I glanced at my watch. It was already two in the afternoon. No wonder I was famished.

I rubbed my empty belly while I contemplated what this news meant. If Tremayne was playing along to continue his cover, then he would have gone directly to the Police. Which he didn't. So, he was either giving up on the charade - but then why return at all? - or something had happened to waylay him.

"You do realise this could all be an insurance scam," I offered.

"It had crossed our minds, but..." he paused, reconsidered whatever he was going to say, then said, "We do know how to investigate a crime, Katie."

I almost rolled my eyes at his imperious tone.

"Of course, darling," I said placatingly. "But Nick didn't do this and you know that, don't you?"

"What I know as a person and what I know as a cop are two entirely different things."

I didn't like the sound of that.

"Something's happened to Tremayne," I said, admitting my thoughts out loud.

"If it has, we have no evidence of foul play," Ryan offered.

"You think he's intentionally been waylaid?" I asked.

"That's one way of putting it. But our current official position, again you've not heard this from me, is that something mundane has delayed him and he will no doubt appear before close of business today. He was not legally required to come directly to the Police Station upon landing in Auckland," he pointed out.

None of it made sense, though. If Pierce was correct, Tremayne was dealing with something willingly before he approached the Police. A delay could be attributed to any number of plausible legal things, as Ryan had insinuated. But if I'd had six million dollars worth of goods stolen, I would be hounding the Police in person until they found my property and returned it to me. Tremayne was not. So, what was he doing?

Fencing the goods? Dealing with a hitch in his supply chain? Covering his tracks elsewhere before the Police turned their attention on him as a suspect? Creating more false trails to ASI and Nick?

"Do you have anything for me, Katie?" Ryan asked, interrupting my train of thought.

My eyes flicked up the street. It had been more than three minutes since I'd done my last scan and I quickly fumbled with the binoculars to ascertain any threats that may have occurred while I was distracted. Ten heart palpitating guilty seconds later all was still clear.

"No," I said a little breathlessly down the line. "Unfortunately, not as yet."

"You sound like you're under pressure, Katie," Pierce pointed out. I sucked in my breath and held it. Now would not be a good time for him to go all chivalrous on me. Ryan had a tendency to want to rescue damsels in distress. "I think it might be best if we ring off here. Let you concentrate on whatever it is you're doing," he finally suggested.

"Good idea," I said, still not breathing.

"You take care, now. You hear?" he said. I just nodded, which of course he couldn't see. But thankfully he didn't wait for a reply and just disconnected the call.

A rush of air left my lips and had me panting for the next lungful in.

Which segued into a yelp as Jason opened the driver's door and slid into his seat.

He took one look at me and then started the car without a word. Once we were several hundred metres past ASI he murmured, "You look guilty, Kate. What did you do?"

"What did you do?" I returned. "Er, find, rather."

"I asked first," he deadpanned.

"I phoned Detective Pierce," I admitted, reluctantly, and then held my breath again.

"Oh, you did, did you?" he asked with a raised eyebrow, but didn't glance in my direction. We were heading for the motorway, and by the looks of it, the South bound lanes.

"I wanted an update on Tremayne. Whether he'd presented himself to the Police yet."

"And he hasn't," Jason supplied.

"No. He landed at ten this morning in Auckland, but they haven't heard from him since."

Jason frowned. "What's Pierce's take on that?"

"Officially, they're not concerned. They expect him to have a viable excuse and turn up on their doorstep by tonight."

"Unofficially?" Jason asked, flicking his gaze towards me.

"Unofficially is a closed book right now. We're on our own."

Jason huffed out a breath of air as he turned the SUV onto the motorway, indeed heading South.

"Where are we going?" Both our homes were back the other way.

"Manurewa. The only property that Tremayne owns, which flies under any official and legal connections to him or his businesses, is a warehouse in Manurewa."

"You think the art might be there," I surmised.

"Or at least a clue to Tremayne's whereabouts. If we're lucky, even Tremayne himself might be there. Pierce, even outside of the official investigation right now, would have looked into his legally owned properties. He and the art are obviously not at one of those. So, that leaves the property in Manurewa."

"And you got all of this off radar?" I asked, intrigued that an underground network of informants could provide such specific information.

"This warehouse being linked to him, yes. But there's more," he added, flicking me another troubled look.

"What?" I didn't want to speculate. Jason's anxiety could mean any number of things. It wasn't worth the worry to work them all out in my mind.

"Tremayne has business dealings with Declan King."

I sucked in a shocked breath of air. "What does that mean?"

"Well, even legit businesses deal with King from time to time. He has his fingers in many different pies. Not all of them are fronts or laundering opportunities for the man. It could be all above board and there was nothing on radar to suggest otherwise. But any connection, legal or not, to Auckland's crime lord, is cause for unease. Especially where Nick and ASI are concerned."

"You think Tremayne is working with King to frame Nick. A revenge type scenario."

"It's the most obvious conclusion to make," Jason agreed.

We exited the motorway in silence, both of us contemplating what this new piece of information could mean. It finally all made sense. Tremayne was the tool with which King could lash out at my brother. For his interference in recent interests King had. For the rescue of Ben Tamati's woman, Abi Monaghan, from King's clutches.

I'd met Abi at a barbecue at Dominic and Genevieve's, the one that Jason had stood me up at. She was courageous and beautiful, a strength of character contained in a soft shell. She seemed fragile and sweet, but from what I'd heard through Nick, she was capable of so much more than looking pretty. And King had wanted to use her, in his turf war with Roan McLaren; Abi's former mob boss in Wellington, where she grew up.

All of this stemmed back to then. To the lock-down. To the operation Pierce was on in Wellington, using ASI, and in particular Ben and Abi, to arrest that horrible man. But things had settled. Nick had arranged an agreement with King, one that should have avoided this outcome. I mean, ASI was partially responsible for getting Roan McLaren out of the way, freeing up King's interests in Wellington and the whole of the North Island of New Zealand. King should have been pleased with ASI's involvement. Should have been thanking Nick, not framing him for a crime.

But whoever said criminal masterminds were sane. In Declan King's mind this was probably all perfectly justifiable. Payback for a slight. Or a warning not to cross him again.

Just then, Jason pulled the SUV onto the side of the road we were on, behind a high chain-link fence bordered by thick bush. We were concealed from whatever stood on the other side. I was guessing, that it was Tremayne's warehouse.

"What if nothing's here?" I asked, peering futilely out of the side of the car.

"Then we go to plan B," Jason said, pulling his cellphone out of his pocket.

"Plan B?"

"Yeah. Pray to God that the Police are better at this than us."

His phone connected to whoever he was trying to contact, which became apparent on his next words.

"Horse. What have you got for me?"

A long pause, where I couldn't hear a word on the other end of the line.

Then Jason said, before hanging up, "I owe you, man."

The phone got pocketed and a gun replaced it in Jason's hand. He checked the chamber, put the safety on and flicked his eyes back up to me.

"Tremayne's here. Has been since not long after he landed back in Auckland. But he had a visitor half an hour after he arrived."

I could guess.

"Declan King."

"Yeah," Jason spat. "But King left and Tremayne didn't." He held my gaze. "Whatever is in there, may not be pretty."

I knew what was coming next.

"I'll keep a look out," I suggested, and saw immediate relief wash his entire face and frame.

He offered me a small smile, picked up my cellphone from between my legs and handing it to me said, "Phone Pierce. This isn't what we think."

But before I could ask him what exactly he meant by that, he was out the door and scaling the fence.

CHAPTER 28

UNDERSTAND?

PIERCE WAS ASSEMBLING A TEAM AND HEADING OUR WAY. HE'D blown a gasket, at the fact Jason had gone in, when the intel from Jason's military contact had indicated possible foul play. He was infinitely relieved to hear I was sitting safely in the SUV outside, hidden from immediate sight.

I wasn't inclined to agree with the detective after he'd pointed all of that out. I'd realised, from Jason's warning of things possibly not being pretty inside the warehouse, that I wouldn't have wanted to witness whatever Jason was uncovering right now. But it hadn't actually occurred to me that he may be in danger. King had left, according to Horse, whom I could only assume had satellite imagery to back up that fact. If King wasn't here, and no one else was seen entering the building, then the only person - or body - inside would be Tremayne's.

But now my mind was racing, making up darker and darker scenarios inside my head, all of which led Jason down a bleak path. I consoled myself with the fact that he was trained for this sort of thing. That although affected by his past, he was not ruled by it. That Jason was more than what most people saw and assumed.

My perfect imperfect man.

There was nothing for me to watch here, no entrance to view through binoculars. The road we were parked on was a side street running parallel to the much larger and well travelled Weymouth Road. There'd been half a dozen cars pass by, but on the whole, the industrial looking area had the feel of slight neglect to it. As though most of the warehouses here were unmanned during the day, or simply abandoned. The economy was not what it used to be.

I started tapping my fingernail, one of the only ones left that I hadn't chewed to the quick, against the handle of the door in an impatient rhythm that matched my elevated heart rate. Jason hadn't made any communication with me through the walkie-talkie since he'd climbed over that fence. Surely, he would have let me know by now if he had found Tremayne or if the warehouse was bare. I had no idea how big the building was from my vantage point inside the car. But I was certain I could get a feel for its size if I stood up and peered through the bushes.

I took a hurried look up and down the road, making sure to survey every direction before I exited the SUV. Inside or outside the car, at this location, was still a safe bet; not a soul walked the street. I approached the fence and peered between the leaves. A rather large blank wall met my eyes. I tried to get a better perception of size, but from the angle I was looking and with the obstruction of the bushes, I couldn't see an end to the vastness of dirty white concrete that loomed through the fence.

I fiddled with the walkie-talkie, trying to decide if I should check up on Jason. Finally anxiety and impatience took their toll and I brought the device to my face, pressed the button and spoke into the receiver.

"Jason? What's happening?"

There was a crackle, as though he was trying to pick his walkie-talkie up, or as though he was frantically trying to turn it down, and then nothing.

Panic seized me. Had I made a mistake contacting him when he was investigating a suspicious location? He hadn't said not to, but then I also hadn't been that stupid when he was inside ASI. Maybe he assumed I understood it was for emergencies only. My nail found my teeth and I gnawed on it for a second, then without anything else to do, I turned back to the SUV to climb inside.

A startled cry escaped my lips as I rotated to face the vehicle and found a man the size of a mountain standing before me. Between me and the car itself. He was huge. And had beady eyes a little too close together and bushy eyebrows arrowed down into a V. However, it wasn't the *Deliverance* facial appearance that sucked all the air from my lungs, but the bulging muscles protruding beneath his too small t-shirt sleeves, the stretch of barrel-shaped chest that stood threateningly in front of my eyes, and the very real looking black gun he held in his beefy hands, pointed at me.

"Ms Anscombe," he said in a gruff voice that matched his physique. "Come with me." The 'with' was pronounced, *wiff.*

OK. Not good. I glanced up and down the street, but still there was no one to see this abduction taking place. I momentarily contemplated flicking a knife at him, but with the gun aimed at my chest and his finger already on the trigger, not to mention the fact that he was probably not alone and Jason was facing off against this goon's counterpart right now, the idea was soon quashed. I'd bide my time. The goon hadn't frisked me, so I was still armed.

And in the theme of his obvious assumption that I was nothing more than a non-threatening woman, I cowered, bit a trembling lip and said in a wavering voice, "Who are you? What do you want?"

"Mr King would like a word," he said, taking a towering step closer.

I shouldn't have been surprised. We'd concluded King's involvement, but we'd had intel advice of his departure. Had he returned? Or was I being taken somewhere else?

A large hand wrapped threateningly around my upper arm, the steel point of the gun was thrust into my side painfully, and the goon pulled me along the length of the fence.

"Where are you taking me?" I demanded, my heart in my throat and the shaking in my legs no longer for appearance sake only.

"To Mr King," the man said, as though I was missing a few brain cells.

The itch to pull a knife and defend myself was enormous. I'd been trained to combat this sort of situation, but reality is a great leveller. The gun felt real. It *was* real. When I'd trained, the weapon used against me had been fake, the outcome; one of bruises and a crushed ego. But here, on the side of a road in South Auckland, I knew if I pulled my Kukri and wasn't fast enough to take the mountain beside me by surprise, there'd be no bruises, only blood. *My blood.*

I had never considered myself a coward, but in that moment, fear for my life overrode all my training. Simply turned me into a victim, not a Kombatan martial arts specialist.

How had Jason survived in a world this real?

Genuine tears trickled down my cheeks, a sense of despondency invaded my mind. I had expected so much more from myself than this. I felt disappointed and disgusted at my weakness.

We entered a gate at the edge of the property and crossed a short, weed strewn, neglected piece of concrete to a closed door at the rear of Tremayne's warehouse. My captor banged three times on the door with a meaty fist, the sound echoing out across the small courtyard and resounding inside my frantic chest. I might have jerked.

The door creaked open, the darkness inside momentarily making it impossible to see who had given us access. By the time I was dragged across the threshold, only the back of another medium build man could be seen, walking away from us towards light at the end of a brief corridor.

A second twitch of my body as the door clanged shut at our backs. I was fast becoming a bundle of nerves and little else. I needed to get a handle on my reactions, settle my mind, ease the drastic clench of my heart. I needed to focus on my training, on Johnson's words of wisdom in my mind.

But all I could hear was Jason. *"If it comes down to it, you do whatever you have to do to stay safe. Even if you have to leave me behind."*

Suddenly, seeing Jason before contemplating anything else was imperative. The need to ensure he was still alive stole all other thoughts from my mind, and replaced all other fears. If I could ensure Jason was still breathing, then I would consider looking out for myself. Retaliating, searching deep within my psyche and finding that place my Kombatan trainer had given me; the strength required to not be a victim, to fight back.

Having something to focus on other than the feel of my too large captor's hand on my arm, or the press of the gun barrel in the side of my torso, was liberating. In a way only being with Jason had ever been. I clasped the sensation, concentrated on my immediate goal, and started surveying my surroundings.

We'd passed several rooms; doors open, revealing office like spaces. Whatever this building had been in the past, it was barely used now. The offices were empty, only gathering dust. No obvious solutions appeared in any of the abandoned spaces.

I turned my attention to the door at the end of the hallway we were in, the one the smaller man had just opened and walked through. Light shone brightly on the other side of the door frame. It had been that light which spilled out from beneath the previously closed door and illuminated the corridor. The blinds were all closed on the empty offices we'd walked past, the only source of lighting came from that room ahead.

I blinked, concentrated on the brightness, willing my pupils to react swiftly so I wouldn't be light blind when I entered the room. Not that I intended to do anything immediately upon arrival there, but somehow the need to be prepared was forefront in my mind. That, and the need to see Jason as soon as possible.

A part of me wished I hadn't been so eager. Because the instant I was hauled through the narrow opening, out into the brighter, larger space, my eyes landed on him. Everything, *everyone*, else vanished. Just me and the crumpled form of Jason several metres away.

He was bloody. I couldn't tell if the blood was someone else's or his, and if it was his, if it was superficial or not. He *was* breathing, but his eyes were closed and his limbs unmoving. He'd been beaten, that much was obvious, and I wondered how anyone could get the drop on Jason, and not wear a few cuts and bruises themselves.

I forced my eyes to leave the shattered looking shape of the man I loved and scanned my environment, looking for evidence that Jason had fought back. Two other men stood in the room. One was the medium built man who had opened the back door, dressed in jeans and a polo shirt, with geek styled mousy brown hair and horn rimmed glasses. The other was tall, distinguished and in an expensive suit. He was also dark skinned.

Declan King.

Neither of them had a scratch on their bodies. Jason had been ambushed, caught unawares. Or had decided fighting back was not possible.

My eyes continued their careful inventory of the room. It was larger than I had expected, large enough to house a basketball court *and* the spectator stands, I should think. Large enough to house all of Tremayne's art, sitting innocuously in one corner. Large enough to house Declan King and his men, with Jason at their feet.

And large enough to house Richard Tremayne. Who looked in similar shape to Jason, but his chest was not rising and falling in the same steady rhythm. My eyes settled on Tremayne's still form, unable to pull away from the sight of a dead body. Of a dead *person* I had known.

If I had thought our lives were in danger before, it was nothing to the realisation of how true that was now. The evidence of just what Declan King was capable of; there on the cold concrete floor, discarded, no longer needed. Terminated.

I flicked a steady gaze back at King.

"Did he renege on your deal?" I asked, surprised at my courage, at the fact I could challenge this man at all.

But a pit of anger had invaded my body, settled in my stomach and spread ice cold tendrils throughout my frame. I was furious. With Tremayne. With the mob boss who stood imperiously before me. With the sight of a once magnificent soldier lying broken on the floor.

It was the type of anger that stole all reason. My head was trying to tell me, *danger, danger, danger.* My body was simply saying, *bring it the fuck on!*

"He was superfluous to requirements, my dear," King said, in an unusual accent; somewhere between Kiwi and a type of French.

"What was he getting out of this?" I asked, needing clarity in something, even if it was only in uncovering Tremayne's motives for now.

"He was not aware of his role, at all," King said, sounding amused and bored at the same time. "Merely a tool I needed to get the job done."

"But you made him approach me?" I couldn't quite work it out. Tremayne had sought me out for a reason, it had to be because of this man.

King let out a loud burst of laughter. It echoed around the room. Jason didn't even stir.

"I would not work with one such as him, Ms Anscombe. But I am not opposed to using his type. Money hungry and elitist. Everything I was not growing up."

Ah. A glimpse into the mind of a megalomaniac crime lord with something to prove.

"But his infatuation with you proved interesting," he went on. "And useful. You do know he was obsessed with you, don't you my dear? Couldn't stop talking about the young, pretty designer he had employed to decorate his new showroom. The plans to have you do the rest of his chain of art stores. The desire to add you to his collection of perfect pieces. For show. For his ego. For his amusement and because he could."

But he couldn't. I'd turned Tremayne down. Had he gone to King and asked for a favour?

"So, he approached you, when he couldn't get what he wanted from me?"

King rocked back on his highly polished expensive Italian made leather shoes, clasped his hands in front of him and smiled a too white toothed grin.

"You don't get it, Ms Anscombe," he said, condescendingly. "I used him. Nothing more. It was for my purposes that his store was burgled. It was for my amusement that your brother's firm was implicated. It was because *I* can. He merely presented an avenue I hadn't considered before. You."

My heart fell. If I hadn't have met Richard Tremayne we wouldn't be here. Nick under question, under threat of arrest, due to a crime he didn't commit. Jason beaten, maybe broken enough to tip him over the edge into that dark abyss. Me facing off against a monster of a man who played with people's lives like a game of chess. And Tremayne, dead.

All because Mrs Montgomery-Smith had told her husband's acquaintance about my work and Richard had liked what he'd seen.

"So, you see, my dear," King said, bringing my focus back to the room. "All roads lead to me. And your brother, with his penchant to interfere in my business. He pulled a gun on me, you know. Fired with intent to kill. How am I not to repay him in kind?"

"Didn't you shoot first?" I asked, trying to stall, trying to give Detective Pierce time to arrive and end this before I had to take that fateful step.

"Only after he stole something that was rightfully mine," King spat. If you could call the way he spoke, spitting.

"Abi is not a possession," I pointed out. It had been while rescuing Abi from King's clutches that a gun fight had broken out. Eva had told me. Another reminder of what sort of world Nicholas Anscombe walked in. A world that overlapped into mine.

My eyes flicked to Jason's on the floor. He was watching me. I tried to still my gasp of breath at seeing him conscious. He gave a small shake of his head, as if to say, *look away, don't react.* Even when he demands with just a glance and no words, I obeyed. Immediately.

My eyes returned swiftly to King's and I held his eager, and quite wrong, gaze. King was crazy. Crazier than Tremayne. Crazier than my ex-soldier. His crazy was on a whole other level, making both Richard and Jason seem down right normal.

"What now, if you don't mind me asking?" I said. So casual. So unaffected. Who would have known I could pull off nonchalant while facing my death, and the death of my lover, so easily.

"A message. A gift, if you will, " King said, straightening his suit sleeve cuffs. Preparing to leave, I think.

Nick had once said that a message from Declan King could be fatal. That a gift definitely was.

I blinked slowly. Took in a measured, calm breath of air. Centred myself using a technique my trainer had taught me. Glanced at Jason, who flicked a gaze at the geek looking guy - the closest man to him in the room and his obvious target. Leaving me both King and his goon of a mountain, who had a gun still pointed at my chest.

The odds weren't good. But I am not your average victim. I may look all sweet and refined. Dressed in my tailored trousers. My designer blouse. My made to measure jacket. And my thousand dollar shoes. I may carry myself like I went to finishing school, as though I belong in the social elite of Auckland city.

But I don't. I am my hard-nosed lawyer father's daughter. My private investigator brother's sister. My soldier boyfriend's woman. I belong in their world, which is a million miles away from the privately educated, socially elite, upper echelons of society that King saw when he looked at me right now.

I smiled. It was slow and calculating and the only warning they would get.

They missed its intention. King taking a step toward the gun toting behemoth beside him, and opening his mouth to issue a command. No doubt something along the lines of, *after you kill her, make sure you dispose of her body well.*

And in a coordinated move, which God alone knows how we achieved it, Jason rolled smoothly to a crouch, while I unleashed two SOG Fusion throwing knives directly at King and mountain-man's chests.

The room squeezed down on us, as though the walls and ceiling began closing in and the air started to freeze. I could still hear. I could still see, although what I saw was no longer normal. I could still feel; the sweat coating my skin, the tremble in my fingers, the sick feeling of inevitability rolling out towards me inside my gut. I swallowed bile, sucked in a choked gulp of air, and reacted.

Despite the fear which gripped me in a claw-like clasp, practice made me move. My training kicked in, even as my mind threatened to rebel at what it was seeing.

Red.

Just a splash, a stripe across pale skin. A drip, suspended in the air as it flew from its origin out towards the ground, gravity pulling it downwards. My knives had found their targets. Clean shots, exacting maximum damage.

But it wasn't enough. A flash of dark clothing told me King was on the move, but his figure was obscured by a mountain of rage. Snarling, spitting fury storming towards me. The glint of artificial lights flashing off the dull black of a weapon.

My heart stalled. My brain faltered. My body took over the fight.

I rolled to the left, out of the responding fire from the huge man's gun, feeling the bullet blast past me in a burst of heated air. The sound momentarily deafened me. The ache of my shoulder slamming into concrete stole all reason. Just for a second of panicked time. I blinked, tried to focus. Tried to get my bearings. Jason was behind the geek, two hands on either side of his head. A short twist, and the body crumpled to the floor.

Then the scene rapidly sped up again, sound returning, so much it left confusion, not clarity in its wake. The yell of rage from the huge mountain staggering towards me. The vile look of death across his face. My head swam with my trainer's instructions, my mind trying futilely to respond to the stimuli it was receiving. Violent anger. Course words of lethal intent. The cold hard floor beneath my knees. The piercing ache in my shoulder where I'd fallen.

For a split second, which felt like forever, I thought I was dead. That the next bullet had already reached me. But while my head was imploding and the world outside my mind was exploding, my body was still acting on auto-pilot. I threw a third, and then a fourth knife in quick succession, into the advancing shape of the infuriated and wounded mob boss's goon. He stumbled, clutched at his chest with one hand and the side of his neck with the other. Futilely trying to staunch the flow of blood.

He would bleed out, my fracturing mind informed me. But my frantically beating heart told me, he was determined to reach me first.

The fifth and sixth knives entered his femoral artery on his right hand side, and his chest on his left. The feel of the ribbed rubber hilts still ghosts of sensations in my cold, clammy palms. My hands shook, my body quaked. My lips trembled as sounds of distress began to whimper out of me. I'd acted as I'd been trained to do, but nothing prepares you for this. Nothing prepares you for death.

Death is real. Death is loud. Death is gritty. Death is final.

The blood loss associated with my well aimed throws would kill this man eventually. If not within the next few seconds. But the knife in the heart stilled all flow of blood completely. I knew this, as I watched the blade flick through the air between me and my target, slowly rotating tip over hilt in a beautiful arc that defied gravity and embraced my will instead. I knew exactly where it would embed itself before it cleaved through flesh, severed arteries, and pierced the organ. I knew.

And I'd aimed true. My intent... *to kill.*

The mountain of a man fell to the ground with a resounding thump. Unmoving.

Shock made the world split apart, adrenaline brought it back into a kind of focus. My trainer's voice a blinding light in amongst the shadows filling my vision.

"It's them or you. Guns kill. But knives can save your life. Use them."

My Kukri was in my hand in the next instant, raised and ready to take on King now that I was an open target. No longer covered by the form of his enormous sidekick.

But was it King who approached me? Softly, carefully, as though I might slice him without even intending to.

"Shhh," someone murmured. "It's OK. It's over, baby. Put down the knife."

My vision warped, colours streaming before my eyes. Shapes coming in and out of focus. I slashed out at the threat, unable to register if the shadowy form before me may be King or not.

"Stay back!" I shouted, just as doors banged open and booted feet pounded across the concrete floor.

My head threatened to split in two, the sound reverberating inside my skull. *Thudda-thudda, thud-thud, thud.* A thousand feet pounding over pavement, tattooing my eardrums, matching the rhythm of my heart.

"Holster your weapons!" someone cried frantically. "I've got this!"

My blood pounded in my ears, beneath my skin, and all I could see were multi-hued shapes. Twisting, turning, creeping forward and pulling back. Nothing made sense, except an overriding need to defend myself. To not die. To not be a victim.

I crab crawled backwards until my back hit a wall, which only escalated the sense of panic and the desire to escape. I made a mewling sound, then strengthened my hold on the knife I wielded before me. Watching distractedly as the lights in the room glinted dimly off the dull blade as it waved back and forth before my eyes.

The leather wrapped hilt felt real. The world around me did not.

"Kate!" a familiar and demanding voice said. "Put the knife down. Now!"

I panted, forcing oxygen into my lungs. Gripping the hilt of the blade as though it was my anchor. If I released it, I would fade into black, slip down the sharp edge I could feel off to the side. The one that seemed so dark.

If the shadow before me stepped closer, I *would* strike. I would not be pushed easily over that verge. I would go down fighting. Just like Nick would. Just like Jason would. I would not give up. I'd die trying.

"I'm going to give you a countdown from three," the voice said, a note of desperation in its tone.

I stopped breathing.

"Three," he said, as though through gritted teeth.

The knife suddenly felt heavy in my grasp. I lowered it slightly, then sucked in a breath of air and straightened my arm.

"Two," the voice murmured, closer.

How did he get closer?

"Come on, baby. Come back to me."

I blinked my eyes, trying to get the hazy images before me to come into focus. But my mind was misfiring, and all I could see were threatening black shadows on the edges of my vision.

"One."

I shook my head to clear the fog, to shake the memory of what had just happened. The vision of blood splattered chests. A jugular vein severed by a knife. A gun firing no less than ten feet away. The sound of the bullet ricocheting off a wall at my back.

My head spun to check the wall I was pressed against. A jagged and broken hole where a bullet had landed was no less than a foot away. I gulped in more air.

"You know what happens at zero, Kate?" the voice asked softly. Almost an intimate whisper.

I shook my head. Zero. I liked zero, didn't I?

"I remind you what you mean to me," the voice whispered, by my ear. "Understand?"

Understand.

Understand.

A shattering, heartbreaking, soul mending breath left me.

Understand.

The knife clattered to the floor and my arms wrapped around Jason, a sobbing, hitched sound escaping my lips.

"Kate," he whispered, burying his face in my neck. "Welcome back, baby."

Welcome back.

I'd been to hell and now I was back. And Jason, my darling, broken, imperfect, perfect man, knew exactly what hell I'd just visited. He'd lived there once too. And just like now, he'd returned to the land of the living. Just like me. He'd used an anchor to bring him back.

I'm Jason Cain's anchor. And he is mine.

Understand?

EPILOGUE

THREE WEEKS LATER

"YOU READY FOR THIS?"

I glanced up at the face before me. A face I'd come to know so well, so intimately, so completely.

For three weeks Jason had not left my side. Conscious that a flashback could happen at any time, determined to be there for me when I needed anchoring. When I needed to be pulled from the torrent of dark images that threatened to suck me down.

I'd had one undeniably life altering and entirely too horrific experience, which had created an untold number of images in my head. Images that were quite happy to run on repeat. When I didn't expect it, I'd see Jason in a bundle of what appeared to be broken bones on the concrete floor. He hadn't been broken, merely ruffled - his words, not mine. He was playing possum, aware that King and his men had spotted me, hoping to give me time to escape.

I hadn't. Therefore the images that popped up uninvited reminding me of that one experience, in technicoloured, surround sound.

Tremayne dead.

King cocky and deranged.

The mountain goon, who I later found out was nicknamed, Truro. Blood. Blood. And more blood. Because of me.

It was all because of me. My design at the Montgomery-Smith's. Tremayne's immediate connection to what I had created, and his consequent attraction and infatuation with me. It all led to Declan King's decision to use his business acquaintance's connection to an Anscombe, to send a message to my brother, Nick.

The message would have been clear. Interfere in my business again, and I'll a find a way to bury you. Whether through a framed crime, or the death of a loved one. Declan King's messages were always severe.

And he wasn't even dead. Or arrested. He'd escaped. Like a phantom, he had returned to Tremayne's warehouse, and then left it again after the events, and somehow managed it all under the scrutiny of Horse in the SAS.

But 'radar' had come up blank. Whoever was hiding Declan King, was doing it well. The Police were on his trail, but it was a trail that seemed to lead nowhere. No one was certain if Declan King would return and exact revenge. He had simply vanished. But we all knew; Nick, ASI, Jason and me, all of us associated to this moment, we *knew* we hadn't seen the last of Declan King.

And still I had flashbacks. Little things would set them off. Inconsequential things. The motorway on ramp at Newmarket. In particular the South bound lanes. The entrance to ASI. My mirror in my walk-in-wardrobe. Any knife, be it a steak knife, a butter knife, or a SOG Fusion throwing knife. Red. But only the shade of red that mimics blood. Loud bangs, sharp retorts. The smell of wet paint.

I have no idea where that last one comes from. Maybe it reminds my subconscious of the decoration at Tremayne Arts. I don't know. But I don't think I would manage to stay long in a room with my builders. But as yet, I've not had to test that theory. I've taken a break from work.

And throughout all of these inconvenient, yet paralysing memories and triggers, I have to remind myself that I only experienced hell once. Jason has multiple experiences to draw on, and yet somehow he handles it so well. Somehow he finds a way out of the memory, into the sunshine. His way back home.

I reached up and cupped his cheek. There was a week's worth of stubble there. He didn't normally let his facial hair become so unruly, but Jason was enjoying life, despite his obvious concern for my mental wellbeing. He was celebrating being alive. Being present. Being with me.

I think I could do the same. With a little more time.

"I'm ready," I said resolutely.

I received a raised eyebrow at that.

"Baby," he started.

"Yes, yes. I know. I'm a terrible liar," I shot back with a smirk. "Only to you, you know."

"I was aware of the effect I have over you, Kate," Jason said smugly. His hands running down both my sides, settling on my waist and then hauling me tight against his groin. He rolled his hips, making me fight a moan at the intimate movement.

Too intimate for the front pathway of Gen and Dom's house.

I went to push away and he grasped my hands, linking our fingers together.

"Do you want to know something?" he asked.

"What?" I replied, unable to hide my smile. He was playing, planning something. I could tell. I'd got very used to Jason's games.

He leaned forward and breathed hot air across my lips, then murmured, "I love you in this dress."

I couldn't stop the moan from slipping out when his lips pressed against mine. I tried to lift my hands to his hair, the first thing I do when Jason kisses me. It's imperative to anchor myself to his body, or I lose all sense of myself. But he gripped my fingers, pulled my hands up between us, and then crushed them between our bodies as he delved his tongue inside my mouth.

It was several delicious, sanity stealing minutes later, that the door opened at the front of Dom's house.

"You two are making a scene. My neighbours might call the cops."

Dominic.

"The cops are already here, my man. No need to dial 111."

Pierce.

"Leave them alone. You'd be no better if you felt in the mood for a kiss."

Genevieve.

"Sweetheart. I'm always in the mood to kiss you."

Dom again.

"Well, I'm in the mood for food. Can't we haul their arses inside so we can serve up dinner."

And that rounds out my siblings. Nick.

"Cowboy! Don't rush a perfect moment. Kisses like that need to be respected."

Eva.

"I'd sure as hell respect anyone who kissed me the way Jase is kissing Katie."

And that would be Kelly. I sighed. Jason chuckled.

"Jealousy will get you nowhere, Kels," he said, dancing chocolate eyes still on me.

I sank willingly into those pools of delicious brown. Blocked out everything else around us. Whether our audience continued to pass comment, I didn't know. I didn't care. All that mattered was Jason and the way he looked at me. As though I was his air. His world.

His anchor.

But Sunday barbecue ritual at Dom and Gen's was not to be delayed. The mouth watering smells of grilled meet wafting out of the open door, making my stomach rumble and Jason laugh even louder.

"My girl needs feeding. Gotta keep your energy levels up," he said with a wicked smirk. Then leaned closer to whisper, "That dress is screaming for attention. My kind of attention. What do you say I squirrel you away down one of Dom's countless hallways and have my delicious way with you?"

My eyes flicked up to his and I offered a wicked smile of my own. "Just say the word, baby. And I'm there."

He let a breath of air out that sounded pained. He shook his head, and said instead, "Food. Inside. Now."

I chuckled to myself as I walked up the steps, relieved to see our audience had retreated inside. We found them in the dining room, helping themselves to overflowing plates of good Kiwi tucker. Barbecued steaks and sausages, fried onion rings, and pasta and loose leaf green salads, Watties tomato sauce, and freshly buttered bread. A feast for friends. For family.

Papa wrapped an arm around my shoulder as I approached the table, giving me a kiss on the head. And then turned to shake Jason's hand. I don't why I had expected him to behave otherwise. Jacob Anscombe was a man who saw what he wanted and set out to take it, claim it and make her his. He recognised the same conviction in Jason. He respected it.

Even after everything my brothers had put my soldier man through, he had still kept coming back for more, just to be with me. And in the end, he proved himself. He had hunted down Tremayne, uncovered King's complicity, and cleared Nick and ASI's names.

Even Nick and Dom couldn't find fault in that.

"So, are you going to come back to work, or what?" Nick suddenly asked, making the whole room hush. All eyes flicked between my brother and Jason.

Jason finished piling a good serving of pasta salad onto his plate. It was my pasta salad. I'd dropped it off earlier in the day, when I swung by to check on Gen. Morning sickness was taking its toll. Once he'd placed the right amount of salad on his plate, Jason lifted his head to offer a steely gaze at Nick.

"I thought I'd take a month off. Take Kate a on holiday. Get away for a bit." I wasn't aware he wanted to take me on holiday, but the thought of sunning it up somewhere, just Jason and me, appealed. I returned his smile when his eyes met mine.

Nick flexed his jaw. The room remained silent, observant, breath-holdingly quiet.

"OK. After that," he said, through gritted teeth. Clearly my brother hadn't quite reached the same level of acceptance that my father had with Jason. That angered me. I took a step closer to Jason, who placed his plate down on the table with care and wrapped an arm around my shoulder.

"Yeah. Maybe after that," Jason replied, levelly.

The room breathed a sigh of relief, which was sucked back in when Nick said, "You moved in with Katie?"

Several shocked gasps and harshly spoken warnings of "Nick!" sounded out around the room. He ignored them, even though the loudest had been from my mother and Eva.

"Son," Papa tried to intervene. Nick just raised his hand to stall him.

"Have you, Cain?"

"Yeah," Jason said slowly, dragging the word out.

"Are you gonna make a decent woman of her?"

Oh good God. My mouth hung open, matched by several others present who were all unable to look away from this disastrous scene unfolding.

Jason crossed his arms over his chest, stood up taller and glared back at Nick.

"You mean, am I going to marry her?"

"Yes, that's exactly what I mean," Nick shot back.

"I think you've said enough, Nicholas," my father announced, in his lawyerly voice.

"Come on, Nick," Dominic murmured, from off to the side, his arm wrapped protectively around a stunned and teary eyed Genevieve. "Just let it go."

"I will not let it go!" Nick almost shouted back. "We all know what he's like. I'd just like to be proven wrong. And a little confirmation that this fucking head case is committed to our sister, wouldn't go astray."

More shouted and disgusted, "Nicks!" sounded out.

Followed by a "Bad call." And a "Not cool." And I think a "Whoa, *e hoa*. Chill."

"Why don't you ask Kate," Jason announced into the uneasy silence that followed that round of reactions.

My hand flew up to my hair and I smoothed my ponytail down. Jason and I had not discussed marriage. Too much had happened, we were still recovering from the warehouse to think long term. I knew I wanted him in my life forever. I was sure he wanted the same with me. But we hadn't addressed it. Did he want me to be the one to take that next step? Was he unable to for some reason? That dark abyss too threatening to consider drawing me permanently into his life?

I'd already decided I would fight for Jason. I would lay down my life to call him back from that bleak edge, if need be. But he'd shown me a strength in himself, in me, I hadn't known had existed. An ability to survive, to overcome experiences, to concentrate on the good that surrounds us, rather than the bad that shadows our minds sometimes.

He'd proven that to me, again and again. I'd willingly accepted who he was, and he'd willingly surrendered to what he felt for me.

So, marriage wasn't out of the realms of possibilities, was it?

"What's on your finger, Katie?" Gen suddenly asked.

I pulled my right arm down and glanced at my naked hand.

"No the other one," Kelly said excitedly.

My left hand met my right in front of me and I gasped.

There, sitting proud and pretty, was a diamond ring. Glinting in the lights of the room, sparkling brightly, dazzlingly, incredibly. And totally unexpectedly. I hadn't had a ring on my finger when I left home. I'm sure there wasn't one on my hand when I got out of Jason's car.

I stared at the obvious engagement ring and didn't say a word.

"Baby?" Jason asked, sounding a little hesitant. "You gonna answer your brother?"

Nick started chuckling, taking a large sip from his bottle of beer, as though this was all perfectly normal. My eyes flicked up to his.

"You knew about this?" I asked. He shrugged his shoulders and then saluted Jason with his bottle of beer.

The whole room started to break into amused and enthusiastic laughter. A few rounds of applause and the odd shout of, "Congratulations!" rang out.

I turned and glared at Jason. He smirked.

"Well?" he whispered, moving closer, his arms wrapping around my waist, but leaving enough space between us so I could still stare at the engagement ring on my finger. "You going to do what you're told, Kate?"

I arched my brow at that.

"Baby," he purred. "Do you need a countdown from three?"

Oh, he would love that wouldn't he?

I sucked in a breath of excited air and glanced back down at the ring. It was beautiful, but not a traditional shaped stone. This one was unique. Elongated with a pointed tip, rounded at the base. Pear shaped I think. Not the precise princess or emerald cut favoured so much these days. But something unusual, something a little less perfect.

An imperfect shaped gem which was simply perfect for me. Like Jason.

"The answer is yes," I said, lifting my eyes back up to an impatient and swiftly becoming nervous ex-military soldier.

"To which question?" he whispered, voice low and rough, and all the more sexy because of it.

"To all of them. To any you ask of me. I'm yours, Jason Cain. Body, heart, mind and soul. I surrender it all to you."

A blindingly beautiful smile spread across his face, which threatened to overshadow the diamond on my ring finger.

"Understand, baby?" I added, my own smile matching his.

Jason huffed out a laugh, leaned forward and kissed me passionately; a full body kiss, tipping me over backwards, while he devoured my mouth with his tongue. Making the room erupt in cheers and claps all over again.

"Kate, Kate, Kate," he murmured against my lips. "I'm going to show you the world, baby. I'm going to light up your life. Like you do mine."

Like you do mine. I had no doubt that he would. Even when the flashbacks threatened, for him and for me, we'd anchor each other, we'd call each other back from the edge of that abyss. We'd never let go, or give up, or walk away. Even when the world seemed to expect it of us.

Jason and I had surrendered. Completely. Mind, body, heart and soul. And once you've done that, nothing else can touch you, ever again.

www.ingramcontent.com/pod-product-compliance
Lightning Source LLC
Chambersburg PA
CBHW070221260626
47160CB00002B/630